Exhibit Alexandra

Natasha Bell grew up in Somerset and studied English Literature at the University of York. She holds an MA in the Humanities from the University of Chicago and an MA in Creative Writing from Goldsmiths College, London. She lives in south-east London and splits her time between writing and working as a projectionist.

Exhibit Alexandra

NATASHA BELL

MICHAEL JOSEPH
an imprint of
PENGUIN BOOKS

MICHAEL JOSEPH

UK | USA | Canada | Ireland | Australia
India | New Zealand | South Africa

Michael Joseph is part of the Penguin Random House group of companies
whose addresses can be found at global.penguinrandomhouse.com

First published 2018

001

Copyright © Natasha Bell, 2018

The moral right of the author has been asserted

Set in 12.84/15.92 pt Bembo book MT Std
Typeset by Jouve (UK), Milton Keynes
Printed in Great Britain by Clays Ltd, St Ives plc

A CIP catalogue record for this book is available from the British Library

HARDBACK ISBN: 978–0–718–18704–0
OM PAPERBACK ISBN: 978–0–718–18706–4

www.greenpenguin.co.uk

MIX
Paper from
responsible sources
FSC
www.fsc.org FSC® C018179

Penguin Random House is committed to a
sustainable future for our business, our readers
and our planet. This book is made from Forest
Stewardship Council® certified paper.

Exhibit Alexandra

Thursday, 21 February 2013
The Beginning

Marc sat on the bottom stair and tried not to think the worst. The voice continued: 'The vast majority of people return safe and well within the first forty-eight hours, Mr Southwood. There's no need to panic.' There was a pause. Marc knew he should take comfort from this. Sit tight and wait for his wife to return with a perfectly reasonable explanation.

The officer said goodnight and the line clicked dead. As if that had solved the problem. As if Marc should have felt better.

Six hours down, forty-two to go.

I wish I could put myself there with him. I'd wrap first my arms and then my legs around his body, cling to him until we lost our balance and tumbled to the hallway floor. Tell him with my touch the one thing he needed to know that night: *I'm here. Right here.*

He stood up and replaced the receiver, severing his fingertip connection to the phone call and his one active plan to do something. The hairs on his arms stood on end as he shivered to a silent beat of *something's wrong, something's wrong, something's wrong.*

Perhaps he shouldn't have phoned the police. After all, I was a grown woman. Perhaps it was over the top to report me missing. It's not as if I had a curfew.

But I was a mother. My children were home and I was not. *It's so unlike her.* Marc had said that to the officer a moment ago. It'd felt like a whine; that childish word laughably impotent in the face of explaining the absolute abnormality of a woman who had always come home, day after day, year after year, not walking through our front door that night.

I was meant to have returned by the time he brought the girls back from swimming. We should have ordered a takeaway. We should have sat with our chow mein, chattering about open days and council cuts.

He tried my phone again. Off as usual. 'My little Luddite,' he'd called me when he asked if I wanted an iPhone for my birthday and I said I was perfectly happy with the two-year-old handset I had. It made calls and showed me my emails – what more did I want? He should have pestered me more. Another man would have given me one anyway, synced our calendars and address books, downloaded an app to keep tabs on me, made sure I couldn't get lost.

'It's Thursday, for God's sake,' Marc said aloud. He paced to the window to peer on to the street again. I wouldn't miss Thursday Takeaway without a reason.

He raised his hand, scratched his left temple.

He'd tried to explain to the officer. Was Jones his name? Officer Jones thought we'd had a fight. People disappeared all the time.

I didn't, though.

I'd spent the day at work. Marc had rung my colleague, Paula, to check. She said we'd walked out of the building together. I'd wished her a good weekend because she had Friday off to attend some family wedding. She'd told me she'd try, though she hated the things, and we'd parted with a wave.

Whole hours had elapsed since that exchange. It was now 11 p.m. It was dark.

Such things bothered my husband. It didn't matter that I'd lived alone in cities before we met. It didn't matter that I'd spent more than a year wandering the streets of Chicago, an optimistic student wearing an armour of Pabst Best against the gangs and gun crime statistics. It didn't matter that I'd once parachuted from a plane, that I'd accidentally hit a black slope the first time

I strapped skis to my feet, that I'd backpacked around India and spent a month living in a roach-infested squat in Alphabet City. My husband saw me as something fragile. He walked me home and met me from trains. He wanted to protect me.

Should he search the streets? Was that what one was supposed to do? Maybe he could ask a neighbour to watch the girls. But where would he go? Did people normally look in pubs and bars?

Marc clung to the idea that we were normal that night. We'd never aspired to be normal before. We'd felt unique. Special. But abnormal things didn't happen to normal people. So we were normal that night. And, in keeping with normality, where everyday anxieties outweigh even the most horrendous fears, my husband continued to care how others perceived us. Behind his concern for me bubbled a multitude of mundane worries: had Officer Jones thought him daft? Had Paula decided he was overbearing? Had he made a fool of himself?

I wouldn't be lounging in a bar, of course; I didn't even drink. Bus shelters? Restaurants? Late-night libraries? This was York in real life, not London in some dramatic episode of *Spooks* we were watching on a boxset binge. This was a picturesque tourist city where the most the police usually had to deal with was fishing stolen bikes out of polluted rivers. Besides, the races had been on and I abhorred town when the cobbled streets and listed bars filled with stumbling gamblers in their glad rags.

He walked into the kitchen to make a cup of tea. *Al would laugh,* he thought. *If she were here.*

I'd have been more likely to roll my eyes, or stick my hands on my hips and give him that 'seriously?' look. But maybe that's me being defensive. Under different circumstances, maybe I would have been amused by my unfailingly British husband. I suppose it's hard to tell from here.

At least Charlotte and Lizzie slept. He'd told them I had to work late. He hated lying to them, I know, but what could he have told a seven- and a ten-year-old? 'I don't know where Mummy is, girls, and I'm trying not to imagine her dead in a ditch, so eat your noodles and we'll find a bedtime story.'

I wasn't dead in a ditch.

He couldn't think like that.

Those things didn't happen.

Not here.

Not to us.

There would be a perfectly rational explanation for my absence and we'd both laugh about it tomorrow. I'd shriek, he thought, when I found out he'd called the police. It'd get pedalled out at dinner parties: the time he lost his head because I fell asleep on a friend's sofa. Our guests would hoot with laughter and he'd blush good-naturedly, happy as ever to play the bashful fool to my leading lady. I can still picture a future that looks like that.

But he'd rung our friends. Patrick first, of course. They'd known each other since university and Marc always turned to him for advice. His wife Susan picked up, though; Patrick was out. He tried Fran and Ollie, the other staples of our little gang of dinner party couples. Patrick had introduced us all years ago, when he and Fran worked in the same surgery, before Fran 'sold out' and accepted a job in a private clinic. We saw these friends every week, went on holidays with them, looked after their kids when they needed help; they were our York family. Mark also tried my old school friend Philippa, then some of the numbers on the PTA phone tree. Nobody had seen me since our Valentine's party. *Fabulous night. Tell Alex I loved her costume.*

Of course, Susan, as soon as I determine she has a pulse, that'll be the first thing out of my mouth.

It wasn't Susan's fault. He shouldn't have snapped. But trust her to play the optimist, to utterly downplay even the most ridiculous of dramas. He made a note to apologize once this was over.

Over.

Despite his panic, he was still thinking in terms of resolution. The very worst things in life, our most fearful nightmares, they don't happen all at once. They creep up, lodge themselves gradually in our brains, worming their way slowly in so that once they become a reality they are already somewhat familiar. If my husband could have known the extent of the horror still to come he wouldn't have survived that night. As it was, he held hope like a pebble in his palm.

The kettle finished boiling, but he no longer wanted tea. He wanted his wife to come home and come to bed. He yawned. He'd had to get up early to finish marking. He hadn't been able to face it last night and the girls had wanted to play board games. I remember I'd sulked because he and Charlotte had formed an alliance, giggling mischievously as they swapped farmers for builders and negotiated defence strategies based on promised hugs and extra marshmallows on hot chocolates. I'd pushed my bottom lip out and batted my eyelashes as if blinking away tears. I remember noticing the new gap in Char's teeth when she grinned, the scab Lizzie kept scratching on her shin, the hole in the heel of Marc's sock, the hitch of the curtain where it'd been drawn hastily over the chair, the slight annoying angle of the Paul Nash print on the wall. The girls hadn't wanted to go to bed, but I'd persuaded them, as I had a thousand times. Then I came back down in Marc's favourite silk and did the same to him.

He crept upstairs to check on the girls now. Charlotte was sprawled face-down across her bed, the Pixar cover kicked to the floor and a brown bear – Puddles, lost thrice, replaced once, worn from a thousand cuddles – hovering precariously near the edge, ready to topple. Marc stepped quietly inside the room, picked the duvet from the carpet and laid it over our daughter's body. He moved Puddles to a safer spot by Char's pillow and touched her dark tangle of hair before retreating to the landing. He stepped along to Lizzie's room and cracked open the door. Our tightly balled eldest breathed evenly on the top bunk. Her face was turned to him and he opened the door further so the light fell on her features. He watched her eyelids flicker with sleep, her lips move silently. She looked like me. Even though she has Marc's fair colouring and everyone always said Char was my double, Lizzie his – as if our genes had been neatly split, offering us one daughter each – I could always see myself in Lizzie too. In the roundness of her face and the line of her lips.

Marc closed the door to Lizzie's room and descended the stairs. What was he supposed to do? He sat down and stood up. Paced from lamp-lit living room to shoe-cluttered hallway, on to Szechuan-smelling kitchen. Tried my mobile once more. He'd called the hospital an hour ago and I hadn't been admitted. Was it time to ring again? He switched on the TV, but heard it through a tunnel. The only sound he wanted to hear was my key in the lock.

I should come clean about something before I go any further. A lot of what I'm writing almost definitely never happened. I wasn't there, obviously. I was missing. Gone. So I can't know Marc put the kettle on, then never poured a cup of tea. I can't tell what thoughts went through his mind the night I never came home.

But I don't know how to tell this story without imagining certain details. And I do know my husband. He's a knowable type of man. Just as I've been described as flighty and impulsive, Marc is a good, honest man whom one can rely on to do and think certain things. He's a man who never deserved to go through everything he has.

So I hope you'll forgive my indulgence. I don't wish to deceive. I'm allowed to listen to the tapes. It's unclear if this is an act of kindness or a form of punishment. But the knowable facts are known to me. I've heard the recording of Marc's phone call to Officer Jones, for instance. And I've seen the credit card statement showing his takeaway purchase at Monkey King. I've sat them in every chair in our house, imagined every combination of crockery they might have used, seen Charlotte animating her chopsticks and Lizzie picking out the onions until I can bear it no more.

I have little choice, though. I'm asked constant questions, prodded to remember and imagine what has occurred beyond these four walls. His motives are unclear. Perhaps he's fucking with me, hoping to turn me crazy by forcing me to bear my family's torture as well as my own. I'm making him do this, he tells me.

'Everyone has a limit,' he says and I see his smile. He gets off on this. 'I'm trying to help you come to terms with your situation,' he says. The situation *he* is responsible for.

I resisted at the start, told him to get lost. But there's nothing else to do and no one else to talk to. I've started answering his questions. Whatever his motives, I'm ready to throw myself into this narrative of partial truths and things I wish were fictions. I'll walk my way through Marc's life since my disappearance. I have little hope it might save me, but the distraction is a comfort. If I could climb inside this story and stay there, I would.

Some things I know first-hand. That my husband was wearing a creased, lightly striped, off-white shirt with one too many buttons left undone that day. He has two that are similar, but this was the one with brown stripes. I watched him button it that morning, contemplating the stripe of dark hairs trailing from his navel to his belt. I'd tried to keep him in bed, but his mind was already on the day ahead. An ironing board lived between the wardrobe and wall, but as normal Marc failed to notice his crumpled attire and I didn't offer.

He also wore dark blue jeans and brown loafers, though I

imagine he switched those for slippers when he arrived home. I'd never owned slippers before I met Marc, but he'd grown up in a shoes-off-at-the-door, slippers-warmed-by-the-radiator kind of house and a part of me loved turning ours into the same.

His hair was freshly washed that morning, so would have still smelled of raspberry shampoo, but it hung slightly too long after yet another week had passed without his getting around to booking an appointment. If things had continued as normal, I'd have marched him to the barbers on Saturday morning and demanded they buzz it far shorter than he liked, arguing that this way he could leave it the extra weeks without my nagging. It was only half a joke. He would roll his eyes but acquiesce and later I'd run my hand through his stunted locks and kiss him on the mouth, freshly amazed by how attractive I found him after a little grooming.

This story I have to tell is more than a collection of basic facts, though. It's more than the 'real-life' shockers you read in the papers and the tell-all exposés of glossy magazines. I have no reason to paint a better or worse picture than what really happened. I've already lost everything. I live within four walls. I've been tied up and drugged. I have no hope of salvation. I've realized I have only this. So despite my ignorance of events I cannot possibly have witnessed, the story recorded here is more honest than the police reports and newspaper articles. If it is not an actual truth, it is very much a human one.

1998

Friday, 28 August

I remember it'd rained, but the sun had come out. There was this freshness in the air, this weird optimism about the empty campus. The students had scurried off home for the summer, leaving the geese and the administrators to run the place. I don't know why I'd ended up there really – a Viking city, a thirteenth-century cathedral, a river and an historically interesting train station, and I'd wandered all the way to the sixties stain that was the university campus. I had such mixed feelings towards York then; the sense of suffocation of the place I'd grown up in was slowly dissolving into something strangely nostalgic. I'd photographed raindrops hitting the polluted lake, clouds fleeing from the concrete canvas. Now I was crouching, my thighs wobbling with the strain, struggling to keep the lens steady, willing that pigeon to make up its mind, to align its wing with the odd staircase spiral, to catch its reflection in that puddle and balance my frame.

'Uh, excuse me.'

'Just a minute,' I said without looking. The voice had been hesitant, unsure, as if apologizing for needing me to shift out of its way. I was squatting in the doorway, I suppose, holding the automatics open as I adjusted my aperture.

'I just need to get by,' came the voice again, a little peevish this time, no?

'Hold on.' I'd taken half a dozen photos already, but I knew none of them were quite right. Then the stupid pigeon finally settled and

I pressed my finger down. My camera clicked and the daft bird fluttered off. 'Got it!' I straightened up, snapped the cap on to my lens and turned around. 'Sorry about that. I mean, thanks for waiting.'

He was tall, easily over six foot, sandy hair and blue eyes. Sort of cute, in a geeky, academic way. I thought he might be a professor, flashed him my little girl smile.

'No problem,' he replied, smiling back. 'I'm Marc by the way.'

Oh. I hadn't expected that. Before I'd really thought about it, I'd ping-ponged back, 'Well hello, Marc-By-The-Way,' and stuck out my tongue. 'I'm Alex-By-The-Way.'

His cheeks coloured and I felt bad. I glanced around for something to distract us, finally noticed the pile of books he was carting out of the library. 'Whoops, those look heavy,' I said. 'I really am sorry.'

'It's nothing,' he said, but judging by the under-developed biceps poking out from the sleeves of his T-shirt, he was lying.

'Kant, Rousseau *and* Hegel,' I said, reading the first three spines. 'You really know how to spend your summer.'

'Um, yes,' he said, shifting his weight. 'I guess it's not the most exciting first impression.'

I laughed and shook my head. 'No, it's fine, but careful you don't get lost in that fog of masculinity. I might need to prescribe some serious feminist theory as an antidote.'

Marc smiled and blushed again. 'Are you a student?' he said.

'Sort of,' I said with a shrug. 'Not here. And not in the lugging books out of the library kind of way.'

Marc frowned. His eyes flicked from mine to focus on something in the distance over my right shoulder. There was a pause, but neither of us made as if to move. Whatever he'd been hurrying out of the library for seemed to have been forgotten.

'Sorry if this is a little odd,' he said finally, looking back at me. 'But do you fancy a cup of tea? Maybe you can tell me what I should be reading instead.'

I examined him properly now, guessed he wasn't a professor at all. He was too old to be a regular student, though. Where had this question come from? Was he the sort to try his luck at any opportune moment? Or was he really the geeky library boy he appeared? Did he actually want me to tell him to read de Beauvoir and Arendt, or had he just this second stepped out of his comfort zone and offered himself up to me of all people? His cheeks were turning from red to purple and an image flickered before me of this man-boy as a peg ready to be thwacked back into place by a child's toy mallet. I, of course, was the mallet-wielding child. This man, I thought, had probably been the type of kid who held out his toys and sweets and pocket money for the bully to take his pick, hoping only for a new best friend. I'm not proud of it, but I was a bitch to kids like that.

I stifled a shame-filled laugh and found myself saying, 'Why not? I guess I owe you for helping me get a good shot.'

I watched the skin around his blue eyes crinkle as he smiled in relief. I imagined running my tongue along the stubble on his jaw, burying my nose in the creases of his skin. I cleared my throat, glanced back towards the library, then again at his pile of books. 'Can I take a couple of those?'

Friday
Fourteen Hours Gone

Marc would have worried whether it was the right thing to do, but he took the girls to school.

'Why isn't Mummy making breakfast?' Lizzie must have whined in the morning. 'You put too much milk in and the cereal goes all soggy.'

'Mummy had to leave early today, sweetie.' Another lie. 'Here, do your own milk.'

'*Where's my maths book?*' I hear Charlotte holler from upstairs.

'*Where you left it!*' Lizzie would have shouted back.

With half-hearted reprimands he'd have bundled them out the door, Lizzie missing a glove and Charlotte moaning that her teacher was going to kill her. My husband would have winced at that word tumbling from her milk-toothed mouth; an involuntary image of me sliced and diced, bloodied and sullied flashing beneath his lids as he blinked in the grey morning light.

They'd have walked together along the terraced streets towards their school. Lizzie might have chatted about looking forward to netball club starting again. Charlotte may have told him she needed new PE shorts. Marc would have nodded and mumbled replies, worrying about being away from the phone. He'd have peered into every car that passed, driven by an absurd superstitious thought that if he missed one it'd contain me. They'd have stopped to wait for the lights. Charlotte would have seen a classmate on the opposite side and tried to step forward. Marc would have yanked her back, fear bringing his surroundings into focus. He'd have shouted at our daughter, his natural inclination towards overprotection shooting into overdrive on this strange morning. Charlotte's eyes would have filled with tears.

'Dad, there wasn't even anything coming,' Lizzie would have groaned, as much in embarrassment as defence of her sister.

The lights would finally have changed and they would have crossed the road. Reaching the kerb, our girls would have shrugged him off, run through the wide gateway towards the chattering uniforms at the bottom of the steps. He'd have waited a moment to see them inside, wanting them to turn back and wave, to smile at their dad, remind him he wasn't alone. A class-room assistant would have closed the door behind the last child and he and the other parents would have turned from the gate, ready to get on with their days. He'd have nodded to a couple of mums he recognized and waited once more for the lights, wishing he could follow them to their meetings and yoga classes, offices and book clubs.

'You're through to North Yorkshire Police. How can I help?' The buzz of an office in the background, phones ringing and instructions being given. The recording is poor, but you can tell my husband feels comforted. They'll do something, he's thinking; they'll help.

'Um, hello. I, uh, called last night because my wife has, well, she hasn't come home.' This must have been the only thought he'd had in fourteen hours, but the words still tasted strange on his tongue. You can hear his hesitation in the recording, sense how surreal he finds all this. 'They said they'd call me this morning, but I just, I thought maybe it might have been forgotten, and I'm really very worried. I can't get hold of her and –'

'Okay, sir,' the well-trained voice responds. 'Can I take your name?'

He gives it to her and she locates the log of his previous call. She asks if he's received any news and they go over the nothing he knows once more. He grows frustrated when she asks if this behaviour is 'out of character' for me, if we've had a fight, if I've done this before. You can hear him taking a breath on the line, thinking before he speaks. That second of silence says far more than his words. *Of course it's fucking out of character – I'd hardly be phoning the police if it wasn't, would I?* Eventually she asks for our address and says she'll dispatch someone to take more information. They'll be with him at midday. He's told to stay by the phone and to think of as many details as he can concerning my last movements.

'Please try not to worry,' the woman says. 'We'll do our best to find your wife.'

The recording ends. I imagine she hung up rather than him. I imagine he sat with the receiver in his hand, the dial tone drowning the chatter in his brain. He couldn't work out what came next. He was meant to wait by the phone, but he couldn't just do nothing. The day before he'd been a competent, functioning man: a moderately well-dressed, happily married male rebelling only mildly at middle age; comfortable in his career; delighted with his daughters. Today, he was a weak bundle of tissue and bone unable to achieve the one thing he desired. A man used to instructing students and staff, juggling timetables and negotiating with publishers, he now found himself at the mercy of officials and red tape. His fists clenched as he realized all he could do was hope some boys in blue could accomplish what he couldn't. He looked down at his shirt and jeans with the disgust of a man who has chosen books over brawn, an intellectual who feels inadequate passing building sites and squealing fire engines. He never trusted that I loved his sensitivity, his lack of clichéd masculinity. I deserved a man, he thought as he sat in our living room, the phone still in his hand, my magazine on the table. A real one who could stride out into the world and return with me beautiful and swooning in his muscular arms.

★

Detective Inspector Jones arrived just before midday. He was a few inches shorter than Marc, maybe six foot one. Clean-shaven. Short, dark hair. Younger too. Thirty-ish perhaps. No ring.

'Mr Southwood?' he said, holding out his hand. Marc reached to shake it, wondered if he should tell him it was *Dr* Southwood.

Marc led him to the living room, noticed how he appraised the décor. Was he judging us, making professional assumptions about our wealth and class, lifestyle and statistical likelihood of disappearing, or did he have a genuine interest in interior design?

'Right, Mr Southwood,' DI Jones said, opening a folder and uncapping the biro with which he made the notes I've read. 'I understand your wife has not been seen since she left work yesterday, is that correct?'

My husband nodded. DI Jones began by explaining that his code of practice recommended filing a missing person report up to seventy-two hours after the last known sighting, but given the circumstances they were bringing the report forward. Marc, no doubt, raised his eyebrows and DI Jones hurried to continue, 'That shouldn't cause you concern. We've no reason to believe anything's happened to Alexandra at this point, we just want to be cautious.'

'Something has happened to her, though,' Marc said. 'Otherwise she would have come home.'

I imagine DI Jones swallowing, continuing cautiously. 'Well, yes, but in all likelihood there's a simple explanation and we'll be able to close the case by this time tomorrow.'

'You think so?' If Marc had a tail, he'd have wagged it. A part of him still didn't believe this was happening, thought it must be a dream, a nightmare he could wake from and find my hot, live limbs on the other side of the mattress. He felt some sceptical part of himself detach from his body, hovering invisibly in the top corner of the room, looking down on and mocking his pathetic, hopeful sincerity.

'I can't make promises, but statistically speaking the odds are that Alexandra will return before the weekend's out,' DI Jones said.

'What if someone's taken her?' my husband blurted, succumbing to that sincerity.

A slow exhale through teeth. 'I know abductions by strangers have a high media profile, Mr Southwood, and I know you're very worried, but such incidents are rare and the circumstances in which most missing persons disappear are not suspicious. All I can do is urge you to keep calm and concentrate your efforts on remembering details.'

Marc nodded and set his mouth in an apologetic line, trying to process the words and assemble his scattered brain. This may be a nightmare, he reminded himself, but it was no dream. He cleared his throat, attempted to speak as DI Jones's equal. 'How do we file this report?'

DI Jones's questions required yes–no answers to begin with. Easy, black and white details. Still, I imagine Marc staring at the corner of our living room, studying the intricate frieze dissecting Almond White from Soft Stone, and wondering who to be in this situation. He felt a need to assert his personality, to define himself as an individual rather than a statistic. He wanted to tell DI Jones that he loved books but had tinkered with cars through his twenties; that his favourite dish was lamb dhansak and he used my shampoo only because it smelled nicer. He wanted to tell him about Lizzie's poetry prize and how he and Charlotte had been quoting *Monty Python* at each other since he introduced her to it last month; that we'd had a nits scare last weekend and he was worried the gutter by the back door needed unblocking. But what if all that was wrong? What if there was a type of man supposed to greet DI Jones at the door of a routine missing person case? What if he didn't fit the bill?

DI Jones asked if I'd been involved in any altercations or

disagreements in the past few weeks, if Marc had noticed anything out of the ordinary.

Marc shook his head. 'Alex likes people to like her,' he said. 'She'd have told me if anything happened. She worries if the postman doesn't return her "good morning".'

'Do you have any reason to believe Alexandra is likely to cause self-harm or attempt suicide?' DI Jones asked.

'Christ, no,' Marc said. 'What sort of question is that? She's happy, *we're* happy. We have two children.'

He was reminded that the more questions they got through, the more thorough the investigation could be. Marc murmured an apology.

He was asked how much I drank, if I took drugs. Marc almost smiled. 'She hasn't had a drink since our wedding day. She'd never do drugs.'

DI Jones looked up. 'She doesn't drink at all?'

Marc shook his head. 'Her mother was an alcoholic.' He watched DI Jones write something down and wondered if he shouldn't have said that. 'Alex has never had a problem,' he added. 'She just saw what it did to her mother, to her family. She said nothing was worth that.'

'Okay,' said DI Jones. 'And is there any medication she might need?'

'She's on the Pill,' Marc said, heat rising to his cheeks. We'd been married nearly thirteen years, but my delicate husband was still embarrassed to imply we sometimes fucked. 'That's it.'

DI Jones has scrawled details here. He must have asked if Marc would mind checking whether my pills were still in the house. Marc sped up two flights of stairs to check the bedside table. When he returned to the living room, DI Jones was standing, inspecting a bookcase littered with dusty photos, nail scissors and pebbles stolen from forgotten beaches. He took my neatly labelled medication, glancing only briefly at the rows of punch-out days interrupted by today's unswallowed Friday, and asked who had seen me last. Marc told him about Paula and left the room again to find my address book – a last helpful vestige of Luddite life, even he might have to admit.

DI Jones was back in the chair. He waited for Marc to sit down. 'Now, I need you to be as detailed as possible, because everything and anything might be relevant. Could you describe the last time you saw your wife and how she seemed?'

Marc told him he'd seen me the previous morning, that I'd seemed fine. He talked about getting the girls ready for school, chatting about a potential holiday, saying goodbye before I cycled on to campus. 'It was a normal day,' he said.

'Can you remember what Alexandra was wearing?'

Marc thought I'd had on jeans and a black and white jumper.

'And did she have a coat?'

'A blue duffel, with a hood. Lizzie and Charlotte have almost identical ones. They thought it would be fun and silly to match.'

'Thank you,' DI Jones said, not even glancing up from his note-pad. Marc knew at that moment he wouldn't tell the police about me packing Lizzie's teddy bear when we went to Paris without her and cart-wheeling around Clifford's Tower without an ounce of alcohol in my system, about the love notes I wrote inside paper aeroplanes then sent soaring to his desk, and my impulsive demands to be surprised, entertained and adored. Everything might be relevant, he said, but many of the things Marc loved most about me felt worryingly fragile, as if merely mentioning them aloud might destroy their magic. The man before him might decide I was odd, unpredictable even. He wouldn't have understood that Marc knew me, that we shared a whole private world.

'Does she have any distinguishing marks: scars, tattoos, piercings?' DI Jones asked.

'She has her ears pierced,' my husband said. 'And a tattoo on her left shoulder blade. A wilting sunflower, like the Van Gogh painting. She got it at uni.' Marc thought of my tattoo, of straddling my legs to massage my back, of pressing his lips to my skin. Then an image surfaced of the cling-film shrouded Laura Palmer in *Twin Peaks*, some anonymous hand turning her over to reveal my wilting sunflower. Marc raised his hand to his mouth, a breath caught on the back of his tongue. We'd rewatched it last year, one episode an evening, late, after the girls had gone to bed, tangling our fingers together and smiling at the nostalgia of the ancient series.

'Are you all right, Mr Southwood?' DI Jones said, narrowing his eyes.

Marc nodded, lowering his hand. 'It's actually Dr,' he said.

DI Jones held his gaze for a moment. 'My mistake.'

They went through my date of birth, height, weight and ethnic background. DI Jones asked if we practised a religion and if my parents lived nearby. Marc told him I'd gone to a Catholic school, my father died a decade ago and my mother lived in the South West but was suffering from late-stage dementia.

DI Jones nodded. 'Is it possible your wife may have gone to visit her mother?'

Marc shook his head. 'Not without telling me. They don't have a good relationship. Al goes down a few times a year, but finds it really distressing. And her mum doesn't react well to changes in routine, so she'd never just turn up.'

'We'll need to make enquiries in any case,' said DI Jones. He shifted his weight. 'Now, do you have any recent photographs I could take away?'

Marc realized he disliked DI Jones but still, strangely, wanted to please him. He fetched his laptop from his bag in the hall.

'We'd also like any items only Alexandra will have touched – her hairbrush, toothbrush and any clothes she's worn recently. And we'll need the details of her bank accounts and mobile phone contract, plus her driving licence and passport.'

While DI Jones clicked through photographs of our family, Marc climbed the stairs to collect the requested items, using gloves as instructed. Our home felt like a crime scene. He pulled a bag from the top of the wardrobe and began packing my things. He rooted through the washing basket, even scooping up my underwear. He put my make-up and hairbrush in my sponge bag and headed down to the office. He grabbed some papers from the top of my desk and peeled off the last Post-it I'd stuck to his keyboard – a lopsided biro heart containing the word 'Mouthwash' – and put them all in the bag. He pulled our filing drawer out on its runners and fished for my bank statements and the driving licence I never used. He flicked to the file labelled passports, but found it empty. He reached his hand into the bottom of the drawer to see if they'd fallen between the folders, then hurriedly shuffled through all of the surrounding files. Confused, he turned back to my desk and hastily hunted under books and hard drives, checked my messy stationery drawers and behind my monitor. 'Fucking hell, Al,' he hissed, panic rising in his chest.

Downstairs, he handed DI Jones the bag and watched as he checked each item against tick boxes on his form. 'Do you have her passport?' he said eventually.

'It's not in the usual place,' Marc said.

DI Jones looked at him with a blank expression.

'Mine's not either, though,' Marc said hurriedly. 'Or the girls'. I mean, they'll be somewhere. Do you have kids? You know what it's like.' He waved his hand, gesturing to our less than tidy house.

DI Jones didn't look around. Marc's face felt hot beneath his gaze.

'I think Al was planning something for the summer,' Marc said. 'Maybe she was booking it as a surprise. She's probably just put them somewhere. They'll turn up.'

'Please let us know as soon as they do,' DI Jones said finally, then glanced down to write something beside one of the tick boxes.

'They're in the house,' Marc said. 'I know they are. It's not like –' He cut himself off. What did DI Jones think? That I'd gone on holiday without telling him? Did some women do that?

DI Jones stood up and thanked Marc for his time. Marc followed him to the door. DI Jones said he'd be in touch. He asked Marc to be careful moving any of my things, to try to preserve everything as I'd left it until they returned. Marc said he'd try, but children lived here. Yes, of course, DI Jones understood, just do his best. My husband was told not to worry for the dozenth time that day. Then he was alone again, which was somehow preferable. It was two o'clock. Twenty-one hours since I was last seen.

The man who keeps me here is as tall as Marc, but a little stooped and much scrawnier than I remember my husband. His hair is growing thin. He looks like he's been sick. He's not conventionally attractive in this wasted form, but he's also not the dead-eyed, anxious type you'd see cast in this role in a film. He's not the sort of man you'd imagine did this kind of thing.

He visits every day, almost on the dot of three. I wonder about his punctuality, about his life outside these walls. Do people notice anything strange about him out in the real world? Would *I* notice anything if we met in the gym, at a bar or outside a library?

This room is stark and bare, like a gallery without an audience. It gives him a gravitas he does not deserve. He's a pathetic man trying to control the mind of a woman. But in here he feels like a god. I'm his object and he gets to animate or break me as his mood dictates.

23

Still, I wait for three o'clock. My heart rate speeds up as I imagine him unlocking the doors. I wait to hear his key in the lock, to see him step through the frame and transform this wretched space. I wonder sometimes what would happen if he didn't come. Would I be relieved? Or would I have to face the truth that there is something even worse than his presence?

'We don't have long,' he says. 'I can't keep you here forever.'

1998

Friday, 28 August

I sat on a plastic chair across from Marc in the empty student café and tried to burble my way through his shyness. I was doing an MFA in Chicago. I told him it was one of those big-deal art schools and I'd had to work really hard to get in. It was true, I was proud to be studying there, but maybe I was also trying to impress. Marc didn't say much, but I watched his expression change as he listened. I kept glancing at the server behind the counter, the geese beyond the window, and playing with the sugar sachets on the table. Marc's steady gaze made me itch. I babbled on and on about my course, working myself up. I was young and ambitious and passionate about the silly pieces I was making. Maybe everyone cringes remembering themselves at that age.

'Why Chicago?' Marc said when I finally paused to take a sip of tea.

I didn't have an answer for him. I already held a BA and an MA from Cambridge. Marc laughed, told me I'd said that as if I was talking about a couple of party dresses I'd purchased on a whim but no longer felt like wearing. I laughed too. It was funny – this guy was funny – but, also, he'd kind of just seen right through me. It made my palms tingle. I smiled and kept talking, worried if I stopped I'd have to ask myself what I was doing.

I described my dad's rage when I left the teaching job I hated to 'go paint pictures for forty thousand dollars a year'. Marc grinned at my impression, but he didn't laugh like my friends in Chicago. He had this crease between his eyebrows. He was trying to figure me out. I'd spent so long cultivating this 'crazy Brit' persona out there, being loud and plummy, always trying to shock and amuse, that I'd forgotten what it was like to be taken seriously. I continued my story, telling it as I always did, willing him to quit trying to connect and just enjoy laughing at me, accept me as the frivolous thing I was.

'What did your mum think?' Marc asked.

'I don't know,' I said, wondering how much of my mess I should land this poor stranger with. 'I haven't spoken to her since I was twelve.'

'Christ, I'm so sorry.' Marc looked stricken. 'I didn't mean to pry.'

'It's fine,' I said. 'It's just the way it is. She's an alcoholic and a cheat. It was better after she left, honestly.'

He frowned.

'Seriously, don't worry. Everyone's parents fuck them up, don't they? It's a wonder anyone wants kids.' I shook my head and returned to my topic. I told Marc I'd won a scholarship to pay for half of my course and I'd made up my mind, so told my dad to sod off. I'd moved to a new city in a new country where nobody knew me to take sculpture, performance, installation and video classes. Marc's frown softened and I thought my plan was working. He said it sounded crazy and bohemian, nothing like his sheltered Welsh upbringing and the cosy life he'd found in academia.

'Don't you want to travel?' I said. 'See the world?'

Marc hesitated. 'Maybe,' he said. 'I'm curious about the world, of course, but I guess I also feel nothing's quite real or enjoyable without a sense of home.'

The way he said the word 'home' made me ache. I had an urge to ask him about what it meant to him, to listen to his

Dylan Thomas lilt. But I couldn't get drawn in. Not today. Instead, I shrugged and told him the only moment I'd questioned myself was on my second day in Chicago when I'd stood outside a Walmart in the middle of some dodgy suburb waiting for a taxi that never came and realized nobody in the city or even the country would notice if anything happened to me.

Marc didn't laugh. He looked more concerned than amused. I didn't know what to do, so I kept talking. I told him I was home for the summer. My course lasted two years and I'd just finished the first. I told him my second would be spent in the studio, creating work for the end-of-year showcase that everyone hoped would secure them a gallery show or a grant. Marc looked genuinely interested in what I was saying. Grad school was amazing, but I'd grown used to everyone walking around in their own bubble of research and obsession. If you found someone whose interests overlapped with yours, you could have a satisfying moment of connection, but only until one of you strayed too far into specifics and the other's eyes glazed over, brain too full to cram in anything not directly relevant to their own research.

We sat in that café for half the afternoon, drinking cup after cup of stale campus tea.

'I have a tutoring appointment,' Marc said and I felt my mood plunge. 'I should have left already.'

'Are you busy later?' I said, then blushed. What was it about this gentle boy?

We met a few hours later, freshly scrubbed and dolled up for dinner in town. I wore the velvet dress I'd found for a dollar on my first trip to the Wicker Park thrift stores and the beat-up Barbarella boots I was in love with that year. Marc had this crumpled shirt on that wasn't quite long enough for his tall torso. We drank cheap red wine, which stained our teeth, and I overheard our waitress call us 'sweet'. I ordered chicken, he ordered pork, but Marc insisted we swap after I said I liked his better.

Marc asked me question after question as if he was genuinely interested in the answers, as if he was trying to learn me. He quizzed me about my likes and dislikes, my school and my family. 'God, you must be so bored,' I said at one point.

'I'm really not,' he said and I had the sensation that his gaze could peel my dress from my skin.

I sipped more wine and crossed my legs beneath the table. 'I've been thinking about my mum again recently,' I found myself saying. 'She moved to the south coast after the divorce. My dad and I stayed in the same house, but the only contact she ever made was one poxy card.'

'That's awful,' Marc said.

I didn't know why I was telling him this. I hadn't discussed my mum with anyone for years. But I realized I liked the concern on Marc's face. His pity was as intoxicating as his fascination. Whatever creature this man saw, that's what I wanted to be.

'What about you?' I said. 'What's your family like?'

'Fairly boring,' he said. 'Only child, parents still together, clinging to a belief in the happily ever after.'

I laughed. 'A regular prince charming looking for his princess, huh?'

Marc blushed.

'Did you ever think it was weird,' I said, 'that all the princes were the same – completely interchangeable from one fairy tale to the next? Even though the women were totally helpless, waiting to be saved by marriage, at least they had personalities.'

'That's true of so much art and literature,' Marc said. 'Men have had power and control and opportunity, but all along their fascination has been with women. We're simple creatures really, obsessed with trying to figure you out.'

I rolled my eyes and asked him about his thesis. He told me

he was writing about time and the quest for knowledge in Romantic poetry. Later I'd ask properly and read bits of his dissertation, but that night I heard the word 'quest' and thought of knights on horseback and long, phallic jousting lances. Marc told me he'd got stuck on the treadmill of academia, beginning his PhD what felt like decades ago but changing topic two years in and only recently feeling like he was reaching the home straight. I told him about my dalliance with serious study and my dad's desire for me to teach warring with my need to create. Marc nodded and said that it was the first time he'd admitted it in years but, though essays and criticism more than satisfied his analytical soul, in his heart of hearts, he wanted to write a novel.

This delighted me. 'I had a feeling you were creative,' I said. 'You should definitely do it.' Then I blathered some more about how expensive my course was and the trouble I was having getting a part-time job because of my visa restrictions.

'It's fucked up, you know?' I said through a mouthful of pork. 'I go to this burrito place and I've been talking to the owner. He's second generation, but he tells me about his family and friends, about how if you're an illegal immigrant there are all these ways of securing American identities, but it's this big joke because you do it so you can get a social security number so you can work, and that number means you start paying taxes, contributing to the State. But if the State finds out, you get locked up or kicked out of the country you've been paying money to. I want to expose it in my final project. You know, show the reality of the ridiculous notion of America being this big melting pot welcoming the tired and hungry masses –'

I cut myself off. Marc was staring at me, his eyes glued to my face, but I got the sense he hadn't heard a word I'd said. I smiled and he smiled back, his features transforming into something quite adorable. He nodded and mumbled his agreement, said

29

he could see how unfair it was, that he'd never considered it before, but yes, I should shed light on it, do everything I could, what a noble thing, what a powerful project and, God, I had pretty eyes.

I laughed and felt my body temperature rise.

Twenty-four Hours Gone

The bell rang and Marc bounded across the carpet to the door. He hesitated. He could make out a woman through the coloured glass, her features mottled by the design. Dare he hope?

'Fran,' he said, clocking our friend's dyed bob and tailored jacket. At her side stood Charlotte, Lizzie, and Fran and Ollie's daughter, Emma.

'Oh God, what time is it?' Marc said, pulling up his sleeve: 4.02. 'Girls, I'm so sorry.'

'It's okay,' Fran said. 'I told them we'd arranged for me to bring them home today. It was a good excuse to get sweets, wasn't it, kids?'

'Thank you,' Marc said. 'What do you say, girls?'

'Thank you, Fran,' Charlotte and Lizzie chimed, their mouths full. They brushed past him, dragging Emma, seemingly unfazed by their abandonment at school. He heard Charlotte cry, 'We are the knights who say Niiiiiiiiiiiiiii,' as they ran up the stairs.

'Really, thank you,' Marc said. 'Um, do you want a cup of tea?'

'I'll make it,' Fran said, placing her hand on Marc's shoulder. 'I take it Al's still not turned up?'

The backs of Marc's eyes prickled as he shook his head. 'I spoke to the police; they've taken a photo and her fingerprints.'

'Oh Marc,' Fran said, wrapping her arms around him. 'I'm sure she's okay. I'm sure there's just some misunderstanding.'

Fran extricated herself to close the front door and led Marc through the house to one of the breakfast stools. My husband watched in silence as our friend bumped around our kitchen filling the kettle and locating tea bags. He wondered what Ollie was doing. It was him we normally saw at pick-up time and arranged to share lifts with. As the full-time parent, Ollie got teased sometimes for their reversed gender roles, but both he and Fran seemed happy. Fran worked long hours as a GP and would've had to have left early to pick up Emma today. Marc wondered if she'd had to cancel appointments, what had prompted the change in their routine, if she was annoyed.

It was cruel to others, but Marc and I always felt lucky. We knew we weren't like everyone else. Sure, we did the same things: I was on the committees and Marc worked late a lot of the time, but we always came back to each other. He kissed the nape of my neck every night before falling asleep. I placed my hand on his back whenever we were speaking to other people. At parties, we had an awareness of where the other was, like an elastic band tied us together. I'd always find him at the end of the night and whisper that I'd like to be taken home, that these people were interesting, I supposed, but they just made me think how lucky I was to have the most interesting one to myself. In fourteen years we'd had only one real fight.

Even though that day Marc felt our elastic band had been stretched perhaps to its absolute limit, looking at Fran making tea, he had the utterly ungenerous thought that Ollie, if he were in Marc's position, would not miss Fran as much as he missed me.

'What have you told the girls?' Fran said, handing him a cup of tea.

'Nothing,' Marc said, only then fully realizing he'd have to think of something.

Fran told him she'd ring Ollie and say she and Emma were staying over. 'You need support,' she said, reaching for her mobile.

'That's really not necessary.' Instantly Marc didn't want her there.

'Nonsense, you're in no fit state to look after the girls tonight. What's your plan for dinner?' She looked him in the eye, waiting for a response.

Admitting he had none, he nodded and she proceeded to dial.

She rummaged through our larder and shuffled pans around the stove to begin making dinner. While it was in the oven she asked Emma if she minded watching a little TV on her own and brought Charlotte and Lizzie into the dining room.

'Your daddy and I have something to tell you,' she said.

'Where's Mummy?' Charlotte said, looking at Marc pleadingly.

'We've got a bit of bad news,' Fran began.

'It's okay,' Marc said. 'I'll do this.'

He reached across the table for our daughters' hands, Lizzie's sporting yellow nail polish that he realized had probably got her in trouble at school. 'I don't want you to panic, girls, because we're doing everything we can, but Mummy didn't come home last night and we're not sure where she is.'

Charlotte's bottom lip began to quiver. Lizzie clenched her jaw and looked at him with her practised 'grown-up' expression.

'I spoke to a police officer today and they're looking for her,' he said. 'They think she'll probably be back in a couple of days. We just have to stay strong and will her to come home.'

He glanced from one pair of wide, silent eyes to another. What could he possibly say to make this better?

'Should we pray?' Lizzie said eventually.

Marc hesitated. We took them to church at Christmas and Easter, but we were not a family who said grace or discussed theology. Her class had just completed a project on different religions, though, and we'd always said we wanted to let them make up their own minds. 'Why not?' he said, wondering if he should have thought of it himself.

Lizzie put her hands together and checked Charlotte was doing the same. 'I'll start.' She bowed her head and began, 'Dear

Lord, I know you're very busy and there are lots of people in the world praying for things, but we have a very important request and if you answer it, I promise not to ask for anything, not even Christmas presents, for a very long time.'

'Me too,' said Charlotte.

'Our mummy didn't come home last night and we need her back.'

Marc lowered his head to hide his tears.

'She belongs in this house with us. We need her to love us and look after us and be our mum.' Lizzie nudged her sister. 'You want to say something?'

Charlotte nodded, her eyes squeezed tight. 'She's the best mummy in the world because she always knows what to do. If we're sad, she makes us happy and if we're hurt, she makes it go away. She cooks the best meals and gives the best cuddles and we miss her so much.'

Charlotte's voice cracked and Lizzie put her arm around her. 'Please, please, *please*,' she said, resuming the prayer. 'Send her home to us. We'll be very good from now on and always say our prayers and go to church and help the poor. Thank you, Amen.'

'Amen,' Marc and Fran echoed.

Charlotte sniffed, tears wetting her cheeks.

Lizzie pulled Charlotte into a sideways cuddle. 'Mummy wouldn't want you to cry,' she said.

Charlotte folded herself into her sister's neck. Lizzie made shh sounds, her own face blank and serious. 'Why don't we go play your knight game?' she said. 'Dad, is that okay?'

Marc gave a stunned nod and Lizzie took Charlotte's hand and led her in search of Emma. Charlotte hesitated, looking back at Marc before disappearing into the hallway.

Marc let out a breath he didn't know he was holding.

'They're remarkably resilient,' Fran said, herself slightly teary.

'Yes,' Marc replied through a sob, wishing he too could go play.

I can tell before he speaks that he's going to say something I don't want to hear. He's leaning against the door, looking down at me. The keys are in his left trouser pocket. I try not to stare. His arms are crossed over his chest. He looks healthier today. There's colour in his cheeks.

'Do you really think your daughters wanted to play after hearing this news?' he says, shaking his head.

'Fuck you,' I say. Why did I even tell him that? Why am I answering his questions, playing his games? My daughters are perfect and beautiful and, yes, they would have been sad when I disappeared, but I can't let myself believe they're damaged beyond repair. Lizzie and Charlotte are strong, intelligent and inspiring young women. I refuse to let him dangle them in front of me as a means of torture.

'Fine,' he says. 'You don't want to talk about your daughters. I'm a reasonable guy. What about Fran? What was she doing there? Do you trust her?' He looks at me, amusement in his eyes. What does he want? For me to talk about another woman taking my place? To torture myself with her presence in my home, with my kids, my husband?

I shrug. I've tried to imagine Marc sitting at home not knowing what to do, then looking at the clock and realizing he needs to pick the girls up, realizing life has to go on, and I just can't picture it. His world would have stopped. I don't want it to – I want to protect him and the girls from everything, to save them from what they've been through, what they're still going through – but it's out of my control. This man knows it's out of my control. He enjoys watching me suffer.

Marc must have been broken without me. So Fran brought the girls home. That's all. There's no greater meaning. I will not let him fuck with my head like this.

'You see,' he says, breaking the silence. 'To me it feels like you're placing another woman in this situation to soften the blow of your absence. To tell me it didn't make a difference, that it *doesn't* make a difference that you're here with me.' He uncrosses his arms and places his hands in his pockets. I hear the jangle of the keys.

'Fuck you,' I repeat, spitting on the concrete between us.

This time he shrugs. 'As you wish. You are your own worst enemy. You know you need to co-operate with me. It'll only get worse if you don't. And I have a limited amount of patience.'

Then he smiles. That slimy, smug smile I see in my nightmares. I've felt that smile pressing to me while I try to scream, while nobody listens. That smile makes me want to vomit.

He turns towards the door, kicking the plastic tray with the crumbs from the stale sandwich I wolfed so desperately earlier. 'This could be much, much worse for you, you know?'

1998

Friday, 28 August

At the end of the night, Marc walked me along the river path to my father's house. I was buzzing with an energy I hadn't felt since my teens. I imagined myself swallowing Marc whole as soon as he made a move, was already wondering if my dad would be asleep, whether he'd hear if I invited Marc in. Was it absurd to sneak a boy into my room in my twenties? I didn't care.

But Marc didn't kiss me, or even attempt to hold my hand on the walk back. He was the perfect gentleman, which only made me want him more. He'd been so attentive all night, drinking me in, making me feel like the centre of the universe. I imagined unbuttoning that ill-fitting shirt and running my lips across his chest, directing his nervous hands, kissing his sweet lips. He was so quiet and contained. I thought I had him pegged as this beautiful, calm man who considered his words before he spoke, who spent his days locked in the library contemplating enormous things. I wanted to unzip him, see what happened when those enormous thoughts spilt out of him. I wanted to be the thing that made him spill.

By the time we turned on to my street I felt almost crazy with desire. I was horny and tipsy and this sweet stranger had flattered me all night. But when we reached my door, Marc said, with a nervousness that suggested he expected me to refuse, that he'd like to see me again. There was such innocence in his face that even I couldn't bring myself to ignore it. I suddenly felt crass and wanton. Marc saw me as a delicate young woman, someone to be treated gently, respected. For the first time in my life, I wanted to be that girl.

I bit my lower lip, took a deep breath and admitted, 'I'm flying back tomorrow.'

Poor Marc just stared at me.

'I should have mentioned that earlier, but we were having so much fun and . . .' I trailed off.

'Oh,' Marc finally said, nothing more.

'I'll – I'll be back for Christmas,' I said. 'Maybe I'll see you then?' I offered him a half-smile.

'Great,' he mumbled, backing away.

'Thank you for today,' I said uselessly as he turned back towards the darkened path. I watched him walk, his shoulders hunched, hands thrust into his pockets. 'Wait!' I shouted and, dropping my bag on the path, ran after him.

Marc turned and I crashed into his torso, launching myself up on to the toes of my boots to press my mouth to his. I reached to run my fingers through his hair. I felt his hands tentatively touch my sides and my back, then wrap around me as if he could hold me there, in England, in York, in that moment.

I couldn't tell you if that kiss lasted seconds or minutes or a lifetime. We pulled apart and I ran back up the street, smiling like an idiot, shouting, 'See you at Christmas!'

It wasn't until I was inside that I realized we hadn't swapped numbers. I didn't even know his last name. I pulled off my dress and lay on my childhood bed, feeling it float and rock on a liquid floor.

Saturday
Forty-eight Hours Gone

Saturday slithered solemnly into existence and the girls slept late. Marc pulled on a pair of jeans and crept downstairs. Bags heavy as bricks hung beneath his lashes. His matted hair desperately needed washing. He made coffee and turned on Radio 4. The *Today* programme wafted through his thoughts as he sipped from a mug and tried to contemplate the day ahead. Fran found him as *Saturday Live* began. Whole hours lost to nothing thoughts. She made toast and told him to eat.

A little after ten the doorbell rang and he found DI Jones on the step. Marc wondered vaguely what hours he worked, whether he'd been called in for the weekend because of us.

'Dr Southwood, how are you?' he asked, removing his gloves.

How do you think I am, you idiot? Marc's mind spat in silent hostility. Outwardly he shrugged.

'I've brought some colleagues with me. We'd like to conduct a search if you don't mind?'

Marc noticed two more officers hovering by the police car. 'Well, yes,' he said, folding his arms. 'My children are asleep.'

'Perhaps we could start downstairs,' said DI Jones, maintaining eye contact.

'I'll get them up,' Fran said from the top of the stairs. 'Why don't I take them swimming, get them out of the way?'

DI Jones offered a grim smile and Marc searched his face for signs of surprise or suspicion. He felt a stab of something like guilt, but if DI Jones was making assumptions about Fran's presence, his features betrayed nothing.

'Thank you,' Marc said to Fran's retreating back, then mumbled to DI Jones about her offering to help out. He hated himself for having to explain, hated this man and his officers for making him feel he must.

DI Jones watched Marc as he spoke, finally cut in, 'Could you show us around?'

'Okay,' Marc said and three pairs of black boots tramped across the threshold. 'Can I ask what you're looking for?'

'Anything that might help,' DI Jones said levelly. 'Has Alexandra's passport turned up?'

Marc caught his eye, tried and failed to determine what he was thinking. 'No,' he said. 'You're welcome to look for it.'

'We submitted an exit check enquiry to the Border Agency yesterday,' DI Jones said, studying Marc's face. My husband scratched his temple, unsure how to respond. 'Her passport doesn't appear to have been used, but we'll have the full report on Monday.'

'I'm telling you, it's here,' Marc said. 'She wouldn't have left.'

The officers were quiet. After a pause, Marc gestured to the rooms on the ground floor. They clomped through to each in turn.

'Is there an attic space?' asked the female officer, her hair so tightly ponytailed it pulled her features into a botoxed squint.

'A little one, but we haven't been up there for years.' Marc stifled a snigger at the idea of me hiding out in the dusty roof, ready to jump out and squeal SURPRISE! 'It's just boxes.'

'We'll need access. And to any locked sheds in the garden,' the stern officer said, scribbling something on her pad.

'I'll get the keys,' Marc said.

DI Jones followed him into the kitchen. 'Would you mind if we went over a couple of things about Thursday morning?' he said.

Marc turned from the key drawer and looked into DI Jones's eyes. 'Anything that will help.'

They sat across the breakfast bar from each other and DI Jones pulled out a notebook. He asked once more about my mood and our conversations, what I was wearing and what time I left. Marc tried to answer without allowing his frustration to seep to the surface. Hadn't they gone over this? After a pause, DI Jones changed tack. He began asking what Marc was doing on Thursday, where he was at specific times. Marc told him he drove to campus; DI Jones asked where he parked. Marc said he walked to his office; DI Jones asked which route, who did he see? Marc described his supervision meetings; DI Jones asked for his timetable. Marc said he visited the library; DI Jones asked what books he checked out. Marc told him he picked up the girls; DI Jones asked about the traffic.

'This is ridiculous,' Marc said eventually. 'You're wasting time. Alex is out there, she needs you to find her.'

'That is exactly what I am trying to do,' DI Jones said.

'Rubbish!' said Marc, his face growing hot. 'You're not going to find anything in this house, you need to be looking out there!'

'I need you to calm down,' DI Jones said. 'We are doing everything we can and everything we need to. This may seem frustrating to you, but these questions and this search are just as important as everything else we're doing.'

'*What* else are you doing, though?' Marc said. 'I don't see you doing *anything* except making me feel like a suspect.'

DI Jones exhaled. 'Please, Dr Southwood. As you know, we're conducting interviews with Alexandra's friends and colleagues. We're searching her route to work and we've scheduled a public appeal for tomorrow afternoon.'

DI Jones glanced down at Marc's fists. Marc moved his hands beneath the counter.

'Right now, though,' DI Jones continued, 'we need to be in this house doing this. Do you understand?'

They stared at each other in silence for a moment. Marc caved first, flicking his eyes to the doorway. He looked through to the dining room, at the table waiting to have a school bag dumped upon it, to be cleared and laid, laughed and chatted over. He looked at the sideboard covered in pens and phone chargers, plastic toys and bills that needed filing. A framed photograph hung on the wall, not of us but another supposedly perfect family, dolled up and posed like stiff Victorians. The project I'd been playing with in my last months in Chicago seems so crass now, but Marc had found it hilarious, insisting this picture was the perfect reminder of what we'd never succumb to. He'd had it blown up and framed as a surprise, given me my own piece of work as a present the day before our wedding. The text beneath the family photograph annotated their glossy happiness with a secret desire they'd each shared only with me: 'I dream about selling up, buying a camper and travelling around India' – 'I wish my sister would wake up one day and all her hair had fallen out' – 'I want to tell my physics teacher I'm in love with her' – 'Sometimes I think about going to Ann Taylor's on a busy Saturday afternoon, taking out a knife and slitting my wrists all over the racks of beige'.

Marc peeled his gaze from the frame and back to the kitchen. He concentrated on levelling his breathing, matching DI Jones's composure. 'Is there anything else?' he said finally.

DI Jones closed his notebook, still looking at Marc. 'Not at this time. Perhaps you'd like to go swimming with your family.'

Half an hour later Marc sat in a café overlooking a pool of screaming children. Lizzie waved at him from the diving board. Marc waved back. He sipped his coffee and thought about DI Jones's questions. He'd watched enough true-crime documentaries in his life to know the police started by looking close to home, but to turn their suspicions to him was ridiculous. He should make a complaint. He'd been nothing but helpful.

Couldn't they see he was concerned, distraught? They shouldn't treat people like that, it added to the trauma. He was okay, he was confident and, anyway, had nothing to hide, but imagine what kind of damage that treatment could do to a less stable person. It wasn't right.

He scanned the pool for Charlotte, spotted her in the shallow end with Fran and a little boy who seemed to be challenging her to a bubble-blowing competition. *Nothing should be this normal right now*, he thought. That fat man in the blue Speedos shouldn't be belly-flopping and the woman with red nails next to him shouldn't be slowly consuming her bodyweight in fresh fruit. He closed his eyes and imagined the treadmills sparking and spinning out of control, worms crawling from the café food and the water in the pool boiling bubbles of blood.

'Fuck!' he said, opening his eyes as hot coffee spilled into his lap. The liquid dripped down his jeans as he stood up and looked helplessly around for something to mop it with. The woman with the red nails continued to chew, staring now at the crumpled paper cup in Marc's hand.

'We're here to appeal for information concerning the location of Mrs Alexandra Southwood, a thirty-seven-year-old part-time Art History lecturer –'

This is the third time I've been shown this video. He's placed a laptop at the end of the bed. There was an incident in the night, so my wrists and ankles are tied. I think he prefers me this way. Bound and helpless. He presses play, watches me as I watch the screen, scrutinizing my reactions.

Marc sits beside DI Jones, microphones and paraphernalia cluttering the desk before them. I watch as DI Jones continues: 'Please refer to your press packs for details of her appearance and the clothes she was last seen wearing, plus a recent photograph. I'm now going to introduce Dr Marc Southwood, Alexandra's husband, who would like to make an appeal in his own words.'

Marc glances at DI Jones and he nods for him to begin. Leaning towards a microphone and looking across the room at the camera lens, my husband clears his throat. His Adam's apple bobs as he swallows. He's trying to hold it together. I don't think my husband had ever entered a police station before all this. My face from a photograph I'd forgotten smiles back at me from posters around the room. I want to turn away, but I can't give him the satisfaction.

'Last Thursday,' Marc says, 'my wife failed to come home from work. She was last seen leaving her office on campus and saying goodbye to her colleague. She would normally have cycled across town to our home in Bootham, but nobody has seen her since she left work. This behaviour is entirely out of character for Alex. We have two young daughters. Our whole family misses her and is extremely worried.'

Marc looks up here, makes eye contact with the camera. I look into my husband's eyes as he says, 'Alex, if somehow you see or read about this, please, I urge you to get in touch. Lizzie and Charlotte need you to come home. I need to know you're safe.'

Journalists stand to take photographs and a female officer touches Marc's arm, presumably in a gesture of comfort, though if I look closely enough, I think I can see it makes him shiver. DI Jones indicates that he'll take questions. I watch Marc's face. His eyes are dark. He hasn't slept. He's clenching his jaw, grinding his teeth, I think. I want to reach into the screen and soften that expression, smooth out his lips, wash away his worries.

'Do you believe she has come to harm?' a journalist asks.

Marc closes his eyes as DI Jones responds. 'We've found no evidence to suggest so thus far, but we're treating the case very seriously.'

The journalist bows his head to scribble on his pad. Another waves his hand briefly in the air and pipes up. 'Is North Yorkshire's Police Force equipped to deal with another major missing persons inquiry?'

'That's hardly a fair question, Ralph,' DI Jones says, amicably. Marc glances at him and I can see he's annoyed. 'We're praying for Alexandra's safe and speedy return –' DI Jones goes on, but I'm watching the vein in Marc's forehead, the line of his lips. He hates this, I think. All of it, of course, but particularly the pomp and procedures, the attention and scrutiny. I wish I could take his hand and lead him home, lock us up with the girls and shut out the world, all of it: the police officers and journalists, this awful room, the psychopath keeping me here and forcing me to watch this, everyone we do and don't know, all of the expectations and responsibilities and every piece of bollocks that ever made either of us doubt the simple perfection of what we had.

'Thank you, ladies and gentlemen,' DI Jones concludes. 'We'll keep you updated on any further developments.'

The screen goes black and he lowers the laptop lid. He stands there, staring at me for full minutes. I stare back, listening to his deep, nasal breaths. His face is etched into my mind, clearer now than Lizzie's or Char's. Am I supposed to say something? Cry? I hold it in until he leaves the room. I hear him click the locks into place, then turn my head to the wall.

1998

Saturday, 26 December

Marc once told me that he spent that autumn 'walking William Blake's fires of Hell'. I laughed, of course, but he said he'd never had to get over someone he hadn't known long enough to discover a single flaw in. He replayed every word we'd said, turning my gestures and expressions into his own personal showreel. Instead of researching his thesis, he spent his hours in the library mulling the beautiful, torturous agony of having fallen for me.

By the time December came around he was so obsessed that he declined his parents' invitation to return to Wales for Christmas, pleading he had too much work to take a break. It wasn't a lie, he had fallen behind, but some shameful part of his psyche that he couldn't bring himself to acknowledge knew he was staying because of me.

He hoped he might run into me again on campus or in the city, but no luck. He grew more and more anxious as the snowy December days approached January. Finally, on Boxing Day of all days, he treated himself to half a bottle of Dutch courage, bought the least sad-looking bunch of freesias from the Jet garage and crunched along the river path. He knocked on the front door and, after a long, chilly pause, my father answered.

'Sorry to disturb you. Is, uh, is Alexandra in?' He told me he felt like a fifteen-year-old, flushed and sweaty palmed.

My father smiled. 'I think she's been expecting you.'

'Marc!' I squealed from the bowels of the house. I'd missed him too. Not in quite such an agonized way perhaps, but I'd thought about him a lot. I'd returned to Chicago and picked up my life there, thrown myself back into my immigration project and hidden from the snow in various people's beds. But I'd also started playing around with a new piece, taking pictures of the families whose dogs I walked for cash and the servers at the restaurants and banks and pharmacies I went to. In exchange for a formal portrait, I asked them to share a secret dream with me, one that didn't have to be realistic or achievable, but the thing they truly desired. I wasn't sure yet what I'd do with this collection of faces and desires, but I had a title – *My Fairy Tale* – and I knew deep down the project had something to do with the gentle man I'd met over the summer. I'd begun making plans to move to Boystown with friends after graduation, filling in applications for jobs and grants, but every time I went to a disappointing show or sat in a bar being bored by someone I probably didn't even want to go home with, I'd think of how much fun I'd had bumming around my dull little hometown with Marc. I'd think about the way his mouth moved when he said the word 'home'.

I raced down the hall and threw my arms around him like he wasn't a man I'd spent only one day with. 'You came!' I said.

I was wearing a threadbare grey jumper and faded jeans. Years later Marc told me that was how he found me most sexy: all wrapped up and warm. I remember punching him in the arm and complaining I must have wasted a small fortune on lingerie, when all I needed was a charity-shop sweater.

Marc had arrived in snow-soaked trainers and this ancient parka his dad had passed down to him. He submitted his frozen limbs to my offered embrace. My dad squeezed my shoulder and gave me a wink before tactfully disappearing through a doorway. I helped Marc shrug off his coat and happily accepted the half-crushed flowers.

He followed me to the dining room where a gathering of our

family friends was assembled around our usual extravagant roast. Marc tried to apologize and back away, but I stopped him. I found a plate and a chair and sat him down next to me. He tentatively forked a slice of turkey on to his plate, which made me laugh. I reached over my not-blood-related Aunt Margaret on my other side and slopped piles of roasted, mashed, braised and sautéed delicacies before him.

My dad laughed at me.

'He looks like he needs feeding up!' I said and turned back to my own not insubstantial plate of food.

We ate and drank and talked until all three activities seemed to require too much effort and everyone at the table slunk, half comatose, into the living room. At some point I laid my head upon Marc's lap and, although he hesitated, perhaps aware of my dad across the room and this strange collection of friends witnessing only our second real date, he placed his hand on my hair and I remember thinking I felt bizarrely content. He slept the night on one of the sofas and I woke him the next morning with a coffee and a kiss.

We spent the rest of my holidays wrapped in each other, devouring time in the most blissful way. I cooked while Marc and my dad jabbered away about critical theory and post-structural analysis and all sorts of yawn-worthy stuff that I secretly loved they could share. After dinner, Marc and I drank from oversized wine glasses late into the night, picking each other's brains as if we were trying to cram the lonely years we'd lived without one another into those short hours. He read me Byron and Keats and I showed him grainy clips of Marina Abramović and Carolee Schneemann performances. I slept late each morning while Marc scribbled in a notebook, composing sentimental poetry about suddenly feeling enlightened to the true essence of Romanticism, his thesis effortlessly rewriting itself, he said. He drove me to Heathrow, wanting to savour every possible second we had left, even if it meant crawl-ing through hellish traffic. He carried my bag to check-in and we kissed at the security gate. We both cried and he had to nudge me forcefully towards the unsympathetic guard.

It was much funnier when we told this story together. We played off each other and had whole dinner parties laughing at Marc's ridiculous appearance on my doorstep with bedraggled flowers and my absurd insistence on photographing that damn pigeon. Marc took over at this point. He said that, after watch-ing me disappear through security, he thought he might hyperventilate. He bought a coffee at one of the kiosks, hoping to calm himself down. He watched other couples and families, tried to guess by their faces whether they were going some-where together or if their hearts were about to be ripped out and stamped along with their loved ones' boarding passes.

Eventually, reluctantly, he returned to his car, getting lost in the maze of levels and cursing the machine for not accepting one of his pound coins. Muttering angrily to himself, he walked to the end of the row where he'd parked and unlocked the door. As he sat down, the passenger door opened and he bit his tongue in surprise.

'Very casually,' I always interrupted here, 'I unfolded myself from where I'd been crouched for what felt like *a year* beside the car and slipped into the seat beside him.'

Our friends always gaped at this. They never saw it coming and I loved it.

'Hey,' I said with a smile.

'W-what?' Marc stuttered, his bitten tongue starting to bleed. He looked at the clock on the dashboard. 'Your plane's leaving in fifteen minutes.'

'I'm not going.' I stared ahead, trying to look as if I was wait-ing for him to turn the key and drive, trying not to smile.

'What are you talking about?'

49

'I decided not to go,' I said with a shrug. Oh, I was so pleased with myself. My heart was pounding and I was still not entirely certain I was doing the right thing, but the amazement on his face made me so happy I wanted to scream. 'I like it here,' I said as levelly as I could. 'With you. I'll ring them tomorrow and tell them I can't finish the year, maybe make up something so they return part of my tuition.'

'But, what about − what are you going to do? What about your work?' Poor Marc was so flustered.

'It doesn't matter, does it?' I said. 'I'm happy with you and I can't face six months on different continents. Maybe I'll try teaching again; it might be better up north. And I don't need some pretentious art school in order to make art. I can do it here if I want.'

'What about your stuff? Your suitcase is on the plane. Your apartment −'

I wrinkled my nose. 'It's just clothes and junk,' I said. 'I can replace it or ship it, or I don't know. I don't care. I'll figure it out.'

'Are you sure you're making the right decision?'

'Don't you want me to stay?' I said, pouting.

'Of course I do!' Marc pulled me into a fierce, uncomfortable hug over the handbrake. 'Oh God, are you really doing this?'

'Yep, I'm really doing this.' I giggled and kissed his bloody mouth.

Monday
Four Days Gone

I've seen a photo of the Family Liaison Officer in the press clippings. She has a kind, freckled face. 'Do you think that's a requirement of the job?' I would have joked to Marc if I'd been there.

She held out her hand and Marc shook it without registering the motion. He opened the door fully and the woman stepped inside, removing her hat to reveal a tidy bun of red hair. They headed to the dining room and she sat with her hands, palms up, on the table. There must have been polite introductions, insignificant small talk, but Marc's mind was too full to absorb anything but the basics. He gathered her name was Nicola Swift, that she was there to help him through this 'difficult time'.

'If you'd like,' she said, 'I can begin by explaining the protocols we're going through and how we're working to locate your wife. Some people find it comforting to know how everything works.'

Marc nodded and she talked about taskforces and agencies and bureaus, how she and DI Jones would liaise to get the best possible response to the search for me. *There's only one response,* Marc thought, but kept quiet. She handed him information on the charity Missing People, telling him that they have a good success rate for finding lost or missing individuals. She offered to help him make the call.

'I'm sure I can manage,' Marc said, struggling to perform himself, but taking the leaflets.

'Of course.' Nicola cleared her throat but maintained eye contact. 'Now, I can't make any promises, of course, but I can give you a few statistics that might ease your mind. Three quarters of all the missing persons cases we deal with are solved within the first week. And where adults are concerned, two thirds of them have left voluntarily as opposed to by force or unintentionally. Four days without contact is not actually very long.'

Marc nodded, then shook his head, unsure what he was agreeing or disagreeing with, feeling only half present or as if his eyes and ears were full of water.

'Having said that,' Nicola continued, 'girls and women across all ages do face higher risks of being involved in crimes, which is why we're taking Alexandra's case seriously, although that is just a precaution at this stage.'

Marc's chest felt tight. He didn't care what the statistics said. He knew me. He knew I wouldn't have left on purpose. But he wasn't ready to face the other options either. Five days ago his life was normal.

'I'm sure your mind is tormenting you with all the high profile cases you've seen in the media,' Nicola said. 'But only 0.6 per cent of missing person cases are resolved by the discovery that the person has died.' She paused, a flicker of alarm fighting through her calmly composed features. Marc wondered how many times she'd done this before, whether perhaps she was quite new at it and maybe there was some handbook telling her the number one rule was never to mention the d-word. She twitched the corner of her mouth in a pinched half-smile and continued, 'I bring that up to try to comfort rather than worry you.'

Marc stared blankly through her, thinking of me sitting in her place last Wednesday and asking what he felt like for dinner. He was drowning in some parallel world and in many ways that felt simpler, more tangible and digestible than whatever his real body was experiencing in our real dining room with this real policewoman.

Misreading the silence, Nicola reached out to touch his arm. 'Do you have any questions yet?'

My husband recoiled. 'I don't think so.'

'I know it's a lot to take in, Dr Southwood,' she said.

'I'm sorry.' Marc scratched his temple and glanced at the clock. 'My children are upstairs, would you mind if I check on them?'

'Of course, I'll be right here.'

He closed the door and paused in the doorway, his mind reeling with statistics. He gulped mouthfuls of stale indoors air. He knew she was only trying to help, but this was the first time anyone had acknowledged aloud that there was a possibility, even a 0.6 per cent possibility, I might be dead. He shook his head and tried to compose himself as he climbed the stairs. I was not dead, I just couldn't be. But wherever I was, I was in trouble. I needed him to find me.

He found Fran dragging a brush through Emma's hair while Lizzie and Charlotte rummaged through an upturned washing basket, both about midway on the pyjama-to-clothes spectrum.

'I need to go home to pick up Emma's homework and I can't be late for work,' Fran said first, turning a creased forehead to Marc.

'Of course.' He attempted an apologetic smile. 'I'm sorry to do this, but is there any way Lizzie and Charlotte could come with you and you could drop them at school? I can pick them all up this afternoon, but there's an officer downstairs who needs to go through more details.'

'Does she know where Mum is?' Lizzie said.

'She's trying to work it out,' Marc replied, hoping his voice sounded reassuring.

He thanked Fran, feeling bad for imposing on her further, then gave each of our girls a squeeze. 'Work hard at school. How do you feel about pizza tonight?'

Lizzie shrugged and Charlotte nodded, biting her lip. He wanted to stay, to step towards our girls, touch them, heal them – take them far, far away from this horrible nightmare. But Fran was handing Char a pair of socks and Officer Swift was downstairs and suddenly he was drowning all over again.

He inhaled deeply before re-entering the dining room. 'Sorry about that, Officer.'

'Please, call me Nicola.'

She checked it was okay, then pulled a small Dictaphone from her pocket. Marc waited while she examined the tape and depressed the red record button.

The rest I know. He's played it for me. Over and over. I've listened to my husband's voice, tried to read between his hesitations, to picture his hands as he speaks. Nicola begins by saying she needs him to help her break down my movements in the weeks leading up to my disappearance. She asks about our work routines, apologizing for the repetition and explaining they need to gather 'the whole picture'.

My husband sighs, but tells her my lecture days vary, that I try to schedule things in school hours so I can collect the girls, but sometimes we take it in turns, that lately I've been staying late to work on a paper for a conference next month. I close my eyes and slip back into our world. I hear our alarm and smell the coffee Marc brews as I rouse the girls. I sit us around the breakfast bar, imagining the canyons carved in the butter and the flakes of cereal spilt on the counter. I pull a jumper over Charlotte's wriggling limbs, feel goodbye kisses on my skin.

'So Alex cycles and you drive?' Nicola says. 'You don't share lifts?'

'No. I mean yes,' my husband says. 'Alex likes the exercise, even in winter.'

'And after your work day?'

'We come home,' Marc says, his exasperation leaking into his tone. How many times has he gone over this by now? 'We have dinner as a family, play games or watch something. All very dull, I'm afraid.'

There's a pause, I think while Nicola scribbles something in her notebook. I always wonder here why my husband feels so apologetic for the life he already misses. I want to reach out and tell him it's okay, I miss it too. I'd give almost anything for one more boring weekday.

'A lot of the time,' Marc says, 'we just play. It sounds daft, but we turn everything into a game for the girls, invent elaborate scenarios to make doing the dishes fun. Sometimes Alex's games take up the whole evening and we're giggling right the way through.'

'Sounds wonderful,' Nicola says. I like her for finding this explanation enchanting rather than ridiculous. Some of our closest friends used to roll their eyes at us, as if we were daft Peter Pan wannabes, destined to land in reality with a thud.

'Now . . . uh, can you think of any breaks in your family's routine? Anything, however tiny?'

You can hear on the tape recording that Marc exhales before speaking. 'Only that she's been working late on this paper. She's been toying with getting a PhD for years and I think she feels this conference is her opportunity to prove she can do it. I mean, everyone else knows she can, it's just her that doesn't believe in herself.'

I had to screw up my eyes the first time I heard that. He was watching me as I listened. I couldn't let my tears fall, couldn't give him the satisfaction of seeing that.

'Okay.' There's the sound of a pencil being tapped on a notebook. 'And you've had no fights? The children haven't been in trouble at school?'

'No, everything's been normal. We're a happy family. I mean, we were.'

It's hard to tell with such a low-quality recording, but I have the impression she wants him to say we had problems. Does Nicola think he's hiding something, protesting too much? Perhaps Marc's supposed to tell her I complained he worked too much or that he worried about the amount I spent on clothes and home furnishings. Perhaps he's meant to talk about Lizzie's attitude problem and the tears I let fall when my daughter disobeyed me, about the spats I had with his mother and how tired he was of mediating between us. Perhaps it would have been simpler if he'd shown her our cracks.

Nicola tells him they've spoken to my mother's carer. 'Given Mrs Carlisle's condition,' she says, 'we haven't made it a priority to interview her, though we may pursue that avenue soon.'

She asks about our friends and Marc tells her where we met them, what they do. My husband sounds like he's not sure what she wants him to say, so he keeps talking until she interrupts.

'Does Alexandra have friends she sees without you?'

'I suppose,' he says. 'She's still in contact with someone she knew at secondary school. They catch up once a month or so. And obviously there are people from work she sometimes goes for a drink with, and she's on the PTA.'

'What about in America? She studied there, yes?'

'Just for a year,' Marc says. 'She's still close to her old roommate, Amelia. They write to each other.'

'By hand?' Nicola says, interested. 'Does Alexandra keep the letters? Would they be here?'

'I've no idea,' Marc says. 'I never asked her.'

'You've never asked your wife about a friend she's stayed in contact with for the past fourteen years?' There's an edge now in Nicola's voice and I don't like her any more. I picture the quiver of Marc's shoulders as his muscles tense.

'That's not what I said,' he replies. 'We talk about her. Al's been following her career as a performance artist. She's shown me her reviews. I just don't know if she keeps her letters. She's fairly prominent. Amelia Heldt?'

A pause, and I picture Nicola showing no sign of recognition. Marc would have been smug at this.

Then a phone rings and Nicola must pause the tape to answer it, because next she's saying, 'That was DI Jones. Alexandra's exit records have come through. Her passport has not been used at any UK airports or ports.'

'Okay,' Marc says.

There are a few moments of silence before Nicola asks, 'Does Alexandra travel frequently?'

'No,' Marc says.

'What about to America? Perhaps to visit her friend?'

'She's only been back a couple of times. The last trip was two or three years ago.'

There's another pause. 'Did you go with her?' Nicola says eventually.

'She only went for a week and a half,' Marc says dully. 'Hardly worth the jet lag.' How surreal it feels to listen to him speak to a policewoman about our life with the same words, the same stock phrases I've heard him use when meeting new colleagues or catching up with the neighbours.

The recording ends soon after that. I imagine Marc standing up to see her to the door, blood rushing to his head and him having to steady himself against the back of his chair.

'Try not to worry, Dr Southwood,' Nicola will have said. 'One way or another, we'll find out what's happened.'

'How tragic that you've lost so much,' he says, ejecting the tape. 'Sounds like you had the true fairy tale.'

I refuse to look at him. I know it sounds like a fairy tale, but

I hate being mocked for it. I know the officers doubted Marc too. Maybe I would have a hard time believing it if someone else told me that after more than a decade of marriage they were as happy as when they met. But it's true. Or was until that Thursday. Our life together wasn't like normal life. I'd seen my parents destroy everything that had ever been lovely between them, so when I got married I vowed never to do that. I vowed to give Marc the happiness he deserved, the future I wanted to believe we both deserved. I worked hard to keep our world light. I didn't see the point of the heaviness and the moods. I made up games to entertain the girls while we loaded the dishwasher or when they started to flag towards the end of a long walk. And I did the same for us too. I didn't want to hold anything back from Marc, but I wanted our love to be about joy and play and pleasure. I'd seen marriages crumble, our friends get so bogged down in the minutiae of life that they forgot how to make each other smile. My mother abandoned my father for the bottle a decade before they divorced; she turned into a different woman and my dad, too, was transformed into a tyrant for her to rebel against. He couldn't even say her name after she left.

So all those things that made Marc worry, I tried to let them wash over me. I tried to see through them and ask what he thought mattered so much. Mortgages and bills, promotions and forms the bank asked us to fill in: what was the point of me stressing about them as well as Marc? I could so easily have been that wife. That nagging, worrying, frowning wife. I could have told him my every thought and grumble. But why? What would it have achieved? Instead, I laughed and said, yeah, we'll do it, but don't forget how amazing the simple fact of you and me and Lizzie and Charlotte holding hands and picking blackberries is.

'Jack and Jill went up the hill to fetch a pail of water,' he sings, invading my thoughts.

I imagine punching the smile off his face, bashing his head

against the wall. I've paced this room a thousand times looking for something to defend myself with, something to use to break out. I know there's more than this door, though. I'd need all of his keys. And where would I find myself? I imagine I'm at the centre of a maze, visited daily by my own personal minotaur.

'Humpty Dumpty sat on the wall,' he says, his voice dropping its sing-song sugar.

'What do you want?' I spit.

He locks his eyes on mine. 'What do we know about fairy tales and nursery rhymes? Humpty Dumpty fell and Jack broke his crown and poor little Alex couldn't be put back together.'

He laughs again. A big, confident belly laugh. He's still laughing as he locks the door behind him, as I curl my knees up to my chest and try to take myself away from this place.

He wants me to believe I deserve this. The happier I tell him we were, the more excited he gets. 'Look where it got you,' he says.

It makes no sense, I know, but I wish I could have been with Marc to help him through that first week. I wish he could be with me now. For fourteen years we faced things together. For fourteen years Marc had someone to turn to, someone to confer with – to share the burden, split the responsibility and divide the pain with. For fourteen years I helped him through. Yet suddenly he was alone. It breaks my heart to imagine that breaking his.

1999

4/16/99
Dearest Al,

Here goes our epistolary exchange. I can't forgive you for leaving me, room-mateless, friendless. You've ripped us apart in the most unnatural of ways. The showcase is next week, for fuck's sake. How am I going to survive without you here? Couldn't you have stayed a few more months? What were you thinking? You could have lived without screwing Prince Charming for one more semester, couldn't you?

I know, I know, he changed your whole perspective on life, blah-blah-cocksucking-blah. I don't buy it. One minute you're an artist with all these rebellious passions. But you go home for a few weeks and all that flutters out of your heart like so much child's play. Suddenly you're a walking cliché. Are you already imagining a nice big house and a dozen von Trapp children?

I want to be happy for you, Al, but how can you change yourself for a man? What happens after this honeymoon period is over, when the artist inside you starts to hack her way out? You'll resent him, you know. That's what happens. Suddenly someone likes this kind of music rather than that, or a person used to scoffing popcorn in front of HBO decides out of the blue that they just love hiking and white-water rafting because their new beau is the outdoorsy type. People wear different clothes, cut their hair, paint their faces, reinvent themselves to meet someone else's idea of perfection. And then one day they wake up and hack their loved one into a hundred pieces and feed them to the dog.

Okay, maybe not, but still. Everyone does it to some extent, but shit, Al, you've gone all out. You're looking for teaching work! You're back in

the country you used to hate. The city you complained was as diverse as
an Oasis concert. You're playing happy families with some guy. All those
nights we spent talking about bringing down the bourgeoisie, about living
beautiful bohemian lives, about attacking the system, challenging the
patriarchy. All the conversations about our duty to do such things, about
the impossibility of just rolling over and accepting this shitty world as it is.
All those lives we were going to lead. I know I'm not impartial, but I
hope you know what you're doing.

   I won't say any more. This is the last time I'll criticize, because maybe
I'm the one that's got it wrong. Maybe you've found your true self with
this Marc and the Al I knew was the performance. I hope so, because I
want you to be happy. It's selfish, but I wish it could be with me.

Love
Am xxx

Thursday, 10 June 1999

The first one arrived on a Thursday. Somehow I knew as soon as
I heard the letterbox fall shut. It made this horrendous squeak,
however much WD-40 we squirted on it. Anyone else would
have thought our first flat a dive. The previous tenant had lived
there for a decade. There was no shower, just a grubby bathtub.
The tiles were coming loose. Every window frame was coated
in a layer of grime. The thin carpets were stained. The place
came furnished, but when Marc placed his thesis file on the desk,
one of the front legs collapsed and we had to hack it up with a
cheap coping saw to get it out of the building.

We didn't care. We saw space for bookshelves made of bricks,
paper snowflakes hung from beams, a real Christmas tree in the
corner, a futon we'd keep permanently in 'bed formation' and a
shelf beside the bathtub for our wine glasses. Patrick and his first
wife, Rebecca, had just moved to York with their two-year-old

daughter, and he and Marc had picked up where they left off after university. They helped us clear the place up, and Rebecca and I hunted in second-hand furniture shops for a replacement desk and strange little objects to make it a home. We splashed out on a coffee machine and settled into a routine of Marc bringing me a steaming mug each morning. He'd coax me to get up and on with applying for jobs, and I'd bully him to crawl back under the duvet and while away the morning. If one of us had to nip out for milk, we'd stop what we were doing to kiss goodbye, lingering as if it might be months before we returned. Marc was meant to be finishing his dissertation and I should have been finding a job. Instead, we frittered entire weeks. We'd look at the clock and it'd be 6 p.m., a whole sumptuous day swallowed by each other. We'd giggle guiltily and ask how the other thought that could have happened.

That day Marc had insisted he needed to go to the library. My pleas had failed and he'd left me with a full coffee pot and instructions to apply for the admin post at the uni that had just been advertised. I knew I should, but my brain was already thinking of other ways to spend the day. I'd been feeling the itch to make something again. I hadn't told Marc because I knew it'd make him worry. Maybe I'd go for a wander with my camera, think about some small project I could work on while he was at the library.

I'd heard him on the phone to his mother last night and wondered if his new work ethic had something to do with her. I remember those first months as blissful, but I know they were also tainted for Marc by his concern that I would regret staying. He tried to hide it, but I knew. He wanted to watch me every second, worried about each frown. I told him over and over that I regretted nothing, but he still couldn't be sure. I think our main problem was other people. To outsiders it seemed absurd and impulsive. Patrick and Rebecca had welcomed me with open arms, but I know Marc's mother kept asking what was going on. She couldn't understand where I'd materialized from and how crazy her son could be about me.

I waited until the postman clanged the gate, then swung my legs out of bed and padded down the stairs. I paused, looking at the envelope on the mat, my name written scrappily in that familiar left-hand scrawl. I considered leaving it there until Marc returned, wanting to validate its existence through his eyes. But he'd ask what was wrong if he arrived home at six and found I hadn't even picked up the post from the mat. He'd fuss over me all night, worrying what I was thinking, if I might be depressed, finally ask if I was having second thoughts. I'd have to soothe and coo and convince him that I wasn't. Because I wasn't, I really wasn't. I was happier than I'd ever been.

So why were my palms sweating as I stared at an envelope on our scratchy doormat?

Wednesday
Six Days Gone

Marc had no idea when he woke how much the day ahead would break him. He dropped the girls at school and drove to campus. He'd rung John yesterday and told him he'd be in for his lecture.

'Are you sure?' his colleague had said. 'You can take as much time as you need.' But Marc wanted to be busy. He couldn't sit around the house for another day feeling this helpless. He couldn't stand living in this limbo state. And, apart from anything, it was pretty hypocritical to force the girls to go to school, abandon their worried faces at the gates, but not make himself do the same. Still, he felt eyes on him as he made his way around the lake to his office. Were people judging him for his presence here?

His lecture was surprisingly full. The roof of his mouth felt dry as he wondered if these teenagers were here to learn about Landscape and the Sublime or just to gawp at the poor sod they'd seen on the telly. He stood at the front finding reasons to fiddle with his bag. Every few moments he cast a furtive glance at the auditorium. He noticed an arm draped over a shoulder, a head slumped on a desk, a flustered commotion as someone hurried in the back and struggled to find a seat. A blonde woman with a ponytail held his gaze until he looked away.

A couple of minutes after eleven he cleared his throat and shuffled his papers on the lectern.

'Right, I think we'll start.'

The voices died to a murmur and then silence. Marc heard the crinkle of a water bottle, a lone phone ping, a cough.

'Thank you all for coming,' he said. He stared out at the rows of expectant faces, pens poised over pads. He swallowed.

'What we, um, right, what we're going to look at today is, uh, the way, uh —'

Marc looked down at his notes. He liked this lecture, gave it every year. Normally he barely had to look at these prompts. Normally he added in a couple of jokes. Normally he enjoyed making a crowd like this titter. He loved glancing up and seeing them all scrawling notes, knowing his words were inspiring different thoughts in each of their brains, his ideas germinating theirs.

But eighty pairs of eyes now sat waiting for him to give them an idea and my poor husband couldn't even move his mouth around his title. He scanned the crowd, looking from face to face, not understanding how all these girls and boys could be sitting here in perfect health, growing bored and impatient, while I was not.

'I'm sorry,' he said, his voice catching in the back of his throat. A murmur rolled through the room as eighty students shifted their weight and exchanged looks with one another.

He bent down, shielding his head behind the lectern. He took a deep breath and then groped for his bag, seeking an alibi for his strange behaviour. Slowly, he unfolded himself and looked back out from behind the lectern, waving a pen in the air.

The room was silent.

'Sorry,' Marc said again. He cleared his throat. 'Where were we?' He scratched his temple and looked down at his lecture. The words swam before his eyes. He blinked and a tear fell into the middle of his page. Marc looked at the students again, his heart thudding in his chest. He saw faces turn away, mouths whispering into ears. There was a commotion on the left side of the room. Marc turned, his vision blurry. The blonde woman with the ponytail was getting out of her seat, climbing towards the end of the row. My husband stared, along with everyone else in the room, as she walked down the stairs and across the small stage towards his lectern.

She was in front of him now. She placed her hand on Marc's arm. He looked down at the fingers on his shirt.

'Are you okay, Dr Southwood?' she said. 'Should I get someone?'

Marc felt the wetness on his cheeks, became aware of his chest rising and falling, of the feeling like there wasn't enough oxygen in the room.

'I need to, um, I need to go,' he said quietly, searching the woman's face in panic.

'Of course,' she said. She stepped behind the lectern and picked up his bag. She opened the flap and placed his lecture notes inside, then held out the handle to him. 'Will you be okay?'

Marc nodded as he took the bag from her, trying to suppress the urge to sprint.

He murmured apologies as he climbed the stairs to the door, heads turning as he passed each row. At the top of the room he touched his temple and turned back to address them. 'This lecture will be rescheduled,' he said, his voice like sandpaper. 'You'll get an email from the department.'

He heard the sound of their voices swelling before the door closed behind him and he hurried along the corridor. He didn't have a plan; he wasn't going anywhere except away. He turned left, then right, out through the automatic doors and along the covered walkway to the next building. He took the first set of stairs, then wove unthinkingly along the first-floor corridor, past closed doors and posters advertising readings and discussion groups. It wasn't until he found himself staring at my name that he realized he'd had a destination all along. He stood outside the office I shared with Rosa, staring at our name plaques and the piece of paper telling him my tutorial hours were Tuesdays and Thursdays between one and three, hers were Mondays and Fridays between ten and twelve. Marc's heart beat in his ears, his kneecaps trembled. What was he doing here? How could he have thought he could give a lecture? What was wrong with him?

A door opened behind him.

'Marc?'

He turned and recognized Paula. She wore a creased man's suit jacket and a thick silver necklace.

'Are you okay?' she said, putting down her satchel.

'I – I just walked out of a lecture,' he said, as if only just realizing that's what he'd done.

'Oh Marc,' Paula said. 'Don't worry about that. Come and sit down.' She ushered him into her office and removed her jacket. 'Take a seat,' she instructed.

Marc sat in the armchair intended for students during supervisions. He almost felt like a scared little eighteen-year-old, unsure how to act in this strangely adult world.

'Does anyone know where you are?'

Marc shook his head.

'Okay,' said Paula. 'Well, I'm going to let the porter know you're okay in case anyone's worried. I'm also just going to nip down the hall and cancel my meeting. I'll be back in one sec, okay?'

Marc nodded and Paula left. He scrunched up his face and willed himself not to lose control. The window was open and he could hear students chatting in the courtyard below. How was it possible everything here was so normal? How could classes and seminars and meetings be going on as if nothing had happened?

Paula returned with two mugs of tea. She handed Marc the one reading Keep Calm and Drink Tea and sat down behind her desk.

She looked at him, her tight, tanned face drawn with concern. 'How are you?'

Marc curled his hand around the mug so Paula wouldn't see the design and feel the need to apologize. 'Fine,' he said. 'That's not what matters, is it?'

'It is,' she said. 'You need to look after yourself.' Her voice was strict and commanding, but oddly reassuring in its absence of false comfort. I loved Paula for her bluntness. She was highly critical and said what she thought, but it meant on the rare occasion she said something positive you knew she was truly impressed.

'Why?' Marc asked. 'What's the point without Al?'

'All the more point,' Paula said and he recognized the sternness for which students had nicknamed her Bulldog. 'You need to remain positive. You need to think of the girls.'

'I'm a husband without a wife,' he said through wet fingers. 'I keep wondering if Alex is alone too. Is it too romantic a notion to draw comfort from the idea that we're alone together? Wherever she is, perhaps she's thinking of me. Is that ridiculous?'

'No,' Paula said. 'It's not ridiculous. I'm sorry, we're all sorry. And we're here for you if you need us.'

They sat in silence for a while, Marc occasionally swallowing a sob and Paula seemingly torn between comforting him and letting him get on with it. He knew he was being morose, knew he should pull himself together and concentrate on helping the police find me. But he felt like he'd been holding it together for days, putting on a brave face for the girls, convincing even himself he was able to work, to function. Paula was the first person who'd asked him how he was that he hadn't felt he needed to bullshit.

She remained at her desk, for which Marc was grateful, imagining his whole body might melt at the lightest of touches. He tried to breathe evenly, focusing his gaze on the image of a lipsticked woman emerging from shards of crystal adorning the cover of a textbook on Paula's desk. How, he wondered, had he come to be bursting into tears in this woman's office, and what must she make of him as a fellow academic?

There was a knock at the door. Marc looked up, panicked. Paula waited while he wiped his eyes and sat up straight, then answered.

It was Veronica, my department secretary, with a couple of young lecturers whose faces Marc recognized but couldn't name.

'We just wanted to say how sorry we are,' Veronica stepped through the partially open door and the others followed awkwardly. 'If there's anything we can do . . .'

'Inspector Jones came to search the offices and interview us yesterday,' Paula said, perhaps worried he'd think she'd gossiped.

'We told them everything we could think of, but none of us can believe this has really happened. It's so *unlike* Alex,' Veronica drawled, a note of excitement in her voice.

'Thank you for your concern,' Marc said without conviction.

'Well, we'll leave you to it,' Veronica said. 'You know where to find us.'

The other two muttered barely audible sympathy and leapt back out of the office. After Paula closed the door, they heard Veronica's shrill voice echo in the hallway: 'I don't know *how* he's coping. He *must* be preparing for the worst. It's only a matter of time before they find a body, don'tcha think?'

'That's if he doesn't already know,' one of the lecturers replied as their voices faded. 'Almost all crimes are committed by someone the victim . . .'

'Ignore them,' Paula said, studying Marc's face for signs of trauma.

'It's okay,' he said. 'I know it's what everyone's thinking.' He gave Paula an awkward smile. She turned to her computer and he allowed his features to fall, his gaze resting back on the textbook. This time he read the title, *Artists in Focus: Marina Abramović*.

'Can I borrow this?' he said.

Paula looked up, then down at the book. She shrugged. 'If you like.'

There was another knock at the door and Paula and Marc made eye contact. 'Perhaps it wasn't such a good idea to tell the porter you're here,' she said.

'It's fine,' Marc said. 'I can't exactly hide from the world.'

Paula frowned, but got up to open the door. Nicola and DI Jones stood on the other side.

'Sorry to disturb you,' DI Jones said. 'Dr Southwood, could we have a word?'

Marc nodded and went to stand up, but Paula gestured for him to stay put. 'I'll give you some privacy,' she said, ushering the officers into the room and gathering a couple of things from her desk. She handed Marc the book. 'I'll be downstairs if you need me,' she told him, then left.

DI Jones and Nicola stood awkwardly between Marc and the desk. 'We have some new information,' DI Jones said. 'It's not conclusive, but I'm afraid it indicates bad news.'

The muscles in Marc's throat contracted.

'We think we've found some of Alexandra's things and we're going to need you to identify them.'

Marc's hands began to shake in his lap. 'W-where?' he managed to stammer.

'By the river,' Nicola said.

'This morning we picked up some teenagers with a number of stolen bicycles,' DI Jones said. 'One of them matched the description you gave of Alexandra's.'

'I don't understand,' Marc said, his breath shallow.

'We brought the youths in for questioning,' DI Jones said. 'One of them admitted to finding the bicycle in question on the riverside path last week. We're keeping him in, but it seems likely he's telling the truth. His description led us to an area just along from Millennium Bridge.'

'Why would Al's things be by the river?' Marc said, his voice suddenly too loud for the room.

'We don't know yet, Dr Southwood. The first step is to positively identify them as Alexandra's.'

'And if they are?'

DI Jones drew a breath, then answered in a softer tone. 'We've also found blood. We're treating it as a crime scene.'

Marc saw students peeking from curtained rooms as he followed DI Jones and Nicola to the police car. They were providing the day's drama. Newsworthy sightings to be indiscreetly disclosed in campus bars and shared kitchens. *Did you see Marc Southwood? Did you hear what happened?* My husband's mind felt like a record player with ten needles trying to play all the tracks at once. He was whizzed through the city, the wordless silence a cacophony in his ears.

Later, he watched the ten o'clock news. DI Jones made the national clips. He stood in front of the river, police tape flapping behind him. 'In light of today's discoveries, we must admit the high probability that Alexandra Southwood has come to harm.'

This is harder than I thought it would be. I wish I could imagine my husband discovering me gone, sobbing for a couple of hours, and then getting on with his life. I wish I could have woken in the night and unstitched myself from his heart, undone all of the things that tied us together, so he wouldn't have had to suffer. I wish the same for our babies too, though I can barely bring myself to think of them. That I may never see my children again is almost impossible to contemplate. He asks what I would say to them if I could, what I hope they'll remember about me. I know he wants me to break. I tell him to get on with it, do what he wants to me, just stop torturing me with these questions. He stands before me in silence, studying me like some specimen he might put in a jar.

1999

Monday, 16 August

'It's strange,' I said, my head on Marc's chest.

He waited for me to finish my sentence, his eyes following a cloud as it morphed leisurely across the summer sky. We had a couple more hours until we should head over to Patrick and Rebecca's. There was a new doctor, Frances, at Patrick's surgery and he'd been talking for weeks about how much we'd get on with her. Rebecca had promised her grandmother's coq au vin for the occasion.

'What's strange?' Marc asked eventually, propping himself on his elbows to look at me. The movement forced me to shift too, prising my eyes from a pair of ducks gliding with the current. Staring at the ducks, I'd been able to imagine us alone on some private riverbank in the middle of nowhere, at harmony with each other and nature. Sitting up, I was forced to acknowledge those we were sharing this privacy with: the dog walkers and cyclists crossing the bridge, the ice-cream truck on the opposite bank and the students picnicking and pretending to study.

'That I'm so happy here,' I replied, turning my attention back to the water. My ducks had gone.

'Why's that strange?' Marc asked, a touch of nervousness in his voice.

'I don't mean bad strange,' I said quickly, swivelling my head so I could meet his eyes. Had I said the wrong thing? I was trying to be honest, to share myself. Perhaps I just needed to explain. 'Not bad strange, but curious. It's an odd feeling for me, being so supremely content, especially so far away from the things I thought would make me happy. I almost feel like a different person.'

Marc tensed. I laid my palm over his heart. 'Don't – please, I mean it, I'm happy. You make me happy. It's just weird when I think about my life last year, about how desperately I wanted to stay in Chicago and live, I don't know, in a way that mattered.'

'Does this not matter?' he said.

'That's not what I mean. You're twisting my words. It's just, for so long I've felt this anger and passion, this need to escape all this *niceness*. I mean, if you'd met me in a seminar having a shouting match with my tutor about the art industry's inherent race and gender biases and told me a year later I'd be lying by the river in York eating grapes from the market and feeling this disgustingly, gushingly in love, I'd have punched you.'

'I didn't mean to interfere with your plans. I'm sorry,' Marc said with a smile, but also an edge in his voice that made me wonder if it was really a joke.

'You should be!' I said, deciding not to push it. I sat up and reached my arms around him. My fingers crawled over his skin, tickling his sides until he squirmed as I panted, 'I. Might. Have. Been. The. Next. Marina. Abramović. Your. Hideously. Amazing. Love. Has. Denied. The. World. My. Art.'

'The next who?' Marc said, gasping for breath between giggles.

'You philistine!' I said, rolling my eyes. 'Fine, the next Andy Warhol or Damien Hirst or Tracey Emin.'

'You wanted to be the next Tracey Emin?' Marc said. 'More like I've spared the world. I'm a hero!'

I growled in frustration and Marc took the opportunity to end the tickling by grabbing my hands and pinning me to the grass.

'I love you,' I said seriously, that second struck by the magnitude of the declaration.

He hovered above me, studying my features. I looked up at him, wishing I could read his thoughts. Was this strange for him too? He seemed so comfortable and at ease. Did he have no angst, no worries, no guilt? How to explain that I'd feel closer to him if he did, if he admitted he didn't have a clue either. We could wade into the murky, mysterious water and glide into the unknown together. But Marc seemed okay. He seemed happy being happy, like it was natural and enough. Like it needed no extra thought.

One Week Gone

Nicola led Marc back along the dead-end path to the right of the bridge. He knew what to expect this time, but his hands still shook in his pockets, his tongue felt swollen in his mouth. At the end of the path, nestled between the trees and the water, there was a square of tape. Inside, my blue coat and grey scarf lay crumpled as if I'd just shed them. Marc had cried out when he saw them the day before, a guttural, almost animal wail. This morning he clenched his teeth and forced himself to keep walking.

My handbag was cordoned off by more tape, tipped upside down and missing various items, including my purse and phone. A tyre print blemished the mud. Closer to the bank lay a shoe and my houndstooth jumper, a dark stain spread along the side of the torso. They sat on an irregular shadow of black mud and leaves. Smaller bits of tape marked other shadows.

'Is that bl—' Marc had tried to ask yesterday, but crumpled before he could say the word. DI Jones hadn't answered. Instead he'd quietly asked if Marc was sure the belongings were mine. All my husband had been able to do was nod.

'We're continuing to question the individual who took the bike,' Nicola said now. 'We need to establish a timeline. He says he found the bike last Friday, but denies ransacking the bag. He says he didn't see the blood. It's possible he's telling the truth, but he may just be scared –'

'What if he's lying?' I imagine Marc interrupting. Nicola and DI Jones had looked at the evidence and settled on a narrative, but my husband couldn't do the same. As obvious as it seemed

76

and as tempting as a conclusive explanation was right then, I know that even with my blood and belongings displayed before him Marc was ready to clutch at anything. He was desperate for an answer that didn't lie in the depths of the Ouse.

'What if this guy did something to Alex?' Marc said. 'Or took her somewhere? Who is he? What do you know about him?'

Nicola couldn't tell him much except that the individual in question was a minor with no prior convictions and he appeared to be co-operating fully. 'We're not discounting anything at this stage,' she said. 'But we're working on the assumption that these items have been here since last Thursday and that both the bike and Alexandra's belongings were taken sometime on Friday, before any appeals went out. After that it seems likely the thief or thieves may have been too worried to report what they found.'

Every hour or so DI Jones came over to give my husband an update on their progress. Four officers bobbed along in kayaks, while six more waded through the brown water in industrial diving suits. Nicola told Marc the ones in suits were called Frogmen. 'If there's anything in the water, they'll find it,' she said.

'They can't search every inch, though, can they?' he said.

'Actually, dredging a river of this size is remarkably effective. Bodies naturally float, so you just have to disturb the bottom really.'

Marc wished he hadn't asked.

On the other side of the tape he could see camera crews and reporters as well as a collection of curious passers-by. Nicola told him they'd cancelled the Red Boats for the day and they intended to search a mile downriver. Marc wondered how many people's days they were disturbing.

The work was slow and methodical, nothing like the hectic drama of film and television. I can imagine my husband sitting there, itchy in his own skin, unable to take his eyes from the water. What was he hoping for? Not a body, of course, but some conclusive piece of evidence that would tell them where I was. For me to drift up like a mermaid and sun myself on one of the barges. For an answer to the questions he was too afraid to ask.

Nicola told him he should go home, that they'd phone if they discovered anything. But he couldn't leave. I know my husband. He would have needed to be there. We saluted single magpies, threw salt over our shoulders and told the girls watched pots would never boil. If they'd have let Marc wade into the brown water, he would have.

Around four, one of the officers manning the cordons tapped him on the shoulder. 'Sorry to interrupt,' he said, bowing his head. 'There's a woman over there says she knows you.'

Marc turned and saw Susan sandwiched between two reporters with oversized cameras eagerly snapping in his direction. Marc nodded and watched the officer let her through. He felt a stab of guilt at not having checked in with her and Patrick since that first night.

'Marc!' she said as she approached. 'My God, are you okay?' She pulled him into a suffocating hug, filling his nostrils with her floral perfume. He saw Nicola retreat to talk to another officer.

'I can't believe it,' Susan said, straightening her thick woollen coat. 'This can't be happening.'

Marc once confessed to me that he struggled to talk to Susan when it was just the two of them, that he liked her, of course, but they had nothing in common. I took offence at the time, especially given how happy she and Patrick seemed together. It had been hard for us all when Rebecca left; she and Patrick had been a constant in our lives for so long. But I was proud of having introduced him to Susan, of having been the one to successfully matchmake Marc's oldest friend, especially after everything he'd been through. I'd met Susan at a pottery class and had this strange, intense premonition that this ditzy, hippy teacher was exactly what Patrick needed.

What was Marc supposed to say to her, though, while he sat by the river waiting for someone to pull my swollen cadaver from its depths? While he tried and failed to prepare for the worst?

Observing her twisting her rings and running her hands through her tangled hair, he realized she might actually be suffering. So far my disappearance had seemed like his private tragedy. The girls' too, of course, but contained within immediate family.

'Are Lizzie and Charlotte with Fran?' Susan said. Marc realized our friends must have talked. Of course they would have, but it made him uneasy.

He shook his head. 'My parents drove up this morning.'

'That's good,' Susan said, touching his hand. 'You need support.'

Marc didn't respond. He returned his gaze to the water, watched a Frogman inspect a clump of weeds.

'Do they think she's in there?'

Marc dug his nails into his palm. 'Just because her things are here, it doesn't necessarily mean . . .' He trailed off, unable to say it.

He felt Susan's eyes on him. After a moment she said softly, 'It's been over a week. Fran said there was blood –' She faltered. 'I mean, we've probably got to prepare for the worst. What other explanation is there? The best-case scenario is that she had a terrible, tragic accident –'

'Don't,' he said, cutting her off. He felt like someone had punched him in the kidneys. What kind of accident would involve me leaving my clothes and blood on the bank? What scenario exactly did she think that was better than? 'Please, I just can't believe that. Not yet.'

'Sorry,' she said, touching him again. He drew away.

She sat with him for a while, watching the policemen stir up nothing in the murky water. With a primary school teacher's aptitude for small talk, she told him the Ouse isn't as dirty as it looks, that it gets its colour from the peat fields it drains, that all of York's drinking water comes from it. Her voice filled the silent air, but Marc's attention never left the water. Eventually she kissed him on the cheek and promised she and Patrick would pop round to check up on him. He hoped they'd forget. He knew I didn't belong solely to him, but his head hurt when he tried to think of all the people in my life, all those he might be expected to speak to or receive sympathy from.

They kept searching, shuffling the police tape along the pathway and into town until dusk settled. DI Jones explained they'd pack up for the day and resume at dawn. Nicola drove Marc home and he let himself into a house smelling of his mother's cooking.

'Your time's almost up,' he said today.

I was lying on the bed when he came in, my face pressed to the pillow.

'Look at me,' he commanded. My shirt twisted as I rolled over and I saw his eyes land on my stomach, on the long purple scar. I pulled the fabric down to cover myself, but his eyes remained there. I curled around myself, remembering the pain, the slice of the knife through my flesh.

'What do you want?' I said, no fight in me today.

He looked dishevelled. There were shadows beneath his eyes. I sat up, my curiosity piqued. What was he worried about?

'I can't keep you here indefinitely,' he said. 'I need to make a decision.'

He says I have one more month to convince him I'm worth

saving. Whatever that means in his warped little mind. Four more weeks to figure out the rules and learn to play his game. And if I can't? What then? Where will he send me? What does he have planned?

How much more is it possible to lose?

2000

1/14/00

Hey sweets,

I suppose the first thing to say is congratufuckinglations. Are you simply drowning in happiness? Will you change your name? Alexandra South-wood, wife and former individual.

Sorry, I said I wouldn't criticize, didn't I? As long as you're happy, then I'm happy. What else is going on with you? Are you embracing your nice British life? Is teaching everything you dreaded?

I'm okay, I think. A bit lonely. Sometimes I don't know what I'm doing or who I am. Life was simple when there were semesters and dead-lines and lectures to wake up for. Without that and without you, I've lost my structure. Let's build a magical, Narnia-esque portal between 'old' and 'New' York so I don't have to bum around this callous city alone.

Don't get me wrong, I love Manhattan. I'm in crisis, but I'm also enjoying it. Does that make sense? I've always thought the best art comes from misery. That's my excuse for these hangovers anyway. I think maybe I should give up drinking. I worry I can't enjoy just one, that I'm looking for oblivion. I wake up in the morning with that terrible shame in the pit of my stomach where I wonder if I've made an ass of myself, exposed too much of who I really am. I lie beneath the blankets working through what I remember, terrified I might have divulged my deepest darkest secrets to someone. Alcohol makes me feel both smart and confessional – perhaps not the best mix for someone like me.

Maybe I'm not so smart anyway. I'm making very little. My head's so full of other stuff that art gets further and further away. Art's what I want, what makes me feel alive, but it seems like the stupidest thing to pursue. Obviously, rationally, it is. It's never going to pay my rent. I look at you getting married and settling down, with your teaching job and your real life, and I feel dumb for wanting to keep running after that stupid little dream we had at art school. It seems insane.

On the other hand, when I quiet my mind, I realize I don't have a choice. If I don't run after it, what the hell were either of us there for? What was the point? The terrible, torturous, beautiful truth is that I can't see myself being happy without creativity. Without rebellion. Without an avenue of protest.

I guess because I don't yet know where art fits into life and life into art, I'm playing with these ideas of invisibility. Pieces as part of the reality people live in, so that maybe they're not aware they're even experiencing art but it influences their lives nonetheless. It's all about what I can get away with, probably more prankster than artist, but it feels like an appropriate way to begin to make my mark on the city. I send instructions to people. Usually I'm not even there at the time, so it's kinda me influencing the place from afar. I tell delivery boys to leave five boxes of pizza around the corner from where I know this one homeless guy sleeps, or I pay a student to leave a trail of M&Ms all around the East Village. Then I post challenges on this amateur photography forum asking readers to photograph specific streets at certain times and upload what they see. It's great because some of the photographers are so oblivious that they take these arty shots of empty chip packets and graffiti tags, but you can still see the piece in the background. Others think it's just a weird New York coincidence and snap happily away. There's this great shot of a bakery owner coming out and throwing all the pizzas in the trash. Like, what the cock? Another time, though, someone caught a passer-by carrying them over to the homeless dude.

What else? Last month I wrote to the Postal Service and asked if they could write me a letter. They sent back an automatically generated reply on headed paper saying they were unable to respond to my enquiry. It's pointless, I know, but it's kinda fun and makes me feel less like the world is slurping my brain through a straw.

Love
Am x

I nodded and called him an idiot. We grabbed each other over the spiky crustaceans. The toes of our shoes dipped in the rock pools, our jeans soaking up seaweed slime. It was winter. The icy wind whipped off the sea. I shivered and smiled. We sat there most of the day, huddled in our coats, watching the tide head out and people come and go. We could have gone to a pub, but we didn't want to move. Every now and again I'd slip my left glove off to inspect the antique ring. I looked at the opal and wondered who had worn it before me, who they were, who I would be with it on my finger. Because this made it definite, didn't it? This was who I was now: Marc's fiancée, some day his wife. I'd chosen my fairy tale, my future. I thought these thoughts not with regret or uncertainty, but with a sense of awe. I'd made a decision.

I grinned at the ring and murmured about my happiness until my fingers turned blue. Marc replaced my glove, rubbed my hand between his.

'Stay here,' he said and climbed off the rock. I sat alone, watching a small dog hop in and out of the surf, its owner striding ahead. I listened to the seagulls circling above me and the roar of the waves. I tried to picture Chicago out on the horizon, the hurry of the streets and the sound of the traffic, the ice on the lake and the slush puddles at the end of every sidewalk. I thought of the lions outside the Art Institute and the view from the top of the Hancock Tower, the rush of wind as you stood on the platform between the tracks at the red line stop on Washington and State. The images felt distant, like poorly reproduced postcards with trite sentiments scrawled on the back. I wanted to press my bruises and imagine for a second what my other life looked like, but I couldn't. It belonged already to the past, to a different century, a different millennium even. All I could see now were the waves and the rocks before me; all I could feel was here.

Marc returned with fish and chips and polystyrene cups of tea. We fed each other, calling ourselves Mr and Mrs, catching colds that kept us in bed for the first week of the year.

March
Nine Days Gone

I liked Marc's parents, but we were never close. His mum in particular, I felt, always held me at arm's length. Their presence was a relief for Marc, though. The second day of dredging had turned up nothing, but DI Jones and Nicola were reluctant to allow Marc to see this as a positive. Today they were tracing my possible routes from campus to the river with sniffer dogs. His mum was advising him to look at the facts, prepare for the worst. Marc walked out of the room, unable to hear another person's advice that he give up on me. Still, it was better to have people around. His dad didn't say much, but proved adept at entertaining the girls. They leapt on his lap, squealing as his arthritic hands tickled their tummies.

I guess their presence must have reminded Marc of my family too, because while the girls watched TV with Nana and Grandpa, my husband finally picked up the phone and dialled my mum's number. What was he expecting from that conversation? He hadn't spoken to the woman since our wedding day. When she contacted me to say she was ill, he'd offered like the perfect husband he was to come with me. I only had to look at his face, though, to know his anger hadn't abated. I guess mine hadn't either. But, despite everything, when your mother tells you she's losing her memory, the child inside you takes over. Marc said he understood, though I know it was hard for him to watch me go to her.

'Hello?' A muffled voice answered after six rings.

'I'd like to speak to Mrs Carlisle.'

A pause. A throat cleared. 'Wh-who's speaking, please?'

'Her son-in-law, Marc.'

Another pause. 'Marc. I'm Caitlin, Mrs Carlisle's carer.' The line was bad; she sounded far away. 'I'm sorry, but I'm afraid Mrs Carlisle is not well enough to speak on the phone. Is there something I can help with?'

'I need to speak to her. It's about her daughter.'

'I'm sorry, I can try to pass on a message, but –'

'Look, if you could just put me on with her –'

'I don't know how much you know about your mother-in-law's health, Marc, but phone conversations in particular make her very agitated. She's in no state to be disturbed by bad news.'

'Bad news? Her daughter is missing! That's more than just a bit of fucking bad news!' He hadn't meant to shout.

'I know,' Caitlin said. 'I'm so sorry, Marc.'

He tried to soften his tone. 'Look, my wife is missing and they've found –' He swallowed. 'It was on the news. I think her mother has a right to know, however agitated it might make her.'

The woman on the other end was quiet for a moment, then in a whisper: 'The police already called. I don't know what else I can do for you, Marc.'

Marc pinched the bridge of his nose. 'Will you just, will you promise to talk to her? To help her understand?'

Caitlin was quiet.

'Please?' Marc said.

'I'll try,' said Caitlin.

Marc hung up wondering if he'd done the right thing. She did have a right to know, didn't she? I'd told him she barely recognized me any more, called me all sorts of names. Sometimes I'd arrive home from those trips and forget to answer my own for a day or so. But deep down no one can forget their family, can they?

★

He left the girls with his parents and drove across town to join the search. Nicola spotted him as he climbed out of the car and extracted herself from a flurry of frenzied activity. He watched with interest and horror as uniformed officers tramped the pavements with dogs, pointing them at hedges and ditches, hunting through bins.

'You don't need to be here,' Nicola said.

'I want to help.'

'This is a police investigation, Marc. Anything we find has to be preserved. We can't have you here.'

My husband looked into her face. He wondered if DI Jones would have been so polite in telling him to leave. 'There must be something I can do,' he said. 'I need to help find Alex.'

Nicola sighed. 'We've made up some flyers,' she said. 'You can hand them out, but you need to stay out of the way.'

Marc nodded.

'Do you have some friends you can call? Why don't you go into town, pass them out at the train station, supermarkets, anywhere busy.'

'Will it help?' Marc said.

Nicola hesitated. 'The statistics show that public appeals work. We don't know what we're looking for yet, Marc, but if anyone out there has information we need them to come forward.'

'Should we be doing more?' he asked.

'If you want to widen the appeal,' Nicola said, glancing back at DI Jones and the officers behind her, 'I can help you arrange putting Alex's information on things like milk cartons and coffee cups.'

'Yes, let's do it.'

'It could be pricey,' Nicola said.

As if that was a concern. If it brought me back, my husband would have paid anything. He told Nicola to go ahead with it, then followed her to her car to collect a stack of flyers. He called Patrick and Fran, met them by Boots to begin handing them out. The day exhausted him, but at least it was activity. If the police were looking not for me, but only for evidence and someone to blame, then the real search was down to Marc.

That evening, Lizzie helped her nana run a bath for Charlotte, claiming she was suddenly too old to share. Marc tried to remember if it was just two Mondays ago that I'd sat on the toilet seat and read them both the final chapters of *The Hobbit* while they soaked together. How could our daughter have grown up in a week and a half? His mother patted him on the shoulder and told him it was natural for Lizzie to want to play mum. Was it also natural, he wondered, that he hadn't seen her cry? That she hadn't come to him? Charlotte screamed and beat her fists against his chest, and that at the time felt like the most terrible thing in the world. But it was nothing compared to watching our eldest trying to cope alone.

Feeling helpless, he descended to the silent living room and sat on the sofa with Paula's borrowed book. I wonder what he expected to find in it, what links he was beginning to make. He turned to a page at random. A stark black and white photograph confronted him: a simply dressed woman with a severe expression held a bow and leant backwards. Opposite her, a similarly dressed man held his weight against the bow's string, pointing an arrow at her chest. 'Ulay / Abramović, *Rest Energy*, 1980.' He flicked to the text and read that the artists held this provocatively balanced pose for four minutes. Skimming back a few pages, he learnt the two were lovers, drawn to one another because of identical hair accessories and a shared birthday. He smiled, thinking I must have enjoyed that detail, and read on. Each in possession of solo careers before their meeting, they thrust both their personal and professional lives passionately together. Abramović left her husband and job to explore Europe with Ulay. 'I could not even breathe from love,' Marc read, the corners of his mouth twitching in recognition.

His romantic identification gave way to a dirty unease as he read about their collaborative works: breathing one breath back and forth for nineteen minutes; running at one another to slam their naked bodies together over and over until she fell and he sliced his feet on shards of glass; competing to entice a four-foot-long python to choose between them; sitting immobile and staring at one another for a gallery's entire opening hours, then repeating the performance ninety times, each losing weight and developing serious medical complications. For their final piece, he read, the pair separated, marking the event by walking the Great Wall of China in opposite directions, bidding their final goodbyes as they met in the middle. Initially conceived in a more romantic light, the performance was supposed to see the lovers walk to one another and marry in the middle. But in the time it took to plan the event, both parties had affairs and, so Marc read, the final straw for Abramović came in discovering Ulay had a fifteen-year-old son he had neither mentioned nor met.

Marc stopped reading for a moment, trying and failing to imagine someone keeping a secret like that.

In a passing comment, the book's author noted Abramović terminated a pregnancy in 1976, claiming, 'I'm a full blood artist and it's not possible for me to share my emotions for being an artist with a child.' His distaste mounting, my husband flicked through images of her solo work, much of it involving cutting, knives and blood staining white backgrounds. At the top of a page he found:

To read Abramović's use of pain as masochism is to grossly over-simplify the process in which she uses it as a means of achieving an alternative level of consciousness: one in which she can transcend mundane physical suffering and thus master it.

Marc turned the pages indifferently, landing on an image of Ulay colliding with a wall. He sighed, thinking himself pathetic for imagining he might find me between the pages of a book about such inconsequential acts. It was years since the day he'd teased me about wanting to be the next Marina Abramović or Tracey Emin. We'd built an entire life over those silly dreams; even *I* must have struggled to find meaning in the strange gestures of Ulay and Abramović now we had a family, a house, a world of our own.

He placed the open book on the coffee table and pushed himself from the sofa, intending to see how his parents were getting on with the girls. As he did, he couldn't help reading the caption beneath the image:

> *Interruption in Space* saw the artists running at each other with a metre-thick wall between them. After forty-five minutes, Abramović became convinced Ulay had stopped and left the scene. Unaware, Ulay continued running at the wall alone.

Marc thought little of this climbing the stairs, composing a smile for our girls or dredging funny voices from his aching chest to animate a bedtime story. But, later, awake in the dark, he remembered the image and those words and wondered if he too was running at a wall alone.

I remember one of the joys of going away for a few days used to be reclaiming ownership of my own space. I loved that in a hotel I could wake up and find everything exactly where I'd left it. I thought for years I was one of life's messy people, that I could never live in a pristine home. I even judged our friends who did. Fran and Ollie's house was always soullessly immaculate, Emma's room the only sign of life. I thought heaps of clothes in the corner and empty loo roll tubes hanging around the bathroom for days, last night's washing-up on the counter and little piles on the stairs of things waiting to be taken up were signs of vitality, of creative minds and contented individuals. But I had this realization once, staying on my own for a few days, that it took absolutely no effort to hang my clothes up as I took them off. And that if I did I'd wake up and the room would be neat. I realized I left my clothes on the floor because Marc did. That I forgot to recycle the loo roll and left the washing-up because he and the girls did too. That I wasn't bothered by these things because they weren't. And that, when I had a few stolen days alone, I could be a completely different type of person.

Now, though, I'd give anything to wake up to Marc's socks on this concrete floor. To Charlotte's toys and Lizzie's homework abandoned by my narrow bed. To see their shampoos and shower gels by the cold sink, their hairs coiled around the blackened plug hole.

I wait as long as I can before opening my eyes each morning. Even in the deadened silence and with the scratch of this thin blanket against my skin, I can sometimes pretend I'm waking in our bed. That it's a weekend or a holiday and Marc is still asleep beside me. In a moment I'll hear the girls thundering up the stairs and they'll throw themselves on us. I'll feel their bodies, hot and solid in my arms, hear my husband's sleepy protests. I'll run them a bath full of bubbles. Lizzie will take ten minutes to get in, dipping her feet in and out, then finally, inch by inch, sink her skin into the water. Char will already be lounging, one foot hooked over the side, waiting for me to begin *The Fellowship of the Ring*.

I cry, of course, when I do finally open my eyes and see only the corners and edges of this confined existence. I know without looking that there's a tray with two anaemic slices of toast, an apple and a glass of water. It's three steps to the door, five to the sink, seven from one wall to the other. Some days I try to think positively. I jog between the walls, counting into the thousands. Sit-ups on the floor even though the concrete hurts my back. Other days I hardly move. I lie with my face to the wall, wondering about the cyanide concentration in apple seeds, if I'd ever be able to save enough.

2000

Saturday, 2 September

In one week I'd be buttoning myself into the ivory dress waiting in Fran's spare bedroom. I'd have my hair pinned and my eyebrows plucked, Marc's grandmother's necklace clipped around my throat and my dad's hopefully clean blue hanky hidden at the last minute in my purse. This morning, however, I was sweating beneath our duvet, last night's make-up crusted around my eyes, wondering what sort of idiot I'd been not to bring a glass of water to bed with me last night.

My friends had wrapped a feather boa around my neck and marched me from pub to pub, insisting I drink everything they put in front of me. My head throbbed and I had that horrible sick feeling of knowing I'd done something bad. I crept through my sodden memory trying to piece together snippets of conversation. I'd definitely talked too long to the guy at the bar, touched his arm too often, but was that why I felt like this? Had I said something I shouldn't have to Philippa? Where was my handbag? I couldn't remember getting home.

Marc pushed the bedroom door open with his elbow and picked his way across the clothes-scattered floor, carrying a tray. He set it down on the chest of drawers and I gently elbowed myself up on the pillows.

'How are you feeling?' he said, handing me a cup of tea and a strip of paracetamol.

'Like I never want to drink again,' I said, popping two tablets from the foil. Marc smiled and placed a glass of orange juice and a plate with two slices of toast on the bedside table. 'And like I don't deserve you.'

He leant down and kissed me on the temple. 'You were very sweet when you got in.'

I groaned. 'Please don't tell me what I was like.'

He laughed.

'Really,' I said, suddenly close to tears, 'I don't deserve you. Why on earth would you want to marry me?'

Marc sat on top of the covers. 'Because you're the best person I know.'

I shook my head, winced. 'But what if you don't really know me? What if I have this – this, I don't know, darkness?'

Marc laughed.

'I'm serious. I shouldn't drink, should I? I know what it's done to my mum. And then I get into this state –'

'You're not your mother,' Marc said, frowning now.

'What if I am? What if I'm not who you think I am? What if I break your heart?'

'You won't,' he said. He reached to stroke my hair. 'I know this is just the hangover, but it scares me when you talk like this. You're brilliant and kind and creative and beautiful.'

'I'm not any of those things.'

Marc smiled, that patient, confident smile. 'You are. And it doesn't matter if you don't see it, because I do.'

In a week I'd be dressing tables with ribbon-wrapped vases, draping bunting and laying place settings. I thought, not for the first time recently, about the faded album I knew still lived in my dad's attic, of my parents' smiling faces, the flowers and the veil, the happiness locked in negatives long lost. In a week I'd be standing before this man and promising him my world. 'What if you're wrong?' I said.

Marc locked his eyes so intently to mine that I almost laughed. 'I'm not,' he said. 'I see you, Alex. I love you.'

I swallowed, a part of me wanting to break eye contact, to run away to the shower and get on with my day, to tell myself everything was fine.

Marc held my eye. 'I know who you are. So maybe it's my job to be here to remind you when you forget.'

I looked into his calm, insistent face. I'd talked too much last night, wittered on far too freely, but I didn't think I'd said anything too terrible to Philippa. I'd text her later to make sure we were okay. I shouldn't put myself in this position, though. I needed to be more careful. It was dangerous to lose control.

Marc stroked my leg beneath the duvet. 'You're just feeling low. Eat some toast, go back to sleep. I'll check on you in a bit.'

Thursday
Fourteen Days Gone

Twice as many reporters sit in front of the microphones at the second press conference. You can hear the clicks of their cameras and see the flickers of the flashes while DI Jones speaks about the reclassification of my case to a murder investigation. When Marc's turn comes, he sets his jaw and says he doesn't believe I'm dead, that he still hopes to find me and restore our family. DI Jones and Nicola stand beside him, their faces serious. I wonder what they were thinking in that moment, how Marc's unwavering faith made him seem to them. Was he just a husband clinging to the smallest hope, or did they read more into the steadiness of his voice, the stubbornness of his words?

'Someone out there must know where she is,' he finishes, staring directly at the lens behind the rows of journalists. 'Someone saw her or spoke to her or took her. I don't care what you did, I just want her back.'

The journalists' questions swim leisurely to his end of the room. They think them probing, perhaps, seeking a reaction, but my husband has absented himself this time. He's left behind the pathetic bereaved husband the cameras want him to be, the desperate two-dimensional face pleading empty words from television sets. Instead, he stands on a pebbly beach, their questions lapping icily at his naked toes but telling nothing of the black ocean before him. I am in that ocean, deep-sea diving in an air bubble of mystery, waiting for him to rescue me. All he sees, though, are these reporters, baby waves tossing tiny pebbles and asking if he shouldn't be preparing himself and our children for the worst. He answers as best he can, feeling numb. They need to keep finding a new angle and he knows it helps him, helps us, if they do because it'll keep my face in the papers, but to my husband the story hasn't changed. His wife has disappeared and he needs her to come home. You can see, though, on the video that he's beginning to understand the game. He already feels wiser, jaded by his recent experiences and less naïve in front of their stinging jellyfish tails.

I can't imagine his parents staying long, especially in the face of his dogged hope. The contradiction of it would have driven Ruth potty. 'I'm sorry, sweetheart,' she would have said. 'We don't want to abandon you, but we're not sure what to do.' They'd have offered to come back if he wanted, of course, or to take the girls for a while, even, but their minds would have been racing towards Frank's appointments, Ruth's church commitments. What an inconvenience having a missing daughter-in-law and a son who refused to accept she was gone must have been for them.

'Have you thought about what you'll do next?' Ruth asked.

'What do you mean?'

'Well, the police think she's –'

'Don't,' Marc pleaded. 'They haven't found a body. There was nothing in the river. She's still out there, I know she is.'

'Sweetheart, you must admit,' his mother carried on and the child in him wanted to stick his fingers in his ears. 'With her things where they were, and now they've let that boy go, the only logical explanations are that –'

'She's not dead,' Marc said. 'I know she's not.'

'Well then,' his mother said with a sigh. 'Alexandra's always been impulsive, we know that.'

'What's that supposed to mean?' Marc said.

She shrugged. 'I don't know. It's just strange, isn't it? What was she doing by the river anyway?'

'What are you saying?'

'Nothing,' Ruth said. They held each other's gaze for a moment.

'This is bullshit!' Marc shouted. 'I can't believe you. You want this to be Alex's fault, don't you? She's been fucking taken, for Christ's sake! She has to have been. She's somewhere out there in real trouble and you're sat there saying she –' Marc turned away as his voice cracked. He leant over the sink, breathing through his mouth.

'Sweetheart –'

'It drives you insane, doesn't it?' Marc interrupted, turning back to face her. 'That we're actually happy together. That we love each other. Christ, if you think that, why don't you just fuck off right now? What the hell are you doing here anyway?'

'Don't speak to your mother that way,' his father said.

'We came to help,' Ruth said, wiping a finger beneath each eye.

The shock of being told off by his father for the first time in decades knocked Marc's anger from him. He took a deep breath and attempted a calm tone. 'I'm sorry, Mum. I didn't mean that. But I just need to think she's out there, I need her to come home.'

'We know it's hard, son,' his father said. 'We're only trying to make you think practically.'

'I know, Dad, I do, but you just, you can't possibly understand.'

They really couldn't. Marc felt he knew what he was getting into from the beginning, but his mum especially always had trouble understanding me. She threw her arms up the year I decided not to celebrate Christmas, and he told me she was genuinely hurt when I said her generation couldn't understand modern feminism. He'd spent the past decade defending my actions, but even he was aware that they sometimes collected collateral damage. Fran and I didn't speak for a year after I took

Emma to get her ears pierced. 'It wasn't a big deal,' I insisted. Eight was old enough, I thought, for a child to make up her own mind. But Fran hit the roof, said she and Ollie had expressly forbidden it and I had undermined their parental authority, that it was the worst kind of insult. I think I actually told Fran to chill out, which didn't go down well. It wasn't until the following Easter, when Ollie insisted and Marc spent an hour convincing me to go, that we buried the hatchet beneath a three-course dinner and some mutual territory shifts. Marc was very tactful, trying to support me, but generally staying out of it. He thought I should apologize, but told me it wasn't his place to insist and agreed that Fran *had* overreacted.

It was harder for him to remain neutral more recently when I helped Patrick's daughter with her art project. For a while Pip would turn up every Saturday to work secretly away on her GCSE coursework in our garage. Patrick was delighted. Pip was going through a 'difficult' stage, he said, having been thrown out by her mum. My interest in her was really a positive influence, he thought. That's not what he said when he saw her work in the showcase, though. How could I encourage her to do *that*? he asked. 'It's self-expression,' I replied calmly as the stupid head teacher and the idiot art director flapped around Pip's work trying to avert the attention of the younger members of the audience. 'She's violated herself,' wailed Susan, prudishly horrified to see her new step-daughter's sixteen-year-old form splashed across canvases slashed by knives, smeared with menstrual blood and scrawled with angst. 'This is not appropriate,' muttered the head, while I stood back, amused and proud of the havoc Pip and I had wrought.

'She's not a child,' I told Marc later. 'She felt those things and needed an outlet. Her work was far more honest and provocative, far more worthy than any of the fruit-bowl still lives and "Grandpa in a chair" crap on the other walls. I can't help it if her parents and her school want to suppress creativity, curtail originality.'

It blew over in the end. Pip got an A, which cheered Patrick and Susan up, and somehow they moved beyond my refusal to apologize.

During our one and only row, Marc called me 'myopic'. That's always stuck with me. It was years ago, not long after Lizzie was born. I probably still had a cocktail of hormones rushing around my body. I started it, deciding to poke a non-existent bruise. I didn't really want to move us or change anything, but I'd got it into my head that everything about our relationship, our life, was on Marc's terms. I wanted to see if he'd make sacrifices for me. So instead of sitting down and talking to my husband, like a proper little wife should, I went ahead and applied for a teaching job at an international school in Cambodia.

'*Cambodia!*' Marc shouted when I told him, perfectly calmly, that they'd accepted my application and offered to pay to move our whole family out to Phnom Penh as long as I could start within a month.

'Why on earth would we move to Cambodia? What am I supposed to do in Cambodia? Who takes a *newborn* to Cambodia?' Marc trundled out question after rhetorical question.

It wasn't about Cambodia, of course. I didn't really want to go there, not more than anywhere else anyway. I just wanted to feel like I could still have adventures, like I wasn't destined to be in the safe, middle-class town I'd grown up in for the rest of my life. Marc didn't understand. He shouted about his job, about responsibilities, about the house, about everything. It would have been comical if I hadn't been so angry and hurt by his immediate dismissal of the notion that we might change our lives for *me*, might move for *my* career, *my* passions.

'You're utterly myopic,' he finally said more quietly. I watched him shake his head before leaving the room. I couldn't let him be the one to leave, so I scooped myself off the settee and marched into the hallway, thrust my feet into boots and left the house, slamming the front door. I heard Lizzie wake from the noise, start screaming from her cot and I felt satisfied that Marc would have to rush upstairs and comfort her rather than chase me.

I had nowhere to go. I walked to the corner shop, bought a packet of cigarettes and some gum, smoked one sat on the low wall by the bus stop. It tasted disgusting. I stubbed it out thinking of my milk poisoning my baby. What was I doing? How could I have thought of taking her to Cambodia? What kind of mother was I? I ran back to the house furiously chewing the flavour from my gum.

I brought it up later, though, in that gently passive-aggressive way you mention stuff that's been on your mind as if it's no big deal. 'But I'm myopic,' you say with a smile when your husband asks if you can see what he means.

Marc sighed and said sorry, he never really meant that and if he did it's just that I had a different way of looking at the world, that he understood it, loved me for it even, because I saw things he didn't. I laughed and we kissed, a happy family again. I guess, though, I kind of liked the description. Maybe I do see the world a little strangely. Which is why Marc could never explain me to his mum and dad.

The best they could do that morning was agree to disagree. That was the subtext of their stilted goodbyes. Marc and the girls waved until the car turned the corner and, deep down, my husband was happy to see them go.

He was less happy to be interrupted that afternoon by a phone call from a reporter asking him to give a statement about police proficiency.

'Do you feel North Yorkshire Police are doing enough? Are you worried budget cuts and staffing problems are affecting the search for your wife? Are you aware of the department's track record in missing persons investigations?'

Marc had been warned he may receive these kinds of calls and briefed on how to deal with them. Nevertheless, the reporter's queries burrowed into his brain, chattering away with the things he'd wanted to say to his mum until he was vibrating with anger and uncertainty. He grabbed the phone once more and dialled Nicola's extension at the station.

'We're following all potential leads,' she said when he asked exactly what DI Jones was doing.

'But what does that mean?'

Nicola exhaled. 'I can't disclose that information, Marc. It's confidential and could jeopardize the investigation.'

'How could telling me what's going on possibly jeopardize the investigation?' he said, infuriated. 'I'm on the investigation's side!'

Nicola was silent on the other end of the line.

'This is bullshit,' he said. 'How am I supposed to trust you if you won't even talk to me?'

'Marc,' she said curtly, 'it's going to be a lot easier if you let us do our jobs.'

'Then bloody do them, will you!' he shouted and hung up, feeling only marginally better.

My upper arms feel so tender I can barely rearrange myself on the bed without crying out. My legs and side are bruised too. Perhaps it's good I don't have a mirror. I think I'll be black and blue in the morning. It was my fault, he told me. I made him do it. Maybe I did. Maybe I knew what would happen.

I didn't really think it through, though. I heard his key in the lock and I grabbed the food tray. I positioned myself to the right of the door, so he couldn't see me until he took a step forward. I caught him just below the eye, drew blood. He swore like a sailor, not what you expect from a man with his control. But he didn't even hesitate before grabbing me and tackling me to the ground. For a split second I was impressed by his reflexes. Where did he learn to defend himself like that? Was it specifically to deal with me?

He pinned me there, his knee in my stomach. I could smell his sweat, sweet and familiar. We stared at each other as our panting turned to breathing. He wanted me to feel the whole force of him, to understand my place.

Maybe now I do.

2000

9/28/00

Dear Al,

How are you? I have a few hours to myself and I'm thinking of you. How is married life? I'm sorry about what happened with your mom. You were right about her, of course. I guess Marc thought he was doing a good thing, but he just can't understand. Maybe no one can understand someone else's family. Although I suppose he is your family now. Am I family too? I'm not quite sure.

Sorry, I'm in an odd mood. I had an email from an advertising agency earlier. I contacted them about curating a space in their offices and they seem interested. Weird, huh? I mean, it's what I wanted, but part of me is always surprised when anyone responds to me as if I'm an adult. I feel like a kid wearing my mother's make-up and high heels. Any moment I'm expecting to feel a tap on my shoulder and turn around to find a stern teacher ready to haul me off. These guys seem to be taking me seriously, though. I want to build a 'Reception Gallery' — a venue for emerging artists to connect the language of art directly with advertising and pop culture. I'm thinking if the big galleries are closing their doors to recent grads and there's no room for new artists to compete with the Establishment, then we need to find our own route. I want to put this chalkboard wall up in the agency and ask exhibiting artists to challenge the line between art and industry. And I want to film the people who work there, too, ask them what they think art is, what they think the difference is between what we do and they do. I have this other idea about building a paper house, or maybe a whole miniature paper town, about thinking about the concept of home as both a part of ourselves, our souls, and also a commodity, a concept to be sold and resold.

I don't know if it's enough yet. I don't know if I'm enough. I want to be an artist. I want my life to mean something. In Artur Barrio's manifesto, he writes: 'What I look for is contact with reality in its totality, everything that is rejected, everything that is set aside because of its contentious character . . .' I mean, that should be everyone's manifesto for life, not just art, right? Your mom is the ultimate contentious character, but you can't ignore her impact on your life, can you? Her blood runs through your veins and somehow you have to accept that and turn it into something good. Too many people wander through the world without contacting anything or anyone, even themselves. They barely open their eyes for fear of seeing something challenging or disturbing. Instead they just tie fluffy bows around all that's disagreeable and tell themselves their lives are perfect. There must be another way to live. I don't want to be one of those people.

Am I? Am I Am, Am is I, but Am I?

Am x

Saturday, 9 September 2000

Marc didn't tell me he'd sent the invitation until the night before our wedding. I think he'd considered not telling me at all, just letting me see my mum's face as I walked down the aisle, but thankfully he chickened out. Strangely, I didn't get mad. I looked at Marc's sweet, hopeful eyes and felt a deep sense of sadness at his misplaced optimism.

'She's sober now,' Marc said, clearly picturing a Kodak reunion we'd one day tell our grandchildren about.

'So she says,' I replied. Then, 'What have you done about the seating plan? She can't be anywhere near my dad.'

'Don't worry,' Marc said. 'It's all sorted out. They're at opposite ends and I've spoken to your dad. There will be no drama.'

He was wrong, of course.

People talk of butterflies and jitters, but I wasn't at all pre-pared for the shakes and stomach ache that clutched me before I walked down the aisle.

'Are you okay?' my dad asked. My face was pale, my palm damp in his. I swallowed, my throat scratchy.

'Just nervous,' I said.

He squeezed my hand.

'Hold on,' I said. I unlaced my hand and reached down to remove my shoes. They were elegant and satin and ridiculously uncomfortable. 'That's better,' I said and my dad led me to meet my groom.

For Marc's mother, walking barefoot down the aisle was only the first of my infractions that day. For years she talked about my hand-made decorations as 'quaint', told people in the indulgent tone you use to explain a child's scribble that her daughter-in-law used to be an 'artist'. After the ceremony we had canapés on the lawn and, while Marc and I were posed and moulded for photographs, Ruth sidled up to my mother. Dis-covering we hadn't yet said hello, she dragged my mum across the lawn and into the frame of one of our portraits, demanding a reunion in a much less subtle version of Marc's optimism. My mum and I hugged awkwardly, the photographer snap-ping away.

'Thank you for coming,' I said.

'Thank you for inviting me,' she said, her eyes narrowed.

'I assume your mother will be at the top table?' said Ruth and my mouth flapped. I reached for Marc's hand.

'We were limited on numbers,' Marc said, coming to my res-cue. He turned to my mum. 'You're on a table with our good friends. Here, let me introduce you to Patrick and Rebecca.'

'Nonsense,' said Ruth as Marc led my mum away. 'I won't hear of her sitting at a friends' table. I'm sure we can squeeze another chair in, I'll talk to someone.'

'Please,' I said, touching Ruth's arm. 'It's not fair on my dad.'

Ruth hesitated. She looked across the lawn at my handsome dad. They'd met a few times and no one who met my dad had any reaction other than sheer adoration. I could almost see the cogs in Ruth's brain as she tried to square her love for my dad with the intense five-minute bond she'd just formed with his ex-wife.

'Marc's handling it,' I added and Ruth nodded her assent.

I saw my mum make a show of refusing the champagne and the wine with dinner, but somewhere along the way she must have found some liquid refreshment. I watched her flirt with every male member of the waiting staff. By the speeches, she was slumped on her arm, her eyes drooping just as they used to when she picked me up from primary school. I stared at her in horror, afraid of what might come. I barely heard Marc or Patrick's speeches. But it was a wedding, everyone was merry. The only person in that room I could have pointed my mum out to and got the appropriate reaction from was my dad and I hoped beyond anything that he hadn't yet noticed. He stood up beside me and cleared his throat. I read his typed-up speech later and it made me cry. But on the day my brilliant dad can't have got more than six or seven lines in before my mum started making a low moaning noise. People looked around, curious at first. Then they began shuffling in their seats. My dad carried on, doing his best to ignore her. Marc put his arm around me. Her moan continued, low and persistent. I felt my body temperature rise, my heartbeat increase. I wanted to moan too, to wail and shout. I pushed back my chair and stumbled around our table. My dad finally stopped speaking and our guests paused in a collective hush. My mum moaned on. I tugged at her shoulder to make her sit up.

'You need to leave,' I said.

She looked at me with watery eyes. She blinked and moved

her sagging mouth into an approximate smile. 'My baby, you look so beautiful.'

'Darling,' my dad said behind me. 'Alex, leave it.'

I shook my head, stared into my mother's eyes. 'Get out. You're a disgrace.'

She stood up then, wobbling on her heels. She'd put on weight over the years, loomed over me. I felt like a child in my silly white dress.

'You're making a mistake,' my mum said. She looked around. Every face was turned towards us. 'You're all deluded. Marriage is a joke.'

'Mum,' I said, pleading now.

She turned back to me. 'Baby, it's not too late. You know you're not like these people, you can't pretend. You'll never be happy. Not like this.'

'Mum, please.'

She reached out and clutched my wrist. Her hand was hot and sweaty. 'Come home with me. Don't give yourself away, don't waste your life with this man. Come home with your mummy.'

I shook her off. 'You need to leave,' I said, tears on my cheeks but my anger bubbling once more.

Her expression dropped. 'Ungrateful bitch.' She raised her right hand and I felt the sting of her palm on my cheek.

The slap was like the flick of a switch. Suddenly our guests were on their feet. Marc and my dad rushed around the top table and grabbed my mum by each arm. They led her out of the building while Fran fussed around me, protecting me from the crowd. I was persuaded to shuffle towards the bathrooms. 'We just need a minute,' Fran told those around us. We reached the landing and I saw Marc coming up the stairs. I thought about my dad alone with my mum outside.

'Are you okay?' Marc said, scooping his arms around me. 'I'm so sorry.'

I nodded. 'It's not your fault.'

'I just, I thought having her here might make this the perfect day.'

I managed to laugh.

'I'm really sorry,' he said again.

'Don't be,' I said, feeling the warmth of his arms, the pull of his touch. Fran retreated.

'I wanted things to be special,' Marc said.

'They are,' I said, looking up at his face. 'You don't need to try so hard.'

He leant down and we kissed with our eyes open. *This man is my husband*, I thought. *My family.*

'I can't believe you're my wife,' Marc said.

I smiled and kissed him again.

'What do we do now?' he said, frowning.

He looked so serious and sad that I couldn't help but laugh. 'I think we're supposed to cut the cake.'

Marc laughed too and then, for some reason, we couldn't stop laughing. My dad came up the stairs to find us in fits of giggles and even he managed a smile. I reached for his hand and wrapped my arms around him. 'I love you, Dad,' I said.

'I love you too, sweetheart.'

We walked back into the hall, my dad on one side and my husband on the other. My mum was in a taxi somewhere in the city, nodding off no doubt and in for an unremarkable hangover, but I was in a room with the people I loved most in the world and for a strange second I thought maybe this was the perfect day.

One Month Gone

'Is there news?' Marc said.

'Not as such,' DI Jones said, stepping into the hall. Nicola followed. Marc pointed them towards the living room.

'We've come to return Alexandra's things and ask a few more questions.'

Marc sat in the chair by the bay window.

'Here.' Nicola thrust a clear plastic bag at him. He could see folded fabric, a bra strap, papers from my desk, my toothbrush. 'We thought you'd want these back.'

'Th-thanks.'

'There's also –' Nicola paused and began again, 'I thought you might like to know Alexandra's going to be featured on a special edition of *Crimewatch* this evening.'

'Great,' he replied, the small delights of his day dramatically different to just a few weeks ago.

'Yes,' DI Jones said. 'Sometimes it helps, but we have to be prepared for a lot of time-wasting responses in an appeal like this. I'd advise you not to get your hopes up.'

'Okay,' Marc said.

DI Jones cleared his throat. 'We've received the lab reports back from the river.'

Marc looked at him, a breath caught in his throat.

'We estimate Alexandra lost two to three pints of blood on the bank there.'

Marc's torso crumpled. He held his hands over his head, his breathing rapid and shallow.

'I know this is hard to hear,' DI Jones continued. 'But we're now working on the theory that your wife's body was moved after the incident at the river.'

Marc's knees began to tremble. He still held his head in his hands, shaking it from side to side. 'No, no, no, no,' he murmured. 'You're wrong.'

Nicola uncrossed her legs. DI Jones glanced at the clock on the mantelpiece.

Marc looked up, his eyes red but his gaze steady. 'What does two to three pints mean? Could she have survived?'

DI Jones hesitated. 'It's a significant amount, Dr Southwood.'

'Is it fatal?' Marc said.

'Not conclusively so,' said Nicola. 'But it's enough to lead to a loss of consciousness. It's —'

'So she could be alive?' Marc said, cutting her off.

Nicola and DI Jones exchanged a look.

'She could be alive,' Marc said again. 'Why aren't you out there looking for her?'

DI Jones leant forward. 'Dr Southwood, if somehow your wife is alive, we will find her, but we will only do that by being realistic about what the evidence indicates. Do you understand?'

Marc's nostrils flared, but he nodded. He watched DI Jones's mouth move as he told him only our family's DNA had been found on my clothing, that there was a trace of something on my handbag, but it could belong to the thief who stole its contents. 'The next step,' he said, 'is to petition for Alexandra's phone and digital records, to try to build as clear a picture of her last movements as possible. We'd also like permission to access yours as well.'

'Mine?' Marc said.

DI Jones looked him straight in the eye and Marc felt heat rise to his cheeks.

'It's routine,' Nicola said softly.

Marc scratched his temple. 'I've got nothing to hide.'

DI Jones stared at him for a moment longer. 'While we're here,' he said eventually, 'I want to ask about your wife's work.'

Marc nodded.

'You said she was going to do a PhD?'

'Yes,' Marc said curtly.

'Why now?'

Marc shrugged. 'The girls are a bit older. Alex has been talking about working full-time again and a PhD would allow her to get a senior lectureship.'

'So you'd say Alexandra was ambitious?'

'Of course. She's the smartest person I know.'

'And what she wanted was a senior lectureship?'

Marc nodded.

'It's strange, isn't it, for such a clever, ambitious woman to have waited this long to pursue something she's so passionate about?'

'Excuse me?' said Marc.

'It's just, we've talked to some of your friends and they've painted a slightly different picture.'

Marc narrowed his eyes. 'Who has? What did they say?'

'Did you and your wife ever discuss who would stay home with your children?' DI Jones said, ignoring Marc's questions.

Marc glared at him.

'It's in everyone's interest that you co-operate with us, Dr Southwood. All I'm trying to do is establish if Alexandra was as happy with your arrangements as you say she was.'

'Of course she was,' Marc said. 'Why would I lie? We share the parenting. We support each other.'

'But you're the head of your department – that must involve a lot of long hours. It must help to have a wife willing to work part-time.'

'What are you getting at?' Marc said, his temper flaring. 'What exactly has been said?'

'We're not getting at anything, Marc,' said Nicola, exchanging a glance with DI Jones. 'We're just trying to fill in some gaps.'

Marc looked from Nicola to DI Jones and back again, feeling like more than a coffee table separated them.

After they left, he returned to the living room and picked up the bag of my things. He extracted my toothbrush and clothes, laid them on the table before him. He fished back in the bag and retrieved two crinkled sheets of typed paper. They were single spaced and lacking page numbers and footnotes. An early draft. The title at the top read: 'Are Aesthetic Emotions More or Less "Real" Than Those Experienced in Life?' Underneath, hand-scrawled in biro, it said: *Or, I Miss Tony Soprano??*

I'd told him a little about the paper I planned to write. We discussed it briefly, but realized we were unlikely to agree. I wanted to do something fun, to depart from the fusty norms of Art History conferences, with their endless slides and attention to the minutest details of the most ancient of paintings. When I got enthusiastic about becoming what I called a 'real' academic, I'd dream of being a public intellectual, of writing kooky columns in the *Guardian* and *The New Yorker*. Marc teased that wasn't exactly the highest of academic aspirations and I poked my tongue out and complained he was too boring to understand. He was fully supportive of me doing a PhD, but we both knew he was one of those fusty academics I wanted to riot against. He liked real papers that addressed serious topics. He wanted citations and bibliographies, texts containing actual text, not critical analyses of *Big Brother* and Katie Price. I rolled my eyes when he complained about his students' tenuous theses, before kissing him on the lips and saying, 'I love you anyway, Dr Bore.' There was a kind of equilibrium, we joked, in our academic incompatibility.

He pushed thoughts of the blood by the river and DI Jones's questions and who on earth might have said we weren't happy to the depths of his mind and folded himself on to the sofa, his slippered feet resting on the opposite arm. *Okay, Al,* he thought. *I'll give your kooky academia a go. My mind's open.*

Are Aesthetic Emotions More or Less 'Real' Than Those Experienced in Life?
Or, I Miss Tony Soprano??

Over a period of months last year, my husband and I watched the box set, series 1 to 6, of *The Sopranos*. Like others across the globe, the characters infiltrated our lives like friends and enemies. We spoke about their motivations and predicaments, debated their options and futures. Then they were gone.

With an unsettlingly abrupt final episode and the last depression of our player's eject button, they were out of our lives. We discussed the ending for a few days, then moved on to *American Horror Story*. Now, twelve months later, I still miss the character of Tony Soprano. I miss his presence in my conscious psyche; I miss knowing I can return to his world at the end of a long day.

I also miss my father, who gave up a long fight with cancer a decade ago. I miss those sweets that tasted like soap, which I was only allowed on holiday when I was a child. I miss my daughters when they're at school and I miss my student days, when I felt I could achieve anything. I miss being able to read Jane Austen for the first time and fall in love with the characters afresh. I miss Father Christmas and vampires, unicorns and digital watches.

I miss dozens of things, real and imagined, to varying degrees and with no or a full desire to have them returned to me. But are some of these emotions of a different class? Of differing importance?

Ed S. Tan distinguishes between A- and R-emotions: Aesthetic and Real emotions. In other words, Art-world and Life-world emotions. He goes on to discuss the differences between emotions related to actual artworks and those related to the things represented within the artworks. I'll call these A- and A2-emotions. Missing Tony Soprano, who is not a real person and whom I have never met, is an A2 emotion, while mourning the end of the HBO series, which was a feature in my real life, is an A-emotion.

All very amusing, but why are both sets of A-emotions considered less worthy than their R- counterparts? Sure, it doesn't have a truly physical impact on my life if the final blackout ending of *The Sopranos* means Tony Soprano was shot, whereas my world *would* spin into turmoil if one of my close friends was hit by a bullet while eating dinner in a restaurant with his family. But is crying during your favourite soap opera really any more ridiculous than shedding tears while reading a tragic story in the newspaper?

'Real' is a judgemental label, which I blame for some of the value imbalance between R- and A-emotions, but I think it goes deeper. It's ingrained in our social constructs that, whatever job we choose, religion we sign up to or life philosophy we decide to pursue, we should expect to live essentially like our neighbours: in cookie-cutter moulds of birth-to-death cycles. Perhaps it's a product of capitalism or something more innate. Either way, I'd argue that there's something quite absurd about holding R-emotions so high above A-s when the R-s are only those that everyone else experiences. On the whole, you and I and the kids down the road will all fall in love, be let down, feel rejected by someone we care about, achieve something we've wanted, bury our parents, hold our children, question our god . . . and so on.

There is a finite number of R-emotions – a very large finite number, but a finite number nonetheless – from which each of us will lucky-dip only a tiny percentage. But the A-s are different. Artists have been working for millennia to manipulate our emotional responses to their work: to create a whole new pool of emotions and feelings, and to seek original thought and unique experiences. Surely, for that reason alone, the A-s should have a higher place on the shelf of worth.

I'm not saying R-s do not hurt and sting and make your flesh ache with longing, but why must we cling to them when they have been felt over and over for centuries with no evolution? Would it not be more sensible to pursue the unknown? To seek the edge of human experience, experiment with manipulating and controlling emotions rather than sitting back and waiting for the world to tell us what to feel? The artist who makes me cry shows far more talent, far more skill, than the boyfriend who dumps me. One has thought with precision about her product, considered its impact on me, the viewer, rehearsing and tweaking her performance, while the other has simply followed some gut instinct, some evolutionary impulse to cut his losses and flee. And while the inadvertently Darwinian of the two might crush my heart and seem like the most tragic thing in the world for some minuscule moment in my trivial existence, the artist and her art, should it be of suitable worth, will live on beyond my heartbreak and beyond her own lifetime, framed in galleries, reperformed for decades, or merely played on screens across the globe. Sad as the implications about individual human worth might be, I'd hazard a guess that more people miss Tony Soprano than my dad.

The draft ended there. Marc stared at the pages in his hands. I'd touched these sheets, typed the words and thought the thoughts. He wanted them to connect me to him, to bleed through his fingertips and bring me back. But was I really arguing manufactured happiness and pain had more worth than the real things? Where did that leave him now? Should he have been heading off to a gallery and revelling in conceptual genius rather than worrying about my whereabouts? Should he write me off like DI Jones so clearly had and go find some emotional catharsis at the cinema?

'Fucking hell, Al,' he said aloud, crumpling the papers in his hands. He bundled my clothes and toothbrush from the table and carried them upstairs. He dumped everything on the bed and reached for the overnight bags above the wardrobe. They were packed one inside another and he pulled them apart until he had all four gaping wide on the bed. Hands shaking, he shoved the things the police had returned in one, then turned to my dressing table with another. He scooped my hairbrush and moisturizers and make-up unceremoniously into the bag, tears wetting his cheeks. He sank to the floor, the bag in his lap. He closed his eyes and saw blood and gangsters and TV violence on the backs of his lids. My husband's limbs shook as he gave way to those real emotions I'd tried to dismiss. The bag fell from his lap, my things spilling over the floor. He opened his eyes and scrambled to pick them up, fumbling with the fabric of the bag. His fingers touched something hard in the lining. Something small and rectangular and distinctively familiar. He felt around for the hidden zip to the inside pocket and pulled out three burgundy passports. He thumbed them each clumsily open, looking for the photographs, checking what he probably already suspected. He saw Lizzie's face, Charlotte's and his own.

I've been alone with my thoughts for too long. He hasn't visited me for three days. There's a tray with food waiting each morning when I wake up, but I've had no human contact. I tried to stay up last night, to see the tray being brought, but I couldn't. Even when I'm awake, my thoughts are foggy.

I imagined it would be a relief if he stopped coming, but it's worse. I want to disappear into my memories, to snooze and dream of my life before. Instead, I have nightmares, both asleep and awake. I try to hold on to what we had, to think of our happiness, our home, our beautiful family, but it's like I see it through a broken window. The cracks distort everything. The hours bleed into each other, nothing to punctuate my torturous thoughts. I keep thinking I hear his laugh or the key in the lock. I turn, but it's just in my mind. *He's* in my mind. I can't escape.

I'm going to stop eating. It's the only control I have. It'll be hard, but I've endured worse. I think of those who have done it before me. The body is just a tool. So far he's used mine against me. Now it's my turn.

2001

Saturday, 24 February

Patrick had neither shaved nor dressed when we arrived. He flipped the latch and let the front door swing on its hinges as he padded barefoot down the hall, his dressing gown billowing behind him. Fran caught my eye as we followed him through. Patrick's brother, Rob, was down the road filling in the paperwork for a rental van and we had both Marc and Fran's cars, but it soon became clear it'd take us multiple trips and most of the day.

Fran put the kettle on and Marc and I sat Patrick down at the dining table to make a list.

'Where should we start?' Marc said. Patrick made a low groaning sound and lay his head on his arms.

Rebecca had taken five-year-old Pip and gone to stay at her mum's. Patrick said she was thinking of moving back to Castleford permanently, commuting to her dance school from there. I thought of the sugar plum fairy I'd helped into her costume backstage last Christmas, of Rebecca running around placating children and parents alike. Patrick started sobbing again, trying and failing to get the words out to tell us what they'd discussed about custody and visitations.

Marc placed his hand on Patrick's shoulder. I wondered if I'd ever seen them touch before. 'Buddy,' Marc said.

Fran and I left them in the kitchen. 'Let's start in the bedroom,' she said and I was relieved to have her take charge.

'How's Ollie?' I asked as we pulled two suitcases from beneath the bed.

'Stuck at work,' Fran said. 'Someone called in sick, so he's on a double. I don't know why he's always the one who gets conned into it, seems like nobody else ever does anything.'

'That's awful,' I said. Fran always complained more about Ollie's work than he did, as if by having her rant about the hours and the way the owner treated her staff, Ollie was somehow free to actually enjoy his job. I loved listening to his animated stories about the stupid things people asked for, about the stresses of life as a chef.

Fran and I took one side of the bed each and began to tackle the wardrobes and drawers. At least clothes were pretty obvious to divide into his and hers, but it felt almost criminal to be in such close proximity to Rebecca's things. I looked at her make-up and lotions, the blonde hairs wrapped around the prongs of her hairbrush.

'It feels like a crime scene,' I said. 'Like their life's frozen in time.'

Fran nodded. 'No wonder he's been in such a state, here in this house alone.'

I knelt to pull another bag from beneath the bed. Inside were leotards in a variety of colours, folded and squashed in with tulle and netting. I thought of the Christmas show again, watching Rebecca waving her arms and whispering from the side of the stage while thirty six- and seven-year-olds stumbled through *pliés* and *pas de chats*. We'd helped her strike the set afterwards, made it to the pub for last orders. Patrick had ordered 'a bottle of this fine establishment's cheapest fizz'. The barman had looked like he was about to deck him. I felt like we'd laughed the entire night.

I zipped up the duffel and pushed it back beneath the bed. We finished with Patrick's clothes and I found Rob in the living room sorting DVDs and books into estimated piles. Patrick came in periodically and plucked one or two to put in a different pile. Marc followed with cardboard boxes and parcel tape. Fran took a box from Marc and began gathering up photographs and trinkets. I watched her dump a slate coaster embossed with the words 'Happily Ever After', then three photo albums without bothering to check their contents. It occurred to me what she was doing and I took a box from Marc to follow suit, scanning shelves and surfaces for the most triggering items.

'What will they do with this stuff?' I asked after Marc had led Patrick upstairs.

Fran shrugged. 'Put it in storage. Throw it away eventually.'

'It's so sad,' I said, thinking of the wedding album on our shelf, the cushion covers I'd made from my dress.

'It is,' said Fran.

We'd had the conversation, of course. The one I'm pretty sure every couple has but can never admit. 'One in three marriages ends in divorce, so who's it going to be?' We'd been sitting on the living room floor, wrapping presents and smiling about how perfect our first Christmas as husband and wife was going to be. Marc snorted when I said it, gave me that 'you can't be serious' look. But I led and tempted him into the conversation and eventually we made a list.

First we went through the most obviously safe. Patrick had been his brother Rob's best man a couple of years ago and we'd been invited to the hour-long ceremony in the Minster, where both Patrick and Rob had once been cherubic choirboys. Just because we didn't have God on our side didn't make our vows less meaningful, we agreed, but there was something rather grave about remembering Rob holding out the ring with an organ playing behind him and tears running down his cheeks. The world would end before he and his wife broke their vows.

Fran and Ollie were a maybe, though neither of us could imagine a scenario that could tip Fran into enough of an emotional state to prompt a break-up. 'What do you think she's like in bed?' I said, making Marc snigger. Patrick's words of warning when he introduced us all had been spot on: 'Fran's a bit doctory but worth the effort.'

There was my school friend, Philippa, of course. She'd married a month before us. Her husband, Charles, was a lawyer like her and seemed nice but a little dull. We'd decided that night that, if it saved our other friends, it was probably okay to write Philippa and Charles off in the name of statistics.

Marc came up behind me and placed his hand on my hip. 'I think we're almost done packing,' he said. 'Rob and I are going to start loading up the van.'

I nodded and leant to kiss his cheek, smelled the aftershave I'd bought him.

Patrick and Rebecca hadn't even come up in that conversation. They'd been together so long they were practically the same person. When I'd first met them, Rebecca had wrapped a long arm around my shoulder and insisted we sit together, leaving the boys to wonder what we were whispering about. She and Patrick had grown up three streets away from each other and dated since they were fifteen. Marc told me they'd broken up at the beginning of their second year at uni, but only for a month. Patrick had been inconsolable during that month, moping in his room and resisting all of Marc's efforts to drag him out to chat up tipsy freshers. I'd never once seen them argue or even snip at each other over some petty thing. Rebecca's phone rang constantly and she was always racing between classes, laughing about a child vomiting in the middle of rehearsal or having to wash nosebleeds out of leotards, but she was also the kind of person who made you feel like she had all the time in the world for you. I missed her. I'd wanted to call her, but it felt disloyal to

Patrick, to Marc. I wondered when I'd next see her, what it would be like when I did. Until two weeks ago, when Patrick had turned up on our doorstep with snot on his cheek and told us Rebecca had met someone else, I'd thought them the perfect couple.

April
Six Weeks Gone

Marc agreed to return to work after Easter. He felt guilty about it, but it was a relief to start planning something familiar. Nicola was keeping him updated on the case, but there had been no new leads – or none they were willing to share with him – and my face had slipped almost completely from the pages of the newspapers. DI Jones had asked about my passport again, saying they'd run a second exit check, but it still hadn't been used at any borders. Marc had told him honestly that it hadn't turned up yet, finding reasons to justify omitting the fact that his and the girls' had. He'd placed them in their correct home in the filing cabinet and run through endless scenarios, of greater and lesser likelihood, of why mine would have ended up elsewhere.

DI Jones had also asked him to make a comprehensive list of all the friends and acquaintances I might have had contact with in the twelve months leading up to my disappearance. Marc had struggled and complained to Patrick that the task was near impossible. 'Could you tell me everyone Susan's spoken to in the past year?' he asked him. Patrick shook his head. 'It's absurd. What a waste of time.' But eventually he'd emailed over a list. A couple of days later DI Jones rang to clarify some of the names. A week after that he called again to ask about one in particular.

'We've spoken to most of the people we're interested in,' he said. 'But we're struggling to locate Amelia Heldt.'

'Okay,' Marc said, leaning back in his office chair. He knew he should feel grateful for their thoroughness, but he didn't understand the point of this line of enquiry and he didn't feel like talking to DI Jones right now.

'Is there anything you can suggest?' DI Jones said. 'Anything you know about her that might help?'

'Not really. She's Alex's friend, not mine.'

'You said Alex wrote to her, didn't you?'

'Yes,' Marc said, scrolling through the day's headlines on the screen in front of him.

'Which makes it quite strange there was no address in the address book, doesn't it?'

'I suppose.'

'We've checked both her university and private email accounts, and there's nothing from Amelia Heldt there.'

'I don't know what to say,' Marc said. 'They went to art school together.'

'It would really help if you could think of a way we might contact her. Even online, Ms Heldt seems to guard her privacy.'

'I'm sorry,' Marc said, opening a new window and typing 'contact Amelia Heldt' into a search engine.

'You say Alex visited her just twice?'

'Yes.' The first thing that came up was a *Washington Post* article titled 'The Cult of Anonymity'.

'Definitely no more?' DI Jones said.

'Why are you asking this again?' Marc said, clicking on the article.

'Is there anyone else Alex is still in contact with in America?'

Amelia's name was mentioned in the first paragraph alongside Banksy, Elena Ferrante, Daft Punk and Sia as artists choosing obscurity over the perks of celebrity. 'No,' Marc said.

'Not that you know of?' DI Jones prompted.

'Not that I know of,' Marc repeated, peevish now. The reporter seemed to be praising these figures for leading the way for those sick of the narcissism of the art and entertainment industries. *Rebelling against Warhol's claim that everyone wants their fifteen minutes,* he read, *they're carving out a new, more sincere and ultimately more admirable kind of fame: one that refuses fame itself.*

'And you feel like you would know,' DI Jones said, 'if your wife had stayed in contact with or perhaps even visited anyone else?'

'Of course.' *For some,* the article continued, *this is too difficult a concept to understand. The large sums being offered to journalists able to 'out' these artists raise questions about whether the public has a right to know whose work they are consuming.*

'Even an old boyfriend,' DI Jones said. 'Someone she was perhaps worried you might be jealous of?'

Marc stopped reading. 'This is ridiculous.'

DI Jones was silent on the other end of the line.

'We have no secrets,' Marc said. 'I've no reason to be jealous.'

'Okay, Dr Southwood. Well, please let us know if you think of a way we might contact Ms Heldt.'

Marc hung up, feeling annoyed. He read absently through the rest of the article, unconvinced. He was no fan of seeing our girls gush and gossip about pop and reality stars, but neither could he see any great social virtue in choosing to hide behind a mask or a pseudonym. Still, if Amelia's anonymity was causing DI Jones a headache, then he was pleased. What was the point in tracking down my old friends? Why wasn't he out there looking for me?

My husband clung to his conviction that I was alive like a child with a security blanket. As the days and weeks passed, though, often the only way to maintain hope was by not looking directly at it. He dropped the girls off in the car one morning, then drove through the drizzle to the retail park. There was a loose washer on the upstairs sink and Charlotte had spilt blackcurrant juice on her bedroom carpet, which now wouldn't come out. Our friends had been checking in and dropping off food and supplies, but he felt he was using up their goodwill. They were running danger-ously low on essential items and he'd finally come to the realization that he needed to offer the girls more variety than pasta, takeaway or chicken nuggets for dinner.

He parked outside Sainsbury's, placed his pound in the slot and wheeled a trolley through the sliding doors. He filled the end of the cart with fruit and veg, planning healthy meals for the girls and trying to think up non-junk-food snacks to offer them. Perhaps he'd get popcorn, though, and they could have a film night. He turned into the wine aisle, thinking maybe he should have a few bottles in the house to offer their friends' parents should they stop by after a playdate. As he did, he saw me.

I had my back to him, studying the label on a bottle of Zin-fandel. A black hat covered most of my head, but he could see a few stray curls tickling the back of my neck. I wore a thick car-digan wrapped around my body in place of a coat. He recognized my stance, weight slightly to the right, left knee bent. My arms moved with familiar fluidity as I replaced the bottle and reached for another from a higher shelf. He caught a glimpse of my cheekbone, pale and freckled. He imagined my lashes brushing against skin as my blue eyes scanned the label.

He stopped at the end of the aisle. People wove their trolleys around him, impatient to finish their shopping and get on with their days. I seemed in no hurry. I placed the bottle in my basket and moved down a few shelves to inspect the reds.

It didn't strike him as particularly odd that he might run into me here. Perhaps it made sense that I'd come back to him as his spirits began to lift a little, just as he'd stopped moping. I wouldn't want him sobbing on the sofa and poring pathetically over old photographs, would I? A man in mourning is hardly a catch, and every child knows you only get what you want when you stop nagging your parents for it. His heart hammered. He inhaled for the first time since seeing me and wheeled his trolley slowly forward, never taking his eyes off my back.

'Watch out,' someone growled as he forced them out of his path. Was that a Rioja I was fingering?

Behind me now, he could smell my perfume, unfamiliar but pleasing. He reached out his hand, placed it lightly on my shoulder. 'Al?'

The woman jumped. Her shoulder shuddered beneath his touch and a gasp escaped her lips as she simultaneously turned to face him and let go of the bottle. He withdrew his arm as if her cardigan was aflame. The wine smashed on the floor. The woman with my hair but another person's mouth and eyes glared at him.

'*What on earth?*' she said, looking down at her sodden shoes and back up to Marc's disappointed face.

A heady aroma filled his nostrils as he slipped from his trance. For a moment he saw himself as if from above. What had he been thinking? Why would his teetotal wife be buying wine? Why would she be shopping in a supermarket after not coming home for six weeks?

'I'm terribly sorry,' he muttered pathetically. 'I thought you were someone else.'

'SPILLAGE IN AISLE FOURTEEN,' the tannoy echoed. Other shoppers stared.

'You're . . .' the woman began, then stopped herself.

Marc nodded. 'I really am sorry.' He stumbled backwards, needing to create distance between him and this woman who was not me but with whom he'd shared the most intimate moment he'd had since I disappeared.

'It's okay,' the woman said. 'No harm done.'

An employee paced around the corner of the aisle with a mop and bucket and ushered them out of the way. Marc offered to pay for the bottle, but after looking him up and down and glancing at the woman for a moment, the employee said that wouldn't be necessary, they could put it through as accidental.

'Thanks,' he mumbled and steered his trolley towards the checkouts. He felt the woman watching as he walked away and was relieved to spot a free checkout at the other end of the shop. He bagged his purchases and wheeled them to the boot, slammed the door and sped from the car park.

A second, smaller appeal aired on *Crimewatch* that evening. Nicola had discussed the need to keep me in the news, how the papers tended to get bored with a missing-person story as soon as the new revelations dried up. Marc watched. My case seemed unsensational, bookended between an international manhunt for a guy who killed two women and the search for a rapist who attacked a young girl as she left school.

Nicola hadn't been too hopeful that the new appeal would result in people coming forward with witness reports, but she rang minutes after the broadcast. There had already been an extraordinarily large response in terms of donations. Someone had just made a £50,000 payment via the link on the website. Anonymously, Nicola said. A PayPal account registered in North America. Usually, she explained, those offering large donations wanted the publicity too. 'This is highly unusual in my experience,' she said.

'But good?' Marc said. As crass as it felt, money had begun to worry him. The milk bottles and flyers all had a price and running a household on one salary when we'd been used to two wasn't easy. The university had frozen my income and informed him they couldn't make a survivor benefits pay-out without a body. All of our accounts were confused too. Marc had had to cut off the phone line and get it reconnected because they wouldn't let him transfer it into his name without my permission. The woman on the end of the phone had been sympathetic, even as he growled at her incompetence, but she'd explained they had no procedures in place to deal with missing people. The home insurance was the same. Marc had tried to cancel and renew the policy in his name, but the guy said, 'Sorry, we need Mrs Southwood to write to us to confirm.'

'Are you fucking stupid?' he'd said. 'How can she write to you if she's not fucking here?' The bloke on the phone had said he didn't have to tolerate that kind of language and hung up.

The donation wouldn't solve everything, but at least it could take the pressure off; at least it meant they had a steady fund to keep paying for posters and adverts, to keep me in people's minds.

'The money is useful,' Nicola said carefully. 'But the circumstances are strange. DI Jones wants to investigate, see if we can trace the source.'

'You think it's a lead?' said Marc, suddenly alert. He stood up to close the living room door in case the girls walked by. 'That the person who took –'

Nicola cut him off. 'We don't know if it's anything yet, but we're treating it as suspicious.'

Marc stared at the muted television, trying to balance the surge of adrenalin that something was finally happening with Nicola's obvious warning that he not get his hopes up.

'While I've got you,' she said before they hung up, 'there's something else. Have you tried to get in touch with your mother-in-law recently?'

'No,' Marc said. Should he have done? Was it crass and uncaring of him to forget about the woman? No, he thought, she didn't deserve his care. She didn't deserve me as a daughter. Marc's face was always so horrified when I talked about her drinking, about the things she'd screamed at me, about the men she'd entertained while I was playing upstairs, about discovering she'd snapped the heads off all of my dolls and my desperate

131

attempts to hide the truth from my dad. The woman had ruined my childhood; Marc owed her nothing.

'Then I'm sorry,' Nicola said. 'But I have some bad news. We telephoned earlier this week to arrange a time to conduct an interview with her and I'm afraid her carer, Miss Morse, answered and said Mrs Carlisle passed away.'

Marc stared at the bright, flickering images on the TV. What was he supposed to feel?

'I'm so sorry, Marc.'

'It's – it's okay,' he finally managed. 'I barely knew her. It's just . . . a shock, I suppose.'

'Of course,' Nicola said. 'Was Alex close to her mother?'

Marc closed his eyes and pinched the top of his nose. 'Not really. They were estranged for a long time, and then with the illness . . .' He trailed off.

'But she visited frequently?' Nicola said.

Marc opened his eyes, stared at the rug we'd picked out from that little shop in Harrogate. He wondered if this was an official question or the polite small talk it sounded like. 'As I've said, she took the train down a few times a year. The trips were stressful, not some happy family reunion. Al would be in a daze for a day or two after returning.'

'It must be unsettling not to be recognized by one's own parent,' Nicola said, sounding genuinely sympathetic. Marc felt a stab of guilt for questioning her motives.

He remained quiet for a moment, unsure how to move the conversation along. He tried to remember which street the shop in Harrogate had been on, wondered if it'd still be there. We'd had cake in Betty's afterwards, Lizzie smearing hers over the table and Charlotte crying so hard I'd had to wheel her pram outside while Marc hunted down our waitress to settle the bill.

He realized Nicola was speaking. 'Without being able to question Mrs Carlisle, we're going to need to go over a few more things with you, Marc. DI Jones is curious about how frequently Alex visited her mother and whether you know of any times she might have travelled elsewhere alone.'

'What do you mean?' Marc said.

'Any holidays or trips, any time she stayed overnight or left the country.'

'We've been over this. We do things as a family.'

'If you could just have a think, Marc, and compile a list of dates over the past few years, that would really help us cross-reference.'

'Cross-reference what?'

Nicola didn't answer.

'What is this about?' Marc growled into the receiver.

'Even if we find Alexandra alive,' Nicola said, 'you may have to face some unpleasant facts . . .'

Marc couldn't listen to this. Nicola continued talking, but he stared at the muted TV and slipped inside his head. The more he talked to Nicola and DI Jones, the less he felt they were on his side. They had information they were keeping from him, thoughts and ideas about our family that didn't match his own. That didn't match us. But Marc knew us; he knew me. The police were burrowing down the wrong rabbit holes. He kept trying to tell them, but they didn't understand. They didn't have access to our world. They couldn't glide, like Marc, into our memories. Nicola couldn't rewind ten years like he could right now. She couldn't follow him to Edinburgh to walk beside me along the Royal Mile, to discuss the terrible piece of Beckett we'd just witnessed in a makeshift basement theatre. We were batting away windswept actors offering us flyers, on the cusp of our new lives, my swelling stomach making me a harsher critic than usual. We were heading back to our hotel, debating jacket potatoes on the way. We had no other thoughts. We were happy.

My husband had lost me. That's what he wanted to say. But it was what you said when somebody died too. Only they were not lost. They were very firmly found: present and correct in their coffins or urns. The people left behind knew where they stood. They could grieve. But he had no idea. He had lost his soulmate. But was that right? It sounded like he'd misplaced me, put me down and forgotten where he left me, like it was his doing. Had someone else contributed to it? Was I stolen from him in far more violating circumstances than someone smashing our bathroom window and rifling through our belongings? Was I in need of his help?

Or should he be considering Nicola's advice? That the best-case scenario was that I was somehow complicit in remaining gone? If I myself knew where I was, was I lost at all? Was I lost to anyone but him? He couldn't believe he was thinking this, not about me. He'd watched all the videos on the Missing People website and felt sorry for the poor parents and children willing their loved ones to return. He thought it sad that they cried over people cruel enough to leave on purpose. But he couldn't relate that to himself. He couldn't imagine that being me. It didn't even make sense, with my blood and belongings found on the riverbank.

Nicola wouldn't let him ignore it, kept saying if he was sure I was alive, then it was a possibility he must consider. But I wouldn't desert them. I *couldn't* abandon the girls. He knew me. If there was any way I could have got in touch, I'd have taken it.

'And why hasn't she got in touch?' he said, his voice too loud for the quiet house. Why, if I wasn't being held somewhere against my will, tortured and – and – all sorts of things my husband couldn't bring himself to imagine, why wouldn't I have rung? It was absurd. Nobody could do that to their family. The woman was insane if she thought I could put them through this voluntarily. He shouted. I had to have been taken. Nicola said they'd discuss it another day. They would not. There was no discussion.

'Find my wife!' He shouted that too and hung up.

I wake holding my stomach. I know it wasn't real, but still I am sobbing. Marc was there. We were at the hospital. I was pregnant, just a little at the start, then more and more like some giant blown-up balloon. I floated through the corridors, glowing and proud, and lay on the bed for the nurse to cover me in jelly. But her little screen stayed blank. Then the doctors and Marc and Lizzie and Charlotte all started poking me, shouting, 'Where is it? What have you done with it?' And my balloon stomach popped, leaving me splayed before them like a gutted fish.

I try to breathe evenly. It was just a dream. This sense of emptiness isn't real. My babies are safe. I roll over and see the tray. My stomach cramps. It's only been four days without food. Pathetic, really. I stare at the slices of toast, focusing and unfocusing my eyes until the room swims like a kaleidoscope.

My time used to be regimented. Structured around school days and term-times, clubs and appointments. I had calendars and diaries. Now I have a little sliver of light telling me a new day has arrived, a clock ticking round and round with nothing but his visits to distinguish the hours. I try to remember what I used to think about, how I filled my days, entertained my brain. But it's a muscle, isn't it? I tried to jog between the walls yesterday, collapsed after a dozen back and forths.

There are cultures that believe enduring bodily deprivation is the only route to the Other, be that a god or one's own subconscious. Physical suffering can be transmuted into power. To control suffering is to control everything.

2001

12/11/01

Al,

You've no idea what New York is like right now. The whole city is walking around in a fog. People are being kind to strangers, holding doors and letting each other get on the subway first. It's surreal. I toyed for a day or two after the event with making a piece, but couldn't bring myself to even brainstorm without feeling dirty and crass. I think it needs leaving to the heavyweights. Laurie Anderson played the gig she had scheduled for September 11th. Or maybe it was the day after, I'm not sure. Either way, it was labelled an elegant move, a beautiful decision. I doubt anything I could come up with would be elegant or beautiful, just angry and confused.

I've been thinking a lot about loss, though. About how losing someone steals not only the person, but the memory of the person too. Imagine if you lost someone as suddenly as in the towers, how it would affect your perception of them as a person. The day before you might have been struck by a twenty-year-old memory of something lovely but insignificant while doing the dishes. But the day after, your love is tragic and all you can feel is the loss. All you can remember is their death. I bet not one of those people left behind could conjure a random, happy memory right now. What haunts them is their loved one's suffering and their own loneliness. How long will it be before they take a moment to smile at the memory of a hand held or a kiss hello?

This is sounding tragically sentimental, isn't it? Not like me at all. Perhaps I'm going soft in my old age. I guess it's this city at the moment. It's full of pain, but it strikes me everyone feeling sad about losing someone

136

is only capable of that emotion because they had a bond special enough to lose. It seems doubly tragic if they forget that too.

So don't forget it, okay? You're about to create the most intense bond there is. And, as long as you don't get so bogged down in puke and poop that you forget about me, I truly hope it makes you happy. Maybe we could turn your baby into a piece. I mean, he'll be your creation, right? (Do you want a girl or a boy?) Allan Kaprow: 'The line between art and life should be kept as fluid, and perhaps indistinct as possible.' There's nothing more lifelike than pushing a 10lb baby out of your cooch, now is there?

I've started doing these little video projects with my mom. I'm still meditating on those fairy-tale narratives we used to talk about and the expectations they create that are totally inaccessible to most people. We've had a difficult time in the past, my mom and I, but she reached out again and, with the world as it is right now, I'm glad I gave her another chance. She's being weirdly supportive. I put her in front of the camera and she tries anything I ask, doesn't care if I'm manipulating her or pressing old bruises. Afterwards she says she gets it, she understands it's about the art and she wants me to push myself, to be the best I can be. I think she secretly resented being a housewife and giving up her career ambitions for my dad. She moved to be with him and then just ended up hanging out at home with me. She used to paint when I was really little, so maybe me being an artist makes up for her not sticking at it. I remember I used to scream at her that she didn't 'get' me, that she didn't have any idea who I was and that she was trying to control me. Now I wonder if she's the only one who truly understands.

The idea is to get her to act like herself on camera by re-enacting ideal-ized versions of herself as a mother. We've started watching all these clichéd films – things like The Sound of Music, Steel Magnolias, Stepmom, Anywhere But Here – anything with a mother figure, anything that might have contributed to the totally saccharine cultural image we have of 'MOM'. I've had her watching and staging some of the scenes and developing models of self-construction and social interaction, *monitoring the relationship between her in front of the camera and me behind it. Even when she's acting from a script, there's this very visible subtext of the real person performing for her real daughter, which I find kind of exciting. I want to examine how the fairy-tale narrative we eat up from films has this passive agenda in our real lives, how damaging it is to roll it out in this one-size-fits-all way. I want to highlight and exploit the gaze of the camera (mine and the movie-maker's) by addressing it directly, turning a private relationship into a public performance, hopefully to create a sense of invited voyeurism.*

I don't know what I'll do with the videos, they might end up being research for something else, but this whole mother–daughter thing is so rich, so complex. I hated my mom for years, but now, when it seems we might not have many years left, she's begun to surprise me. She's been amazing really; in a weird way, I'm not sure my life would be possible right now without her.

I hope your baby grows up to feel the same about you. I worry I'm neither selfless nor selfish enough to give everything I have to a child. When you're a mom, you have to sacrifice all your dreams for theirs and all the world for you and your own. I hope you can do that.

Am x

Sunday, 6 May 2001

'When we win the lottery,' I said, twisting Marc's fingers between mine, 'we should buy this place and turn it into an arts centre.'

'We don't even play the lottery,' he said.

I looked at the side of his face and then back to the building. I pulled my hand from his. 'Let's look inside.'

'Don't be ridiculous,' he said. 'Come on, we're already late for lunch.' He continued pacing towards town, confident I'd reappear by his side any moment.

Instead, I pulled at the boards covering one of the ground-floor windows until one came loose at the bottom. I cast a glance around, checking for witnesses, then thrust my right leg through the hole. Finding my footing on the other side, I pulled my torso and head through, my left leg following and the board banging shut behind me. I blinked, waiting for my eyes to adjust to the darkness. Sucking my bottom lip between my teeth, I tiptoed across the debris-littered floor.

'Alex!' I heard Marc hiss from outside. He must finally have looked around. 'Alex! Get out of there!'

'You come in,' I said. 'It's amazing.'

'You'll get us arrested.'

'Only if you keep standing there like an idiot. Come on, I want to explore.'

I heard him mumbling about rotten floorboards, health and safety requirements and our friends waiting for us, but eventually I saw a leg appear through the entrance I'd used, followed by the rest of him.

'Over here,' I said, thrilled he'd actually followed. 'Isn't it beautiful?' I reached for him through the gloom, placed a kiss on his pursed lips. 'Look,' I said, leading him further inside. 'We could make this a theatre space and upstairs we'd have artists' studios. And a kitsch American-style diner over here, with the waiters on roller skates –'

'Al –' Marc said.

'No, listen,' I said, unlinking my fingers from his and cutting him off. 'Artists would come and stay and work in the diner or whatever for a couple of hours a day to earn their room and food, but the rest of the time they'd just make art. We'd have actors and playwrights and workshops and installations all around the building – anyone could just rock up and try something out. The whole place would have this magical air of experimentation. Naturally, everything would also be brilliant, so the critics would love us and there'd be a waiting list and funding would just pour in . . .'

I'd wandered away from Marc, towards the bowels of the building. I navigated an area of missing flooring and wove through a narrow doorway into an even darker room. I stepped towards the far windows, seeking a crack in the boards to peer out on to the river and the path opposite. My heart continued to hammer with the adrenalin of adventure and the excitement of imaginings, even as my brain began to wind down and remind me that I'd never have the millions necessary to do anything like that and, anyway, York was not exactly renowned for being on the cutting edge of anything. I thought about Fran and Ollie waiting for us at the restaurant. I thought about our flat and the letter that had been sitting on the dining table since Monday morning. I thought about my mum's thick handwriting. About the slim chance of her being sober when she'd written it. About her apologies and pleas and how even after everything a part of me still wanted to believe them. I thought about the phrase she'd used, so medical and detached, yet impossible to read without a flood of emotion. About what it must have been like to write those words to the daughter who hated her. About the uneasy feeling that I may have inherited more than her cheekbones and hair colour.

Early-onset Alzheimer's.

Turning back to the derelict room, I was temporarily blinded.

'Marc?' I said.

'I'm here,' he replied from the darkness.

I heard him step towards me, imagined him drawn by the silent code of my heart and the secret language of husband and wife. Then I heard a thud and the tumble of limbs.

'Shit!' he shouted.

'Marc!' I raced back into the other room, grabbing the splintered door frame to steady myself around the missing flooring.

Marc was on the ground by one shadowy wall, a string of swear words tumbling from his mouth.

'Shit, are you okay?'

'Do I look fucking okay?' he yelled. 'I think I caught my arm on a nail. I'm bleeding.'

'Oh God, what do we do?'

'It's okay,' he said, his voice calmer but strained with pain. 'Just, uh, I need to put pressure –'

'Yes,' I said, adrenalin kicking in, realizing my role. I tried to remember the first aid course work had sent me on. I shrugged off my jacket, but it was all zips and pockets. I pulled off my T-shirt and knelt beside him in the gloom. He held up his arm for me. Palm to elbow was wet and black. 'Fuck, there's so much blood.'

'What not to say when giving first aid,' Marc said weakly.

'Sorry.' I pressed my T-shirt to his skin. 'I can't see. We need to get you out of here. I think we need to go to hospital.'

Marc groaned, but managed to lean on me with his other arm and stumble to his feet.

'Keep it elevated,' I said as we picked our way back to the window. I pulled at the boards and got two fully loose so Marc could climb out a little more gracefully than we'd entered. Outside, I took his arm and inspected the gash. It was deep, running from the knuckle of his little finger all the way down the side of his wrist. I pressed my bloodied T-shirt more firmly to the wound, placed Marc's good hand over it to hold it there. 'Should we call an ambulance?' I said.

Marc shook his head. His face was pale. 'Let's just get a taxi,' he said. Then he attempted a smile. 'You can't go like that, though.'

I looked down at myself. I was standing in the middle of the pavement in my bra, Marc's blood smeared on my skin. I could have burst into tears, but instead I started to laugh and Marc did too. I looked at my husband, holding both his arms above his head like an ungainly dancer. I thought of my jacket abandoned in the gloom, of Marc's DNA dripped on the dusty floorboards, of how mad Fran must be growing waiting for us. I thought of the cocktail of genes my parents had shaken to create exactly me, and the equally baffling genetic accident that had formed the exact man before me. I thought of the natures and nurtures and the flows of fate that had brought us to this exact moment together, yet the strange unknowns of our future.

'Marc?' I said.

'Yes?'

'I think I want to have a baby.'

Two Months Gone

Marc phoned Dorset once more. Caitlin answered, said he was lucky to catch her, she was sorting through my mum's things. He tried to picture the house I'd described, wondered what would happen to its contents. The first time I visited after the diagnosis, I got back on the train after only a few hours in her company. We'd tried to sit in a café, neutral territory, but found ourselves sniping at each other, each waiting for apologies the other wasn't willing to give. Eventually she'd burst into tears. I'd stared at her, wondering what right this woman had to cry. Then I'd grabbed my bag and left her there, making my peace on the journey home with the idea that I'd lost my mother a long time ago, that I was already an orphan. But she persisted. She wrote to me, again and again, finally saying the words I'd waited almost a lifetime to hear. I wrote back and, eventually, against Marc's advice, we tried again. We spent a weekend walking the cliffs and sobbing. Nothing was resolved or forgiven, I told Marc, but she *was* finally sober and I'd agreed to return. On my next visits, I told him, we spent time making food and watching films, neither discussing nor quite ignoring the hurt between us.

The line was bad again. Marc didn't know how to ask Caitlin what he wanted to know. He rubbed the scar on his little finger, finally blurted, 'Is there a will?'

She was silent on the other end of the phone.

'Do I need to do anything?' Marc asked to fill the silence. 'Execute something? Sell the house?'

'I'm sorry, Mr Southwood, but unless your wife has returned I'm not at liberty to discuss such things with you.'

Marc drew in a sharp breath. 'Shouldn't you at least have called me when it happened?'

'I'm sorry you weren't told, but I'm not responsible for such things,' she replied.

'But someone has to inform the next of kin, don't they?'

'You're not next of kin. Your wife is. I believe efforts have been made to contact her, but if she doesn't come forward then the estate will be divided between the other beneficiaries.'

'Who are?'

'I'm not at liberty to disclose that.'

'Jesus, I'm the father of the woman's grandchildren. Did you even tell her Alex was missing?'

Caitlin was silent.

Marc hung up the phone and stared at the kitchen counter. He took some deep breaths and finally unclenched his fists. He wondered if he should have asked about the funeral. If he should tell the girls. Hadn't they been through enough?

Patrick convinced him they needed a break before term started. He picked them up on Saturday morning and they crawled through the weekend traffic as the kids played I spy.

They arrived in a sprawling converted barn in the Lake District. Thick wooden beams dissected airy living areas and a sweeping staircase led from a long dining area to an elegant sitting room. Marc's first thought was that I would have loved it. He said it aloud, wanting to establish me as an okay topic of conversation. He'd decided at home that he needed to be my husband this weekend, not some lonely sap everyone had to tip-toe around.

Patrick paused, then said, 'She would have, wouldn't she?' Marc smiled a thank you and they hauled their cases from the boot.

The others arrived and they sat in the kitchen drinking tea

and catching up while the children explored the garden. Barring a few awkward pauses, it felt almost normal. Patrick told them about his recent private sector offer and how torn he felt. Marc interrupted to tease him about their idealistic student days. Susan laughed and said she'd always be overworked and under-paid, so whatever he decided, their marriage would have ethical equilibrium.

'Would come in handy for tuition fees,' Patrick said, nudging Pip, who briefly looked up from her phone.

It might have felt strange or uncomfortable to be alone amongst couples, but mostly Marc found it a relief to be with those who knew him, who knew us. These were our oldest and best friends; he didn't need to perform or bluster or tell them he was okay.

Fran suggested they open a bottle. Ollie jumped up and bowed at the waist muttering, 'Mi-lady.' Everyone except Fran laughed. Talk turned to the kids. Ollie said they were consider-ing sending Emma to a private tutor for her Year 6 SATs, which launched Susan on a rant about the pointless pressure put on kids at such a young age. Marc's mind was wandering. He looked around the table and, despite the languid pull of early alcohol and relaxation, felt a jolt at the normalcy of it all. How could they be here? How could they talk about this? How could my absence not be present in every second?

Marc excused himself to check for messages. Fleetingly reas-sured, he shrugged on his jacket and joined the others for a walk. They headed into the vast green landscape, the girls running ahead with Emma, laughing and shouting. Marc was glad they'd come. They trekked over stiles and through mud puddles, con-versation ebbing and flowing as they each traversed their own thought patterns.

Marc found himself at the back of the group with Pip. 'How are the applications going?' he said.

'Okay,' she said, glancing at him. 'I've got three offers.'

'That's great.'

'Yeah, maybe, I don't know which I want. Dad says I should put the one with the highest offer down as my first choice, but I don't know if I liked the art department there.'

'Tricky decision,' Marc said.

'I wish I could talk to Alex about it.'

Marc looked away. He cleared his throat. 'She'd have some good advice.'

'Sorry,' Pip said. 'I didn't mean –'

'It's okay,' Marc said. 'It really is.'

'I miss her.'

Marc put his arm awkwardly around Pip's bony shoulders. 'Me too.'

They caught up with the others at the top of a hill, surveying the fields and waters below.

'Alex would have wanted us to *roll* back down,' he said and crouched as if to inspect the ground for nettles.

'You what?' said Pip.

The others laughed a little unsurely, but Fran of all people replied in her plummy accent, 'Why the *hell* not?' and sat on the grass beside Marc.

He noticed her pink nails and diamond stud earrings as she stretched out and launched herself down the uneven slope. Susan gasped, Pip giggled and Ollie gave a sort of pained yelp as his wife careened towards the fields and hedges below, gaining momentum and collecting bracken in her hair. They heard her shrieks and watched her roll over and over, finally reaching the flatter ground and slowing to a stop just before what looked suspiciously like a cowpat. Marc squinted nervously at the fragile body below until it threw out its arms in a gleeful star shape. The wind carried her laughter back to the top.

'Christ,' said Ollie. 'She could have broken her neck.'

'What a legend,' said Pip.

'Chickens!' Fran shouted, scrambling to her feet.

Marc looked at Patrick, who glanced down at Fran, then back to Marc.

'Remember jumping from the bridge during finals?' Patrick said. 'This is nothing.'

Marc snorted. But recalling the foolhardy things they'd subjected their bodies to in their twenties, he zipped his jacket and lay down. The women giggled as Patrick followed suit and they launched themselves down the hill, slightly out of sync, cries of terror and elation tangling in the churned air. Halfway down, the world spinning from ground to sky and back again, Marc heard cries of a higher pitch and realized Pip and Susan were behind them. Marc imagined serious walkers seeking tranquil escapes looking over and seeing their multi-coloured coats avalanching down the opposite hill.

Hearing the adults' screams, the children sprinted back to leap on them.

'Daddy, can I have a go?' asked Char, jumping on Marc's stomach.

He shook his head and watched her screw up her forehead and thrust out her bottom lip. She always looked so adorable when she did that; half the time I'd relent and give her what she wanted. Marc just smiled at her, though, his heart beating in his ears. He heard Emma complaining to his left that she was almost an adult, so she should be allowed. Ollie, who'd walked down behind them, told her to be quiet. Amidst parental refusals, Marc heard infectious giggles and deep, contented sighs.

They were finally encouraged by the disappointed children to heave themselves from the ground. As they paced back over fields and through metal gates, they reminisced about other daring exploits. Marc blushed as Patrick described his running from campus security guards with a traffic sign under his arm.

Then, as if it was the most natural thing in the world, someone mentioned me. They remembered my midnight run through the snow to the jacuzzi in Austria, the precarious pose I struck for a goofy photograph on a jutting rock halfway up Arthur's Seat, and the time I insisted they all take part in a flash mob slurping coffee conspicuously loudly in Betty's. Laughing with friends and talking about me as if I were just not able to make this weekend, as if I'd be home to welcome Marc on Sunday and we might all go out for a meal next Thursday, felt like the universe slotting back into place for a moment.

'A while ago,' Pip said, 'she told me she'd had an idea for something big.'

'Like what?' Patrick said.

Pip shook her head. 'She wouldn't say, said she was still planning it, but that she'd need all of our help with it.'

Fran turned to Pip. 'What do you think it was?'

Pip shrugged.

'Something fabulous, no doubt,' Susan said.

Back at the house, Marc headed to his room. He lay on top of the floral quilt and spoke aloud to me, his words coming breathlessly between hot tears. 'Come back to me. Please. Please come back.' He chanted uninspired prayers, whisking his pain into thick, fluffy egg-white peaks.

He fell asleep and woke with aches in his back and legs. He splashed his face with water, then headed towards the kitchen, pausing as he heard voices.

'– it's the not knowing that's tearing him apart. It's not good for the girls either.'

'Yeah, I mean, I don't want to admit she's gone either, but I think it's pretty obvious –'

'They need to find a body, then he can start dealing with it.'

Marc stepped back into the shadowy hallway. *They're only concerned for you,* he heard my voice in his ear. He closed his eyes and felt my arms around him, my lips on his neck.

Ollie took charge of the meal, which they devoured, making appreciative noises and repeating that he should go on *Masterchef* or open his own restaurant. Conversation remained light, meandering through work, the news, local politics, books, and landing as so often on TV and film.

'We went to see the new Woody Allen last week,' Ollie said.

'Any good?' Marc said.

'How can you justify watching anything that man does?' Susan said, her cheeks pink from the wine.

'Oh come on,' Ollie said. 'You can't dismiss his entire work because of a scandal. It's not like he's been convicted of anything.'

'Neither has Polanski,' Patrick said.

'And they're both great film-makers,' Ollie persisted. 'Did you see *Carnage*?'

Susan shook her head. 'It doesn't matter. We shouldn't be supporting these men making money and collecting awards.'

'I sort of agree with you,' Fran said. 'But I remember having a conversation with Alex about this kind of stuff, and she had a pretty good argument for why it's all much less black and white. Marc, you can probably explain this better than me. She started talking about Kant, I think, which I didn't really follow, but it was something about it being okay to assess things differently on different levels.'

Marc nodded. He'd heard me repeat myself often enough. 'The idea is that aesthetic value and moral value are distinct but interlinked. You can have different opinions about both, but if you prioritize one over the other you're heading towards absolutism.'

'Does anyone have a clue what he just said?' Patrick poured himself another glass of wine. 'We're not in the classroom, you know, buddy, you can speak in English.'

'Can I not just be absolutely disgusted?' Susan said, ignoring her husband.

Marc laughed. 'Of course, but Al would argue that by doing so you're failing to engage with the work and thus failing to have a proper stance. To really protest the sexism of Hollywood or whatever it is, you need to engage with these films on both a moral *and* an aesthetic level. Al would say you need to see them to critique them.'

'And do you agree?' Patrick asked.

Marc pinched the stem of his glass. 'Um –'

'Ha! See?' said Patrick. 'Even you have to admit, Alex talked some weird shit sometimes.'

Marc looked at his friend, the muscles in his neck tensing.

'I don't think any of that's shit,' said Pip. 'It makes sense.'

'That's what worries me,' Patrick said, throwing his arm around his daughter. Marc was still staring at Patrick. He finally met his gaze. 'What's up?'

Marc took a breath. His voice was soft and controlled. 'Please don't speak about my wife in the past tense.'

Ollie stopped stacking the plates and Susan held her glass before her mouth.

'Oh Marc, buddy, I'm –'

'No,' Marc cut him off. He looked around at the faces of our friends. 'I heard you all earlier. I know what you think, but you're wrong. I can't just move on and pretend Al's dead. I know what it looks like, I know what the evidence suggests and maybe I even accept that if I was my friend I'd think the same as you. But deep down I know she's out there. I know she's in trouble and she needs us to find her.'

A hush drifted over the table. Marc sensed the words 'It'll be okay,' dancing on our friends' lips. Thankfully no one was crass enough to utter them. Eventually Susan suggested they adjourn to the sitting room for a nightcap.

An hour or so later, heading towards the bathroom with his toothbrush, Marc bumped into Pip. Her bedroom was at the other end of the barn and he wondered if she'd been waiting for him.

'Hey,' Marc said.

'Hey,' she said.

'You okay?'

Pip nodded.

'Do you need anything?'

She shook her head. 'No, I just, I was thinking about my coursework and – it doesn't matter.' She turned to go.

'Do you want a chat?' Marc said and she turned back to face him.

He led her into his room. There was nowhere to sit but the twin beds, so they each took one, facing one another awkwardly.

'What's up?' Marc said.

Pip twisted the end of her sleeve. 'I just, I wish I could talk to Alex.'

Marc swallowed. 'About your school work?'

She nodded.

'Might I do?'

She shrugged.

'Go on, try me. I might be able to help.'

She looked at him for a moment before speaking. 'Do you think artists can ever have a right to be cruel?'

Marc frowned. 'Um, no,' he said. 'Artists have the same responsibilities as everyone else. No one has a right to be cruel.'

Pip wrinkled her nose. 'Never mind.' She went to stand up.

'Wait,' Marc said, realizing she was looking for me and he'd just sounded like her dad. 'That's only my opinion. Al would have liked the question. Is this about the films we were talking about?'

Pip sat back down. 'Not really. I just, I'm wondering if an end can ever justify the means.' She picked at her nail polish. 'I mean, what if an artist truly felt the work they needed to do involved hurting someone else? Then perhaps their responsibility to their art would outweigh the responsibility they had to an individual.'

'That doesn't sound terribly ethical,' Marc said.

'But,' Pip said, gesturing with her hands and reminding him of me when I got passionate about something, 'if you look at the world as a whole and all the suffering and prejudice and cruelty in it, then you can't feel sentimental about the pain of just one individual, can you? Especially if his or her suffering serves a higher purpose.'

'What sort of higher purpose?' Marc said.

'I don't know. Maybe if it's used to highlight an issue or make a statement. Like if you sacrifice one person to save many.'

'Is this really for school?' Marc said, wondering if he shouldn't have encouraged this conversation after all. 'What sort of project are you working on?'

Pip chewed her lip. 'I just, I dunno. I was thinking, what if a murderer killed someone as an aesthetic act?'

'Excuse me?' Marc said, his voice raised.

Pip blinked, but decided to go on. 'Alex and I used to talk about this kind of thing and I know you want to believe she's out there, but I just thought –'

'Alex is an academic, Pip,' Marc said, cutting her off. He stood up, towering over the teenager. 'She talks and thinks about all sorts of things. She likes playing devil's advocate.'

'I know,' Pip said, looking up into his face, her eyes wide. 'It's just, what if . . .' She trailed off.

'What if what?' Marc challenged, his face growing red. 'What are you suggesting? That she was some sort of sacrificial lamb?'

'No,' Pip said, looking hurt. 'I don't know. I just wondered if there was a connection.'

Marc shook his head. 'This is ridiculous. There's a difference between the art world and the real one, Pip. It's interesting to think about this stuff, to debate whether to go and see a film or not, but when you're older you'll understand there are much more important things in life.'

He walked around the beds and held the door open for her. 'You should be asleep,' he said, as if telling off a child.

He came today. It's been almost a week. He stood over me, arms folded, and asked why I wasn't eating. I don't know why, but I burst into tears.

He watched me for a while, then said, 'I know this is difficult for you.'

I wanted to hate him, to spit on him or scream at him. But I was so weak. My arms were covered in goosebumps. My stomach had been cramping all night. When I slept, my dreams were about food.

He pulled a little plastic-wrapped packet of tissues from his pocket and held one out for me. I stared at it and then him, trying to put together a thought. Why was he being nice? What did he want? My mind kept flicking. I couldn't concentrate, even on hating him.

'Take it,' he said, and I heard the familiar frustration in his voice. A part of me wished he would hit me.

'Thank you,' I said, taking the tissue. I wiped my tears, blew my nose. On the backs of my eyelids I saw Ann Moore, the Fasting Woman of Tutbury, shaking her head at me from the nineteenth century. I saw Kafka's hunger artist and the paying crowd gawping at his forty-day stamina all folding their arms in disgust at my failure. It had only been a week, but it was such a relief to see him. To hear his voice. He pulled up the plastic chair, sat down facing me. I lay back against the lumpy pillow. I had an urge to fall asleep while he watched.

'Are you ready to co-operate now?' he said.

I nodded and saw Marina Abramović and Tehching Hsieh turn their backs on me.

2002

8/19/02

Al,

I miss you. I know I'm not supposed to say that. I'm not supposed to make you feel guilty or question your choices. Not now. There's no going back for you, is there? You have a child. You've created life. That's so much more real than anything I'll ever create, isn't it? That probably makes you more real than me. But I can't help grieving for you. Is being a mother really everything the world says it is? Is it really our sole purpose? Don't you resent Marc just a little bit for being able to hold his child proudly and also go off to work and have it affect nothing for him?

Sorry, I'm being an angry feminist. You must have so many hormones racing around your body still that you barely know what to think. It's cruel for me to worm my way in when you're vulnerable. In a way, I feel vulnerable too. I have these bits of work coming together, but the moments in between — I have whole periods of doubt, of not knowing, of feeling invisible or inconsequential. I get this unease in the pit of my stomach. What will people think of me? How will they react to my work? I know I need to be open to criticism, but I'm not sure I can handle rejection.

What if everything I've done, everything I'm doing, is condemned? Will anyone other than you understand? Sometimes I have this suspicion that I'm a bad person. I list all the non-bad things I do: the acts of kindness, the things I volunteer for, the money I give to charity, the stuff I sacrifice. But then I wonder if maybe I only do those things to mask my true self. What if, deep down, I'm just not nice?

Do you have the same fears? Do you worry about being your mother's child? About your own? Do you think about nature versus nurture?

I'm scared of losing you, Al. I'm scared you'll give your whole self to your child. I'm scared there'll be nothing left for me.

Am x

Thursday, 4 July 2002

The nurse showed me how to wash my hands and arms, then wheeled me over to the frightening plastic box. The label on the side read 'Baby Southwood'. Her tiny, shrivelled limbs were a deep pink, her slit-like eyes fused closed. A cannula ran across her face into her nostrils. I watched her chest rise and fall with the machine, her delicate hand pierced with tubes.

I reached forwards on my chair, feeling the movement in every butchered muscle between my chest and thighs. I slipped my gloved hands through the openings in the side of the box.

'I'll give you some time,' the nurse said and I heard her slip out of the door.

I'd been in labour for twenty-two hours, four weeks too early. Still only four centimetres dilated, I began to haemorrhage and the midwife said the baby's heartbeat was rising. A doctor was called. Marc was ushered away to put on scrubs and I was wheeled into surgery.

I'd been begging the nurse since I woke up to let me come. Finally, she'd checked my stitches and said it would be safe to visit the neonatal ward in a wheelchair. 'Your husband's asleep in the lounge,' she said. 'Should I wake him?'

I shook my head. Marc was exhausted. He'd been worrying about both of us, dozing mostly in the chair beside my bed, waking as soon as I moved a finger. He needed to sleep.

I looked at my daughter, wired up like an alien, and felt like

I'd never felt before. *Please*, I thought. *I promise* . . . What did I promise that evening? I can't remember my words, but I know it was everything. I promised to devote my life to her. To do anything she needed. To keep her safe and warm. To make her happy and strong. To protect her from and prepare her for everything she might encounter. To love her always.

'I'm sorry,' I said aloud. This was my fault. It had to be. This was my punishment for worrying about what would change, for not enjoying my pregnancy. For drinking coffee and eating unpasteurized cheese. For continuing to work. For feeling stressed. For thinking of myself. For trying to have it all.

Please, I thought, touching my baby through a latex barrier, *please just let her live.*

May
Ten Weeks Gone

I don't know how, but eventually Marc found the letters.

Nicola was ringing him every few days to give an update, but there was rarely any news. My phone records had come through, but my last communications were nothing out of the ordinary: a call from my mobile network, a text message to Marc about the girls' swimming lesson, an unanswered call to Fran, another from a colleague. That was it: no communications after my disappearance. If the phone was stolen along with my wallet, Nicola said, the thief probably inserted a new SIM card.

With the police offering nothing for him to pin his hopes on, he couldn't help but feel the pressure of everyone's advice. No one explicitly told him to give up or move on, of course, but it was there in every question about the girls and work and how he was. Gentle reminders that this couldn't continue forever; life somehow had to go on. Perhaps he was thinking of the girls, realizing he needed to offer them a home rather than a shrine. I imagine he sent them to his parents for a weekend and determined to have the house cleared by the time they returned. He wouldn't have wanted to, but he had no choice.

He won't have got rid of anything, but I imagine him packing my things into boxes and hauling them up the little ladder to the attic. Maybe he hesitated, wondering why on earth I'd bought a metallic silver T-shirt and when he last saw me in the peach suspender belt. Maybe he placed my jewellery close to the hatch, unable to consciously contemplate a life without me, but subconsciously already imagining Lizzie wanting to wear my diamond pendant to a school ball, Charlotte claiming my grandmother's brooch as a memento before going off to uni.

He wondered if he should take our photographs down. Where did one stop? My voice was on the outgoing message. He didn't want to erase it, but knew how morbid it must sound to anyone who phoned.

The house was full of my things. He couldn't box them all. But he couldn't leave my mud-crusted walking boots in the rack beside the front door to morosely greet everyone from the postman to Charlotte's new best friend. Patrick and he had plans to watch the Grand Prix and Marc had told himself he needed to have worked it out by then.

He heaved the last box up through the hatch and tried not to think about how long my stuff would be up here. He decided that didn't matter right now. He had to think about today, about this one step, not the many that may or may not need to follow.

He climbed through the hatch and knelt on the chipboard panels to stack the boxes to one side. I wonder if he looked around, trying to remember what was in the other boxes up there, whether we still had the cot and the buggy, what we'd done with Charlotte's train set and Lizzie's toy kitchen. Did he sit under the bare bulb thinking about our family? About the years we'd spent in the house below. Changing nappies and sleepwalking through scream-filled nights. Fixing the banister Lizzie kicked out during a tantrum and patching Charlotte up after she toddled into the CD rack. Yelling up and down the stairs. Chasing them through the hallway, around the breakfast bar and out into the garden until they were pinned against the apple tree and had nowhere to hide from our tickles. Plastering grazed knees, cutting chewing gum from hair, wiping tears from cheeks, carrying them to bed and worrying through fevers. Marc looked around the dusty attic, surveying the remnants of what we once were. His eyes scanned the boxes and the junk, landing finally on a black lidded archive box. It was stacked discreetly beneath two boxes of old curtains and with the sleeping bags and the tent piled on top. It looked perfectly normal, not out of place, not something anyone would notice. Except Marc. He knew we'd never bought archive boxes. And he had these same ones on his shelves at work. Everyone did; I guess they must have been cheap for the university to buy in bulk. I must have pinched one from work, he realized, but how had it found its way up here? He moved the sleeping bags and lifted the curtain boxes. Perhaps he thought he was going to find more of my essays. Perhaps he was hoping for a box of art books or lecture notes or ancient bits of student work.

He lifted the lid and saw a stack of faded manila folders. The top one bulged, its flap only just closed. From its left corner, in my thick Sharpie lettering, he read *MARC*. He stared at his name, his heart pounding. He lifted it up and found another beneath it reading *CHAR,* another beneath that reading *LIZZIE.* He opened the flap of his own file and a supermarket receipt fell out. He scanned down the list of items, then turned it over to see his own writing. *Back late, love you.* He flipped it back over. The date on the receipt was 2005. He pulled everything out of the folder and spread it on the floor. I'd kept every note, letter and birthday card he'd ever written to me. I know Marc has a similar collection in a shoebox on his side of the office. I found it years ago, but never mentioned it. Sometimes, if he was out, I'd open the box and just look. He too kept every reminder I tacked to the fridge and every postcard I wrote while I was away but, not trusting the post, carried home in my luggage. He kept every note, every message I pinned to doors or hid in books, every paper aeroplane I folded and flew to distract him. Daft words and messages I'd barely thought through. A thousand simple *I love you*s and a hundred *Darling*s. Neither of us were sentimental hoarders, but how could we throw away such things? I'd look at a tiny torn-out scrap with Marc's heart crudely scratched in biro and know I couldn't relegate it to the bin. Such things didn't belong in refuse sacks to be manhandled by men in work boots at seven on a Tuesday morning, slopped into the back of a lorry and brutally upturned at the tip. I'd imagine them wriggling free from their neighbouring newspapers and food scraps, fluttering in the wind and seeking something to devote their sentiment to in a loveless landfill. So I kept them. A whole folder of notes he probably had no recollection of writing. For the briefest of moments, crouched in our attic, realizing we'd shared the same romantic dilemma, Marc would have felt us whole again.

He wiped his cheeks and picked up Charlotte and Lizzie's files. Drawings and Mother's Day cards, hospital bands and crumpled crayon messages. Beneath these was a file labelled *SCHOOL* containing an old art book, notes passed in class with Philippa, a certificate of achievement. My father had a file too: letters he wrote to me, but also printouts of the scans following his chemo. My mother's file was almost empty: a photograph of a rosy-cheeked young woman with a baby, and the one card she'd sent when I left for university.

At the bottom, he discovered a bulging folder labelled *AMELIA*. He recognized the name of my Chicago room-mate and, curiosity welling, lifted the file from the box. He froze. There on the cardboard at the bottom of the box, lay a passport.

He put the folder down and reached for the passport. He flipped to the photo. I looked out at him, young and serious. Was I twenty-eight, twenty-nine in that photograph? My hair was longer, hanging loose over my shoulders, tucked behind both ears, emphasizing the point of my chin. Not a flattering image, but it still made his stomach flip.

What went through my husband's mind? What pieces was he

starting to put together? Of course, his first question had to be: *What on earth is her passport doing in the bottom of a box in the attic?* Had it fallen in when I was packing these things up? Had it been accidentally scooped from my messy desk with these folders? When had I packed them away? Why, if these things were so sentimental, had I put them in the attic?

I don't know how Marc reconciled these mysteries that afternoon, whether he shrugged and said it must have been an accident, one that would have been annoying and costly when I did get round to booking our next holiday and we turned the house upside down before I admitted defeat and had to go to the passport office for reissue. Or whether doubt began to worm its way in even then.

Either way, he placed my passport in his pocket and turned back to Amelia's folder. Inside were a couple of hundred hand-written letters. The scratchy writing was familiar to him from the envelopes that periodically arrived on the doormat. Marc removed one at random and smoothed its folds on his thighs. It was postmarked May 2003. I'd visited Amelia that summer, taking the still breastfeeding Lizzie on that nightmare seven-hour flight. I arrived back exhausted but gushing with stories about my friend's success. Marc remembered picking me up from the airport and kissing my tears as I embraced him. 'It's only been a week,' he teased, but he spent the whole evening with both Lizzie and me in his arms, as if he was afraid we might vanish once more.

I was brought a cup of tea today, sweet with sugar, the bag left in longer than most people prefer, just like my husband knew to make it. He sits with me when I eat now, watches me chew. I sleep for long periods of time, wake with no memory of my dreams. I don't have the energy to fight his questions any more. Today he asked me to describe our sex life. I wonder what he does with this information. Files it away for his private fantasies, perhaps. What does he achieve by getting me to talk? Isn't it enough that he is keeping me here? That I am his plaything? It's like owning me physically is not enough for him; he must get inside my mind, root around and leave me nothing.

He hasn't touched me since I hit him with the tray, though. The cut on his cheek is almost healed. My bruises too are fading to a pale yellow. Soon they'll be gone.

I think a lot about where he goes when he's not with me, who he talks to, how he holds himself. Does he think about me? I like the idea that a part of me slips out of the door behind him, follows him through the locks and into his life. He doesn't get to do this to me and simply leave me behind when he feels like it. I hope I'm with him always, whatever his life is out there now.

2003

5/4/03

Al,

You're coming to New York! I can't wait. I have a show opening, so you can help me set up and spy on all the important fuckers. Your baby will be a great disguise – nobody pays attention to mothers, do they? The idea of domesticity erases any notion of creativity.

How are you doing? I know it's so hard for you right now, I know you're still grieving, but I'm pleased you're coming. I couldn't do this without you. In his way, I'm sure your dad would have understood that too. I think he would have been proud of us both. The timing of this show is bad, but I couldn't say no. It's what we dreamed of back at grad school. It's the tittyfucking Whitney! I hope they like my stuff. I mean, I guess they must, because they already friggin' asked me, didn't they? But I still have to pinch myself and check this is real. It terrifies me that it's a new piece. If they like it, it should help me get a grant, but if they don't, my whole career could just fizzle and die. What would happen to me then? I'd probably fizzle and die too. I used to think I didn't care, that I made things just for me. But now the stakes are higher, turns out I really do.

Will it be weird to leave Marc? Or secretly a relief? It'll be the longest you've looked after Lizzie alone, right? Does it worry you that you've got seventeen more years of this? I feel trapped if I work on a performance piece for longer than a month. I could never do a Linda Montano. I mean, it's not the most difficult thing to wear the same coloured clothing every day and live in a one-coloured room, but still. It's the dedication, the kind of meditation on your art: deciding to live it every second of every day, whether or not anybody's looking. I'm too bad at making decisions and sticking to them. I mean, I'm earning money now and getting commissions, but I still don't always wake up feeling like an artist. Does that make you laugh? I'm not anything else, am I? Not like you: mother, wife, teacher.

I bet ORLAN wakes up feeling like an artist. All that plastic surgery to give her the Mona Lisa's brow protrusions, the chin of Botticelli's Venus, Diana's eyes – it's a genius concept, but what does it feel like to be the Frankenstein's monster of idealized female beauty? Can you imagine transforming your flesh for art? Making that kind of commitment? I suppose you have transformed your flesh. Somehow doing it for a child seems more acceptable than what ORLAN does. I love that someone's out there doing it – I mean, I think we need it to exist for art's sake – but everyone I know is like, 'Yeah, she's doing cool work, but I'd never go that far.'

Mostly I just like being anonymous. I had a fight with the Whitney's PR guy because he wanted me to send a picture for the flyer. I like being able to sit with the audience and experience what they're experiencing. More than that, I want my identity to be an irrelevance. It's getting increasingly hard to remain private, though. People want to put a face to the work, to draw meaning from who you are, place you in a safe little box and say they understand you. I'm like, what the cock? I feel like my face's lack of celebrity is as much of an accomplishment as if I was plastered all over billboards. You have to work to be stealthy in this city. What if we don't all want to be Andy Warhol? I mean, it's bad enough that your skin colour and the way you talk and where you went to school and the parts between your legs influence the interpretation; now it's all about your online presence and building a brand. Vito Acconci said he stopped doing live performance because he felt like everyone knowing what he looked like put more emphasis on the cult of his celebrity than on his actions.

I'm getting a bit obsessed with this life-as-art-as-celebrity thing. Britney may not have an output beyond cheesy pop and a kiss with Madonna, but she's a living performance, isn't she? She's more committed to the character she's created than I am to any of my pieces. I leave *them in the gallery or on the street and move on. She's still partying and performing wherever she goes. And we're all watching, like she's there for our consumption. Wouldn't it be ridiculous if kids end up studying celebrities alongside Montano's* Seven Years of Living Art?

It's such a delicious mindfuck. I need you to help me work it out. I need you, period, actually. Sometimes I think I need you more than anyone needs you, Al. More than Lizzie and Marc and your silly students. I can't wait to have you here.

See you very soon, babe.

Am x

Monday, 6 January 2003

I glanced at the old woman's face. Who was she? A neighbour, perhaps. Marc was by my side and I entertained a brief fantasy that he might lift me up, carry me away from this woman, away from all these solemn strangers eating canapés and spouting clichés.

'It was a lovely service,' she said.

'Thank you,' I said. Marc was watching me. That morning I'd sobbed so violently I'd fallen to the kitchen floor. He'd tried to catch me, ended up crouching and cradling my crumpled form. I loved him for it, but it wasn't enough to stop me crying. He was trying to be my rock, I knew. But what use is a bloody rock when you're burying your father? He'd held my hand during the service and now, at the wake, he'd appointed himself my personal bodyguard. He was ready to whisk me away as soon as I gave the nod, as soon as he thought I couldn't stand it any more. And his presence, well, it meant the world to me, even if it couldn't actually fix the world.

A couple, now, were giving me their condolences. I nodded

and said the right things, but my mind was wandering. I was thinking about last night, when I'd found Marc standing over Lizzie's cot, deep in thought. I'd wanted to ask what he was thinking, but hesitated. These past few weeks I too had stood over our child and thought the unthinkable. My warped mind had tried to picture our beautiful little girl one day sitting on a wooden pew sobbing for us. How could I reconcile my own mortality with my love for my child? Or my husband? I didn't want to have these thoughts, but they barged their way into my brain. Would it be better to be the one buried or burying? Could I cope with going through this again? With Marc in the coffin? With nobody by my side, nobody to catch me when I fell to the kitchen floor or bring me fresh tissues and tell me I was still beautiful even with snot running down my face?

I blinked and realized I was about to cry. I said a flustered thank you to the couple before me and turned to Marc with a panicked expression. He understood. He placed a protective arm around my shoulders and led me towards the door. I slumped into his torso and imagined the respectfully apologetic expression he was directing towards anyone trying to interrupt our exit. Once, I thought, I'd been an independent, capable woman. I'd flown off around the world, taken risks, felt like my life was my own. Today, though, I needed this man. I needed our family, our life. The relief of submission was absolute.

Marc led me to his car. He strapped me into the passenger seat and kissed my forehead before walking around to the driver's side. I looked over at him releasing the handbrake and checking his mirrors and let out a sob. If I couldn't live without Marc, I realized, the only alternative would be to leave him to bury me. To condemn his heart to be broken and him to face all this, plus the rest of a lifetime alone. Could I do that to him? Maybe we could die simultaneously, so romantically co-dependent that one heart could not continue beating without the other. Could that happen except in a film? And what about our daughter then, left to bury both her parents at once?

'We're home,' Marc said as we pulled into our street. 'Let's go inside and send the babysitter home. We can lock all the doors, snuggle up with Lizzie and shut out the world.'

I nodded and offered a weak smile. The answer was obvious really. Marc knew what to do, how to act, how to cope. I, on the other hand, would be lost without him.

Three Months Gone

My ninety-third day missing was Charlotte's birthday. Marc knew it was just another date on the calendar, but it seemed more significant somehow. He wondered if I noticed the day, wherever I was. He was struggling so much that he almost forgot it altogether until Fran caught up with him at the school gates a few days before and asked what he had planned. Seeing the flash of panic on his face, she took pity on him. They spent the rest of the week in whispered phone conversations concocting a last-minute party.

He searched high and low for our daughters' smiles on the day. He roped Lizzie in on the plan and she told him with a roll of her eyes that Char wouldn't want princesses, balloons or anything pink. She offered to make breakfast and brought a tray up to our room with three soft-boiled eggs accompanied by soldiers with Marmite heads, like I used to make them every weekend.

Char's bottom lip trembled as she looked down at her plate, but Lizzie squeezed her sister's hand and told her she should open her presents.

She'd been sent home on Friday with gifts from her school friends, and Nana and Grandpa had posted an enormous box of presents. She unwrapped clothes, books, DVDs and a magic kit. Lizzie had made her a chalkboard sign to put on her door, reading 'Current Mood . . .'

'I've got one too,' Lizzie said. 'It's so Dad doesn't have to keep asking how we are.'

Charlotte giggled, but Marc studied Lizzie's face, unsure how much of a joke it was.

He gave Char a digital camera. She'd asked for one like Lizzie's for Christmas and we'd said it was too expensive, she'd have to wait until she was older. She beamed as she tore the paper and, once Marc had helped her install the memory card, began snapping away. Marc and Lizzie hid beneath the duvet shouting, 'Paparazzi, Paparazzi!'

They headed into town so Char could take pictures of the river and the boats. 'Let's start on the bridge,' Marc suggested as they walked past the old fire station and towards the opera house. They collided with an alighting crowd at the bus stop, and Marc and Lizzie lagged back so Char could step around the corner first. It had the desired effect. She turned and saw six of her school friends standing at the front of the queue for the Dungeons. She swivelled back to him and began to say, 'Look, Daddy, Emma and Rose and Becky are he—' but her friends interrupted, jumping up and down and shouting, 'SURPRISE!' Fran offered a conspiratorial wink from the back of the group.

They were given a private dungeon tour, complete with jump-worthy zombies and hideous prosthetics. Charlotte clung to him a couple of times, but then she saw an actor with blood-stained sleeves flapping where his arms should be and cried, 'It's just a flesh wound!' She dissolved into such rolling giggles that even the actor cracked a smile.

At the end of the tour, the guide gave Charlotte a souvenir book and each child got a goodie bag. He ushered them into place in front of a gruesome hanging scene for a group photograph and they waited as they printed eight copies. Marc thought the party a success, but studying the photograph later, he found an unmistakable frown pasted to Lizzie's face.

Back at home, with the girls plonked in front of a film, Marc and Fran retreated to the kitchen for a cup of tea.

'Thank you,' he said, handing her a steaming mug. 'Seriously, thank you so much. For today and, you know, everything.'

'My pleasure.' She smiled and he noticed dark shadows hiding beneath her foundation.

'Are you . . .' he began unsurely. 'It's a long time since I've asked this of anyone, but are you okay?'

'Me? Yes, fine!' Her lips curled less convincingly this time. 'Just, you know, a little fight with Ollie, that's all.'

'I'm sorry,' he said, not wanting to hear the details.

'How about you?'

Marc wondered if she could sense his indifference and felt a pang of guilt. 'As expected, I suppose.'

'What are the police saying?'

Marc shrugged. 'To prepare for the worst. I seem to ping-pong between accepting that this might be the way it is now and rebelling against all such thoughts. It's hardest on Lizzie, I think.'

'She seems okay,' Fran said, reaching to touch his arm. 'She had a good time today and she's such a good sister to Char.'

Marc nodded. 'Thank you for organizing all this. Really, you've been a godsend. I've been asking far too much of you. If there's anything I can do in return —'

'It's nothing,' she said. 'I want to help. My heart is breaking for you, you know? You don't deserve this.'

Marc watched a frown flash across her face.

'Are you sure you're okay?' he asked, more sincerely this time, and placed his hand on her shoulder.

Fran folded into him. He prised the mug from her fingers and placed it on the counter, then wrapped his arms around her back, feeling strange about touching an adult like this for the first time in months.

'I'm sorry,' she said into his shoulder. 'I shouldn't be doing this to you.'

'It's okay,' he said, smoothing his hand over her back.

'It's not. Nothing's okay.'

Marc patted her thin cardigan and made shh noises while she sobbed into his shoulder, but still wasn't sure he cared. For months he'd barely registered other people's lives except to grow envious of their simplicity. Marital arguments and petty jealousies, financial headaches and personal grievances didn't seem important any more. If I came back, he knew he'd never worry about such things. Even while holding Fran, trying to comfort her, he tasted disgust upon his tongue, as if her unhappiness, whatever its cause, was unsavoury. A cruel part of his brain wanted to push her away, shake her by the biceps and tell her to go home and make up with Ollie, because at least she still could.

He kept holding her, though. The quiet crying continued and he wondered if it'd be rude to reach for his tea and sip it over her head.

'Alex and I used to grumble about the little things,' Fran said through her tears. 'About being torn between what we wanted for ourselves and for our families. But she had you. Ollie just doesn't understand.'

My sweet husband resisted the urge to roll his eyes.

'It's simply not fair, when someone like you –' Fran stopped herself and Marc stiffened. She pulled her head from his shoulder, but still clung to his torso. She looked up into his face, all puffy-eyed, mascara flecking her cheeks.

'It'll be okay,' he said.

'Alex never appreciated you.'

Marc frowned. He knew Fran was hurting, knew her words were about her and Ollie and not us, but still. He held his tongue, conscious of trying to support our friend in this moment.

A beat went by when perhaps he knew what was coming, but it still came as a shock when Fran launched herself on to tiptoes and pressed her hot, fleshy lips to his.

172

He pushed her away, but not before registering her lipstick on his skin, the sensation of her urgent, desperate kiss.

'What are you doing?' he said, wanting to gag.

'I'm sorry,' she said and backed away, fear in her eyes.

'What kind of sorry slut are you?' he shouted, forgetting the children in the next room.

Fresh tears came to her eyes, but she flashed him a stony look. She shook her head. 'Maybe I was wrong, maybe you're just the same. You men are so fucking oblivious. You deserve everything you get.'

Fran stalked out of the kitchen. Marc followed her into the hallway. 'What's that supposed to mean?'

She turned to face him and gave a dry laugh. 'You act like it's this great surprise, like we've suddenly woken up and changed overnight, but you must have been walking around with your eyes closed not to realize how unhappy we've been.'

'Who's we?' Marc said, his voice angry but fear creeping down the back of his neck. 'I'm sorry you and Ollie are having problems, but Alex and I were –'

'Happy?' she said, cutting him off with a sarcastic smile. 'Perfect? Just as in love as when you met?'

'Why are you doing this?'

'I'm not doing anything,' she said. 'I just can't stand to see you moping over Alex like she was some sort of saint. You need to wake up, Marc. Alex wasn't the smiling doll you think she was. She used to cry on my shoulder about how fucking dull everything was. She hated this city, she hated her job, she even said she hated this house.'

'That's not true,' Marc said, shaking his head. 'Alex loves –'

'Isn't it?' Fran said, a cruel smile playing on her lips. 'Your wife told me she hated her life.'

Marc felt like he'd been winded. He stared at our friend as if she was a stranger. Where was the woman who'd helped us paint the dining room, who'd held our children when they were tiny, who'd driven to pick us up when we broke down halfway to Newcastle, who he'd watched me wrap in my arms the day she found out she'd miscarried?

'Emma!' Fran shouted, her eyes still locked with Marc's. 'Come on, we're leaving!'

Marc watched Emma tie her shoelaces, aware Lizzie and Charlotte were hovering curiously in the doorway. Fran pinched her mouth into a smile and said goodbye to the girls, then dragged Emma out on to the pavement. Marc closed the door behind them and stared at the stained glass panels, imagining he could still taste her lips. He wanted to scrub layers of his skin away with the memory. *Alex is no longer the last person you kissed,* he kept thinking in horror.

'You really think Fran offered herself up like that?' he says, amused. He's been asking about our life, like it gets him hard to think about the sweet, gentle husband I've lost. I'm tired of fighting him, though. Answering his questions is easier than the alternative.

'Well?'

I shrug. Why not? I saw the way women looked at Marc.

'Okay, fine,' he says. I wonder if he's jealous. The husband I sit here picturing is attractive and sexy and desirable, while the man before me has to lock a woman in a room to get her to talk to him.

'Maybe she did,' he muses. 'Maybe Nicola threw herself on him too, maybe there was a queue down the street. But what makes you so sure he pushed them away? The man loses you for what looks like forever and you still want him to remain pure and true?'

'What do you want?' I say, too exhausted to scream. 'For me to imagine them fucking on our kitchen floor? Someone moving in, looking after our kids, taking my place?'

As I say it I realize that is what he wants. *Exactly* what he wants. For me to picture my family without me. He looks at me as if he knows me, as if he sees what's going on in my head.

He laughs and turns towards the door. 'Time's running out, Alexandra. Your time is running out.'

2004

9/27/04

Dear Al,

How are you? How is little Lizzie? How's being back at work? It must feel like you've had your brain handed back to you now you're allowed to discuss more than poop and potty training!

Sorry, I only tease. But you need to talk to Marc. I know he wants another kid and I know you want to give him what he wants, but you can't do that to yourself, babe. And you can't just keep taking birth control and not telling him. Your desires are just as important as his — more so when it involves your body. He needs to respect what you've gone through, what you've sacrificed. I mean, it's enough for any woman, but you in particular. Becoming a mom after what yours did to you is not nothing. You've achieved an enormous amount. I don't know many women who would be able to move on from that. I remember your face in that tattoo shop in Boystown as your scar was finally replaced by something beautiful. I remember you saying you never wanted kids. I know all that's changed and Lizzie is the light of your life, but just because you changed your mind once doesn't mean you can't trust it now. You're in a great place: you have a child and an opportunity to reclaim some of yourself. Don't give it up because Marc has some idea about the perfect happy family.

I'll shut up now, I've said my piece.

I don't want to jinx anything, but I too am finally in a positive place. I feel like I'm finding a balance between the things I love. I'm in the final stages of tying pretty pink ribbons around something to present to a gallery, and I also have this other, tiny piece that I initially thought was a bit of fun that's totally spiralled and become this thing every motherfucker's talking about. I was looking through the videos I made with my mom a year or two ago and felt the urge to play with the project some more. I came up with this installation board game based on the film Terms of Endearment. *(Have you seen it? It's this terrible, totally wonderful film that everyone loves here — all schmaltzy, weepy, family stuff with a mother and daughter who fall out and marry and divorce and get cancer and make up and fall out and make up and et cetera, puke-my-guts-out-and-wipe-my-face-in-it, et cetera. Won all the Oscars, obviously.)* I pitched it to PS1 and they had this last-minute opening, so I set it up within a couple of weeks. I thought it'd be there for ten days and that'd be it, but it's been two months now and every day more and more people seem to be schlepping across the river to sit and play my game. It's a simple dice-roll thing for moms to play with their daughters, but each square asks them to face something personal about their relationship, to share a secret or ask something they've been afraid to say. I figured hardly anyone would be willing to volunteer, but apparently most days there's a queue. All these assholes acting out their private therapy sessions for the crowd. They're paying me to keep it going and there's word a couple of museums are interested. Plus I got a write-up in The New York Times and now every snot-nosed journalist wants a piece of me. *(I'm being very coy and telling them I'm 'unavailable for interview'.)*

Also, the advertising house where I used to have my Reception Gallery contacted me a few days ago to tell me they have companies interested in 'alternative' advertising that would like to work in conjunction with a performance artist. They're paying me just for a phone consultation, so if all goes well this could be a nice little cushion.

It's so exciting to feel busy and stretched again, like waking up after a long sleep. If we were together, we could have shrieked and giggled and danced in celebration of our new freedoms. Perhaps this is our year, Al.

Am xx

I pedalled furiously up Heslington Road, cursing the cars that crawled up my back wheel to overtake then slammed on their brakes right in my face when they reached a speed bump. I was thinking of my nine o'clock seminar and that we needed to send in the meter readings this week and that we were running low on Calpol and if I was going to the chemist there were probably other things we needed so I should make a list and – and my legs slowed their pumping as something occurred to me and I tried to remember the date and count backwards and think when was the last time.

'Watch out!' shouted a pedestrian I'd just cut off on the zebra crossing, pulling my focus back to the road. I checked behind me, lifted my right arm, and pulled across the traffic towards campus. I locked my bike in the usual place and hurried to my class.

It was almost three by the time I managed to extricate myself from students and departmental meetings, and then only for half an hour. I hurried through the colleges to the tiny campus supermarket, praying they'd have what I needed. Having to ask the pimply student to retrieve the test from behind the counter was mortifying and I wondered why nobody had thought to put dispensers next to the tampons and pheromones and condoms in all university loos. I was tight on time, but keen for as much privacy as possible, so I took the lift up to the fifth floor of the library and headed for the toilet behind the stacks.

I peed and waited, gingerly holding the plastic stick in a wad of toilet roll. I counted backwards again, trying – and praying – to remember if I'd bled over freshers' week and just somehow forgotten. I thought about the strip of pills hidden in the bottom of my make-up bag and wondered if I could possibly have forgotten, if there was a day I might have taken one late. How could I have been so careless? Marc had been going on about Lizzie needing a playmate for months. I'd argued it was too soon, there was too much going on, we needed to focus on work and ourselves for a bit, but Marc had made those puppy dog eyes and somehow we'd agreed to 'wait and see' and 'let nature take its course'. I hadn't told him I'd been renewing my contraceptive prescription and thinking we should leave it at least another year, maybe more. Marc and I were both only children, I argued to myself – was it really so bad? I loved Lizzie to pieces, but I'd just got my life back. Things were starting to happen. These past few weeks I'd remembered I was more than just a pair of tits and a soothing voice, more than just a mother.

I stopped waving the stick and looked down at the two blue lines.

June
Fourteen Weeks Gone

Marc read Amelia's letters before he went to sleep each evening. She wrote frequently, often repetitively, meditating on the same themes and projects, moaning again and again about our distance and divergent lives. Marc remembered my excitement upon receiving the letters. Now and again I'd told him fragments of their contents and he'd tried to understand my enthusiasm for my friend's weird-sounding creations, but he was never curious before. Now, like my essay, they offered a window to a lost world. They were something tangible he could clutch in his hands. Proof that I existed.

Sometimes Marc grew bored, other times Amelia's words kept him awake. He was devastated to discover how reluctant I'd been to have a second child. We'd talked about it, of course, but I hadn't raised my objections enough. I wonder if he lay in our bed trying to remember the times we fucked that autumn, him thinking we might be creating something, me knowing I'd made it an impossibility. Only I hadn't. I'd missed a day and that was all it took. Marc remembered the evening I came home with the wiped down stick in my handbag and told him our three would become four. He remembered popping champagne and making love to me that night, the happiest and most virile a man could be.

He thought about my tattoo as well, wondered why I'd never told him it was covering something, wondered what exactly was beneath. I'd talked about my mother's emotional and psychological abuse, about finding her in pools of her own vomit and being screamed at for hours through my bedroom door, but I'd never said she was violent. Clearly I'd told Amelia more than I'd told him. I'd shared my most painful secrets not with my husband, but with a woman across an ocean. It must have hurt him to realize this. Reading her letters chronologically, Amelia struck Marc as a tragic character. He doubted she'd let anyone say that without swearing at them, but as far as he could tell she was serially single and occupied only by her work and herself. She barely talked about family and never mentioned friends. Marc thought her crass and critical, a man-hating misanthrope. What had I written back? Words he'd never know. He hated the idea of Amelia knowing about our life, of me sharing my thoughts and feelings with this stranger.

Sometime at the beginning of June, he reached 2005, the year Charlotte was born. It wasn't a great year, he remembered. My mother had started to deteriorate rapidly and I had to keep travelling down to see her, leaving him and the girls with a fridge stocked with expressed milk. It was around then that I got pneumonia too. I returned from one of my trips to see my mum and just collapsed. Marc rushed me to hospital, panicked and terrified, but I got my strength back within a couple of weeks. Those memories seemed impossibly far away by the time he read about Amelia's strange ideas and installations.

A few days later he opened the paper to find James Gandolfini had died. He scanned the article, learning the actor was in Italy with his family. After a day of sightseeing in Rome, his son discovered him collapsed on the bathroom floor of his hotel room. He'd had a heart attack and died some time later in hospital. Despite the freshness of Amelia's sneers at celebrity culture and despite knowing nothing about James Gandolfini beyond the roles he played, Marc felt sad. More than that. Reading quotes from politicians and producers, directors and other actors, all paying tribute to the 'ferocious actor', 'gentle soul' and 'genuinely funny man', Marc's eyes began to fill with tears.

'You're ridiculous,' he told himself and wiped his nose on his sleeve. He *was* ridiculous. He could only have seen James Gandolfini in a handful of roles, most memorably of course as Tony Soprano, which yes, he'd enjoyed as much as I had, but that didn't mean he had any link to the man himself. The death of the real actor had nothing to do with the character he played, however good the series. Before reading it in the paper that day, he might even have struggled to name the man. Yet, the sadness he felt was real. It stayed with him as he read the rest of the paper, lingered throughout the day. In the shower and again while waiting for the kettle to boil, he was struck afresh by the horror of a child finding his father unconscious. He thought about Charlotte and Lizzie, about being their only parent, their sole guardian. He made himself a salad for lunch, wasted twenty minutes reading an old *Independent* article about the best exercise for a healthy heart, then consciously walked fast enough to work up a sweat and feel his heart rate rise on the way to pick them up.

Char met him at the gate first, a grin on her face but mud scuffed from ankle to knee of her trousers.

'What on earth happened?' Marc said in dismay. It was a Tuesday, he'd only just washed her uniform.

'She scored the winning goal,' Lizzie said as she walked up, a touch of pride in her voice.

'That's great, sweetie, but you'll have to wear your skirt tomorrow.'

'No way,' said Charlotte.

Thrown by her uncharacteristic stubbornness, Marc faltered, but eventually murmured less than authoritatively, 'I can try to wash your trousers tonight, but I don't know if they'll be dry by tomorrow.'

Char crossed her arms and stared at him.

They walked home in almost silence. When they got through the door, Char dumped her bag in the hallway and raced up the stairs to her room. A few minutes later she descended in a pair of tracksuit bottoms and handed Marc her folded school trousers, before silently returning to her room.

'Is there something wrong with Char?' Marc asked her sister.

Lizzie shrugged. 'She likes playing football with the boys, I guess she can't do that in a skirt. Did I tell you she got in trouble last week for kicking an older boy in the shin and making him cry?'

'No, you didn't,' Marc said.

Lizzie smiled, apparently rather pleased with her tough little sister.

Marc spent the evening scrutinizing Char. Was she becoming a tomboy? Did it matter if she was? He couldn't tell any more what normal parental concerns felt like. He found himself on hyper alert, looking out for the smallest changes in our children, wondering if they were natural or a result of my disappearance. Was Char attention seeking? With me gone and him her only parent, was she trying to emulate her dad, not her mum? Or was he reading too much into too little? It felt impossible to tell when to worry. They seemed to have accepted the situation. They talked about me and sometimes they grew sad, but Marc was careful not to let them give up hope. He'd started a book of things we could do once I got back. Lizzie had sat in silence as he explained the concept, but Char had dutifully filled a page with a list of games and holidays and outings.

Maybe they clung to him more than he saw their peers doing to their parents. Lizzie, usually so calm and collected, had refused to go on the Year 6 camping trip and when he'd coaxed the reason from her she'd said she didn't want to leave in case anything happened while she was away. He'd asked what could possibly happen and she'd looked at him like he was stupid and said, 'You might disappear.'

He tried to knock on her door when he thought she might be feeling down, but he was turned away as often as he was allowed in. When he did cross the threshold, he sat nervously beside her, holding our daughter as she sobbed and feeling that perhaps she wished he wouldn't. He was not enough; that was the simple fact of it. It was what Lizzie was thinking and what caused her to cry, but our little girl was far too sensitive to tell him, so she pretended he comforted her even as he contributed to her sadness. Such moments of helpless intimacy with Lizzie were perhaps the hardest of this time, trumping the leg-kicking tantrums of Charlotte when she refused to comprehend the situation and wiping the floor with any discomfort he felt before TV crews and inquisitive police officers. They were his lowest hours, hammered even lower by the mortification a man feels when failing his family.

After what had happened with Fran and the awkwardness of our interwoven friendships, the only person Marc spoke to about his fears was Paula. They'd grown close since his return to work. At first he thought she was knocking on his door just to check up on him, a strange sense of benevolent duty badgering her conscience. But over sandwiches and coffees he began to realize they had a rapport. He started to see what had made us friends. We weren't obvious companions: a frivolous, bicycling, Dada-loving lecturer and a stern, seriously academic, suit-wearing feminist. Paula smiled infrequently, more inclined to analyse the grammatical ambiguities of his rhetoric than to latch on to a punch line. But beneath the wrinkled frown and severely cut bob he discovered a kind, straight-talking and intimidatingly intelligent woman. While those he'd known for years tiptoed around his feelings and whispered behind his back, he found in her a frank and refreshingly unsympathetic new friend. 'You're doing fine,' she told him repeatedly. 'The girls are lucky to have you.'

Apart from the obvious comforts of support, Marc also enjoyed talking to someone again. With all the drama and heartache of missing me as a wife and mother, he'd forgotten the simpler fact of missing intelligent conversation, intellectual companionship. Paula's bangles clattered on her arm when she got excited about a PhD proposal for next year and she fingered the collar of her jacket as they grew heated on the topic of the impact of the Industrial Revolution on art and literature. I would yawn, he thought, if I could hear some of their conversations – proper stuffy academic geekiness, the kind I worked so hard to persuade my students wasn't the only option.

They talked about me too, about the stagnating search and the impossibility of accepting the blindingly obvious. Marc hadn't told DI Jones about finding my passport and the box of files, but he shared his progress with Amelia's letters with Paula. He phoned her one night after completing one. It was late and he thought he'd probably wake her, but he knew he'd get no sleep unless he could discuss Amelia's words.

'She *betrayed* her friend,' he said into the receiver.

'Marc? What time is it?'

'Sorry, I needed to talk to someone.'

Paula sighed. 'What's up?'

'Well, sorry, maybe it's not that big a deal. Go back to sleep, we can discuss it tomorrow.'

'No,' she replied. 'You've woken me up now, you'd better go on.'

'I just finished one of Amelia's letters and she describes this piece that won her some award,' he said. 'But I'm struggling to see how it's art or even ethical. I know it doesn't really matter if I understand it and Alex would probably laugh at me for not getting it, but something in my brain won't let it go.'

'What's the piece?' Paula said.

'She used a friend of hers – her agent, I think, but it sounds like they were close too. The woman had just broken up with her fiancé and was clearly in a bad place, but Amelia decided to use her as art. She paid a psychology student to befriend her friend and document their relationship as if they were therapy sessions. All without the agent knowing. She got talking to this woman in a coffee shop and poured her heart out to her because they were apparently going through similar things. She thought they'd become close, but all the while the therapist was writing Amelia nightly reports on her friend's "condition". And then Amelia set up all the documents and some photographs of the friend and the therapist in a gallery, all alongside photocopies of the cheques she wrote the therapist to prove it had been a monetary transaction rather than a human connection. And without telling the agent what she was seeing, she sent her tickets to the opening and had someone film her reactions to discovering the betrayal and then put *that* in the gallery the next day.'

'How did the agent react?' Paula said, displaying none of the outrage bubbling in him.

'Amelia says she flipped out. She seems kind of surprised, like she expected her to find it funny or something, but the woman burst into tears and is no longer returning her calls. Here, let me read it.' He scanned down the page on his lap and read Amelia's words into the receiver: '"Obviously a huge part of the piece was observing her response after everyone else in the gallery had read the therapy reports. She was mad. Which made the piece really successful, but sort of upset me. A lot. I'm a bad friend, Al. But a good artist, I think. I guess that's something."'

Paula laughed.

'She sounds sorry to some extent, doesn't she?' Marc said. 'But not enough to regret it. And later she admits that the filmed reaction is what made the piece so compelling and probably what won her the award.'

186

'It poses some interesting questions,' Paula said.

'But imagine seeing details of your broken relationship on a gallery wall – intimate things you told someone in confidence, someone you thought liked you but you then find out was being paid to be your friend. It's cruel.'

'Yes,' Paula said hesitantly. 'But no one said art has to be nice. Artists do cruel things to prove a point all the time.'

'But I don't see *any* point in this, it's just mean.'

'I don't know, I'd have to know more about the piece, but maybe it's a comment on capitalism, or therapy, or women's relationships, or trust. Or perhaps she's simply pushing the boundaries of art in general, proving the very point you've just picked up on: that art is cruel and artists can't be trusted not to use anything you offer them, even yourself, for their work.'

'But how could Alex be friends with someone like that?'

'Come on, Marc, you know Alex liked work that provoked a reaction. I don't know if she'd have approved of Amelia's methods, but I imagine she'd have been interested in the piece. You know about Guillermo Vargas starving a dog in an art gallery, right?'

'Wasn't that a hoax?'

'It didn't matter, the point was that people thought a dog was being starved to death for art and got so outraged that they started a petition to complain, but not a single person tried to free or feed the dog in the actual gallery.'

'So you're saying while they thought it terrible and cruel, they still accepted it as art?'

'Yes, it *was* art,' Paula replied. 'As, I suppose, was Amelia betraying her friend. A stray dog starving in the street in Nicaragua is just life, but Vargas's dog dying in a gallery was elevated to something more and thus thrust into the minds of people around the globe. I suppose, equally, friends fall out all the time over large and small things and it's nothing special, but Amelia

187

has elevated the destruction of one of her friendships into art, turning the simple point of whether the agent forgives her or not into a much more complex act of aesthetics. She's turned the people in her life into unwitting performers, objects to be scrutinized.'

'How is that okay, though?' Marc said.

'Maybe it's not,' Paula said, stifling a yawn. 'It's for the public and critics to decide. But that's an interesting thing too, because as far as I'm aware no artist to date has done anything quite despicable enough to provoke a unanimous outcry. I imagine at some point someone will push the boundaries that bit too far and someone will have to turn around and say: "Enough! This is no longer art." But as soon as they say that, I suppose it will go down in the history books as the *ultimate* piece of art.'

'So there are no limits?' Marc said, thinking about Pip's questions about morality and art. Had I told her about Amelia, described this piece? 'What about as a human being? Art can't just trump pain and feelings and empathy. Alex would never have accepted that. How could she be friends with this woman?'

Paula sighed. 'I don't know. Look, Marc, it's late and I'm conjecturing off the top of my head. Can we continue this tomorrow?'

'Of course,' he said, wincing at his insensitivity. 'Sorry, thank you, sorry!'

'Don't be sorry,' Paula said. She hesitated, then added, 'Marc, I'm worried about you. Maybe you should give the letters a rest for a bit.'

Marc hung up and sank back into his pillows, trying to make sense of Paula's justifications and wondering if he should take her advice. He tried to imagine what I would have contributed to the conversation. He pictured me laughing at his old-fashioned views of what constituted art, but he couldn't imagine me condoning Amelia's actions. He knew me as a friend. I was loyal and trustworthy. I bent over backwards not to renege on my word. He wanted to know how I replied to this letter, whether I felt reservations in congratulating my friend on her latest success, why I'd never mentioned this piece to him. He lay awake for a long time before reaching for his phone. 'Amelia Heldt friendship piece' brought up a dozen reviews of varying enthusiasm. One had a photograph of and a quote from the agent, naming her as Serena Graves, Gallerist. A few more clicks brought up a professional profile. Without thinking too much about his motives or the consequences, Marc sent a short email mentioning me and Amelia and asking her to get in touch. As dawn approached, he fell into a fitful sleep, his dreams tormented by yapping terriers and sobbing women.

'I have something for you.'

He looks different. Expectant.

'Aren't you curious?' he says.

I try to keep my face still. The backs of my eyes prickle. My tongue scrapes on the roof of my mouth.

He hands me a folded newspaper clipping.

I smooth out the crease and look at an inky picture of six schoolchildren holding certificates. Second to the left is my daughter. She's taller than the boy next to her. She's shot up. And her face is thinner, those chubby cheeks smoothing over the bones. Her smile is the same, though. My baby grinning out at me. I read the caption. She got a silver in the Junior Maths Challenge, placed in the national top fifty.

'Clever little Lizzie,' he says and I want to scrub the name from his lips.

I place my finger over her face, try to picture how I would have congratulated her. I can't hold back my tears.

'You can't keep it, I'm afraid,' he says.

I look up. 'Why not?'

He just stares at me, that patiently patronizing look, as if the rules of this place – his rules – are obvious.

2005

11/3/05
Al!

How are you? How are Marc and the girls? Is Charlotte letting you sleep yet? I'm sorry your mom's getting so much worse. I know your feelings about her are complex, but you really don't owe her anything, you know? You have every right to prioritize yourself, even now. Especially now.

Congratulations on Marc's promotion. I guess that's kind of a big deal for him. You're good to be such a supportive wife. Behind every great man and all that . . . Seriously, you are a supportive wife. I know you doubt yourself, I know you think Marc's some saintly being who's just the most brilliant dad while you're fumbling around getting everything wrong, but you're better than you think, Al. As a wife, as a mother, as a teacher, as a friend.

There's a class being taught about me, can you believe it? Not just me, of course, but my work in context with some other modern performance artists. Can you picture our old professors doling out handouts with my name at the top, analysing my performances from whatever perspective? It almost makes me feel like an adult, you know, a proper artist. Not really, though.

The piece I just set up is totally childish. A little gallery in Chelsea asked me to do something for them and I really had no ideas. I had, like, four days before I was flying out of New York and I had to come up with something. I was staying in a hotel uptown. I'd decided to explore the city from a tourist's perspective, you know? Stay in a hotel, strap my camera to my neck and get in line for the Empire State Building, hop the Staten Island Ferry, find inspiration somewhere along the way.

But I caught this terrible fever and woke up on that first morning feeling like death. I ordered room service and stayed in bed watching cable. So, I watched, like, three days of trash reality TV. On the fourth day I still felt hideous, but I had to summon the energy to talk to the gallery people. I had nothing, not a single idea in my cotton-candy head. So I pick up the phone and they're all like, 'Dahling this, Dahling that,' and I was like, Jeez, I'm dealing with this *type. But I opened my mouth and this bullshit idea came pouring out. I told them I wanted to put a rifle up in the roof (they've got this high ceiling in the gallery and this gorgeous balcony around the perimeter), like properly stealth and serious-looking. The gallery visitors would be privately invited by an attendant, one at a time, to climb up to the spot and choose their victim. They'd be encouraged to aim at anyone in the gallery and pull the trigger, with no idea what would happen if they did. If they had the balls to do it, then the gun would rain down paper confetti on their victim. The piece would be called* A Shot at Love *and documented by hidden cameras. I blathered about making a social comment on the commodification of love and combining America's gun worship with its embracement of the world of celebrity.*

I mean, shit, I was doped up on Tylenol, I could have been saying anything, but my head was pounding and I had the shivers and I just didn't care. Anyway, those dumbfuck dahling types ate it up. They loved it, so the piece is going ahead. I felt like a student again, pulling something out of my ass at the last minute.

I'm curious to see what it produces, though. One of the curators worried nobody would actually shoot the gun. I disagree. I think, deep down, we all have the ability to pull a trigger; we're just looking to be told it's okay.

Anyway, my DAHLING, I'll let you get back to your lovely life. Kiss the rugrats from Auntie Amelia, tell them how fabulous I am and that one day I'll come and steal them away so they can live like artists in the much more fun New York.

Love you!
Am x

Thursday, 22 September 2005

I stepped through the front door and paused. Charlotte was asleep. I shook my arms from my coat, toed off my shoes and snuggled my feet into slippers. I picked Marc's slippers from the floor, placed them on the radiator. I stroked Charlotte's soft hair and headed for the kitchen. I filled the kettle, checked the clock. I had forty-five minutes before I needed to pick up Lizzie from the childminder. Marc should be home in about an hour, two if he was going for a drink. If I turned on my phone, there'd probably be a message letting me know. I'd left my bag in the hall, though.

I poured myself tea, cupped my hands around the mug to warm my fingers. I could make a start on dinner, plan something nice, set the table and light candles. I could lie on the sofa and make use of Charlotte's nap to have one of my own. But time alone was rare. I lifted Char gently from her pram and carried her up to her cot. She stirred and gurgled but didn't wake. I left the door open and stepped into the office. I sat down and reached to the back of the middle drawer for Amelia's last letter. I placed it on the keyboard and took a blank sheet of paper from Marc's printer. I thought about New York and her latest gallery show, about the distance between being reviewed in *The New York Times* and wiping shit from the changing table. Amelia was filling in grant applications and being invited to parties. My life was listening to Lizzie's jealous screams as Charlotte sucked my nipples raw. I picked up a biro, rolled it between my fingers a couple of times.

I posted the letter on the way to the childminder's, stopped to buy a pizza from the supermarket on the way back. Lizzie had a tantrum in the dairy aisle because I wouldn't let her out of the pushchair. I reached down to soothe her and she bit my arm, leaving a neat circle of teeth marks on my skin.

'You fucking little –' I found myself shouting before I could stop myself, then hurried to the checkout, aware of strangers' stares. Marc was home by the time I wheeled the pushchair through the door, Lizzie still screaming and pulling at the straps holding her in. Charlotte had kicked off her socks.

'How was your day?' Marc said, kissing me on the lips before crouching down to release Lizzie. She calmed to a whimper in her daddy's arms, nuzzling into his neck.

I rolled my eyes. 'Fine,' I said. 'Char and I went to group, sang "Incy Wincy Spider" several hundred times, took a walk along the river, cried at a goose. Pretty standard.'

Marc laughed. 'And what's all this about?' he said into Lizzie's hair. She let out a little moan.

'I wouldn't let her run around the supermarket, so she bit me,' I said, showing him my arm. This was so often how our evenings started: me relaying all the ways our daughter had tormented me, while she nuzzled, sweet as an angel, into Marc's forgiving arms.

'How was your day?' I said, attempting to shake my mood.

'Well,' Marc said, lifting Lizzie to the ceiling and making her giggle through her tears. 'It was pretty good actually. Richard has finally decided to retire at the end of this year. I spoke to the dean and he said he wants me to apply for head of department.'

'Wow,' I said, stretching my cheeks into a smile. I dug inside for my 'proud wife' performance, the one I'd perfected at faculty dinners, family occasions and every time Marc published a paper. *Tonight, Matthew, I'm going to be a woman who's delighted her husband has a thriving career while she sits home with their children.*

I stepped over to kiss Marc. He shifted Lizzie to his hip and she leant away to watch as he reached his hand up to cup my cheek. I felt the slight roughness of the scar on his little finger, the jolt of a memory making me turn to our daughter. Her cheeks were still red from crying, but her mood had lifted and she looked sweet and adorable in Marc's arm. What was wrong with me? This was great news. I *was* delighted for Marc, for both of us. I smiled at Lizzie and she smiled back. 'That's amazing,' I said, wondering what I could concoct that would be more celebratory than oven pizza for dinner, how I might properly congratulate Marc once the girls were in bed.

'Samazing,' said Lizzie, making us both laugh.

July
Five Months Gone

On Friday, 26 July Marc received news. He'd wanted and feared news for almost five months, but when it arrived he didn't know how to categorize it. It fell into neither the good nor the bad pile, just the general heap of confusion that was his life.

Nicola and DI Jones said little as he let them in and refused cups of tea for the first time since their original interviews back in February. He wondered if their visit had anything to do with the email he'd woken up to that morning. More than a month after he'd contacted her, he'd finally received a reply from Serena Graves. He'd read it multiple times, but still couldn't make proper sense of it.

Dear Mr Southwood

I kindly ask you respect my privacy and make no further contact with me regarding Amelia Heldt. I have already made the same request to the British police and was, therefore, distressed to be contacted by you as well. I have suffered a great deal at the hands of Amelia and I advise you to stay away from her. If your wife is involved with Amelia, then I feel sorry for both her and you. The woman is not to be trusted. She's dangerous and I want nothing further to do with her or you.

On the advice of my legal representative, I need to inform you that should you harass me further I will be taking legal action.

Sincerely
Serena Graves

Marc perched on the sofa feeling foolish. Of course DI Jones would have got in touch with Serena Graves before him; it hadn't exactly been hard to find her details. What other avenues had they already explored? Who else had they talked to? How much did they know that he didn't?

But DI Jones and Nicola weren't there to talk about Serena. It took a while for what they were saying to make sense. Even once Marc had deciphered the meaning of each individual word, their sentences remained incomprehensible. But they showed him a copy of the death certificate, so it had to be true.

My mother had been dead since 2007. She died in hospital, after being brought from her home. She did have dementia, but she didn't live long enough for it to progress as far as I'd implied.

'We discovered through a cross-referencing coincidence,' Nicola told him. 'We made some enquiries at the beginning of the investigation, but had no reason to question the death that was reported this year.'

An unrelated inquiry by a different jurisdiction, however, had cause to examine records at Bridport hospital. 'By chance,' Nicola said, 'one of the officers assigned to that case has recently moved from the North Yorkshire force. He was speaking to a nurse at Bridport hospital who brought up your wife's case and asked if he'd worked on it. She said she was asking because she remembered meeting your wife when her mother was brought in. Our officer asked her if she was sure. She said she was certain and she remembered it because the name Carlisle stuck in her head because it was where she was from.'

Nicola paused and DI Jones cut in impatiently: 'The nurse dug out the records and they show Alexandra's mother had a stroke on the seventh of April, 2007.'

'I knew that already,' Marc said. He focused his attention on Nicola, but felt DI Jones's eyes on him.

'She died two days later,' Nicola said.

Marc stared at the certificate. Nicola and DI Jones were silent. Marc wondered if they could read his thoughts. His skin felt hot.

'What does this mean?' he said, eventually. He knew he should tell them about the letters, about the things he'd learnt about my mother, about my scar. But, he rationalized, what difference would it make now? The woman was dead.

DI Jones cleared his throat. 'Are you positive Alexandra said her mother was alive?'

'Of course,' Marc said, too fast, too defensive. 'She went to visit her.'

'How long ago was her last visit?' Nicola said.

Marc frowned as what they'd told him finally sank in. I'd lied to him. Not just about my mother's death – which frankly he didn't care too much about – but about where I'd been going for almost six years.

'It would really help if you could remember,' Nicola said gently.

'December,' he said, his brain in emergency shut-down. 'After term broke up but before Christmas. She spent five days with her.'

Nicola and DI Jones exchanged a look.

'It seems your wife wasn't entirely honest with you.'

Was Marc imagining it, or did DI Jones seem pleased? 'She wouldn't . . .' he began, but trailed off.

'We don't know what it means yet,' Nicola said. 'It could indicate a number of things.'

'We'll begin by investigating the area around Alexandra's mother's home. It seems she never sold the house, so perhaps she did visit at some point. It would be helpful if you could give us the exact dates of her trips. Ultimately, we'd like to determine what your wife's intentions were.' The word 'intentions' made

Marc look into DI Jones's face again. He imagined he could see another word – 'affair' – playing on his lips.

'What about the carer? She told me . . .' Marc couldn't finish. His thoughts felt like they had knots in them.

'We'll certainly be looking to speak to Miss Morse. If nothing else, she gave misleading information to an ongoing investigation, which could lead to charges for perverting the course of justice and wasting police time. We'll be looking to establish her motive for lying and what links her to your wife.'

Marc stared at him. He didn't want to talk about motives or ongoing investigations; he wanted to know right then what the fuck all of this meant. He wanted to shake DI Jones until the truth rattled out of him. He wanted to punch his patronizing, insinuating, perfectly calm face. He wanted to cry out and scream and smash something and ask me what on earth I was thinking keeping something like this from him.

He had a hard time sleeping that night. He'd scanned through all of the letters he'd read, looking for any and all mentions of my mum, relieved if nothing else that I didn't seem to have disclosed the truth to Amelia either. He wasn't sure if he felt upset or angry or what, but he lay awake, his eyes closed while his mind tried desperately to arrange the puzzle pieces of our marriage into something recognizable. Eventually he gave up and crept down to the office. He opened the archive box he'd heaved from the attic and shuffled through the files until he found my mother's. He stared at the photograph, studying the trees in the background for clues. When was it taken? 1975, he supposed. The baby must have been me, but it was so small, still in that alien, personless form. He concentrated instead on the woman. He searched for something to recognize. She looked a little like me, he thought, perhaps in the nose and mouth, but maybe he only wanted her to. She had thick, straight, dark hair, bobbed at her shoulders, a black turtleneck making her pale face float in a shadowy frame, only her pink cheeks fighting the monochrome as she smiled at the person behind the camera. My father? Marc wondered what he looked like back then. He knew him as an old man, wearing Argyle and corduroy, bespectacled and respectable. What was he like when I was young, when my parents shared a house, when my mother remembered me? What was my parents' life together before my mother started drinking? Were they happy? Did they take one another for granted? I'd told Marc one of the saddest things I felt after they split up was that all the good times, all my childhood memories, every moment of affection, had to be erased to make way for the present. Nothing could survive the nuclear holocaust that was their divorce. What would my father have done back then, though, if his wife had not come home one day?

With a warped sense of logic, Marc wondered, if he'd been beside me for this woman's death, whether I'd still be with him now. It's what we marry for, isn't it? Sickness and health, good and bad. Maybe he should have offered to go with me more, been more insistent. He had, of course, when she was first diagnosed, but I'd told him no, that one of us had to stay with the girls. He'd said we could take the girls with us, that he wanted to be there for me. I'd smiled and told him he was lovely, but creased my forehead and said it was my responsibility, I didn't want our daughters involved in my mum's mess. He'd swallowed my reasoning. He'd wanted to support me, but I'd said I didn't need him in this. Why hadn't he tried harder?

He slipped the photograph back into the file and pulled out the card. It was hand-painted. A simple flower on the front, the strokes delicate, the colours chosen to complement. The message inside was short: *Good luck at university, darling. Love always, Mama.* He wondered what I'd felt when it had arrived. She didn't write, I'd told him. She made no effort to contact me after packing her things and driving away. So this card must have arrived out of the blue and sunk its claws into me just as I was about to start a new life. Why had I kept it? My mother was not the woman in the photograph, the lady who had kissed me better when I grazed my knee and cooked me soup when I caught a cold. She wasn't the loving 'Mama' that wished her child well as she left home to study. My mother was a troubled woman at the other end of the country, struggling through illness and old age, who only sometimes remembered her daughter.

But even that wasn't true, was it? She had been, but not since 2007. She hadn't been anyone since then. And I hadn't even bothered to tell him. Where on earth had I been going for all those years? Why had I lied? What else had I been keeping from him?

Marc dropped the card and reached back into the box for the folder with his name on it. He climbed to his feet and carried it down the stairs and through the kitchen, stopping to take a box of matches from the drawer by the fridge. He let himself out of the back door and picked his way to the bottom of the garden. It took six matches to light the thick cardboard. He watched the flame flicker and lick, eating through the folder's flap before beginning on its contents. He should have been wondering about Caitlin, why some strange carer would go to the effort to lie. He should have been questioning so much more than he did. Instead, my husband stood in our garden, tears rolling down his cheeks as he watched his own words twist and distort. The dawn chorus struck up around him, but he stood until every note and Post-it, every scrap of paper and Christmas card, every word of love was gone.

I dreamt about him again. I've always wondered if other people have the same debauched imaginations. At school I thought I must be some kind of freak. Our gross, lecherous PE teacher would give assemblies wearing these tiny little shorts and scratching his arse and I wouldn't hear a word he said because I'd be trying to picture the thing beneath the fabric, the thick member that must be there, just like it must be in the trousers of all the boys sitting cross-legged around me, just like it must be between the legs of my tutor, my doctor, my piano teacher, my father even. And then I'd realize I was thinking about my own dad's dick and I'd feel so gross, so embarrassed. I'd look around, my cheeks burning, wondering if anyone could read my thoughts. Did the other girls in those assemblies have similar things going through their heads? I couldn't imagine they did. It was inconceivable. But did that make me a freak?

I wondered the same when Marc and I first moved in together. Our sex was great, don't get me wrong, but I would have wasted whole days, weeks even, in our sheets, while Marc insisted we had to get up, had to behave like adults. I began having dreams about our friends, my colleagues, anyone I'd met in the day and thought about pressing myself to. I felt so guilty waking up next to Marc with these thoughts. I knew I didn't want to do any of those things in real life, but I couldn't help my imagination. Giving up drinking helped a bit, but the urges were still there.

In my dream last night we were in the university library. Odd that's where my subconscious took us. I was naked, sat on a chair by one of the windows while he peered at me and asked what I was thinking. Then he came over to me and unzipped his fly, asked what I felt, what I thought I deserved.

I guess it's understandable. He's the only man in my life these days. But also there's this part of my brain I've never truly had control of, a part that's always popped up at the most inappropriate moments to shove an image of my boss's erect member or Lizzie's teacher's splayed thighs before my eyes. Are other people the same? Perhaps it's a British thing. We're so repressed about sex, so insistent that it must be kept separate from the rest of life, that it thrusts its way into all parts of it.

I never thought I'd get married. Or, if I did, I had an inkling I'd be the kind to cheat. I didn't want to; I'd seen what my mum's infidelity did to my dad, but I couldn't help feeling I had this instinct inside me. I had a friend at Cambridge who once told me that sex was all right, but she'd rather have a nice cup of tea. I thought her mad. Sex was everything to me then: it was woven into the literature I loved, present in every performance I saw, every work of art I admired. Sex wasn't a separate thing, but part of all elements of life. The ever-present Eros. I was watching a lot of Italian cinema, wandering my college pretending I was Monica Vitti. I devoured the Marquis de Sade.

Marc was so different. So pure. For him, everything was compartmentalized. He got uncomfortable if I tried to flirt in inappropriate places. He didn't enjoy being teased. If he was concentrating on work, then he was concentrating on work and there was no space for me, no room for my flesh. I suppose I just fell into line. I didn't notice at first because I was happy, and then of course having children becomes your world, but eventually I realized I was missing something. I'd forgotten what it was like to walk down the street and feel the chill of air tingle across my skin, to allow a melody to melt into me, to feel laughter and sadness, affection and annoyance all drain to my crotch. When I remembered these things, I felt gauche and embarrassed, but also angry. Marc seemed so sorted, so mature. In comparison, I was some sex-mad creature. It took me a long time to realize I liked being that creature.

I can't be the only one. What if we were all adults and admitted we had these thoughts? What if I told him I dreamt about him last night? What if he nodded and said, 'Yes, I think about sticking my thick dick in your mouth and holding your head until you gag too. I want you bent over and pushed up against bookshelves, crying out for me to punish you harder, to teach you the error of your ways'? Or would my honesty spoil the illusion? Would it shatter his fantasies to find I'm not just the cowering woman he keeps in captivity?

2007

4/22/07

Al,

I cannot work today. I have two stolen hours, yet I sit here with no thoughts. I feel chained to this desk, to this room. All my worries and paranoias scratch at the insides of my temples. I could be happy, I think. I have the capacity. Yet, I swear no one in this city is as miserable as me right now.

Someone stopped me in the street earlier to ask if I'd seen the light. She was some nutcase talking about God, obviously, but her words followed me home. Have I? Have you? What if the light is the truth? What if spirituality is just figuring it all out? My light and your light might be totally different, but does that mean we can't share it? I don't really know what I'm saying. When I got home, I dumped my groceries and sat on the floor and cried. I'm worried I have no light. I'm worried I've made all the wrong decisions, that one day I will regret everything. What if all my work, all the things I pretend give me purpose, are big felt-tip pens scribbling over the light? What if all artists are selfish? What if we create light only by stealing it from others? Sometimes I wonder, if I died, would anyone care but you?

I wish you'd come out and spend some time here. I could help, I know I could. We could process things together. There's no one in your life who understands as much as I do. We know each other, Al, we can tell each other everything.

Am x

A hand touched my shoulder. 'Al?'

'Huh?' I jumped and swivelled with an air of annoyance. Slowly, though, I registered Marc's features and my own softened. 'Sorry. Hi, darling.' I smiled weakly, shifted my bag so I could lean in for a kiss.

'You were miles away. I was practically shouting your name.'

I stared at him, registering that he was cross but unable to summon the necessary words to placate him. In fact, worse than that, I was cross too. Why was that? What had I been thinking before he interrupted? I raised my hand to rub my left eye, but my face stretched into a yawn and I diverted the hand to cover my mouth instead. What time was it? Christ, I was tired. If only I could curl up and deal with everything later. I might even remember what I'd been thinking. It had been important, maybe anyway. An idea, perhaps. Dammit, it was gone.

Marc watched as I stumbled through these thoughts, seeing only a series of unreadable emotions flickering behind my eyes. The platform emptied as the rest of the passengers from my train made their way towards the exits. Regretting his tone, he tried again. 'Sorry, hi, you must be tired.' He leant to kiss me and I resisted the urge to withdraw from his prickly stubble, his familiar scent. 'How was your trip? How's your mum?'

I blinked and opened my mouth, struggling to find my voice. 'I, uh, yeah, she's um, she's okay. She's home. Not great, but okay.'

'She's home?' he said. 'That's great, isn't it? Have they arranged someone to come in then?'

'Um, yeah,' I said, trying hard to maintain his eye contact. I wanted to shower and change and brush my teeth and drink a large mug of tea and lie down for a few hours. Then maybe I'd be ready for this. Marc was looking at me, though, waiting for me to elaborate. 'Yeah,' I said again. 'Someone's going by every day. She's being looked after.'

Marc reached to fold me into his arms. 'Oh Al, you poor thing. I wish you'd let me come with you.'

'It wouldn't help,' I murmured into his jumper, breathing deeply as if his scent might ground me back here, back to us. Another train pulled into the platform and I leant away from his body but reached for his hand. 'Come on, we're in everyone's way. Let's go home. I want to see the girls.' Holding his fingers in mine I felt a surge of energy and clarity. 'You can't imagine how much I've missed you all.'

August
Six Months Gone

The summer spun into a blur of children pacing through the house, rifling through the fridge and staring at dull television programmes. Marc knew he should have made more of an effort to enrol the girls in classes or trips or all those things I usually took care of, but when he asked Lizzie and Charlotte what they wanted to do, they said they'd rather stay home. And Marc, for his part, was relieved by their answer. They tried to keep occupied. He and Lizzie planted flowers in the pots in the garden, while Charlotte followed them around fanning a deck of cards, insisting they pick again and again so she could practise her magic tricks. They took a trip to Bridlington for fish and chips, and drove out to Brimham Rocks so Marc could have a heart attack as Lizzie waved from the top of a deathly-looking structure of stones.

For all their activities, though, Marc still felt the days melt into one another. He remembered the feeling from his own childhood. He didn't have computers and PlayStations back then, but despite the technology, Lizzie and Char still looked just as bored as he did kicking through his sleepy Welsh town all summer. And this year he joined them. They lounged around, waiting for me to come home and give them something to do, to tell them their purpose in life. Marc had some work to be getting on with and Nicola came around occasionally to ask the same questions and update him on the stagnating case, but generally he padded after the girls, trying to learn their complicated video games or insisting they return to the last century to play a round of Monopoly. Or they baked cakes and ate the whole batch sprawled in front of the television, channel-hopping blindly through cartoons and soaps, absorbed by nothing. When they retired to bed, Marc paced and lounged some more, zoned out in front of an uninteresting film, then crawled upstairs to escape to Amelia's letters. Time didn't feel like time. He didn't read a paper or speak to another adult except the checkout lady for a whole week. They lived in a bubble. And, in a way, my husband liked it.

When he finally emerged from his cocoon, drove across town to drop the girls off at friends' houses and sat sipping tea in Patrick and Susan's living room, he discovered a whole world had continued to spin while he lounged in stasis. As Susan tidied a pile of Pip's sketchbooks from the coffee table and Patrick peeled the film from a packet of Bourbons, he learnt how utterly self-absorbed he'd been.

'They didn't want to worry you,' Susan said. 'I think it's been on the cards for a while, but it's still not simple.'

'Why did no one tell me?'

'You've had so much to deal with,' Patrick said. 'And we were hoping they'd sort it out.'

'How long ago?' Marc said, thinking about Charlotte's birthday.

'Fran moved out a few weeks after we went to the Lakes,' Susan said. 'Maybe it always seems that way from the outside, but it felt pretty sudden.'

'How's Ollie doing?' Marc said, feeling rather sick.

'As expected, I suppose.' Patrick sat back on the couch. 'Emma's living with him and he and Fran are talking, but we've had a couple of beers and once he relaxes his guard he starts lamenting the loss of his soulmate. He's broken, really.'

Marc tried to arrange his thoughts as they drove back around the ring road. He understood he hadn't been the most

209

approachable chum lately, but it hurt that his friends had kept this from him. He wondered if it was more than just respect for his grief, if Fran had told anyone about the kiss. He shook the thought away. He'd done nothing wrong.

He welled with compassion for Ollie, suddenly facing life alone, but something else bubbled beneath his empathy. Rationally he could accept marriages broke down, couples grew apart, but for two of our friends to allow their union to crumble in the same year ours had been brutally ripped apart felt like a personal betrayal. *They should have tried harder*, he thought. *For Emma, for Alex, for me.* And now Ollie was sobbing into his pints about soulmates. What gave him the right to do that while he still had a chance to fix his relationship, while Fran resided only a ten-minute walk away and I was God knows where?

He visited Ollie later in the week, not to berate him with his selfish accusations or absolve his niggling guilt, but to be the friend he'd failed to be since February.

'How are you doing? Do you need to talk? Can I help?' These were the questions he asked, the same useless words people had directed at him for months. But what else was there? Ollie gave non-committal answers, then laughed self-consciously at himself and batted the questions back to Marc.

Finally, after a few beers, they spoke properly. Ollie rubbed between his eyes and yawned.

'I keep thinking this has to be temporary,' he said, gesturing around the room.

Marc nodded, realizing how helpless everyone must have felt talking to him over the past few months. 'Are you sure it's not? Can't you work it out?'

Ollie shook his head. 'I think it's pretty permanent.'

'What happened?'

'I don't know,' Ollie said. 'I thought we were fine, happy, you know, in our way. And then Fran just started griping, pointing things out, complaining that I didn't understand her.'

Marc sipped his beer. Should he have come to Ollie after the kiss, told him what Fran had said? Would it have helped?

'I told her I wanted to understand her, to give me a chance. But she just brushed me off, said it was a woman's dilemma, having to choose between family and career. I got angry then. I mean, I've sacrificed everything for her career. I'm the fucking embodiment of the feminist male and then she turns around and says I can't possibly know how she's feeling –' Ollie cut himself off, his anger giving way to sadness.

They sat in silence for a while, each lost in their own thoughts.

Marc spoke first. 'Did she mention anything about Alex?'

Ollie looked up at him. 'Why do you ask that?'

Something about his tone made Marc nervous. He almost shrugged and said never mind, it didn't matter. 'Just curious,' he said. 'Fran said some of those things to me a while ago too.'

'She did?' Ollie said, his voice laced with surprise or suspicion, Marc couldn't tell.

'Just in passing,' Marc said, his eyes falling to his drink.

'She said they'd talked about it,' Ollie said. 'About the guilt of wanting something more but also being happy with what they had. Fran had this theory.'

Marc looked up, but Ollie had stopped talking. 'What theory?'

'It's nothing, I shouldn't have said anything.' Ollie stood up. 'Do you want another beer? Anything to eat?'

Marc tried to catch his eye, but Ollie looked away. 'What theory?'

Ollie sat back down and buried his head in his hands. 'Jesus, it's not important now, is it?'

Marc exhaled. 'Tell me.'

'We argued about it. It wasn't the only thing, but it

contributed. It made me see a side of Fran I didn't like. And she was furious that I didn't believe her.'

'Didn't believe her about what?'

Ollie groaned. 'Trust me, you don't want to know.'

'Ollie, I do! If this is important, you *have* to tell me.'

Ollie finally made eye contact. 'Fran thinks Alex was going to leave you.'

The room swallowed the words and they sat quietly for a moment. There were questions Marc wanted to ask, but no words formed in his mind. Ollie heard them through the silence and carried on. 'She thinks she was going to do it soon. They'd been talking for a while, apparently. I didn't even know they were close, especially after that thing with Emma's ears –' Ollie hesitated.

Marc set his empty bottle on the coffee table, cleared his throat. 'What exactly did Fran say?'

'She said that behind her smiles and your brilliant parties, Alex was just as unhappy as her. That they both agreed they were stuck, trapped by an "inherently patriarchal system".'

Marc blinked at Ollie's gestured quotation marks. He almost laughed at the idea of me using that phrase. It would have had to be in jest, surely.

'I told Fran to buy a fucking magazine,' Ollie said, growing animated. 'You know, all the headlines are about "having it all" and "striking the balance". I couldn't believe we were having this conversation in the twenty-first century. I mean, Fran has her career, she had her family too, what more could she want? She said she was still made to feel guilty. That's why she understood Alex. She told me a woman could only feel truly understood by another woman. It sounded like the bloody seventies: "Feminism is the theory, lesbianism is the practice." Fran raised her eyebrows when I said that and I laughed. I thought she was telling me she'd met a woman. "Not me," she said and I asked if she meant Alex. She said she didn't know, but that she wouldn't be surprised. I thought she was mad, just being cruel because we were fighting. But she insisted that she thought Alex was planning to leave.'

Marc bowed his head and shielded his face with his hand. He searched for words to shout or tears to cry. Neither came.

'Fran wanted to tell the police,' Ollie said, more softly now. 'I didn't believe her, but I drove with her to the station. They took her statement. She came out furious.'

Beneath his fingers and his flopped-down hair, behind his limp tongue and dry eyes, a realization penetrated Marc's frozen thoughts. DI Jones and Nicola had heard all this, had told him nothing. 'It was her,' Marc said, looking up. 'She was the one who told them we were unhappy. I couldn't figure out who would have said it. DI Jones turned up treating me like a suspect. But Fran knew us. *You* knew us, Ollie. You were meant to be our friends.'

Ollie swallowed, looking everywhere except at Marc. 'For what it's worth, they didn't believe her. She said they grilled her, asked her to remember the exact words of their conversations, asked if she had any more evidence, any names or specifics. They told her they'd take it "under consideration", but she felt they'd been patronizing her. I could see why.'

He waited for Marc to say something. When he didn't, Ollie continued: 'I thought that was the end of it, but she wouldn't let it go. She wanted to tell you. I told her she couldn't put you through that, not without proof. I tried to reason with her, argue it from her perspective. I told her it wasn't important now, if someone –' Ollie hesitated. His cheek twitched. 'You know, whatever happened at the river, well, it didn't matter what she was thinking about doing before, did it? If I was in your position, the last thing I would want to hear was some crazy conspiracy about my wife not being happy.'

Marc looked up at his friend. Ollie had leant back in his chair and crossed his left ankle over his right knee. He looked almost relaxed. It must have been a relief to have this off his chest. When Marc spoke, it was slow and controlled: 'You can't possibly imagine what you'd want in my position.'

Ollie stiffened. 'I'm sorry,' he said, getting to his feet as Marc stood and reached for his coat. 'I was trying to protect you.'

Marc didn't respond. He walked into the hall and out of the house in silence. Thoughts wriggled around his brain as he started the car and pulled on to the road. He felt numb. Fran's version of me as unhappy didn't match his knowledge of the weeks and months before my disappearance. He knew me better than she did, better than anyone. We were best friends. Even if he belonged to the enemy sex. But doubt was creeping in.

I'm naked when he comes today.

'What are you doing?' he says, standing by the door. He actually looks uncomfortable. I've made him feel uncomfortable.

I look him in the eye. 'This is how you want me, isn't it? Baring all.'

'Put some clothes on,' he says, turning his head.

I don't move.

'I said put some clothes on.' His voice has an edge that makes the hairs on my arms stand on end.

'*Now* you're prudish?' I say with a smile. 'You want to know everything, don't you? Well, this is everything.'

'I'm going to count to ten,' he says. 'One –'

'Here,' I say, spreading my legs, thinking of Annie Sprinkle offering the audience a speculum and a flashlight to examine her cunt in her *Public Cervix Announcement* performance. 'Take a good look, get your magnifying glass out. You want to know my secrets? They're all in here.'

He's only at six, but he turns and unlocks the door. I listen to the key on the other side and his footsteps fading away. I close my legs. I'm shaking and my heart is thudding in my ears, but for the first time in forever I almost feel like laughing.

2009

4/8/09

Al,

I thought of you the other day. I wandered into Tiffany's just to play at feeling like the sort of woman who shops there. I was looking at all the shiny things and there in the center of one of the cases was this little silver pendant in the shape of a tiny paper plane. I thought how perfectly saccharine it would be if Marc had seen it rather than me and bought it to encase your throat in the iconography of your love.

I'm alone, Al. Is that funny? I always have been, but it's like it's just hit me. No one will ever walk into Tiffany's and see a pendant that represents the purity of what they feel for me. I don't know if I can stand it much longer. I walk down busy streets and I want to scream. Everyone is just out of reach. And I know I'll never be able to change that. I'll never be able to connect.

It's not about sex. I could have my petites morts if I wanted. It's about possibility. It's about the freedom to be who I want to be. About sharing that freedom with someone who understands. I'm making a silly amount of money now, getting more commissions than I can handle, but it feels pointless when I'm this isolated.

Every decision we make ties us in tighter and tighter knots. I live for praise and I bury myself beneath criticism. Yet the more successful my work is and the more important and real I become, the more confined I feel. Once upon a time I could have been anyone. Now I am Amelia Heldt. In the eyes of everyone I don't know, I am someone. Some One. Just one.

I have this idea for a piece about loneliness and identity. About the layers that we wrap around ourselves and secretly wish the person we love would peel away. Do you think all secrets hope eventually to be discovered? I think the loneliest thing in the world might be to never be known.

But I've made my choices, haven't I? I'm living this one life and there's no going back. For either of us. We must make do with what we have, find our joys where we can, count our blessings. But I can't help dreaming of another way. Imagine a world where our identities weren't so set.

I don't know if the piece will go anywhere. I guess I'm still working out whether I can go anywhere.

Am x

Monday, 19 January 2009

I don't suppose it's top of many people's wish lists for their thirty-third birthday to be sitting on a soggy bath mat bathing a poorly three-year-old, but in a weird way it wasn't so bad. Lizzie had caught the bug first, then on the very day she managed to keep down a bowl of plain pasta, Charlotte had spewed down both the front and back of Marc's shirt. We'd had more than a week of vomit and here I was waving goodbye to another year of my life propping Char up in the bath while I tried to get it out of her hair.

Charlotte looked at me. 'Mummy smile,' she said and I did.

'This is a pretty good birthday, isn't it?' I said, rinsing off the remaining suds.

Charlotte nodded. Then her little body shuddered in my hands and I knew what was coming, but still wasn't fast enough to prepare for the puke that shot over the side of the tub and on to my jeans and the liquid brown that emerged from her other end.

'Christ,' I shouted as Charlotte began to yell.

Marc hurried in, observed the two of us and began to laugh.

'It's not funny,' I said.

'I'm sorry, I know. It just –' He held his hand over his mouth to stop himself laughing more. 'Here,' he said, crouching down by the tub to take Char from me. 'I've got this. You get cleaned up and go see what Lizzie's up to.'

I relinquished the still screaming Charlotte to his control and climbed to my feet. 'Thanks,' I said.

'Happy birthday!' he said with a grin that I couldn't help but return.

I pulled my clothes off and left them in a pile, then climbed the stairs to our en suite. Washed and dressed for the second time that morning, I found Lizzie playing with her dolls in her room. 'Can I play too?'

She scooted her little bum over to make space for me.

'What's the story today?' I said.

'Barbie and Ken are getting married,' she said.

'Again? I thought they did that yesterday.'

Lizzie looked at me, her mouth a straight line. It had been more than a month now since Marc's cousin's wedding, but it was still all Lizzie could talk about.

'Sorry,' I said. Lizzie's behaviour had been improving and I had no intention of rocking the tantrum boat today. 'Okay. Where are they going on their honeymoon?'

'New York,' she said.

'Oh great, they're going to have so much fun.'

'And then they're going to have a baby and Ken's going to go to work and they're going to live happily ever after.'

'Is Barbie going to go to work too?' I said.

'Nope. She has to stay home so the baby doesn't get lonely.'

'Okay,' I said, feeling a stab of guilt. Marc would tell me to leave it. Even now she was at school most of the time, Lizzie hated that both Marc and I went to work. If I had to mark essays in the evenings or at the weekends, she'd bang on the office door until I thought my brain might explode. When I came out to go to the bathroom, she'd wrap her arms around my ankle and force me to drag her along the carpet.

I took a breath and picked up two dolls with straight blonde hair. 'Are these the wedding guests?'

'Yes,' Lizzie said.

I rummaged in her Tupperware of clothes and stretched dresses on their pointy limbs. I stood them on their tiny toes, bending their arms around each other's waists. 'Okay,' I said. 'They're ready to go to the wedding.'

'They need dates,' Lizzie said.

'Can't they be each other's dates?'

Lizzie gave me that look again, like I was the stupidest person she'd met. She twisted her torso and reached for two bears from her bed. 'Here, they can go with Podge and Ted.'

I looked at my dressed up dolls and the fat, naked bears. I held one of the dolls up to my ear and nodded while Lizzie watched me. 'Savannah says she wants to go with Michelle,' I said. 'She says Podge and Ted would rather go together as well. They say love is love and shouldn't be dictated by convention or prejudice.'

I watched my daughter as she tried to make sense of this. Her mouth was set in that frighteningly straight line and now her eyebrows creased together. Her nostrils flared and then she opened her lips and screamed, 'Noooooooooooooooooooooo ooooooo!'

'Elizabeth,' I said in my first warning voice.

'No, no, no, no, no! Why do you have to ruin everything?' She swept her arms over the carpet, knocking all of the dolls and bears over, destroying her scene. 'I never want to play with you again!'

'Right,' I said, dropping Savannah and getting to my feet. 'You need a time out.'

'I don't care,' Lizzie said, her face red. 'I hate you!'

'I'm going to shut this door and leave you to think about

what you just said. You've got ten minutes and when I come back I want an apology.'

I made it out of the door before my first tears fell. Marc was on the landing. Charlotte, clean and snuggled in new pyjamas, sat on his hip sucking her thumb. 'What happened?' he said.

I shook my head, unable to speak, too mortified to admit I'd fucked it up again.

September
Seven Months Gone

It will come as no surprise to some that Lizzie fell in with a difficult crowd at the beginning of her first term at secondary school. It did, however, come as a surprise to my husband, and it was weeks before he noticed. If it wasn't for Paula, he might not have. She caught up with him in Langwith one afternoon and asked if he still had her Marina Abramović book.

'Shit,' he said, embarrassed to have hung on to it for so long. 'I'll get it back to you tomorrow.'

But that night he couldn't find it. He turned the office upside down and wracked his brain to remember where he'd left it. It was nowhere. The next day he sheepishly apologized to Paula and ordered her a new copy. A week later, though, he took a hot chocolate up to Lizzie and there it was, on the floor by her bed, tossed beside magazines and nail polish.

'I just borrowed it!' she said as he picked it up. 'Hannah wanted me to show it to her.'

Confused by her defensiveness and worried some of the content might not be entirely appropriate for Year 7 lunch breaks, Marc lowered himself on to the edge of her bed and asked why Hannah had wanted to see it.

'I told her about the star and she said it was cool.' Lizzie looked away from him.

'What star?' he said.

Reluctantly, she took the book and turned to a still from the performance *The Lips of Thomas*. My husband digested the image of Abramović's bloodied belly.

'Do you understand the context of this, sweetie?' he said.

'Pain makes her feel better?'

'I think it's a bit more complicated than that,' he said, terrified of pushing our daughter out of reach. 'There's a lot of symbolism and texture to this performance; it's about much more than whipping and cutting herself. I can understand that you might want to read this book because Mummy likes performance art, but I'm confused why Hannah was interested in this.'

'It's nothing to do with Mum,' she said.

He took a breath. 'Can you tell me what it is to do with?'

Our daughter spoke into her lap. 'If you really must know, Hannah wanted to do one herself. There you go, are you happy? Now she's never going to want to be my friend.'

'Do what herself?'

Lizzie shrugged.

Working on instinct now, Marc took her shoulders and made her face him. 'This is serious, darling. You need to tell me what's going on.'

She blinked at him, trying to maintain an attitude of defiance but struggling with her natural instinct. Thank God for that instinct. In those seconds he imagined the next decade spent impotently on the other side of a slammed door, frantic for an insolent, monosyllabic, drug-taking, nose-piercing, tattooed teenager. But finally she melted and he had our beautiful, wonderful, kind and sensible daughter before him once more. She told him Hannah and Katy tried cutting their upper arms over the summer. They'd shown her in the girls' toilets, smug at the secret they'd kept from parents and teachers. They'd told Lizzie the scars meant they were true friends forever, never to be separated. Trying to impress them, Lizzie had described the book she'd found in our living room, told them her mum had been 'into' that kind of thing. 'So cool,' Marc could almost hear them uttering in the empty bathroom. Lizzie had taken the book to school the next day and immediately been afforded guest privileges in their little gang.

'I need to ring Hannah's mum, you know that, don't you?'

Lizzie nodded.

'And I have to ask,' he said, willing his voice not to crack. 'You're not – I mean, you haven't hurt yourself, have you?'

Lizzie shook her head silently and folded into his arms.

'Thank God. Promise me, baby, promise me you'll come to me. Promise you won't ever do anything like that.'

'I promise,' she said into his jumper. Marc clutched the flesh we'd made, his lungs ready to burst.

A few days later he made his final trip to the police station. Nicola met him in the gloomy linoleum reception and led him to one of the sparse meeting rooms. DI Jones was already waiting. Marc spied a stack of formal-looking letters on the table. He'd given little thought to the dotted lines Nicola had directed him to in the past, but as he stepped into the solemn, cell-like conference room he realized they must be to do with malpractice suits. Whatever Nicola and DI Jones were about to tell him, they needed to cover their backs and make sure he didn't sue them in the future for overlooking something.

'Dr Southwood.' DI Jones stood up to shake his hand across the table. 'Take a seat.' He motioned towards the chair opposite and Nicola stepped around the room to sit beside him.

DI Jones cleared his throat and began to talk about the case. He tiptoed around the subject of my mother, saying they'd made 'enquiries', but found little 'conclusive evidence'.

'What does that mean?' Marc asked.

'Well,' Nicola said, crossing her legs beneath the table. 'We've searched Alexandra's mother's house and examined the phone and electricity records –'

'But . . .' Marc prompted, his patience thin.

'*But,*' she said, nodding, 'there's nothing definite. The house is full of her mother's things. She was an artist, wasn't she? There are canvases and bits of junk. We think that, by the state of the dust on them and a few items of clothing found in the house, that Alexandra must have stayed there at certain points since 2007, but the electricity meter over the past few years shows minimal usage, not even enough to suggest a kettle was boiled. There's a smashed window at the back of the property, but no other signs of vandalism or theft. None of the neighbours have noticed anything, but they also couldn't say for certain that the property was empty for the whole period. A lot of the houses around there are holiday rentals and apparently Mrs Carlisle wasn't the most sociable of people whilst alive.'

'What about the carer?' Marc said. 'Who the hell is she?'

DI Jones cleared his throat once more. Marc clenched his fist beneath the table. 'Just be straight with me, will you?' he said.

'Look, Dr Southwood, I'm not going to lie. Things look increasingly circumspect. We haven't been able to locate the carer. In fact, we can find no record of a Caitlin Morse in the area at all. We examined the phone line and it's still connected, so we contacted the telephone company and their records show not only that there have been no incoming or outgoing calls except from you and our precinct in the past twelve months, but also that a call forward has been set up.'

'A what?'

'An instruction for all calls to be forwarded to a Skype account. It means the woman who picked up the phone and claimed to be Miss Morse could have been answering from any-where in the country, anywhere in the world even.'

'So you think –'

'We have a lot of questions right now,' DI Jones said, cutting him off. 'And it seems someone has gone to a lot of effort to keep them unanswered. As a precaution, we've run another exit check. Alexandra's passport has still not been used.'

Marc tried to match DI Jones's gaze, but glanced away, his

eyes landing on the camera in the corner of the room. He swallowed, wondering if DI Jones could tell he already knew my passport hadn't been used, because it was sitting in our office.

DI Jones coughed. 'I need to make clear nothing has changed the evidence found at the river. We're investigating a suspected murder, Dr Southwood.'

Marc shook his head slightly, as if he could shrug off DI Jones's words. 'What about before she disappeared?' he said, trying to keep the desperation from his voice. 'You must be able to find out whether she went to Dorset when she said she did?'

DI Jones and Nicola exchanged a look. 'We're working on a couple of theories about where she might have gone in those periods, but what we're struggling to put together is *how*.'

'What theories?' Marc said, panic rising in his throat.

'We've checked the records of Alexandra's personal account,' DI Jones continued, ignoring Marc's question, 'as well as your joint account and credit cards, but there's no trace of Alexandra travelling or staying anywhere during those time periods. Not even any moderately large withdrawals that would be consistent with her paying cash.'

'Meaning?'

'Meaning it may not have been her who paid for it.'

'But –'

'We're working on the assumption,' DI Jones said, 'that wherever Alexandra went, somebody else must have been funding her.'

'Who else could have?' Marc said, his voice rising. 'What are these theories? What aren't you telling me?'

DI Jones cleared his throat. Nicola avoided Marc's eye.

'We're looking into links with the PayPal donation we received for the appeal. Whoever's involved clearly has both funds available and an interest in keeping an eye on our case.'

'You think she was having an affair, don't you?' Marc said, less incredulously than he'd have liked.

Neither Nicola nor DI Jones spoke. Marc felt the silence wrap around his throat and chest. He believed in me, he truly did. He loved me. He trusted me. But like a mantra uttered until the sounds run into one, these phrases were beginning to lose their sense. As much as he willed his faith in me to remain unshakable, he couldn't help but feel the panic of our world unravelling. Though I'd been gone for months, until they found out about my mother, he'd still felt me close by, in his heart and imagination if not in body. But now he saw only blurred reflections rippled by raindrops in a once still pond. He'd stopped sleeping.

'Look, Dr Southwood,' said DI Jones, 'we're not trying to make this more difficult for you. We know these things are hard to hear. But we have to look at the evidence. Your wife lied to you about her mother, told you repeatedly that she was staying with her. Then on top of that someone posed as her mother's carer to continue the lie after Alexandra's disappearance. The theory we've been examining is that Alexandra may have had plans for another short break but something went wrong. Maybe her accomplice changed his or her mind and something went sour. We don't know.'

Marc looked at him. Why did he say 'her'? Marc wanted to ask, but couldn't without admitting his own suspicions, without examining Fran's accusations. He quashed the thought. 'The other times,' he said, following another thread, 'she told me where she was going and how long she'd be. She didn't want us to worry. Whatever she was doing, she still cared enough to protect me and the girls. But that night we were expecting her home, we –'

'Which is why we think something went wrong,' Nicola said. 'Perhaps the other person surprised Alexandra, perhaps there was a confrontation. Marc, none of this changes the fact that it's incredibly unlikely Alexandra is still alive.'

'What's the next step?' he asked, ignoring her tone.

Nicola's eyes flitted away from him.

'We've already explored a couple more avenues,' DI Jones said, pushing a printed report across the table. 'But we've tied up a lot of our resources in searching for Alexandra over the past few months.'

Marc looked up from the papers. 'What does that mean? You're giving up?'

'No,' DI Jones said, looking Marc in the eye. 'We will continue to review the case and as and when anything further develops we will reassess the need for resources, but right now we're going to reassign it to our non-immediate cases. It will be headed by a centralized missing persons officer for the North.'

Marc stared back at him dumbly. Nicola's head was lowered.

'We need you to sign a couple of forms to state you understand the procedure.' DI Jones pushed more papers and a biro towards him.

As he was leaving, Nicola handed him the card for the centralized office and suggested he get back in touch with the Missing People charity.

'I'm sorry, Marc. I only found out yesterday.'

He sat in his car for a long time, unable to turn the ignition. Back at home, he mulled Nicola's advice and clicked through to the Missing People website. He read about a now twenty-four-year-old, missing from Peckham since 22 December 2006: five foot three inches tall, of medium build with brown eyes and black hair in a ponytail. Marc stared at the sad eyes and glossed lips of the photo and imagined a family still desperate to find her. Next to hers was a photo of a smiling seventy-six-year-old woman, a garden visible in the background. Case reference number 13-000981: missing from Boston, Lincolnshire, since 12 April 2003. Next, a twenty-five-year-old with long dark hair, posed without a smile on an overcast cliff-top somewhere: missing from Southampton since 19 May 2013.

Marc kept clicking, the page loading six articles at a time. He glanced over the mostly male faces looking out at him, homing in on the women, wondering what their stories entailed, what their husbands and children and parents were feeling. A sixteen-year-old from Coventry, gazing quizzically at him from a photo booth, missing since 28 May. A thirty-nine-year-old grinning in a bathing suit, on holiday with someone she loved, Marc thought, missing from Wrexham since 19 August. A fifty-eight-year-old with a piercing stare and a lipstick frown, missing from Enfield since 22 July, a single line beneath her description: 'Lorraine, we would love to hear from you.' A twenty-two-year-old who could be one of his students, elegantly dressed, sunglasses propped atop her head, expression curious, missing from Edinburgh since 7 June.

They continued. He was surprised to see so many reported missing during 2013. All of these women had disappeared this year. In the months he'd lost to missing me, others had misplaced those they loved too. *Yet I feel so alone,* he thought.

From a column on the left of the screen he selected 'Join the Search'. An image of the British Isles appeared. Scrolling over it with the mouse, he could see who was being searched for in any area. 'We are currently publicizing thirty-two missing from Yorkshire and seven thought to be in the area.' He clicked the link and there on the first page of six photos he saw me. That over-published image they took from his laptop on the first visit to the house. 'Age at disappearance: thirty-seven. Alexandra Southwood has been missing from York since 21 February 2013. There is great concern for Alexandra as her disappearance is out of character. Alexandra is urged to call our confidential service Message Home for advice and support. Alexandra is five foot, four inches, of slim build with short, dark brown curly hair and blue eyes. She wears a wedding ring.'

He leant back in his chair and returned my gaze. The more he looked, the more I resembled those other unfamiliar faces, the more I seemed to belong to their world rather than his.

'Are you out there, Al?' he asked aloud. 'What don't I know? What don't I understand?'

Locking me up in my sixty-five-word profile, he left the office and descended the stairs to tie his shoes. He shrugged on his jacket and locked the door behind him. The grey sky danced behind the oranges and reds left on the branches. He breathed in the wet air and flexed his fingers in the cold. He'd never admit it to Nicola or DI Jones, but a tiny part of him was beginning to believe in their version of me.

That's it then. He's had enough of me trying to raise a reaction. He reminded me that everything he's done and everything he's doing is to try to help. To 'straighten me out'. We only have a couple of weeks, he reminds me. A couple of weeks until he makes a decision about my future.

'I don't care if I live or die!' I shout. It's true, I realize. All I care about now are my children. He chuckles and tells me I have a strange way of showing it.

So no more. He says he won't come every day, that I don't deserve his sympathy or care. He says he'll treat me as I'm asking to be treated.

'You think I'm your enemy,' he says. 'But I'm all you have left.'

He leaves and I lie on the bed and close my eyes. I wish I could slide myself into Marc's world, slip on to his tongue and fizzle his pain away like a living Alka-Seltzer. This might have ended so differently if I could have maintained his faith in me. If I could have sat beside him through those miserable weeks and months as he flicked through every channel, scanned the papers and read every quote from students, waiters and paperboys. He was desperate to know what they knew, convinced there was one person out there with the information he needed. His mind wandered from one second to the next. At times, he started to believe the evidence. It felt like a betrayal to contemplate it, but what if I *was* dead? Should he try to accept it?

I imagine Marc closed his eyes when he saw himself on screen. Unshaven and pathetic-looking, pleading for the one person who knew what had happened to come forward. How far were my husband's imaginings from my truth now? Did his imagination stretch to see me banging against these walls, unheard in this reinforced room? Did he see my matted hair and chapped lips?

I lie here wondering what the Marc I remember would do if he got hold of my captor. I dream about my husband plucking out his eyes. I ache to be rescued.

2010

4/19/10

Al,

How's it going? Did you guys finish the kitchen extension yet? Is it everything you dreamed of?

I'm still living in my crappy flat, of course. Nothing quite as exciting as designing my own space. Some fun things still happen to your old friend, though. I was asked to give a lecture at NYU this month. I had to turn it down, of course — it'd be pretty difficult to give a lecture without revealing your face — but it was nice to be asked.

Actually, scratch that, it made me really sad to turn it down. Imagine standing before those students and being able to tell them something real. Imagine if just one of them heard what I was saying and took it away with them. Obviously I can't regret anything I've done. My name is out there, it means something. I've got more money in the bank than I ever imagined. And mostly I still like keeping my face hidden, I really do. But every now and again I sort of wonder what I could achieve if I stepped out from my own shadow. What sort of platform I could have.

I miss you, Al. I want to spend the day walking the city with you. I want to go to museums and performances, plays and films. I want to feed our brains and then gorge ourselves on junk food, spin on the rides on Coney Island and stand in the middle of the Brooklyn Bridge like the giddiest of tourists. I miss being able to talk with you, laugh with you, rage with you. Abandon myself fully in your presence. It's not the same with anyone else.

Am x

'We have to see this,' I said, still devouring the article before me. 'At the Whitechapel next month.' I looked up from the paper in excitement, willing my husband to meet my gaze, match my enthusiasm.

'Hmm?' he said, spooning coffee into the cafetière.

'Sophie Calle's new piece,' I said. 'It's called *Take Care of Yourself*. The title's from a break-up email someone sent her. She's got a load of women to reperform her own rejection. How brilliant is that? The private made public, the personal universal — it's so rich.'

Despite everything the past decade of knowing this man should have taught me, my own excitement had temporarily blinded me such that sitting two feet from my husband, the *Guardian* spread over our John Lewis countertops, and M&S bagels toasting in our Kenwood four-slice toaster, I found myself truly expecting Marc to be affected by this news. I wasn't asking him to drop the coffee pot, shatter the glass over the Italian slate we'd just had fitted and cause a minor catastrophe in our otherwise perfect morning. But I did need him to climb at least a few rungs on my ladder of excitement, to hesitate and ask the dates, wonder about the ethics, show some — *any* — kind of interest.

Marc smiled and reached for the kettle. He poured the boiled-not-boiling water over the coffee grinds in a circular motion, taking care to cover each granule. He continued pouring until the water reached the lower lip of the outer metal casing, then delicately balanced the plunger on top of the concoction and glanced at the Jones & Co clock above the cooker, noting, I knew, to plunge the filter in exactly four minutes.

Finally he turned to me and spoke. 'Is she the creepy stalker?'

My lips pursed. He was teasing me, just as we both might

tease our daughters if they bounced into the room squealing over their magazines, thrilled by the latest bit of Justin Bieber gossip. 'You're a shit, you know that?' I said, trying but failing to match his light tone. My disappointment was not feigned. 'She's not a bloody stalker. She's totally seminal. She's the *queen* of the unexpected.'

Marc folded his arms. 'But she stalked someone, right?'

I exhaled through my teeth. 'She examines identity by pushing the boundaries of privacy. She used a lost address book to create a picture of a person from those who knew him. It was an *aesthetic* act —'

'Didn't he sue her?' Marc interrupted.

'That's *so* not the point,' I said. 'Or if it is, then it's exactly the point. Her performances are about crossing that line, about invading privacy and working within the space that makes us strangers. We all think we're walking around in these bubbles; we forget someone might be watching us.'

'I don't see how that's not creepy.'

'Just because you can only get excited by dead poets rotting in their graves. Christ, this is like you reading that Byron just woke up as a vampire and invited you to a laudanum party.'

Marc's shoulders shook with laughter. 'I was joking, darling. It sounds exciting — as does the laudanum party. Shall we go to both?'

I glared at him. I actually hated him right then.

Marc began apologizing, asking when the exhibition opened, making reference to the Paul Auster novel I'd given him one Christmas — offering something, I supposed, to prove he took me seriously. I was barely listening. None of this mattered, I reminded myself. What mattered was that today was Sunday, that I needed to get the girls' uniforms in the machine so they'd have time to dry on the line, that we had to nip out to get wrapping paper for Emma's present before the party at three, that if there was time this evening we should look at booking a hotel for Ruth's sixtieth. That I loved my husband and my family and my life.

Marc turned to plunge the cafetière. I let him pour me a mug and took it upstairs. Charlotte was in her room, crayons and paper spread over the carpet. 'What are you drawing, sweetie?' I said, sitting on the edge of her bed.

'A princess,' she said, spreading her pages out to show me. 'This is her horse and that's going to be the castle where the prince lives.'

'Great work,' I said.

'Mummy, do you know any princesses?'

'Sure,' I said. 'Loads.'

'Who?'

I scratched my head. 'Oh, well, let me think. There's Princess Pip and Princess Fran and Princess Lizzie and Princess Charlotte.'

'No, I mean *real* princesses,' Charlotte said, picking up a blue crayon. 'Not just people we know.'

'Okay, sorry,' I said. I looked at my daughter colouring a cloud-dotted sky for a moment. 'There is this one princess, Princess Amelia, who's not like any of the princesses you've seen in your storybooks.'

Charlotte looked up from her pictures. 'Why not?'

'Well, she used to be like them, like your princess here. She was looking for her prince and dreaming of a castle. But then one day she realized she didn't need a prince or a castle to make her happy, because she had everything she needed already within her.'

'What did she do?'

'She lived happily ever after, of course.'

I sipped my coffee and watched Char scratch her knee before returning to her drawing.

October
Eight Months Gone

'Tell me what you told the police,' Marc said.

Fran folded her arms and glared at him on her doorstep. 'Hello to you too,' she said.

Marc wanted to shake her. 'Alex phoned you,' he said. 'Just before –'

'I missed the call,' Fran said softly. 'She didn't leave a message.'

Marc searched her face, but Fran looked genuinely sad.

'You'd better come in,' she said and Marc followed her into the immaculate flat. 'It wasn't weird, her calling me,' she said, putting the kettle on. 'We shared a lot of things, Alex and I.'

'So I hear,' Marc said. He sat on a hard dining chair.

'I take it you've spoken to Ollie,' Fran said, turning to face him. 'I'd told Alex I wanted to leave him. She was probably phoning to see how I was. It was just a coincidence.'

'When did you get so close?'

'Why does it matter?' she said.

'*Why does it matter?* Because you told the police –' Marc took a breath, tried to calm himself. 'I want to know what Al said.'

Fran carried two cups of tea over to the table and sat opposite him. 'Marc, about Charlotte's birthday –'

Marc shook his head. 'I don't care about that. I just want to hear what you told the police.'

'The police are pricks,' Fran said.

'So why didn't you come to me?'

Fran looked at him like he was a child asking her to simplify the mysteries of the world. 'Would you have listened? Last time I saw you, you threw me out of your house.'

The muscles in Marc's neck tensed. 'I'm sorry,' he said with some effort. 'I shouldn't have said . . . I'm listening now.'

Fran stared at him for a moment, her hands cupped around her tea. 'I still don't know if it's anything,' she said. 'Ages ago, we were having drinks in town. It must have been before Christmas because I remember the lights had just gone up. Alex asked me if I'd look out for the girls if she wasn't around, if anything happened to her. I said sure, if she'd do the same for me.'

'Is that it?' Marc said.

'I know it doesn't sound like much, but it's what I remembered when she disappeared. She was so serious when she said it, like it had been playing on her mind.'

'So why didn't you tell me?'

Fran sighed. 'The police didn't seem to care and then they found Alex's blood by the river. Ollie told me to think about what it would do to you if I pushed it. He was right. Obviously something awful happened to her, so I put it out of my mind. I couldn't see the point of dragging all this up if it wasn't relevant. I decided, even if it was significant, if somehow Alex knew what was going to happen to her, then what she said must have been in confidence. She talked to me because she knew she could trust me, she knew I could understand.'

'Understand what? Fucking hell, Fran. How would she have known? You had one morbid conversation and you think Alex had some psychic premonition?'

Fran leant away from him. His clenched fists and raised voice seemed to confirm her position. 'I told you, Marc, Alex wasn't happy,' she said. 'Not really.'

Marc took an exasperated breath, tried to calm his frustration. He swallowed a mouthful of saliva and dared himself to ask the question he was most afraid of. 'Was there someone else?'

Fran shook her head. 'All I know is she felt torn. We spoke

about our love for our families warring against our hopes for ourselves, our ambitions: our *identities*. Alex wanted more –'

'But we talked about that,' Marc said. 'She was going to do her PhD.'

Fran shrugged. 'Was that her dream or yours?'

Marc studied her, taking in her tailored suit and neat hair, not recognizing the woman he knew.

'We used to talk about why it's like this,' she said. 'Why men can't understand how much a woman sacrifices. I told the police about all this and they didn't care. They thought I was just some whiny woman. I know it seems like things are evening out, that both parties now have to compromise, that every newspaper has an article about "striking the balance", but even that's just a subtler form of oppression, just the newest way to pacify us. It's still always the woman who changes her desires to meet the man's. It's still a world built for you and not us.'

'Bullshit!' Marc said. 'Do you know how patronizing this is?'

'Is it?' Fran said, challenging him to meet her gaze. 'Would you have given up your PhD to move to Chicago with Alex? Would you have stayed at home to bring up the girls while she climbed the career ladder? Why was it only this year that she was concentrating on her own thesis?'

'Alex never asked me to do any of those things. They were choices she made. What she wanted.'

'She didn't need to ask. You'd never have done them. The most you would have offered would have been some moderated version: a long-distance relationship or full-time childcare. Alex knew the only way to live your lives as you did was for her to make those choices. So she changed what she wanted. Women do it all the time. We adapt our wants and desires to meet those of our families, while men adapt the structures of their families to meet their wants and desires.'

'What about you and Ollie, then?' Marc said. 'He's a stay-at-home dad, you can't say he hasn't sacrificed anything.'

Fran laughed. 'Come on, he was working in a pub kitchen when I got pregnant, he was hardly going to support us as a family. That fell to me, but just because I kept my career doesn't mean I got everything I wanted. Alex and I joked that between us we were one complete woman. Between us we had a full life.'

Marc tried to speak, but Fran cut him off. 'I'd have liked to take Emma to nursery sometimes, you know? To be the parent she ran to. I'd have liked to share the financial responsibility too. To be the carer now and again, the softer side of us as a couple: the one that wowed our friends with delicious meals and who they called to ask for favours, not the cranky one always getting in late from work and thinking of practicalities. This wasn't how I saw my life. I wanted a partner, someone to *share* it with, not dole it out fifty-fifty.'

'Why couldn't you just have told us?' Marc said.

'You wouldn't have understood,' she said. 'It's not that we were ever unhappy, ever choosing anything we didn't want. But constantly changing what you want – who you are – takes its toll. And I really think that's something only women can understand: the rewriting of our dreams to fit the world around us. It's sewn into history.'

Marc pinched the bridge of his nose. 'So, you think that because Alex couldn't talk to me, she found someone else?' He hesitated, unsure if he could finish the question. 'A woman?'

Fran looked at him with pity. 'I'm sorry, I know this is hard. I know you're a good guy, Marc. Maybe you would have tried to understand if Alex had given you a chance. She never said anything specific. I just got the impression she felt there was another option – somewhere and perhaps someone with whom she could pursue herself.'

They were both quiet for a moment.

'And I don't think it could have been a man,' Fran finally said. 'Regardless of all this, she loved you. That was what was so hard for her. She hated lying to you about these feelings. She wanted them out in the open.'

Marc wanted to argue with her, pick holes in her logic, shout and growl if he had to, but deep down he sensed the futility. 'Did you know about her mum?' he asked before he left.

'No,' Fran replied. 'But I'd be lying if I said I was surprised. Alex was more complicated than she let any of us know.'

'Is there anything you want to say to me?'

I stare at the floor, pray he'll leave. I don't have the energy for this today. I dreamt about Lizzie and Charlotte. One of those lovely, normal dreams where we're playing in a park and laughing as if no tragedy could ever touch us; one that is utterly devastating to wake from.

'Suit yourself,' he says. 'I'm almost done with you anyway. You've got a week left here and then . . .' He trails off and waits for me to look up, then gives what I assume is meant to be a meaningful stare. I catch his eye, breathe through my nose.

If I squint my vision, I can almost see my husband before me: the colour of the light on his hair, the line of his jaw, the way the shirt hangs from his shoulders. But then this monster clears his throat and the illusion is lost. He can threaten me all he wants. I refuse to show him my fear. Deep down he's a weak man who, like the rest of them, is deluded into thinking he's in control. I am stronger than him. I've been through more than he can possibly imagine. I will get through this.

3/6/12

Al,

I can't do this any more. Remember that song that goes, 'If loving you is wrong, I don't want to be right'? I feel kind of like that. If all this is wrong, then I'm not sure I want to be right. I don't want to rationalize it and realize everything I've worked towards is total bullshit. I just want to go on thinking it's right. Because it feels right. It's the only thing that does. I know you understand. I know you have all these other thoughts that complicate everything and stop you thinking clearly. I know you have responsibilities and fears. But I also know you can figure it out. I know you'll choose the right thing in the end. You have to. Because I can't keep doing this. I won't survive. That's a promise. I need you more than anyone. I will die if you don't figure this out. How will you feel then?

Think about it.

Am x

Saturday, 18 February 2012

Charlotte had just begun her brief stint at Saturday morning karate, which Lizzie told us she had 'zero interest' in getting involved in. Marc had volunteered to drive Charlotte, suggesting perhaps he could take her out for lunch afterwards and maybe Lizzie and I could spend the day together. He was being sweet, I knew, but it irritated me that he felt the need to orchestrate time between us. Lizzie was only nine, but I could already feel that teenage attitude rolling in like a bad storm. She was such a Daddy's girl that Marc didn't see it, but lately I'd been subjected to worryingly frequent eye rolls and door slams.

'Why don't you go to the cinema together or something?' Marc said.

I nodded, but thought to myself I could do better than that. I had an idea. Lizzie's class had been drawing still life for a couple of weeks and it amused me that I kept coming down to find our fruit bowl arranged next to a jam jar and a bottle of squash.

'Pop some clothes on, Liz,' I said after the other two had left. 'We're going out.'

'Where?' she asked suspiciously, but did eventually head upstairs to get dressed.

'Bring your sketch book,' I said when she re-emerged.

We caught the 10.23, arriving in Manchester just before midday.

'What are we doing?' Lizzie asked for the dozenth time, an unmistakable note of excitement in her voice. 'Are we shopping?'

I shook my head and we wound through the busy streets to the art gallery.

'Oh,' she said when we stopped outside.

'Come on, it'll be fun.'

She followed me obediently inside and I picked up a leaflet with a map. 'We don't have to see everything, I just want to show you some different versions of still life. Then we can go shopping if you like. Okay?'

Lizzie sighed, but nodded.

We wandered through the rooms, honing in on fruit bowls and objects arranged before windows. Lizzie wasn't totally disengaged, I noted happily. We talked about the things her teacher had said about light and shadow and I took a moment to study my daughter's serious profile as she gazed at a Vanessa Bell.

'I like that you can't see what's rolled up in the papers,' she

241

said. 'It's like it's just from someone's house and they might come home and pick them up at any minute.'

I glanced from Lizzie to the painting and back again. I almost wished Marc was here to witness this. I tentatively put my arm around Lizzie's shoulders and kissed the side of her head. She didn't return the hug, but she did lean slightly into me. Then she pulled away and walked towards the next room.

'How about this one?' I said, grabbing her hand and turning her towards a canvas of flat, irregular blocks of colour.

Lizzie rolled her eyes. 'That's not a still life.'

I pointed towards the writing next to the painting: '1946 (composition, still life) Ben Nicholson'.

'It's just colours, though,' Lizzie said.

'It's abstract,' I said. 'Look, there's a mug there. See the handle?'

Lizzie folded her arms. 'I don't like this kind of thing.'

'What kind of thing?'

'Anything like this.'

'That's quite a blanket statement,' I said.

She shrugged.

'It's okay not to like this one painting,' I said, 'but you should be careful about dismissing things you haven't even seen yet.'

'Mum, I like *normal* art.'

I frowned. 'What's normal? Why is this not normal?'

'Because it's not. It's stupid.' She snapped. 'You like stupid art and you want everyone else to like it too, but me and Dad and Char like normal stuff.'

I turned to face Lizzie, unsure what had just happened. 'That's not a very nice way to put it,' I said. 'People are allowed different tastes, it doesn't mean they're stupid.'

'It does,' Lizzie said, her cheeks growing red. 'You don't see how stupid it is that you try so hard to be different all the time. Why can't you just be normal? Why won't you let *us* be normal?'

242

I blinked at my daughter, aware of the other people around us. 'What is this about?' I whispered.

Lizzie shrugged. 'I feel like you want me to go back to school and draw something like this,' she said, waving at the painting. 'But can you even imagine how badly I'd get laughed at? Do you even care?'

I frowned. 'I don't want you to do anything,' I said. 'I just want you to open your mind a bit, think a little differently.'

Lizzie shook her head. 'Everybody hates you if you think differently.'

'That's not true. The world is shaped by those who do.'

Lizzie snorted. 'Not in my class. Your life is made miserable if you're different.'

'That's really sad,' I said, looking at Lizzie's clenched jaw and pursed lips. 'But it's still not a reason to wish you were normal.'

Lizzie glared at me.

'Most people who do anything worthwhile in this world have probably been miserable at some point,' I said. 'But sometimes pain has a higher purpose and it can lead to something good in the end. If every artist and inventor, every activist and revolutionary had given up at their first moment of misery, the world would be a very different place.'

Lizzie rolled her eyes. 'Mum, you don't know what it's like.'

'You might be surprised,' I said, hoping I sounded soft and caring.

'Urrgh!' Lizzie sighed in frustration. A woman on the other side of the room glanced at us. 'You don't! I just want to be liked and not have to worry about who's going to hang out with me at lunchtime and whether they're whispering about me behind my back.'

'Baby,' I said, leaning forward to take her hand. Lizzie shrugged me off. 'Anyone who's whispering behind your back doesn't deserve to be your friend. I know it's hard to believe now, but this is all going to make you stronger. You're going to do brilliant things.'

'What?' she said. 'Like you?'

'What's that supposed to mean?'

'What have you ever done that's brilliant?' she said. 'I want to do something important and interesting and worthwhile with my life. I want to have a job that makes a difference, to help people or discover things or save lives. I'd rather be like Fran than you.' Lizzie's face was pink, her nostrils quivering.

I stood up straight. 'I'm not really sure how we got to this from still life,' I said, trying to keep my voice even. 'I'm glad you have dreams and ambitions, but Fran's not the only one doing something important with her life, you know? And it's not like she hasn't made choices to sacrifice things too.'

Lizzie folded her arms across her narrow chest and moved her eyes in a long, slow circle.

'Bloody hell,' I said. 'You can be a real brat sometimes. You're spoilt and ungrateful and –' I clamped my mouth shut and lowered the hand I hadn't realized I'd raised. I turned away from my daughter, saw the door to the next room and walked towards it. Then I kept walking, following the exit signs until I was on the street. I turned right and right again and kept moving my feet until I was crossing the tram tracks and scooped into the middle of a bustle of shoppers, being washed with their wave into a shop full of fabric and mannequins. There were voices all around me, snippets of conversations bombarding my ears, the security tag alarm screeching by the door, cars sounding their horns outside. I rested my hand on a pile of folded T-shirts and closed my eyes.

'Why are you crying?' I heard an exasperated mother shout from across the store. 'Just stop it.'

'Stop it.' I heard my own mum then. 'Stop crying, will you?' Her voice was slurred and the wine sloshed against the side of her glass, threatening to spill. I was nine years old and I'd spent the evening trying not to listen to my parents shouting at each other. At half past eight there had been an enormous crash, followed by the slam of the front door and then silence. I'd waited another half an hour before venturing to the top of the stairs. I didn't know who had left, my mum or my dad, but their argument had preceded dinner and my stomach was cramping with hunger. I tiptoed down and along the hallway to the kitchen, but stopped in the doorway. The dining table was on its side, cutlery and plates and what I assumed was meant to have been our meal mashed on to the lino. My mother was leaning against a counter, taking long, methodical gulps from a glass.

'Sorry about dinner, darling,' she said slowly, her eyes struggling to focus. 'Want some cheese on toast?'

I hovered in the doorway as she pulled four slices from the bread bin and hunted in the fridge for the Cheddar. While it was under the grill, she placed her glass on the side and used both hands to right the table. She set two chairs at the end, then laid two new plates from the cupboard, fresh cutlery and a new bottle of wine. When I refused to step over the mess of broken crockery and food, she picked her way to me and carried me to my seat.

As we ate our cheese and toast, I felt the tears roll down my cheeks. By the time my plate was cleared I was sniffling and struggling to take full breaths.

'Why are you crying?' she asked, sweetly at first. 'What can Mummy do?' But when I couldn't answer, she grew impatient. 'Stop it,' she said. 'You're driving me mad.' She grabbed my shoulders and shook me.

Then she placed her lips right by my ear and shouted, 'WHY ARE YOU CRYING?'

Fresh tears came along with a ringing in my ears. I looked up at my mother's blotched and puffy face and shouted back, 'BECAUSE YOU'RE DRUNK!'

I froze. I'd brought her glasses of water when she couldn't get out of bed before, fed her little pellets of bread and gathered up her stained and soiled clothing to hide in the washing basket before Dad could see them, but never before had I challenged her. Never once had I named the thing that was destroying us.

For a moment I thought she was taking her hands away, regretting shaking me, ready to apologize and ask my forgiveness. But then I felt the full force of my mother's palms connect with my shoulders as she shoved me away from her. I felt my chair tip back and to one side, until I was wobbling on just one leg, my arms flying out, grabbing at the air. I crashed into the ground, landing on the mess of our uneaten dinner, the prongs of a fork stabbing my arm, a glass slicing my thigh and the thick shard of a broken plate penetrating the flesh beneath my left shoulder blade.

I opened my eyes, the skin beneath my tattoo itching with the memory. The exasperated mother and her wailing child were gone. Other shoppers wove around me, inspecting jackets and tops, jeans and leggings. Suddenly I realized where I was. What I'd done.

I elbowed my way back on to the street and tried to run through the crowds, took a wrong turn. My heart was thudding in my ears and I could hardly breathe, but I managed to ask for directions, sprinted back towards the gallery.

Lizzie was in the lobby, standing next to a security guard, her eyes red from crying.

'Oh my God,' I said, running up to her, wrapping my arms around her shoulders and head and anything I could cling to. I felt her body stiffen in my arms.

'Is this your child?' the guard said. 'We found her wandering around alone; she was quite upset.'

'I'm so sorry,' I said to both Lizzie and the guard.

'I'm going to need you to tell me what happened,' said the guard.

Lizzie leant away from me and extracted herself from my grasp. 'It's my fault,' she said. 'I ran off. I shouldn't have done it.'

I looked at Lizzie and she looked back at me, her eyes dark and unreadable.

'Is that what happened?' the guard asked.

I turned to face him, struggling to break eye contact with Lizzie. 'Um, yes, that's what happened.'

December
Ten Months Gone

Marc woke on Christmas morning in his childhood bedroom. He could hear the girls chuckling excitedly with his parents next door. He'd worried his mother might chide that they were too old to be barging into adults' beds in the mornings, but she seemed to enjoy having them around.

'Are you sure you should stay in that house?' she asked as she stabbed a slice of turkey.

He glanced pointedly at the girls and muttered that maybe they could discuss this another time.

'I was only making conversation,' she said.

Carrying the plates through, he tried to tell her he couldn't move, even if he wanted to.

'So you're going to stay there forever? Just in case she comes back? Do you know how ludicrous that sounds?'

He didn't have the energy to fight with her, and a part of him did know how ludicrous it sounded, how morbid and cruel it was to force the girls to stew in the remnants of our old life, especially given what he'd learnt about that life. Would he be a ninety-year-old man with a stair-lift and a mobility scooter, still feeling his heart pound every time the doorbell chimed?

But what if? What if, despite DI Jones and Fran's accusations, despite his own growing suspicions, despite knowing the odds were a million to one, what if I tried to reach them and found another family in their place? If they moved, it'd be like nailing my coffin without first checking my pulse. It'd mean giving up, saying there was no point hoping I'd find them because they'd accepted I wasn't out there to look.

They returned to York and Emma invited the girls ice-skating. Home alone and on his second glass of wine at just three in the afternoon, my husband sat in our office and read Amelia's final letter.

12/14/12
Al

I'm finally in a good place. I feel so calm and focused. I've signed a lease for an apartment and invested some of my Reception Gallery money, which means all I really have to worry about now is concentrating on making my life mean something. I've finally decided that's the point. And while it's kind of scary to take the plunge, it's also liberating. I've been messing around for years and it's now time to truly commit.

I went to this little art festival the other day. Half the stuff was no better than the turgid things we used to fuck around with at the Art Institute. Do you remember when Nico stood outside the library in her underwear with a sheet over her head and whipped herself with a piece of rope until the security guards came and carried her away? I swear this twenty-year-old with an eyebrow piercing was doing almost the exact same thing. She was wearing a burka instead of a sheet and had all these plaques around putting her act into context, but to me that made it less rather than more compelling. Am I getting old when I'm no longer amused by youngsters' art? It's events like that that make me glad I haven't paraded my face out there with my art. I saw the eyebrow girl recognize an artist and approach him to ask for feedback. His eyes skitted about and he mumbled a few things about subtlety and interpretation. I almost went up and told her her piece was no better than shit on a dick and maybe she should go back to art school. Am I cruel? I'm definitely

crude. You'd never have that thought, would you? You'd have looked at
her and seen her as somebody's child, somebody's love.

But life is too short, Al. We only get to do this once. I want to help
you. Think what a relief it will be to finally allow yourself your thoughts,
to say what's on your mind, to give in to your desires. I want you to try
it. I want you to be who you want to be. I just need you to trust me.

Always yours
Am x

Marc had traced our friendship from beginning to premature
end. This was the last and most recent letter, posted just a couple of
months before I disappeared. This, surely, had been his destination
all along. But arrival brought with it a fresh sense of loss. Not only
had this journey failed to produce his missing wife, but the slivers
of information imparted along its way had left him desperate for
more. What went before these letters? What slotted in between?

He shuffled back to the first letter and tried to imagine me
reading it in our first flat. We were happy, weren't we? Our lives
felt full of promise. But at some point an envelope had arrived
and his future wife read that she was making a mistake.

What happens after this honeymoon period is over, when the artist inside
you starts to hack her way out?

Had I laughed? Had I dismissed Amelia's worries? Or had I
stood amongst our things and our life and disappeared into my
head, wondered if maybe my friend had a point?

You'll resent him.

And this last one. I'd sat, probably in this very study, almost a
year ago and been told life was short and my friend wanted to help

me give in to my desires, be my true self. What did that say about the self I had been with him? What did Amelia know that he didn't?

Marc placed both letters on top of the rest and reached for his wine. He couldn't contemplate it. We were happy. He knew we were. Amelia was wrong; I *did* say what I felt. But I felt good things. Amelia may have wanted me to be as crass and cruel and rude as her, but I just wasn't. I was kind and gentle and caring. Marc still couldn't believe my heart was clouded by doubts. Every decision we made, we made it together. I'd always said I was sure. I'd promised him I regretted nothing. I'd missed things and people, of course, which was why I wrote and visited. When a friend said they were planning a trip to the States, I'd give them a list of breakfast places, must-dos and absolutely-cannot-be-misseds. But nostalgia wasn't the same as regret.

There was another, more pressing thing in that first letter, though, that he tried and failed not to analyse. He left the letters in the office and descended the stairs to find the rest of the wine bottle, but the words followed him to the kitchen. He shook the final drops from the bottle and carried his glass to the table before confronting them.

I wish it could be with me.

As hard as his stubborn mind was working to refuse the thought, Marc finally realized that Amelia and I must have been more than just room-mates.

He drained the glass with a wince. Why hadn't I told him? 'It wouldn't have made a difference,' he said, defending himself to the empty room. It wouldn't have changed anything to know I'd left her for him.

You know why Alex didn't tell you, his cruel brain said. Marc's eyelids drooped and his stomach growled. He rested his head on his arms, squeezing his eyes shut, denying his tears.

Then he opened his eyes, remembering something from one of the letters, something he'd logged months ago but never analysed. Amelia signed off with 'I can't wait to have you here.' And in another letter, she'd said she was ill the same time I'd had pneumonia. He'd put it down to coincidence, but how could he have been so stupid? Suddenly his mind ran away from him, threading a flickering movie reel into an ancient projector, forcing him to imagine secret liaisons with my American lover, passionate trysts at the other end of the country, ducking quietly into my dead mother's house and laughing cruelly at my cuckolded husband.

'For fuck's sake,' he muttered, shaking his cloudy head. How could he think like this? He missed me. That was all. These suspicions were just insane, drunken paranoia. He needed to eat something and forget all about them. He needed to continue believing in me.

But instead of walking towards the fridge, he found his legs carrying him back up to the office, his hand reaching for the filing cabinet. From the folder in the front, where they should all have been that first day the police came around, he pulled out my passport. Why hadn't he looked at this before? He'd flicked to the back to mope over my photo, but he'd never checked the front, never questioned where I'd been. His fingers fanned the pages open and there, before him, were a dozen oval stamps. 'Department of Homeland Security US Customs and Border Protection, Admitted NYC.' He read the dates: Aug 4 2003 and May 7 2010 – he'd expected these, but with horror he learnt I'd also entered the US on Oct 14 2005, Jul 17 2006, Jun 8 2007, Sep 22 2008, Jul 14 2009, Sep 19 2010, Feb 28 2011, May 16 2011, Nov 3 2011, Mar 28 2012, Sep 4 2012 and, finally, Dec 18 2012, just two months before I disappeared.

He tells me I need a physical examination. I roll my eyes, but it's not like I have a choice. I'm instructed to take off my clothes.

Hands prod and probe me. He stares at the scar on my stomach for a long time.

'That's quite something,' he says, impressed or proud, I don't know.

I'm left alone to clothe myself once more. I think of the different types of touch, of all the hands my skin has been stroked and held, gripped and hurt by. I think of the ways I have both wanted and feared all of those touches, how I have rarely felt comfortable in my skin unless I could feel another's next to it.

I lie on the ground, feeling the concrete press into my flesh. What touch do I have left to look forward to? What intimacy? Do I really deserve this for what I've done?

2013

Friday, 15 February 2013

I had my hair rolled and pinned and wore this severely cut tweed skirt-suit I'd found in a charity shop. I'd tried to convince Marc to go as Hitler to my Eva Braun, but he'd said that would be taking it too far, so I'd had to get creative with my accessories. Lizzie had rolled her eyes and told me the whole thing was stupid, but Charlotte had helped me paint a cardboard Reichsadler to pin to my breast, tea-stain some identity papers and doctor a tin of mints into fake cyanide capsules.

'I'm not sure how appropriate this is,' Marc had said, walking in on our crafting session. 'What if she tells her teacher she's spent her weekend painting swastikas?'

'It's educational,' I'd said. 'And, anyway, it's no less appropriate than the gross paper hearts her teacher had them cutting out. I've half a mind to complain to the school about their endorsement of such a clichéd, grossly heteronormative holiday invented by capitalist corporations to sell chocolates and greetings cards.'

Marc had raised his eyebrows and left us to our painting.

I'd dubbed the evening our Anti-Valentine Party. The invites had asked our guests to come as 'History's Worst Dates'. I'd managed to get Marc on board by telling him T.S. and Vivienne Eliot had attended parties as Dr Crippen and his mistress Ethel le Neve. 'It's literary!' I'd said, kissing away his frown and trying not to think too hard about the state of Tom and Viv's marriage at the point they donned those costumes.

Fran and Ollie had come as Bonnie and Clyde, while Patrick and Susan made an incongruously paired Dracula and Aileen Wuornos. Marc had opted for Lord Byron, which he'd dressed as for three previous costume parties. I complained he was lazy, but he did look good in his silk cravat and smoking jacket.

Among others, we had a Henry VIII, a Jack the Ripper, a Cleopatra and a Myra Hindley in attendance. I was particularly impressed with Philippa, who'd shed her power suits and convinced her husband to bare almost all with her as Adam and Eve. 'Best or worst date ever? Discuss,' I heard them say as they introduced themselves to a couple of Marc's colleagues.

I did the rounds, topping up drinks and encouraging people to play the silly card and truth games I'd set up throughout the house. Marc had helped me make a Treasure Hunt for the Broken-Hearted, and I'd turned the living room into a Vegas-style Chapel of Love, where guests could bond themselves in the most unholy of matrimonies. I glanced around, wondering if people were having fun, how long it would be until they left.

'What a performance,' Philippa said, sipping the wine I'd dyed with food colouring. 'You've gone to so much effort.'

'So have you,' I said, gesturing towards her paper fig leaves.

The bell went and I slipped through the throng to open the door. I let more guests in, squealing at their outfits, swapping pleasantries and leading them to the kitchen to pour blood-red gin and tonics. After introducing them to our Ripper and Myra, smiling at Susan across the room and refilling a snack bowl, I returned to the kitchen to run myself a glass of water.

'You okay?'

I turned to find Fran standing behind me. She was wearing a beret and holding a plastic gun in one of her gloved hands.

'Never better,' I said with a smile. 'How are you?'

'Getting through,' she said. 'Great party. I think everyone's having fun exploring their dark sides.'

I laughed. 'I guess there's always something new to discover about your friends.'

'Indeed,' Fran said. She looked at me for a moment. 'Are you sure you're okay?'

'Honestly,' I said. She held my gaze until I looked away.

'Okay,' Fran said, lifting her gun to my chest and pretending to shoot me. 'Then we should get back in there.'

I pulled the mint tin from my jacket pocket. 'Cyanide?'

We stepped into the dining room and joined a conversation about the new business park development. I listened for a while, then drifted into the empty hallway, seeking a few minutes alone. After a while Marc came up behind me, placed his hand in the small of my back. He leant towards me and pressed his lips to my ear. '*Fräulein?*' he said. I'd spent the past week messing around with my German accent, longing for Marc to catch on to my teasing. I felt my desire swell; perhaps it was finally working.

'*Ja?*' I said, turning to face him. I touched my fingers to his cravat. '*Alles ist gut?*'

'Yeah,' Marc said, his voice normal again. I dropped my hand. He sounded tipsy. His gaze drifted to the iPhone in my other palm. 'Whose is that?'

'Uh, I don't know. It must have fallen out of someone's coat,' I said, gesturing to the overloaded hooks. I placed the phone on the shelf beneath the mirror and smiled at him. 'How's the party?'

'People seem happy. I might just check on the girls.'

'I'll go,' I said, twisting from his touch.

I found Charlotte sitting at the top of the stairs, picking from a stolen bowl of crisps. 'Hey you, you're meant to be asleep.'

'You're being too loud.'

'I'm sorry, darling. You want to come down for a bit?'

She shook her head.

'Want to sleep in our bed? It'll be quieter up there.'

'Okay.'

I led her up to our room and took my shoes and jacket off to snuggle under the covers with her for a bit.

'Why do you have parties, Mummy?'

'I don't know, sweetie. To see my friends, to bring people together and make them happy.'

'Everyone's just standing around, though.'

I laughed. 'I guess they are. But that seems to be what makes them happy.'

'Does it make *you* happy?'

'Sometimes,' I said. 'Sometimes, though, even if something doesn't make you happy to begin with, then if you just smile and pretend, eventually you find you really are happy.'

Charlotte wrinkled her nose.

'Nothing makes me as happy as sitting up here with you, of course.'

'Will you wait 'til I fall asleep?' she said.

'Of course,' I said, stroking her hair. 'I'll be here just as long as you need me.'

January 2014
Eleven Months Gone

Unthinkably, over the course of January, life took on a routine. The sun rising and setting, the clocks ticking and the calendars turning – Marc knew from the first day I didn't return that these would continue regardless. Back then, though, it had seemed absurd to imagine he would do the same. But the girls and he carved a new existence into the walls of our old one. They trod the same carpets of the same house and breathed the same air of the same rooms. Marc, however, began to walk into those rooms and see only what was there to be seen: Charlotte in a chair or Lizzie with her laptop, rather than the shadow of me watching TV or flicking the pages of a magazine.

Nicola had left him a message saying she wanted to 'check in', but he hadn't called her back. The morning after he found the passport stamps, a realization had seeped through his hangover: the police already knew. They'd ordered their exit checks and received full reports of every time I'd left and entered the country. They'd questioned him about my travels and about Amelia, knowing full well they had more information than him. He'd known all along they were keeping things from him, not telling him every detail of the case, but to have watched him maintain his faith in me for all of those months, to have allowed him to make such a fool of himself, he couldn't forgive Nicola for that.

He'd received valuations from two estate agents and allowed one to hammer a sign into the front garden. The girls weren't keen to change schools, but he'd set his heart on Knaresborough and began dragging them out there to look at houses each weekend.

He still thought of me every day, but woke with a numbness, contemplating the events of the day ahead rather than mourning those of days past. He picked the girls up from school and they chattered about things that had happened, made plans for the weekend or the next holidays. They were learning to cook together, spreading Jamie Oliver or Rick Stein on the counter, Charlotte shouting out measurements while Lizzie rifled through the larder. Char, he found, was particularly good at mashing potatoes for the tops of pies, and he and Lizzie had learnt to make a mean lasagne. On Friday nights Emily, the sixteen-year-old daughter of the couple across the road, arrived in her skinny jeans and thick mascara to babysit. He met Patrick and Ollie at the Swan. Ollie was doing well, considering. Fran had bought a flat inside the city walls and had Emma at week-ends, but Marc hadn't seen her since before Christmas. The girls had swimming on Thursdays, he did the food shopping on Tuesdays, they ordered takeaway on Saturdays, and invariably he frantically shoved their school uniforms in the washing machine on Sunday evenings. The bins went out on Wednes-days to be picked up first thing on Thursday mornings, recycling every other week. Lizzie had to remember to take her flute to school on Fridays, and Charlotte needed something for show and tell every third Monday of the month. They had dental appointments and vitamin schedules, homework planners and birthday diaries. They played Monopoly and Space Dice, read *Harry Potter* all over again, and talked excitedly about the next Marvel release.

When the girls mentioned me, Marc spoke as if I was dead. Not morbidly, but matter-of-factly. 'Mummy would have liked that,' not 'Mummy would like that.' He tried to keep his thoughts pure for them, tried not to linger on his hurt and anger and loss. It was only alone at night, in those moments before sleep, that he allowed himself to picture my blue skin and cold flesh, the slice of somebody's knife. He might never know what happened at the river, never discover why I was there or what role Amelia did or didn't play, but my husband had finally accepted I was gone. And in that, at least, there was a kind of release. My family was coming to the end of the first month of the first year they'd lived without me and, against all odds, they were coping.

By the middle of February there had still been no offers on the house and Marc was fighting a sense of stagnation. Encouraged by Susan, who'd been forwarding him articles about the need to make positive changes and establish new routines, Marc drove over to the animal rescue centre. He spent more than an hour speaking to an enthusiastic volunteer and stroking the soft, black fur of a terrier abandoned by the side of the A64 just after Christmas. The following week he returned and drove the puppy home. Lizzie was meant to be meeting Charlotte after sports club and walking her back, but if he hurried he'd make it in time.

'Oh. My. God,' said Lizzie, dropping her school bag on the pavement. She stared open-mouthed at the puppy on the end of the leash in Marc's hand. 'Is this for real?'

Marc smiled at our daughter, his heart filling to see her so uncomplicatedly happy. The puppy wagged its tail as Lizzie dropped to her knees to pet it.

'What's going on?' said Charlotte, walking up. She skirted around Lizzie's bag, then her eyes landed on the dog. 'Puppy!' she squealed and Marc could barely contain his laughter. Her classmates were noticing the commotion now and pulling away from their parents to crowd and coo. The puppy yapped and twirled in circles.

'Can we keep her?' Charlotte asked.

'Him,' Marc said, nodding.

They said goodbye to the other children and parents and

began walking home. Lizzie took the leash and Charlotte skipped ahead with the puppy dancing around her feet.

'What are we going to call it?' Lizzie asked.

'I don't know,' said Marc. 'We need to think of a name.'

Charlotte turned back to face them. 'What about Princess?' she said. 'Princess Amelia.'

Marc stopped walking. He felt his blood drain towards his shoes.

'It's a boy, dummy,' Lizzie said. 'He can't be a princess.' She turned and saw Marc had stopped. 'Dad, what's wrong?'

The three of them stood in the middle of the pavement, the confused puppy running back to sniff Lizzie's ankles.

'Where did you hear that name?' Marc said.

Charlotte squirmed under Marc's gaze. 'What do you mean?' she said.

Marc tried to keep his voice steady. He knew he was frightening our daughter. 'I need to know where you heard the name Amelia.'

Charlotte frowned, unsure what she'd done wrong. 'In a story Mummy told me,' she said nervously.

'What story?'

'Um, about a princess who realizes she doesn't need a prince to make her happy.'

'It's a dumb name for a dog,' Lizzie said. 'Even if he was a girl. He doesn't look like a prince or a princess, he looks like an otter.'

Both girls were staring at Marc. He could hear his pulse in his ears. They needed to not be on the street right now. He needed to get them home. 'Come on,' he said, as if it had been the girls slowing them down. 'We'll call the dog Otter, that's a great name. Well done, Lizzie.'

The girls spent the evening playing with Otter, keeping out of Marc's way. At eight, when food had still not even been mentioned, Lizzie dug a pizza from the freezer and put it in the oven.

She took two slices up to Marc, knocking tentatively at the office door. Marc sat in the middle of the floor, the filing cabinet and my box of folders emptied around him, bills mixed with letters mixed with scraps of paper. For a moment Marc saw himself through our daughter's eyes, knew what she was seeing was bad. But he was too far inside of himself to conjure more than a simple 'thanks' before she shut the door and retreated downstairs.

The pizza grew cold as he turned the office upside down. His armpits sweated and his eyes prickled as he grew increasingly frantic. He'd tried to ignore this, to numb himself with alcohol and forget about the letters and their implications. He'd told himself to listen to the police, accept the evidence, concentrate on his daughters and the life the three of them could still have. He'd told himself he could move on. But he'd built their new-found stability on a tectonic plate boundary and the volcanoes of my past were far from dormant.

There wasn't a single address on any of Amelia's letters. A couple of the original envelopes floated amongst the pages, but they featured nothing but a New York post stamp. Marc fished out my address book from the things the police had returned, already knowing Amelia's name was absent. He rechecked every scrap of paper, every crumpled shopping list and old bank statement. Eventually he turned to the internet, scrolling past the articles speculating about her anonymity, uninterested in reviews. There was a website with stills of her work. He'd visited it before, but now he lingered on the brief Artist's Statement:

I'm driven by identity, by the solidity it brings to an individual as well as its ability to shift, morph and ultimately elude. People want to know who I am, but the answer is only my work. That I may be the product of immigration, have studied at SAIC and drunk Kool-Aid as a child is less relevant than you think it is. Some refer to those brought up in two or more countries as 'third culture kids'; I'd like to posit myself as a child of the 'fourth culture'. My identity, rather than being a fusion of the things, people and cultures around me, is the distillation of them.

Shaking his head at such incomprehensible gobbledygook, Marc remembered his mission. But of course the site featured no contact details, no address or even information on upcoming shows. Another dead end.

I've got three days. Whatever it is, it's going to happen then. He seems excited. He likes feeling important, I think. In control.

'How do you feel?' he asks.

'About what?' I say, playing dumb.

'Your future. Your fate.'

I shrug. 'You've made it pretty clear it's out of my control.'

'On the contrary,' he says, 'all of this has been in your control.'

I laugh.

'You still don't accept that it's your doing, do you?' He seems disappointed. What has he achieved if he hasn't broken me fully? If I don't grovel at his feet, grateful for whatever tiny reprieve he might offer.

'You chose this, Alex.'

'I did not.'

'Perhaps not explicitly, but everything you did, everything you had, was leading you here. To me. To this moment that will decide the rest of your life. I'd have thought you'd see some beauty in that.'

2013

Thursday, 21 February
My Last Memory

'Five more minutes,' I remember saying, kissing him lazily on the shoulder.

'I have to get up,' Marc said with a groan.

My fingers brushed his belly, tickling their way towards elastic.

'I'm sorry,' he said. He wriggled away, turning to plant a loving but firm kiss upon my pouting lips. 'Tonight? I promise.'

I rolled over and faced the dressing table as Marc pulled himself out of bed and padded towards the bathroom. I bit my bottom lip to keep from crying, lay there as the clock ticked over, knowing soon I'd need to wake the girls, start our routine, but unable to leave these sheets, this bed. Unwilling to accept the day's arrival.

Marc had no idea as he crept back into the room to pull on yesterday's jeans and a crumpled striped shirt over his freshly showered skin that he wouldn't be able keep that promise. Would he have been so keen to hurry down to the office and get stuck into a second year's thoughts on Keats if he'd known that was our last chance?

He found me standing by the sink, rinsing his preferred coffee mug. The girls chewed cereal, still in pyjamas.

'Morning, Daddy,' Charlotte said with her mouth full, then giggled as milk dribbled down her chin.

He kissed each of our daughters' foreheads, then stepped in

my direction, wrapping his arms around me from behind. I felt the warmth of his fingers through my robe, the chill of the tip of his nose as he nuzzled my neck. I clutched the edge of the sink, worried my knees might buckle.

I exhaled a long, silent breath, then turned around. 'Don't forget they have swimming tonight,' I said, pointing to the calendar on the fridge.

'Uhg, do I have to go?' Lizzie said.

'Yes,' said both Marc and I, then caught each other's eye with a smile.

'But they're going to make us do butterfly again. I get water up my nose.'

'Can we go to Center Parcs in the holidays?' Charlotte said.

'That'd be cool,' Lizzie said, sitting up. 'I'm tall enough for the rapids now.'

'I like the roller-skating,' Charlotte said. 'And the pancakes.'

Marc laughed and looked at me. 'Maybe we could?' he said, raising his eyebrows. I suppressed a sudden urge to kiss both those eyebrows, to taste his skin. 'We could get a chalet and see if everyone wants to go,' he said.

'Can Thomas come?' Charlotte said.

'You luuurve him,' Lizzie said.

'I do not!'

'You do! He's your boyfriend!'

'He's not!' Charlotte said, close to tears. 'Mum, tell her not to be mean.'

Lizzie rolled her eyes. 'I'm not being mean. Why are you getting so upset? You're such a baby.'

'I'm not a baby.'

'Are too.'

'Girls!' I said. 'Come on, time to get ready.'

'I'll go,' Marc said.

I stood in the kitchen and listened to Marc usher them upstairs as Charlotte told Lizzie she was not the Messiah but a very naughty boy. I opened and closed my palms. 'Come on,' I said aloud. I grabbed my mug and marched to the top of the house. I undressed and ran the shower until the water was almost too hot to bear. Bracing myself against the tiles, I let the water cascade over my body, opened my mouth so it would trickle to my tongue. I tasted salt and raised my head into the stream.

I dressed in dark jeans and the worn houndstooth jumper Ruth had given me a couple of Christmases ago, then crept down to the first-floor landing. Charlotte's door was ajar. I put my ear to the crack. Marc was in there, searching for a discarded uniform, no doubt.

'What are you doing?' I heard him ask.

'Mr Panda and Mr Potato are getting married and having a baby,' our youngest replied matter-of-factly.

'Give me that Sharpie,' my husband said. 'Now put this on.'

I passed Lizzie's closed and silent door and felt a pang of something, but carried on down to the hall. I laced my shoes then yelled up the stairs that it was almost time to leave.

Waiting for my family now, I turned to the mirror above the key shelf. I studied my reflection, tried to find something familiar there. I ran my finger beneath my left eye, pulling the slackening skin taut.

'Now you're older and I look at your face,' Marc sang as he descended the stairs, still buttoning his shirt. He stepped up behind me and kissed my shoulder. 'Every wrinkle is so easy to place, and I only write them down just in case . . .'

'I should die!' I finished, sticking my tongue out at his reflection. I plucked a hair grip from the shelf and fixed it in my hair, then turned to the girls. 'Right, are we ready?' I leant to finish tying a shoelace, wrapped a scarf around a neck.

Marc opened the door, kissed each of the girls on the cheek. 'Have a good day at school.'

'Bye, Daddy!' they said as I sought their palms. Lizzie shook mine off and walked a couple of steps ahead while Charlotte told me what classes she'd have that day.

'Hey, Liz, wait for us,' I said as she neared the traffic lights.

She looked back and waited for us to catch up before pressing the button. We stood looking at the red man.

'You know you guys always have each other, right?' I felt both pairs of eyes turn to me. 'That's what makes sisters special. Promise me you'll always look after each other. Whatever happens.'

'What's going to happen?' Charlotte said.

'Nothing,' Lizzie said. The lights changed and we started to cross. 'Mum's just telling us not to fight.'

'I don't want to fight,' Charlotte said. 'You always start it.'

I hugged each of them outside the school gate, pressing them to me as they fought to escape my grip. 'I love you,' I called after them. Charlotte turned around to wave. Lizzie sank her shoulders into her coat.

Back at home I found Marc sitting at his desk, still murmuring. 'Take a look at these crows' feet . . . just sitting on the prettiest eyes . . .'

'We need to take in that form about camp next week,' I said.

'Mmmhmm,' he said, eyes on the essay in front of him.

'Looks like it might rain, so I think I'll cycle in now, try to beat it.' I stepped over to rub his shoulders.

He looked up. 'You're welcome to a lift, you know?'

We both smiled.

'Okay.' He sighed as my fingers probed his neck. 'Have a good day.'

I reached around his shoulder. We kissed, awkwardly but passionately.

'What was that for?' he said, eyes squinted in arousal.

'For being you,' I said. I pressed my lips to his once more. 'Bye, I love you.'

'Love you too.'

He turned back to his desk and I disappeared down the stairs. He'd have heard the back door close, the latch of the side gate click back into place as I let myself out.

One Year Gone

Marc didn't tell the girls why or where, he just packed their suit-cases and bundled them and Otter into the car. He'd secured a good last-minute rate. The man on the end of the phone was most helpful, waiving the booking fee and suggesting the best pet-friendly accommodation still available during half-term.

They played I spy, sang along to the *High School Musical* soundtrack and listened to an audiobook as they crawled down the M5. They stopped twice for loo breaks and once for food, stretching the journey to an exhausting seven and a half hours.

'I can see the sea!' Charlotte finally cried, which set Otter barking from the back seat. Marc tapped the brake as they wound down the steep road from Uplyme to Lyme Regis, turned as per his printed directions and pulled into one of three reception bays to pick up the keys. They wove through the town and back up another sharp hill to find the car park overlooking the sea. The girls raced through the cottage, marvelling at the black beams and wonky windows of their temporary home.

'It's like something out of a story, Daddy,' shouted Charlotte from one of the bedrooms.

'Do you like it?' he said, climbing the steep stairs to find them.

He read the rental instructions in a folder by the kettle and cranked the heating up to full. Once they'd settled, they clipped on Otter's lead and walked the few hundred feet to the beach. They looked at the black sea beneath the moon.

'It looks like it could gobble you up and never let you go,' said Charlotte.

'Scaredy cat,' responded Lizzie without enthusiasm.

They bought fish and chips and took them back to the cottage, curled up together on the sofa to watch a film.

'What are we going to do here, Dad?' asked Lizzie, frowning.

'Whatever we want, we're on holiday.'

'But it's winter,' she said. 'It's cold.'

Perhaps, Marc conceded, a seaside holiday in February was odd. It was definitely cold. They paddled one day and had to hurry back to sit by radiators and drink hot chocolates. They tried pitch and putt, but the wind combined with Otter's insistence on chasing and fetching the balls drove them back inside. They did, however, bundle up and walk along the picturesque Cobb to see the fishermen haul their catches on to the rocks. Marc tried to tell the girls how famous the place was, about its literary heritage and filmic representations, but they were more interested in browsing the jewellery and fossil shops. Lizzie bought a rose quartz pendant and Charlotte spent her pocket money in one of the bookshops he made them visit repeatedly. Marc liked browsing the little art galleries too, hidden down windy lanes and displaying their wares on easels. Lizzie liked a pinkish seascape in the window of the gallery opposite their cottage, while Charlotte preferred the portraits in the space by the bakery up the road. They found a café serving cream teas out of season and ate one every day. Marc had hoped they could walk along the beach to Charmouth as he remembered doing once as a child, but big notices told them coastal erosion made it unsafe. The girls seemed relieved and suggested they return to the cottage to finish the puzzle they'd started.

On their third day, he insisted they walk up the far hill. The girls protested about the cold and their aching legs, but he told them Otter needed a proper walk and promised them sweets on the way back. They settled into contented plodding. He was searching for St Georges Hill, off Haye Lane if he'd read the map correctly. With little hassle they found the grand cul-de-sac with views over the bay. The girls looked at him, puzzled. He shrugged and said he wanted to see what it looked like from up there, but his eyes darted away from the view and over the house numbers, finally locating a curly bronze 5. He surveyed the modern building, unexceptional but expensive-looking. He thought about knocking, but knew no one would answer. *Unless I could be legally declared dead, it couldn't be sold. It had belonged to me since my mother's death.* He didn't know what he thought he'd find that the police hadn't, but he longed to look inside. He imagined me peering out of the top window, looking at the sea on one of my pretend trips. He turned back to the girls' questioning faces, unable or unwilling to pursue the thought.

'Sweetie time?' he said.

'Finally,' Lizzie said, her eyes lingering on Marc's face.

I shouldn't have brought them here, he thought.

He put the girls to bed that night and sat outside the door listening for their breathing. As soon as he was sure they were asleep, he crept down to gather his coat and shoes. Otter wagged his tail, hoping for a walk. Marc hesitated at the door, but stepped out into the night, locking our children and the puppy in the strange cottage.

He climbed through the sleeping town, back to the cul-de-sac, and crept around the side path to the rear of the house, looking for the broken window the police had mentioned. He found it boarded loosely, the nails already tampered with. He tugged at the wood, straining silently. Eventually it gave. Feeling ridiculous, he swung one leg, then the other through the small window.

Inside, he realized he hadn't thought further than this. What was he looking for? He fumbled for a light switch and a bulb flickered to reveal a dusty kitchen. He wandered through to the front, then up the stairs, turning on lights and hoping the neighbours really were as unobservant as the police had suggested. Downstairs looked much like he'd imagined his mother-in-law's house: florally upholstered furniture and dusty trinkets on the mantelpiece. Upstairs, he found her bedroom: a neatly made, quilted bed and a wardrobe of undisturbed dresses. The next room was less ordered: an untidy bed and drawers hastily left open. The guest room, he assumed. Or mine. Feeling queasy, he stepped towards one of the drawers and pulled out a woman's shirt. It could have been my size but he didn't recognize it. He rifled some more, discovering underwear and jumpers all mixed in together.

Trying to breathe evenly and keep his thoughts from jumping ahead, he moved to the front bedroom, the one with the view. There was no bed, but a vast floor space littered with blank paper and scattered pens. An easel stood proudly at the curtainless window, nothing on the canvas. It was odd to see such a cluttered and obviously used workspace without even a scrap of work in progress. It looked like someone had taken a rubber to the room, removing all trace of whoever had been there. He stepped over to the built-in wardrobe, wondering if he'd find something more personal. Part of him wanted to discover irrefutable evidence of Amelia, just to know he wasn't losing his mind, but another still clung to the idea that he'd find an old lady's house jacket and a stack of my mother's calm and conventional watercolours.

My husband slammed the wardrobe door. He yanked it to slam it again and again, punching it beyond its hinge, finally letting the splintered wood hang concave in the empty cavity. It was bare. What had he expected? He'd just broken into a dead woman's home hoping to find proof of his wife's sapphic affair. Had he imagined dildos and love letters littered around the place? What was wrong with him? He headed downstairs, turning the lights off as he went, failing to notice the photograph of a pigeon looking into a puddle on the landing, failing to read the title on the cardboard mount: *By the way*. Instead, with a final glance around the kitchen, my husband climbed through the window and hurried back down the hill in the growing dawn, praying our daughters had survived their night alone.

They went for a long, sulky walk the next morning. Marc paced silently ahead with Otter as Charlotte and Lizzie dragged behind, unusually unified by their parent's petulance. 'Look, we're almost there,' Lizzie said, encouraging the flagging Char. They caught up with him, stopped at the tip of the Cobb. Otter sniffed the edge of the concrete. Marc looked at the boulders leading to the black sea. Lizzie pulled the drawstring of her hood tight, hiding from the wind-whipped spray.

'Can we go home?' Char said.

Marc turned and saw her flinch at his expression. Something stabbed deep inside him.

'Of course,' he said, trying to soften his features. Biting back tears. He threw his arm around the shivering Char and turned to the tortoise-shelled Lizzie. 'I'm sorry, girls. Let's go and pack up.'

Lizzie nodded, eyeing him through the hole in her hood. They walked back along the inside edge of the Cobb, sheltering from the wind, Charlotte waving to the fishermen.

They turned into Coombe Street and Marc handed Lizzie Otter's lead so he could fumble in his pocket for the complicated bunch of keys the rental company had given him. Char wandered to the other side of the narrow street to gaze at the pictures in the gallery window. Marc got the door open and turned to call our youngest, but his eye stopped on an image just beyond the display.

'Hold on a sec,' he said and stepped forwards. Peering through the glass, he saw a black and white photograph, blown up and distorted by its lack of definition. The result was more impressionistic than representational. He made out a plump guy with an apron tied around his waist bending to inspect a pile of flat boxes. Something buzzed in my husband's brain, some eerie sense of familiarity. Silently he led the girls inside the gallery, nodding only briefly to the man perched on a stool in the corner before approaching the photograph. Charlotte drifted away to marvel at the canvases on the opposite wall, while Lizzie crouched just inside the door, soothing Otter. Marc left them in the shop as his vision tunnelled and he fell into the photograph. He studied the distended print, its distortion adding to the sense of voyeurism. The man's paunch hung heavily as he bent to the pavement, his chins blurring with his neck, his features unflatteringly mottled. The only items in focus were the boxes he was reaching for. In contrast to the soft moodiness of the rest of the image, here the crisp type boldly announced: 'Papa John's Pizza'. A single line of text had been stuck on the cardboard mount. It read *Neighborhood Watch: What the cock?*

An elastic cord snapped Marc back to the shop in Lyme, to his children, his surroundings and his life . . . *this great shot of a bakery owner coming out and throwing all the pizzas in the trash . . .*

'Wh-where's this from?' Marc asked the man in the corner.

Charlotte and Lizzie turned to watch.

'That one?' the man said, slipping from his stool. 'A lady brought it in years ago. I had it out for ages and it didn't sell. Found it in the back last week and thought I'd give it another go. Kind of a weird one, isn't it? Makes you stop.'

'Do you know who she was?' Marc tried to sound calm, but wondered if the man could hear his hammering heartbeat.

The gallery owner looked at him with more interest than before and pulled lightly at his beard. 'The lady? It was a long time ago. Some woman with curly hair, I think. She said it was her friend's and it'd mean a lot to her if I'd try to sell it. I wouldn't normally have said yes, but I guess I was in a good mood.'

'I'll take it,' Marc said. 'I mean, how much is it? I'd like to buy it.'

The man's mouth curled into a smile. 'Well, great. How does three hundred pounds sound?'

Marc reached for his wallet, aware of the girls gawping at him and that the owner's expression probably meant he was being ripped off. He didn't care.

'Do you have the artist's details?'

'Huh?' said the man, poking numbers into the card machine.

'An address or phone number or something?'

'Uh.' The man looked at him. 'I mean, sure, I've got it written down where to send the sale, but it's not something I'm supposed to give out.'

'I'm interested in buying more,' Marc said, making a quick decision and hoping it was the right one. 'I'm a collector and a huge fan of Amelia Heldt. I'm amazed you've had this piece for so long, it's really special. You see, my problem is her website is down and I don't know if you heard about how she fell out with her agent, but she's very hard to contact. I want to buy more of her work, maybe commission her. So I really don't think she'd mind if you gave me her details. It's going to make her money, after all.'

Marc watched the man process this information. Had he bought it? Some instinct had told Marc this guy wouldn't be taken in by his missing wife sob story, but would he really believe Marc was some rich art collector?

'All right, how much is it worth to you?'

Marc felt blood rush to his fists. He wanted to grab this bearded idiot by the shoulders. He took a breath through his teeth and narrowed his eyes. He'd walked into this. 'Fifty.'

'A hundred,' the man countered. 'Cash.'

'Look,' Marc said, pulling out his wallet once more. 'I've got sixty-five, that's it.'

The gallery owner held out his hand with a smile and Marc reluctantly shook it. The man took the cash and disappeared into the back for a few minutes, returning with a yellow Post-it. Marc quickly read the scrawled address before slipping it into his wallet.

'Can we buy the pink sea picture too?' Lizzie said when they got outside.

'No,' Marc said, leading them into the cottage. He brushed past her to climb the stairs to his bedroom.

Charlotte followed him up. 'Daddy,' she said quietly, 'is the artist the princess? Is she real?'

Marc stopped in the doorway and turned to Charlotte. 'You're too old to believe in fairy tales,' he said and shut the door on her confused face, sacrificing parental responsibility to indulge in a violent Garbo-esque desire. Leaning wearily on the frame, he removed the tissue paper and stared at the latest evidence of my betrayal.

I will never admit it to him, of course, but I am scared now. I don't know when it happened, but I've grown used to this place. Its familiarity has been a comfort. From here, I have managed to leave, to fly away to the family I remember, to my home. What if I lose that tomorrow? What if I lose everything?

April
404 Days Gone

I've imagined the rest in detail. I know it's the months of limbo, of not knowing, of ordinary abnormality that must have been torture for my family. For my husband. But it's the last few days I keep thinking about. I wonder what would have happened if Marc had been able to let go.

That sounds like my meditations are entirely selfish. They're not. I don't think about myself in this. I think about Marc. About my kind, gentle husband who never deserved any of this, but who loved me too much to give up; who couldn't help but be changed by all this. I dream about him. I see him, walk beside him. His flight touches down and he feels exhilarated to be in the city, perhaps a few dozen blocks from Amelia. This is New York, the city that never sleeps: all those clichés, songs, films and Beat poems, all the crime figures and homelessness statistics. All the tales I gushed about manic metropolises and a cosmopolitan chic more sophisticated than a Brit could possibly imagine.

He stumbles from the plane through passport and visa control, through customs and imports. The familiar strangers he's followed from his flight disappear towards friends and relatives, taxis, trains and buses. He follows arrows to a shuttle to the subway, passes through the stile and takes the elevator to the platform. He watches through the scratched window as they stop and start, picking up passengers. Van Siclen, Liberty, Broadway, Rockaway, Lafayette and into a tunnel that takes them under the East River. Finally, 59th Street: Columbus Circle. He swims with the crowd to another platform, slumps into another seat. Three stops and he straightens his stiff legs, lifts his bag and steps on to Manhattan concrete.

He finds his hotel a couple of blocks from the subway, checks in and takes the stairs to his room. A small box painted a cheery yellow with a bed, a low plastic nightstand and a crooked lamp. He brushes his fuzzy teeth, gulps a mouthful of water.

By 1 p.m. he's found a diner around the corner, complete with fluorescent lights and checked plastic booths, and ordered his first American breakfast, pancakes and all. He's awake but only in that tired-behind-the-eyes sort of way. He drinks a cup of coffee and the waitress returns with the pot.

His plan was to go straight to Amelia's address, but here in Manhattan he's suddenly nervous. How does one go about confronting a woman who may have killed your wife? Who definitely fucked her? He thinks about the agent's warning. What if jet lag makes him incoherent? What if she's dangerous? Perhaps he should wait until he's slept.

By the time he reaches this decision he's drunk a small reservoir of coffee. It's sunny and warm outside. He could walk through the park, take in a museum on the other side. That's what people do when they come to New York, isn't it? He feels strangely detached from himself, like he isn't Marc Southwood here, but some other, normal person borrowing his body. He wonders how our girls are doing. They'll have finished school and be eating dinner with his parents. He should be with them really, sorting out their new school applications, making sure everything's okay with the buyers, booking a surveyor. But while life in York continues as always, Marc is here, taking a holiday from himself.

His jet-lagged thoughts freeform their way to the faces on the Missing People website. He's always contemplated the poor families left behind, the bereaved individuals searching for their loved ones. The statistics say many left on purpose. Sitting here, where no one knows him and no one cares what he does next, Marc almost sees the appeal. He loves our children and of course he'd never leave, but he doesn't love his life any more. It's liberating to sit alone and feel that for one afternoon he can forget who he is. He can do anything here and it won't matter to a single soul, not even his own.

He walks through the park to the Met. He follows tourists and schoolchildren into rooms of famous paintings, stands alone in front of other, more obscure pieces. Every so often he has to turn away and take a breath. His connection to some of these works is so entwined with my passions that it's impossible for him to stand before Hokusai's *The Great Wave Off Kanagawa*, Jasper Johns's *White Flag* or the intricate splatters of a Jackson Pollock without hearing my voice. He moves on to *The Blind Man's Meal* and is so struck by the cold loneliness of the painting that he shivers before it. Is he Picasso's blind man, fumbling ineffectively for his wife in this cruel city? After that everything seems tainted: Georgia O'Keeffe mocks his impotent manhood, Roy Lichtenstein splashes artificial colour on his scrambled world and Modigliani's *Juan Gris* looks out of the canvas with the same pity he's seen on the neighbours' faces.

He buys a pretzel from a cart on the steps and walks. He crosses at any green light, zigzagging to Times Square, where the crowds and the billboards spin his brain. He escapes down a side street, then another, a horn blaring when he walks on to a crosswalk with a red hand telling him to stop. His stomach growling, he ducks into a brightly lit shop and buys a hot dog drenched in toxic dressings. His feet ache. He paces back towards the hotel, studying the hurrying people he passes. He sees a woman in spike heels hail a yellow taxi and thinks of Joni Mitchell. An Asian boy who looks too young to be wandering around alone bumps into Marc, runs off without apology. A couple speaking heatedly in Spanish overtakes him. Eyes peer at him from beneath hoods and behind sunglasses. He feel conspicuous, like everyone around knows more of this world than he does. What does my poor husband have in common with these hardened New Yorkers? His eyes and ears and brain too full of stimuli to process anything more, he finds the hotel and lets himself back into his room. He flops on to the bed and falls immediately to sleep in his clothes.

He wakes at four thirty the next morning. He dresses and waits impatiently in the cramped room for a decent hour. As the birds chirp the city into life and the streetlamps flicker off for another day, he walks back to the same diner. He eats French toast drenched in maple syrup, thinking the girls would be jealous. He tries to focus. He's going to find Amelia today.

He pays his bill and heads towards the subway. One transfer and two stops bring him to Penn Station. He's carried with the crowd around a corner and up a flight of stairs to a fluorescently lit walkway leading in every direction. He chooses an exit at random.

The sun shines white on the blistering pavement and he smells concrete mixed with roasting nuts and bile. His brain flicks through thoughts of September 11 and London's 7 July. A childish voice chatters about why he's always chosen cities like Durham and York, why men like him don't fly across oceans to confront their wives' lovers. He senses someone behind, impatient for him to move out of their way, to stop ruining their morning with his feeble existence. He picks up his pace. Hurrying pedestrians, trees growing from the sidewalk, bus shelters plastered with posters and random blocks of concrete all provide obstacles for his directionless journey. Eventually, confident no one is about to barge into the three feet in front of him, he looks up. There, mistily blurred above the dead straight street, he sees the immediately recognizable silhouette of the Empire State Building.

'Watch it, asshole,' growls a passing suit. He's slowed almost to a stop staring at the iconic building. *What's wrong with you?* he growls at himself this time, *Of course you're seeing the Empire State Building, you're in New York – you* are *an asshole.*

He looks across four lanes of taxis and horns. He reaches an intersection and peers to his right to decipher a blue sign, its white lettering declaring Fashion Avenue. On the diagonal, a fairy-lit billboard reads MACY'S. Underneath, revolving doors swallow and spew out bag-laden shoppers. He watches for a moment, his pulse calming, then turns down 7th Avenue. He walks until the elegant boutiques give way to eye-popping neon signs. By the fifth intersection he feels he's walked into a different city. The street signs are less embellished, the crosswalk lights lower and a grimy yellow rather than sleek black. This feels more like what he's looking for. He turns on to West 29th.

Fewer people dash along this stretch of pavement, but he has to navigate cars turning in and out of parking garages, scaffolding clinging to facades and red fire hydrants sticking up in the middle of the sidewalk. As he walks, businesses morph into apartment blocks. He passes 329 and digs in his pocket for the creased address, double-checking what he already has burnt into his brain: 522 West 29th Street.

At the next corner he finds a blue bar called Tom&Fi's and wonders how young and cool you have to be to step in there. Without slowing his pace, he peers through the darkened glass and thinks he makes out people already sitting at the bar. *Does Amelia hang out here?* he wonders. The door swings open and he jumps, feeling conspicuous.

'See you tomorrow,' a leggy young woman shouts behind her as she exits the bar. She flicks a dark braid out of her face and catches Marc's eye. She says nothing but doesn't look away, just glares in a kind of bemused way. Do strange men often look at her in the street? Has she developed some kind of staring contest defence mechanism? It's clear he's going to look away first, that her tactic will work, but before he does he registers the tank top that finishes inches before her jeans begin, the long, tight stretch of her neck, the metal stud beneath her cupid mouth and the scattering of freckles on her high cheekbones. All that in a guilty split second where he feels like a dirty old man, though all he's done is glance into a bar. He adjusts his rucksack and turns away, continues to the crosswalk where, humiliatingly, he has to wait for the lights.

Staring at the other side of the street, he realizes he's only a couple of blocks away and wonders for the first time about the woman he's searching for. What will she look like? How will she dress? Will her hair be long or short? So far he's modelled his imaginings of her on my friends in the UK: the mums at school in their practical jeans, Philippa in her expensive suits and court heels, Susan with her silver rings and summer dresses. He's assumed Amelia will be the same: a woman in her late thirties or early forties, adapting fashions and taste to the growing respon- sibilities of age. But what if she's not? Perhaps her difference is what attracted me to her. She's an artist with no children and no responsibilities other than to herself. *Not since Al, anyway*, his cruel brain reminds him. He forces the thought to the back of his mind and tries again to picture Amelia physically. Will she be wearing paint-spattered dungarees and have her uncut, tan- gled hair piled in a messy bun? Forgetting the decade, he pictures her as a Doris Lessing character or perhaps a moderately dragged Radclyffe Hall. What will she be doing at midday on a Friday? Standing at an easel listening to Tchaikovsky? Lying in bed smoking clove cigarettes with a much younger lover? Marc looks down at his dark jeans and leather shoes. He feels a million miles from himself. What does he know about artists and New York and the life Amelia might be living? What is he going to say to this alien being when she answers the door? He scratches his temple. Sweat forms around his collar. Will she even be there? What if she's sitting in that bar downing neat whiskies right now? Or uptown at MOMA installing her next piece of fabulously incomprehensible art? What will he do if he finds no one in?

He passes through a badly lit tunnel, blinks in the sunlight on the other side. The tall buildings have fallen away and he can see the sky caressing parking lifts and railway bridges. An abandoned jacket hangs from a scrawny street tree. Posters half ripped from railings and temporary barriers tell him to 'Just Dance'. He passes an orange storage shop with 517 painted on the glass. Next comes a blank grey building with 525 efficiently stamped to the heavily bolted door.

'It must be on the other side,' he murmurs, turning to face across the street. Opposite stands a squat, utilitarian, one-storey building painted two shades of grey with opaque windows reflecting Marc back to himself. He looks left and right, then steps across the road. A small vertical sign reads 'Alison Graves Gallery'. His heart sinks. Is it just a gallery address? It doesn't even look open.

He peers further up the street. He can see two American flags and a sign reading 'Jesus is the Light of the World'. He feels sick. What is he doing here? What if Amelia really was involved in what happened at the river? He should have gone to DI Jones; he should have let the police handle it.

The Graves block dominates about a third of the street, but he can't see a number. He walks back towards 10th Avenue. Next to the military gallery, divided by only a thin column of brick, he finds a dented, graffiti-plastered door with 522 stamped at head height. To its left is a metal block of buttons beside apartment numbers. He scans the tiny paper slips, but her name is not there. Marc punches the wall in front of him, regretting the act as pain soars from his knuckles.

You've come all this way, you can't give up now.

He scans back up the list of names, lingering on the one reading Apartment Manager. He presses the circular metal button.

A moment of silence, then the crackle of an intercom and a gruff, 'Yes?'

'H-hello,' Marc says self-consciously into the wall. 'I'm looking for someone I was told lived at this address, but she doesn't seem to be on the list of names.'

'So? Maybe she moved,' comes the terse reply.

'Yes, that's what I thought. Her name's Amelia Heldt. You wouldn't by any chance have a forwarding address, would you?'

There's a pause. 'Amelia?' the voice finally says.

'Yes,' Marc says, his excitement audible.

'Hold on.' A click and then nothing. Marc waits on the doorstep for five or six minutes, inspecting his grazed and swelling knuckles, wondering if he's been forgotten. Just as he's contemplating the buzzer again, the heavy door swings open and a short, grey, unshaven man in a tatty dressing gown stands before him.

'Amelia's never lived here,' the man says, squinting and shaking his head. 'She pays me to pick up her mail and send it to her, that's all. How'd you get this address?'

'From a gallery owner,' Marc says, adding, 'I've come from England.'

'Thought I heard an accent,' the man says with a serious nod.

'I'm trying to contact her. It's urgent.'

The man shrugs his sagging shoulders. 'I have no idea where she is. I get her mail, then I post it uptown.'

'Can you tell me where?' Marc says.

'I guess. It's not an address, though, it's a mailbox number, so I don't know if that'll help.'

'That seems odd,' Marc says.

The man sniffs. 'She moves around a lot, says it's easier this way. She pays me cash and she's a nice girl, so what do I care?'

'She comes here?' Marc says. He doesn't want to hear about Amelia being nice.

'Yeah, you know, she stops by when she's in the neighbour-hood to see if she can save me the hassle. I make coffee and she tells me about her gallery stuff. I used to take pictures, you know? Before my eyes got bad.'

'Oh right,' says Marc, shuffling his feet. 'I'm sorry.'

'That's how we met. She bought one of my pictures, wanted to use it for some project. Most of the time I don't understand what she's talking about, but she's a good lady, passionate and caring. She asks about my kids.'

Marc stares at the old man, feeling both sorry for and a little revolted by him. How has he ended up like this, spilling his guts to a stranger on the doorstep? Marc tries not to wonder if he's looking at a version of his own fate. 'How long has this been going on?' he says.

'Jeez, ten years maybe. No, more than that, maybe like four-teen or fifteen. I don't remember, you know.'

'That's okay.'

'After I sold her the picture, she asked if I could do her a favour,' the man says to the air above Marc's head. 'I didn't see why not, thought it'd be for a few months 'til she got a place, but I guess those months stretched out. The years blur, the tenants come and go and even my daughters forget to send birthday cards. But not Amelia. She always remembers. Known her since she was a fresh little thing, all bubbling about art school and wanting to make a name for herself. Say, are you the one who writes to her from England? I always notice the stamps with the little Queen's head on, but Amelia never told me who they were from.'

Marc swallows. 'That was my wife,' he says. 'She studied with Amelia.'

'I see,' the man mumbles.

'My wife's gone,' Marc says.

The man's watery eyes meet Marc's. 'And now you're trying to find Amelia?'

Marc nods.

'She doesn't like to be easily tracked down,' the old man says. 'Scared of commitment if you ask me. If she stayed in one place for too long, she'd have a dozen guys lining up to propose. Who can blame her, though? My marriage fell apart. They all seem to these days –'

'You really have no idea where she is?' Marc says.

'Sorry.' He sniffs again. 'I wish I could help. You could try at the galleries around here. They know her next door, I think.'

'When was the last time you saw her?' Marc presses.

'Oh, a month or two ago. She had an exhibition coming up.'

'Do you know where?'

The old man shakes his head. 'SoHo somewhere. I don't keep up with these things. I might if I could go, you know, but it's difficult these days. It's not so bad, so long as there's something on TV, I keep myself occupied.'

'Sorry,' Marc says, hoping to mask his frustration with a sympathetic smile.

'I'm sorry too.' The old man looks genuinely sad. 'Look, I'll get you that mailbox number.'

'Thank you,' Marc says when he returns. 'You've been a lot of help.'

'I hope you find her,' the man offers before turning back to his gloomy hallway.

Marc looks back at the door for a moment, then walks the ten steps back to the gallery. It's dark inside. He cups his hands around his face and peers through the glass but sees only an empty desk with a sagging orchid. He knocks, tentatively at first, then bangs with full-fisted frustration.

He stomps back and forth on the pavement, wondering what

to do next. Eventually he reaches into his rucksack and tears a page from his notebook. He scrawls a message asking someone to get in touch urgently. He hesitates, then mentions Amelia and scribbles the name of his hotel.

He slips the note through the vertical letterbox and watches it disappear into the abyss. Is that the extent of his plan? Now what?

He rubs his eyes. He's still jet-lagged. His stomach rumbles. He'll find something to eat, then take the subway to the mailbox address, see if there's anyone to talk to there. He wanders to a small park, chews a sandwich and then heads uptown.

Amelia's mailbox is in a large facility with a suited reception-ist who tells Marc the company's reputation is built on their ability to provide a discreet, private service. He refuses to enter into further conversation and threatens to call security if Marc doesn't vacate the premises. Unsure what else to do or what else he expected, Marc leaves. He steps back over the yellow bobbles on the platform and into a subway carriage. He stares at the scuffed metal grill beneath the seats and the graffitied windows above other passengers' heads, avoiding eye contact. They stop, he thinks at Columbus Circle, but the announcer's voice is muffled. Marc's heart pummels in his chest. He prays he won't cry. A guy by the metal pole closest to him plucks a ukulele. It begins softly, gentle notes offered tentatively to the crowd. He plucks a few bars, then a couple more, parts his lips and lilts qui-etly and solemnly: 'Some-wheeere . . . oh-ver the rain-bow . . .' The guy opposite Marc crosses his legs with a sigh. 'Some-wheeere . . . oh-ver the . . .' The musician taps his foot, picks up pace: 'Some-day-I'll-wish-upon-a-star-and-wake-up-where-the-clouds-are-far-behiiind mee . . .' The train slows to a crawl in the blackened tunnel as the man resumes his melancholy prayer. A woman a few seats down coughs. The train shudders back to full speed and the busker takes a breath before launching into a belting entreaty of the carriage. 'If-happy-little-bluebirds-fly-beyond-the-rainbow-Oh whhhy can't IIIIII?' He tips his baseball cap and clears his throat. The other passengers study the floor, gaze through the opaque glass. 'Thank you ladies and gentlemen, I'm a student at Julliard and trying to pay my tuition, so any donations are much appreciated.'

Marc stares at his lap as the man passes through the carriage, his pulse pounding in his ears. The woman next to him places a folded five-dollar bill in the guy's hat. 'Thank you, thank you,' beams the student. Marc clenches his fists, his grazed knuckles throb. They reach his stop. He tumbles through the carriage, through the turnstile, through the grey corridors, out from the concrete hole and up the stairs into the real world. To his left is the park, the green, the trees, the dog walkers. The blue sky makes his eyes sting. A piece of newspaper hits his foot. He runs up the last two steps gasping for air, wondering if he might be sick. There are no rainbows and no bluebirds and I am not out there to be found.

'Which way is Ninety-first Street?' asks an overweight man with a camera.

'I don't know, I'm English,' Marc says, as if it's a defence. *How should I know? I don't belong here.* He turns his back on the park and paces towards his hotel. *I shouldn't even be here.*

He falls asleep in the middle of the afternoon, entering a suffocating dream world until 2 a.m. He reads while the sun rises through the hotel window. Finally 7 a.m. arrives and he hurries, wide awake and freshly shaved, down the stairs to consult the yawning receptionist.

'Good morning,' he says. 'How are you?'

'Are there any messages?' Marc asks. 'Room two-one-two.'

'Lemme check.' The receptionist turns to the desk behind him. 'Two-one-two? Yeah, someone called for you yesterday afternoon. We knocked but there was no answer.'

'Did they leave a message?'

'Um, no, looks like they didn't –'

Marc's excitement plummets.

'There's a number, though.' The receptionist begins to pass him a scrap of paper and Marc snatches it out of his hand. The guy nods towards a wall-mounted receiver next to a tattered leather chair in the corner.

'Thanks,' Marc says, already halfway to the phone.

It's not until after he's dialled the nine digits that he remembers it's rather early to be phoning strangers. His finger hovers, ready to hang up, but halfway through the second ring a groggy male voice answers, 'Hello?'

Marc's throat feels suddenly dry. He swallows.

'Who is this?' muffled by a yawn.

'Hi, I'm Marc Southwood. You rang me yesterday. I left a note –'

'Oh Christ, man,' the voice says and it sounds as if its owner has flopped back into bed. 'What time is it?'

'I'm sorry. Did I wake you? I've only been here a couple of days, I'm still getting used to the time difference.'

'S'okay, man,' is offered as an aural shrug and Marc imagines this guy, whoever he is, sitting up again and trying to tap the sleep from his brain. 'Your note sounded urgent, so I guess I'll let you off. How can I help?'

'I'm looking for Amelia Heldt. I'd like to talk to her.'

The voice chuckles. 'Ah, Amelia.'

'You know her?'

'Sort of, I guess,' the stranger says, his words travelling at an excruciating snail's pace to Marc's ears. 'But you don't just get to talk to Amelia whenever you want, you know? Only when she wants.'

'Whatdoyoumean?' Marc asks, desperate to extract the information he needs.

'She's a free spirit,' the voice says in a higher register, a smile playing on its owner's lips. 'A fucking genius but, you know, a bit whack too.'

'But you do know her?'

'Kind of,' the guy says.

'Kind of?'

'Well, we – I mean, the gallery – we represented her some-times. She contacted us years ago to ask if we were interested in arranging some of her shows.' He pauses, then adds, 'I think she probably had a similar set-up with a couple of other places, but she paid us well and it was good publicity for the gallery.'

'Was?'

'Yeah, well, there was a bit of an issue between her and my boss. I guess Amelia kinda used their friendship and some pretty personal stuff in one of her pieces and my boss didn't really like that so much.'

'Oh,' Marc says, his mind groping to match the detail to the descriptions in Amelia's letters. 'Wait, Alison Graves Gallery – is your boss related to Serena Graves, Amelia's agent?'

'You could say that. Alison's her middle name. She changed the name of the gallery after the scandal. It was a total night-mare, to be honest. I almost quit.'

Marc scratches his temple. He may not have found Amelia, but he's relieved to find her world slotting into place. 'Do you know how to contact Amelia?'

'Well, no,' the guy says. 'They haven't spoken for a few years now, but even if that wasn't the case, I probably couldn't help you. I'm telling you, man, Amelia's a bit of a fruit loop. She never actually came to the gallery. I never met her and neither did anyone who worked there except my boss. And it was pretty unclear how close they ever were, especially after her so-called 'Friendship' piece. She called us, that was all. We arranged everything by phone and she never gave us a number or address to contact her on. It was all a bit mysterious. Why are you trying to find her? Are you a reporter or something?'

'No. My wife went to art school with her,' Marc says a little angrily.

'No way!'

Marc winces from the receiver.

'That's awesome. I mean, my boss says she's certifiably insane, but that's kinda cool. Your wife must have some stories.'

'So you don't have any contact details for Amelia?'

'Sorry dude, no.'

'What about your boss? Would she talk to me?'

'No way. Man, she'd go postal on you if you even mentioned Amelia's name. Trust me, she has no links to the woman any more and it's not worth your life to try. You're lucky I found your note and not her. She'd fucking kill me if she knew I was even talking to you.'

Marc has one final idea. 'Do you at least know where Amelia's last show was?'

'Oh yeah, I can totally help you with that,' the guy says. 'I didn't tell my boss, obviously, but I went to it last month. It's still running, got another week or two left if you want to check it out.'

'Really? Do you think Amelia might be there?'

'Unlikely. She's not exactly the meet and greet type.'

'Oh.'

'It's at Space38, anyway. On Greene Street, third floor. It's a cool piece, I took my girlfriend.'

'Right, thanks,' Marc says, his interest in the individual on the end of the line dwindling rapidly now he has his next destination.

Hanging up, he tries to quash the feeling in his gut that this whole trip is turning into a wild goose chase. He's reached his third day in New York and all he's learnt is Amelia's some kind of kooky recluse. He has an address, a direction in which to take the subway, but will it reveal any more than a gallery of her work? Still, despite his frustration, he's curious to see Amelia's show. He climbs the stairs back to his room, throws his wallet and notebook into a rucksack, locks the door and hurries out into the morning. He switches to the A and rides the five stops to Canal Street. The gallery proves simple to find, but an A4 page Blu-Tacked to the inside of the window tells him it doesn't open for another hour. Impatience rises in his stomach, but he feels strangely calm. He's here, at least. At some point today these doors will open and he'll learn something about the woman I betrayed him for.

At two minutes to the hour the gallery finally opens. As the thick doors swing outwards, Marc leaps from the step and stands to attention. A skinny white boy with pockmarked cheeks and floppy hair gives him a quizzical look. 'We don't usually have people so eager,' he says as he leads Marc into the elevator. At the top, he holds a door open and Marc steps into an enormous white room.

'You can leave your bag here,' the boy says, pointing to his left. 'Phones and cameras and any recording equipment need to go in the lockers.'

Marc does as he's told, then turns to the space. Occupying the whole corner of the building, the room features rows of large sash windows and a dozen or so vertical pillars holding up the ceiling. That ceiling is criss-crossed with an intricate pattern of pipes and sprinkler systems. Long horizontal radiators run at knee-height around the entire circumference of the room.

'Lemme know if you need anything,' the boy says as he heads to a desk in the corner.

Marc steps further inside, twisting his head to look at the pristine walls. He's reminded of the room full of blank paper at my mother's house and experiences the same eerie feeling of something having been erased. He walks away from the docent's desk, crossing to the other side of the wooden floor, wanting privacy. As Marc moves, the sunlight through the windows shimmers over something on the opposite wall. When he approaches, though, whatever it is disappears. He steps back again, moving his head to catch the right angle and realizes it isn't just the window causing the effect. A series of palm-sized mirrors are arranged at angles on the ceiling and skirting boards. They bounce the light at multiple angles, reflecting off what might be as simple as gloss on matt paint so that as he moves he catches writing on the wall. He dances daftly around the room trying to pick out whole sentences, recognizing snippets of lines and rising on tiptoes to glimpse their authors' names, elaborately scrawled in parentheses beneath their Helvetica statements. A mixture of theorists, writers and celebrities neatly graffiti-ing the walls seemingly at random, sentences running into each other or curling around images of cavemen wielding spears. The words make up lines or part-lines, some taken entirely out of context or with little relevance to their original purpose, but a common theme connects them all:

'A people must have dignity and identity . . .' (Andrew Goodman) 'Identity is performatively constituted by the very "expressions" that are said to be its results . . .' (Judith Butler) 'A strong sense of identity gives man an idea he can do no wrong . . .' (Djuna Barnes) 'My name is my identity and must not be lost . . .' (Lucy Stone) 'I lost my identity and balance . . .' (Mathias Rust) 'Americans may have no identity, but they do have wonderful teeth . . .' (Jean Baudrillard) 'An identity would seem to be arrived at by the way in which the person faces and uses his experience . . .' (James Baldwin) 'Each time this identity announces itself, someone or something cries . . .' (Jacques Derrida) 'Human identity is the most fragile thing that we have . . .' (Alan Rudolph) 'All types of identities, ethnic, national, religious, sexual or whatever else, can become your prison after a while . . .'

(Murathan Mungan) 'The individual, with his identity and characteristics, is the product of a relation of power exercised over bodies, multiplicities, movements, desires, forces . . .' (Michel Foucault) 'This strong, brutal rapist, whatever, identity is my true self . . .' (Slavoj Žižek) 'Like Popeye says, I yam what I yam . . .' (Tony Soprano)

'Cool, huh?' The pock-marked boy has crept up behind him. 'It's like those invisible letters you used to write with lemon juice when you were a kid.'

'Uh-huh,' Marc says.

'You look confused.'

Marc clears his throat. 'Modern art isn't exactly my forte.'

'Oh man, you're missing out,' the boy says, bobbing on his sneakered heels. 'I love this artist. She looks at the world in a different way.'

'Through lemon juice?' Marc says, only half joking. He's thinking about my paper. Did I send Amelia the Tony Soprano quote?

Ignoring Marc's attempt at humour, the boy continues, 'It's meant to be about how, like, the physical fact of the world makes everything pale in comparison, however, like, hard we try to make that not true. Even art and literature and theory and fame, they all mean, like, nothing compared to the ground beneath our feet, the sun in the sky. Our identities feel like everything, but what do they actually mean? What do we have to show for them? If you keep kinda thinking along those lines, you start, like, imagining we're all just stupid little puppy dogs howling to an invisible moon.'

'Or shuffling around an empty room to see something that's not there?' Marc says, wincing at the boy's stumbling syntax, but catching on. He frowns, sceptical that all this can truly exist in some quotes scribbled on a wall. Suddenly my pop-culture thesis seems surprisingly academic. What would Paula make of this piece?

'Right,' says the boy. 'Exactly! So, here, like, the performance becomes the person looking for the art, searching for a meaning that's maybe not there. It's hilarious really.' His grin drops. 'Not that I was, like, laughing at you, you understand. It's just a cool piece to docent for.'

'It's okay,' Marc says.

'I get really, you know, pumped about this piece. And the artist, like, I've sort of been following her work for my final-year project. She's really hot right now. Everyone wants a piece of her, but she's like, "Fuck you all, I'm gonna live this hermit life and you'll never find me." I was so pumped to meet her at the opening, she like never usually goes.'

'Hold on, you've met Amelia?' Marc says, sounding almost as desperately excited as the boy before him.

'Yeah, I know, it's hard to believe, right?'

'Do you have a way to contact her?'

'Are you kidding? Nobody knows how to contact her, that's like her thing. She didn't even tell us she was like coming to the opening, so we weren't prepared. It was just us and a few of the gallery supporters, a couple of reviewers, though press night was the next night. And then, like, around eight thirty, this woman walks in in this *A*-mazing cocktail dress and asks the room how it's enjoying her latest baby. We're all shell-shocked and kinda rush towards her, everyone crying, "Are you Amelia Heldt?" like, in total disbelief. I mean, like, none of us knew what she looked like, how old she was, anything at all, and I guess we all must have painted our own pictures based on our interpretations of her work and our own biases, but I reckon there was not one person in that room who wasn't surprised when we found out who she actually was. Anyway, she's like totally unfazed and kind of shrugs us off and gives an impromptu talk about her influences for the piece. She's so eloquent. Then she claps her hands, gives a kind of giggle, and declares we should all drink more. It became a regular party after that. Even Amelia got wasted. She was like wandering the room, chatting to everyone and then kissing people like full-on on the mouth. I heard she was from Louisiana, but it seemed pretty European to me. But then I was talking to my boss the next day and he had a theory that it was all intentional. Like, when she turned up and started kissing everyone, nobody paid any attention to the art on the walls, we were all like, "WTF! Is she bi or something? Or on drugs?" And, like, the twenty of us that were in the room that night are, like, the only ones who know what Amelia Heldt looks like maybe in the whole of Manhattan. Pretty cool, huh? Although, one of the critics tried to write about it afterwards in *The New York Times* and the next day every other paper was saying he made the whole thing up. So it's like nobody believes us, we're this little club that can never share our experience with anyone outside the club. Like *Fight Club*, only cooler.'

The boy is practically panting by the time he comes to a stop, his dewy eyes focused wide on Marc's face, willing him to share in his excitement.

'You really have no way of contacting her?' Marc says.

'Sorry, man, if I did it'd be worth a fortune. Not just to you, you know?' His features soften into a putty frown as he registers Marc's disappointment. 'Hey, I'm really sorry. Why do you need it so bad anyway? Are you a fan? I could fish out some of the brochures for the opening, I think she signed a couple, if you like.'

Marc opens his mouth to say that's unnecessary, but the boy's already darted to his desk and begun rummaging in a drawer. Marc steps over to join him.

'Here we go.' The boy pulls out a bundle of inexpensively photocopied leaflets. He picks one up to investigate the inside cover, then drops it back on the desk. 'Not that one.' He picks another, then another, discarding them both. As he selects a fourth, a square Polaroid slips from the pages and floats to the top of the pile below, landing face down.

'This one's signed, look,' says the boy as Marc reaches for the picture. He turns it over in his hand and sees a gloomy image of a young woman with long, straight hair pressing her mouth to the crimson lips of a blonde woman. Only half in the shot, the blonde looks stunned, as if she's in the process of backing away, while the other woman seems passionately in the moment, her slanted eyes closed to reveal a thick line of kohl and spidery lashes splaying towards the freckles on her prominent cheekbones.

'Oh wow,' the boy says, leaning over the desk to peer upside down at the photograph. 'I didn't know anyone had a camera. Fuck, that's proof, that's worth a fortune.'

'Is – is this Amelia?' Marc asks, confused.

'Yeah, that's her. See what I mean, she's stunning.'

'But it can't be.'

'Sure, I know. Not many artists look like supermodels, right?' the boy says. 'But that's her. I saw her with my own eyes, kissed her with my own lips.'

Marc looks up at the boy, scanning his face for doubt or confusion. 'It's not that. She just can't be this young. This woman's twenty-five, thirty at most. My wife went to university with Amelia. She has to be closer to forty than thirty.'

'No way!' The boy's eyes pop. 'Wow, then either Amelia Heldt found the elixir of youth or she's got Demi Moore's surgeon on speed-dial.'

Marc looks back at the Polaroid, studying the woman's skin. Could plastic surgery make someone my age look like this? Now he looks more closely, there's something unsettling about the woman, almost familiar – could that be a product of surgery? Does she have some celebrity's nose, another's eyes? Is he recognizing that?

'Can I keep this?' he asks.

The boy gives him an almost cold look. 'Dude, that's like the only proof that what I told you is true. I need to like send it to *The New York Times* or something –'

'I'll pay for it,' Marc interrupts and the boy's expression changes.

They settle on $200, almost all the cash Marc has left. He'll have to use his card now and get stung on the exchange rate as well as the charges. And all for a silly photograph that hasn't got him any closer to finding Amelia. He stares at it some more as he rides the subway back uptown, trying to imagine me with this woman. It's late afternoon. He wanders through Central Park for a while, then finds a dingy restaurant for dinner before returning to his hotel. It takes him a long time to get to sleep, his mind busy trying and failing to come up with a plan for tomorrow. *I can't give up*, he chants beneath his eyelids. But he has one day left and no more leads.

He wakes in a cold sweat with half an erection. He wants to cry and scream and thump the pillow. Not only have his dreams shredded his sanity, but he's waking to a day of nothing. He has twenty-four hours left to find Amelia and no clue except a stupid snapshot. There's no reason today for him to extricate himself from these sheets, no purpose to his being in Manhattan.

Eventually he drops his feet over the edge of the bed and heaves his weary limbs towards the shower. He tries to let the scorching water wash away his negativity. He allows his mind to roam, scanning all the things people have said, all the places he's been, seeking something he's missed. Perhaps he should go back to the landlord, see if he knows anything else. Or he could visit galleries at random. If Amelia did the opening night stunt at one, she might have tried it at others, there might be someone she's made friends with. Even as he thinks these thoughts, the water washes them from his hair to his toes and down the plug-hole as extreme long shots.

He scrubs himself with a towel and wraps it around his waist, pads back into the room. As the door swings into the claustro-phobic space, something catches his eye. Next to the unmade bed, on the low table with the battered lamp and his notebook lies the Polaroid. From this angle, with the faces flattened and alien-looking, his sense of recognition reaches uncanny. He steps towards it, his towel dropping to the floor, and picks it up. Yes, he's seen this woman before, he's sure of it. *Think!* he silently instructs himself. He wants the woman to open her eyes; he's sure he'd know her if he could see her pupils, if she could look at him, if he could connect those cheekbones and that puckered mouth to a gaze. 'A gaze,' he murmurs, stepping hesitantly on to a train of thought, like it might be the right subway car but heading in the wrong direction. *A gaze, a glance, a glare . . .* This is the girl who walked out of the bar on 29th Street, near the first address he had for Amelia. She stared him down like some per-vert wandering the streets. Her expression was hard and mean, but if you softened those features, if you caught her in an act of tenderness, if you unplaited her hair, she'd look like this, wouldn't she?

As certainly as the thought arrives, it begins to retreat. He scrutinizes the photograph, doubting himself. He notices the tiny scar of her empty lip-piercing, almost but not quite invisi-ble beneath her foundation. It can't be, can it? What are the chances? But it's something. And the only something he has, so it has to be worth a try. He dresses in a hurry, grabs his bag and heads out. He'll go to the bar. That's his plan. She'd shouted something about seeing them again, so they must know her. Someone will know how to find her.

He exits Penn Station without so much as a glance at the Empire State Building and pounds down the sidewalk, cursing

299

dawdling tourists and darting across intersections with whichever light says walk. He's back at the blue bar within fifteen minutes. Tom&Fi's, established 1989. The tinted glass door is propped open and the faint sound of Elvis Costello drifts on to the morning street. Catching his breath, he steps into the dark entrance.

His eyes take a moment to adjust to the gloom. To his left is a long bar with a dozen empty stools facing the shiny rows of beer taps. Straight ahead a pool table and a couple of dartboards nestled amongst posters advertising Pabst Best and Coors. The place is empty. Costello keeps crooning. Marc leans across the bar to peer through an archway to the back.

'Uh, hello?' He speaks tentatively at first, then shouts.

A balding man appears.

'Hey. What can I get you?'

'I'm not here for a drink,' he says, fumbling in his pocket for the Polaroid. 'I'm looking for someone.'

'Are you British?' the guy asks with a smile. 'I like your accent.'

'Thanks,' Marc replies automatically. 'This girl, do you know who she is?' He presents the photograph across the bar.

The guy whistles and steps away as if the image might incriminate him. 'You don't want to go showing that around here, man. If Erin's boyfriend sees you waving that thing, you won't know what hit you.'

'Erin?' Marc says, relief flooding through him. 'Is that her name? Do you know her?' He's not crazy, it *is* the woman he saw. Can she really be Amelia, though?

'She works for us sometimes. But seriously, you need to put that away.'

'She works here?' Marc says, frowning. Amelia has money, a life; the woman he's been searching for all week can't work in a grubby bar.

'Just cleaning and stuff,' says Tom. 'She came in looking for bar work, but you know, it's Tom&Fi's joint, you kinda have to only have Tom and Fi tending the bar otherwise it don't make sense, do it? I'm Tom, by the way. Fi's my sister.'

'Marc,' Marc says, taking Tom's offered hand. 'Look, it's important, do you know where Erin is, where I can find her?'

Tom looks him up and down, perhaps trying to determine if he's looking for trouble. He must decide upon the negative. 'Stick around, she'll be in in a bit.'

'Really?'

'Yeah, calm down, she usually comes by before lunch, to see if we need her tonight. Take a seat. Can I get you something to drink?'

'Coffee?' Marc says dubiously.

Tom disappears into the back and returns with a cup of steaming liquid.

As Marc's finishing his coffee, the girl from the photograph stomps into the bar, leans over the counter and hollers for Tom, who's out back once more. She glances up the bar at him, then flicks her hair over her shoulder and looks away.

Intimidated but determined, Marc says, 'Excuse me. You're Erin, aren't you?'

Her head snaps back to him and she scowls. 'Do I know you?'

'Not as such.' He smiles weakly. 'But I, I was wondering if I could have a word with you?'

She scowls some more, but says nothing. Taking this as a positive sign, Marc slips off his stool and approaches her, holding out the Polaroid.

'What the actual fuck?' Erin says, twisting her shoulders to face him square on. She's slender but muscular, a good inch or two taller than him in her chunky heels. 'Where did you get that? What do you want?'

Marc steps away, leaving the photo on the bar between them.

'I don't want to get you in trouble. You can keep the picture. I just want to ask you about that night.'

She narrows her eyes at him, but nods towards a booth on the opposite wall. They sit across from each other in silence, Erin clearly unwilling to speak first.

'I, um, you see,' Marc stumbles under her glare. 'I'm looking for the artist, for Amelia Heldt. I mean, I'm assuming you're not her, though you were pretending to be her that night, weren't you?'

'It was just an acting gig,' she says, holding the glare. 'I was told it would stay private, so I agreed to the weird stuff.' She gestures distastefully towards the image.

'You're an actor?' he says, the cogs in his mind whirring but as yet spitting nothing out.

'Yeah,' she says, her face softening. 'Stage, you know, or at least that's what I want to do eventually.'

'Right. And you were hired by Amelia to play her for the evening?'

'My agent set it up. It seemed kinda shady, going in and just kissing everyone like some big orgy, but the artist had requested me apparently, and I guess I was flattered. They told me there'd be no cameras.' She scowls again, moving her lip piercing back and forth with her tongue. 'I didn't know that was taken.'

'Keep it. I think it's the only one. You've got nothing to worry about.'

'Kieran would kill me if he saw this.' She looks down at the table, her lashes brushing the skin beneath her eyes. Marc feels a pang of sympathy, wondering about the story inside the girl before him. He shakes the thought off.

'Do you know how to contact Amelia? You said she requested you?'

She looks up and shakes her head. 'I only spoke to my agent. She said she'd seen me around was all. I can give you her details if you want, I guess she should have her number.'

'That'd be great,' Marc says, trying to hide his disappointment.

She fishes in her handbag and retrieves a business card. 'Keep it, I've got tons.'

'Thanks.'

'Sure,' Erin says and shrugs.

'Sorry if I scared you.'

'Whatever. Are we done?' she says, already snatching her handbag and the Polaroid. She leans over the bar to shout to Tom that she'll be back at six, then stomps out into the street.

Marc looks at the card. Inside a small black and white image of a clapperboard he reads the contact details for Maxine Stein, Inc. He considers asking Tom if he can borrow his phone, but looking again he realizes the address is only six blocks away. He leaves a handful of dollars on the bar and walks back into the sunshine. He turns up 9th Avenue and walks straight until he hits 35th. He's almost back at Penn Station by the time he finds the entrance. He locates the button for the fourth-floor address and, after a garbled explanation of his business, is buzzed through the door and instructed to take the elevator.

Suite 410 is less luxurious than he imagined, but a rosy-cheeked woman behind the desk gives him a friendly smile as he approaches. He vomits out his reason for being there in one long breath, trying to explain the urgency with which he needs to contact Amelia and how he's traced her here and this really is his last hope. The woman, whose name he learns from a wooden block on her desk is Maria, gives him a sympathetic smile and says she'll call her boss.

'She's at a casting,' she says, dialling.

Marc clutches his hands still behind his back and wills his foot not to tap. Maria speaks through a microphone attached to an earpiece. He can only hear one side of the conversation, but he imagines the person on the other end is not best pleased to be

interrupted by some bizarre tale about a performance artist. Even to him, his story sounds unlikely when he hears another
person repeating it.

'I have a man here who says he knows that artist Erin . . .
Amelia Heldt . . . yes, that one . . . no, he doesn't, that's not why
he's here . . . he's trying to get in touch with her . . . I know, I know
we did, but he really needs to contact her . . . of course, I know,
but he's lost his wife and he's come all the way from England . . .
I'm sorry, I don't know what difference that makes, but . . . yes, I
know . . . uh, huh . . . I understand . . . yes, I promise . . . no, I
won't bother you again . . . thank you for your time.'

She presses a button to hang up and removes her earpiece
before looking up at him. Her mouth is drawn into an apologetic line.

'No?' he says, trying to hold himself together.

'She said we signed a confidentiality agreement with the artist confirming we wouldn't reveal any personal details about her
under any circumstances. I remember now, she almost didn't
hire us because she didn't want to give us any details at all, but
our insurance means we have to cover all bases. You know, if an
actor falls down on someone's set or something to do with neg-
ligence, we have to be able to contact someone immediately, else
we could be liable . . .' She trails off.

'Right.' Marc clears his throat. 'I should leave you to get back
to work then.' He pivots slowly on his heels, remembering as if
drunkenly where he exited the elevator. How can he have come
this close and be turning around? Amelia's address is in this
office somewhere and he's giving up. He wonders what else he
can do. Threaten it out of the receptionist who's been nothing
but sweet to him? He almost turns around, almost clenches his
fist ready to slam it on her desk, almost conjures the words to
frighten her into submission. He's not some spy from a Le Carré
novel, though; he's just a man who's been told no.

'Wait,' Maria says, her cheeks suddenly flushing. 'Oh Jesus, she'll kill me if she finds out I'm doing this, but I'll get you the address. You have to promise not to say where you got it.'

'Really?' Marc says, feeling as if every muscle in his body is an elastic band that has just this second snapped. 'Of course, I promise.'

The woman smiles in spite of herself, shrugs and pushes her chair back to stand up. 'Wait here,' she says and toddles through one side of the heavy double doors behind her. Marc sways excitedly on the balls of his feet, then stuffs his hands in his pockets, pulls them out to scratch his upper arms, and paces around the room inspecting framed headshots. *Finally, I'm getting somewhere*, he thinks, then immediately replaces hope with worry. *What if it's another dead end? Would Amelia have given these people the right address?* A headache begins to throb in his temples as he thinks about the paranoid lengths Amelia's taken to keep herself hidden.

'She'll probably fire me for this,' Maria says as she re-enters the room. 'Still, I'm always talking about quitting.' She looks up and flushes again. 'Here you go.' She holds out a small sheet of headed notepaper with an address scrawled on it. 'It's in the Village,' she says. 'Around Fourth, I think. Do you know the way?'

Marc nods and tries to think of a way to thank her. He wants to hug her, but she's already shuffling back behind her desk.

'You've no idea —' he begins, but she cuts him off.

'Don't mention it, it's my good deed for the day. Now go find her!' She waves him in the direction of the elevator and turns back to her computer.

'Thank you,' he says and does as he's told.

The loopy address reads: 126 MacDougal Street, Apt 6.

Marc rides the E to Washington Square Park and walks along leafy West 4th until he spots a green sign reading MacDougal.

His intestines give a flip as he realizes he's less than a block away. He stops to take in the fire escapes and signs crowding above him, the litter and traffic and noise. A group of youngsters that could have stepped out of one of his classes swarms around him and a woman with a pushchair, enveloping them for a moment in their foreign chatter before crossing the street. Marc reaches out to steady himself against a lamppost, glancing at the non-plussed mother bending over her kid. He thinks of our street and our house and our family, imagines what a horror it must be to have a child in this city. He takes a breath and carries on. Tomorrow he'll be home with our girls, but today he's here for a reason. He counts the numbers down on the left side of the street, crossing over West 3rd and passing an array of restaurants and cafés on the other side. Between something called Silver World and Ali Baba, he finds a black-framed glass door beneath a plastic awning reading 126. Stepping back, he looks up to observe the arched windows towering four or five stories towards the sky. Sucking in his breath, he walks up to the address panel. He runs his index finger down the first five names, then stops. A.H. Apt 6. That has to be her. He's actually here. He's a finger-press away from meeting the woman who's eluded him all week.

He presses. He holds down the buzzer for far longer than necessary, then gives two more short rings for good measure. Forty seconds later, he tries again. Fifteen seconds after that, again. Then every thirty seconds for at least five minutes.

'Bitch!' he says, slamming his fist into the wall beneath the panel. Pain shoots from his already-bruised knuckles along his arm. He looks down and sees blood pricking through the grazed skin. His cheeks are wet with tears.

She's out, that's all, he tries telling himself, but this latest dead end feels more final than those before. This is the end of the road. This was his last chance and it's no good. He stumbles away from the doorway. Turning back the way he came, he takes a few aimless steps and wonders what to do. He could go to the park, check out the Arc de Triomphe rip-off. Will it remind him of Paris? Of being there with me? Kissing on the Eiffel Tower, walking hand in hand down the Champs-Elysées with Lizzie's stuffed toy in my rucksack? Was I betraying him even then? He wipes his eyes on his shirtsleeve. He feels dangerously close to hyperventilating. Or passing out. It's three o'clock and he's eaten nothing all day. Without looking, he steps into the road and crosses to the other side. At the corner of 3rd Street, a turquoise awning announces Ben's Pizzeria. He pushes open the glass door and steps up to the counter. He asks the aproned guy for two slices of pepperoni and a Coke. He sits in a chair by the window and chews methodically, tasting nothing. He stares dumbly at the intersection on the other side of the glass. He doesn't feel better. The cheese sits angrily on the top of his stomach. He wants to throw up. Still, he slurps more Coke. His hand is sore and his head still pounds, but his body doesn't matter right now. Nothing does. He's in New York for no reason at all. It's been a waste of time and money. It doesn't matter what he does next because whatever it does won't bring him any closer to understanding me. We're further from each other now than we've ever been. Amelia has forced him further than he's been from our daughters too. She's turned him into a daft, middle-aged man chasing ghosts in an unfriendly city when he should be at home with what's left of his family. Serena Graves was right, he should have steered clear. He believes her now. Amelia is dangerous.

He sits in the restaurant for a long time. He can't bring himself to leave. He watches people wait at the lights and cross the street, pass by his window without the faintest of glances, then carry on to wherever they're going. He makes a game of studying people's faces, trying to imagine what pain each of them has experienced, whether they've ever lost someone they loved or been deceived, if they've ever felt torn apart, ready to implode. He watches each one disappear on their way and resents them for not feeling what he's feeling. He drains the last of his drink and throws the cup in the bin. Looking back out the window he sees a woman waiting for the lights. Her back is to him. She's wearing a long cardigan and harem trousers. She has sandals on her feet. He traces his eyes up her back, over the canvas bag slung across her right shoulder, and up to her thick, curly hair. It's too long really; I got mine cut every six weeks, always said I'd end up with a mullet if I didn't. And this woman is heavier, isn't she? A tad curvier. And even if she looked just like me and he was to leap out of his chair and run outside, he'd find he's imagining things anyway, wouldn't he? Just like in the supermarket. He'd make a fool of himself and feel even worse than he does now.

The light changes and the woman steps across the street. Barely consciously, he scrapes his chair back and throws his rucksack on his shoulder. He pushes through the glass door and sprints across the street as the lights change back and engines rev. He stops on the other side, panting. She's four, maybe five, steps ahead of him and walking briskly towards the park. He has no desire to call my name. He prays she won't turn around. He wants the illusion to continue. He knows it can't be me, but he feels more alive than he has all week, all year perhaps. He clenches his fists at the thought of this woman turning to reveal a face that's not mine, a life that's not over.

He follows her, keeping an inconspicuous distance and deliberately looking away if he thinks she's about to turn her head. He studies the back of her. How dare she bounce with each step, lift her hand to tuck her hair behind her ear, fill her lungs with this callous city's air? This woman's existence feels malicious to him, but while she keeps her back to him he also finds comfort there. He doesn't want this to end. He doesn't care that it isn't real. He's finally going crazy, but it feels good. At 4th Street, she crosses diagonally over the intersection and enters the park. The dusty greens engulf them. *Alex would like this*, he thinks, remembering how I used to rant about Chicago being the perfect city because it combined the bustle and artistic satisfaction of a metropolis with the tranquillity of miles of lakeside parks. 'I lived two blocks from an "L" stop and four from a beach!' I'd exclaim, as if unequivocally proving the city's utopian properties.

Fake me walks quickly through the park, oblivious to Marc as her shadow. She checks her watch, but doesn't look back. He takes in her dark curls, the shape of her shoulders, the sway of her hips. He morphs every detail with the memories of the wife he hasn't seen in fourteen months. With every step they take, he grows more and more certain that she is me, even while another, saner part of his mind increases its conviction that he's finally lost it. He doesn't notice the roller skater that almost knocks him down and shouts, 'Dickhead!' as he speeds away. He stops caring about their leafy surroundings and barely registers as they skirt around a fountain and emerge from the park at Washington Square Arch, the derogatory monument he'd thought might break his heart. It flecks its shadow over his shoulders as he follows the woman through crowds of camera-clutching tourists. She turns right and walks to the first intersection. Crossing diagonally again, this time on a one-way light and causing a cab to blare its horn to which she flips a ringless middle finger, she disappears into a shop. He hurries across and steps into the deli a couple of minutes behind her. Suddenly conspicuous and more than a little afraid he'll accidentally bump into the front side of his imaginary wife, he takes a basket and selects a shelf at random. He studies an array of pay-by-the-pound cereals, then shuffles carefully to the salad bar at the back of the store.

Cautiously, he turns around and scans what he can see of the shop. There she is. At the cashier. Thankfully facing away. He gazes at the back of her head for a moment, feeling equal measures of hope and despair, then grabs an over-priced muffin and scuttles towards the cashier. By the time he's paid for his alibi purchase, the woman has crossed back towards the park. He hurries to catch up, noticing at the last minute that she's turned to skim the perimeter rather than head back through it. Does she have another errand to run? Is she heading home to her real husband? Marc's headache throbs with his heartbeat. He clenches his jaw with the pain. They pass buildings waving NYU flags. How old is this woman? He wonders if she's even in the same ballpark as me. What can you tell by the back of a head? Maybe she's a student. Maybe she's someone's child, someone who gets to spend Christmases and birthdays with her family. Maybe she has her whole life ahead of her. He sniffs, realizing his eyes are filling with tears. 'You're a fucking mess,' he says aloud and a woman with a pushchair turns to face him. In a split second he feels her take in his crumpled clothes and the dried blood on his knuckles. She hurries away.

The woman he's following crosses the next road and heads into a towering, windowless building. Bobst Library, he reads on the sign. He hovers in the shadow of a tree on the corner, afraid following her into a library he doesn't know might give his game away. While he waits, he tries to talk sense into himself. *I can take the subway back to the hotel, make sure my things are packed, go out to dinner, even see a show if I like. The trip doesn't have to be a waste. I can salvage my last night in New York at least. I can leave this corner right now if I want to. I don't have to act like this. I don't have to be this man.*

It almost works. He steps up to the crosswalk a couple of times, but scurries back to his shadow before the glowing sign says Walk. *I'll follow her to her next stop*, he tells himself. *It'll probably be closer to a subway station anyway. I'll just pretend a little longer.*

He stands in the shadows for nineteen minutes. He knows

310

because he keeps checking his watch. Eventually she emerges. She looks both ways along the street, but he manages to press himself into the tree in time to avoid either of them seeing the other. He knows in his heart he's probably going to follow her until it becomes abundantly obvious she isn't me, but he's not ready for that to be now. Not ready to find out what that realization will make him do.

She turns left, three books hooked under one arm and her deli bag in the other hand. She turns left again on to Sullivan Street. The pavement is almost empty, so he drops back, allowing almost a block to stretch between them. She takes the first right and is almost out of sight by the time he makes the turn. She's heading left a block ahead of him. He quickens his pace, trying to catch up. He reaches the corner, double takes as he recognizes the sign for Ben's Pizzeria, then turns back on to MacDougal Street.

There, up ahead of him, ducking towards the glass door between Silver World and Ali Baba, is the woman with my thick, curly bob. He watches as she transfers her deli bag to the arm with the books and fishes in her canvas bag for keys. He's only a few paces away now. She's about to disappear into the building. This is going to be the end of his fantasy, whatever the outcome.

He opens his mouth to speak. A large, empty breath comes out but no sound. He tries again. What is he trying to say? He's forgotten. Whose name is he calling? A third time and a fourth, and he manages nothing. They're two metres apart now, his legs still working even while his tongue refuses.

Finally, he locates his voice. He parts his lips once more and rolls his breath over his tongue, past his cheeks in order to sound the first 'A' of 'Amelia'. But, before the rest of the name can tumble from his mouth, the woman turns. She whips that iconic bob to the other side of her neck, twisting her shoulders and waist, almost dropping her books and shopping in the process. She swivels to face him, speaking before she's turned, calling out, 'Look, you cocksucking asshole, stop follow—'

But her words seem to choke her. She does drop her books now. And her shopping. Something cracks. Maybe eggs. The breath falls away from her insult, just as it does from the wrong name he's trying to call. Her blue eyes meet his. The air leaves his lungs. His knees feel weak. *I'm not crazy*, is what he thinks as his body hits the pavement. And then I'm rushing over to him, calling his name. 'Marc, Marc! Are you okay?'

He looks up at me, the brownstone with the arched windows towering above my head. 'I found you,' he says, then slips into unconsciousness.

'Have you considered maybe you wanted to be caught?'

I shake my head. He's so fucking smug. He thinks he can see into my psyche. Even now, he still wants to believe he's found a nugget of remorse, prove I never really intended to get away.

'Well,' he says, 'what other explanation do you have for leaving your passport and the letters to be found?'

'I didn't leave them to be found,' I say. This is how he works: he talks his bullshit until I'm so pissed off I can't help but correct him. 'I couldn't take anything with me, but I couldn't bring myself to destroy them either. All I could do was hide them and hope they'd sit collecting dust in the attic until maybe one day I could retrieve them. I thought the police would believe I'd drowned and Marc would move on and that would be that. I didn't think he'd have a reason to go rooting through everything.'

'But you kept your mother's house. You left Amelia's work in a gallery.'

'I tried to sell a photograph years ago, that's all.' I'm almost shouting now. I can feel my face growing red. I hate this man. 'I'd forgotten all about it, okay? And I never thought Marc would go there.'

He folds his arms, shaking his head. 'I think you left a trail.'

I don't know why he is here. It's not a proper session. His statement has been heard; his work is done. In an hour or two, maybe more, maybe less, my fate will be decided and our relationship will be over. He'll go back to his life and his other patients, and I'll head off in search of my next identity. Criminal or insane, what a choice.

I look at him and sigh. It will be strange not seeing him after all this time. 'I was trying to give myself options,' I say. 'I thought

I might want to return to Lyme one day, after it had all blown over. I miscalculated, that's all.'

'How does that make you feel? After all your work, you made a mistake.'

I shrug. 'It was minor. It should have been fine. The police didn't find anything.'

He nods. 'It was only Marc who put everything together, only he cared enough to solve your mysteries.'

We sit in silence for a moment. I have an urge to ask him questions, to find out who he is, why he does this. I wonder if today he might tell me.

He crosses his ankle over his knee and leans forward. 'You like to be in control, Alex, but the most important characteristic of the subconscious is its inability to be controlled. It's scary for someone like you to acknowledge that there's a part of you that's ever-present but ultimately unknowable. You've tried to be the puppetmaster your whole life, but today you're finally having to accept that, like everyone else, you're also a puppet.'

I screw up my face. I want to scream.

'Does it please you that it was Marc?' he says. 'Does it make you feel loved that he went to all that effort? That he tried harder than the authorities to find you?'

The backs of my eyes begin to prickle. I want to tell him to shut up, to leave me the fuck alone. I hate that I made mistakes. I hate that I am here, that this is how it ends. I didn't mean for this to happen. I thought I'd figured it all out. I went over and over everything. After all that planning, I honestly don't know how I missed things.

'I return to my original theory,' he says. 'Deep down, I think you wanted to be found. And, more specifically, you wanted Marc to find you.'

2014

Friday, 4 April
The End

Marc woke on my couch. I'd had to ask a neighbour to help me carry him in. I told them he was a relative from out of town, that the medication he was on made him prone to fainting, that he just needed rest. I don't know if they bought it, but what I like about Manhattan is that nobody pries.

I didn't know what to say now, how to start. Marc had been out for a while, but I hadn't known whether to call an ambulance.

'I wasn't sure if you had medical insurance,' I said. 'It's sorta complicated here. You didn't hit your head, so I thought you'd be okay.'

I winced at my own American twang. Marc looked at me.

'Can I get you a cup of tea?' I asked in a clipped British accent.

He pulled himself into a sitting position. I'd bandaged his hand while he was out. I'd also changed into a long black dress. I'm not sure why now. What had gone through my head as he lay passed out on my sofa? *Must look nice for the husband I abandoned?*

'Is it –' Marc said, his voice betraying a condemned man's hope. 'Is it you?'

I turned away, nodded.

'I –'

Nothing came after that word. I'm not even sure which one of us said it.

I snuck a peek at him. He looked good. I know I had no right to, but I'd missed him. He was rolling his eyes around the apartment. We were in a light, open-plan living room-cum-kitchen. The floors were polished wood, the only frills the lilies on the coffee table and the fake coals in the fireplace. I knew what Marc was thinking: it felt like a show-home.

'It's not much,' I said. 'But it's comfortable.'

'Amelia,' he said, but nothing else.

We were quiet once more. I heard a siren trickle through a crack in the window frame, a far-off whine that increased in urgency as it came closer and closer, eventually howling for attention right beneath us, then fading slowly back into nothing as it headed uptown. The silence in its wake filled the air with treacle.

'You and Amelia.' Marc spoke as if in shock. It wasn't a question. He didn't look at me, he wasn't asking for an answer.

'Marc,' I whispered.

He snapped his head now and I felt his eyes burn into me. He was scrutinizing every inch of me, the strange, mortal body he'd spent months searching for, the simple woman for whom he'd travelled.

'Are you – are you living here?' he asked, this time definitely a question.

'It's not what you think.' My voice came out louder now, breaking through its whisper.

He stood up, knocking the coffee table with his shin. The vase wobbled. 'I need to get out of here,' he said.

'Please,' I said, stepping forwards.

'Get away from me,' he growled, finally making eye contact. I recognized so little in those eyes.

I looked away, backed up to a stool beside the breakfast bar, securing four or five feet of no-man's land between us. 'I wanted to do it differently.'

'Fucking hell, Alex,' he shouted, kicking the coffee table now. It scraped across the floor towards the window. I watched the vase topple, then roll, spilling water and scattering petals. It reached the edge and seemed to hover in the air. My body jolted with the smash.

Marc sat down, hid his face in his hands.

My voice was a whisper. 'I thought and tried and ached not to break your heart, but we were happy.'

He let his hands drop, turned to face me.

'I couldn't tell you I needed to leave, you wouldn't have understood.'

His nostrils flared.

'If I'd told you about this,' I said, gesturing around the room, 'it would have ruined everything we had, you'd have thought I'd lied, that our vows, our life was untrue.' My last word hung in the air for a moment.

'Was it?' he said finally.

'No.'

'I thought you were dead.'

'I'm sorry,' I said. 'I thought it'd be better that way. I left my things by the river.'

'There was blood!' he said, shifting his weight as if he was about to stand up again. I imagined his hands around my throat. I almost wanted him to hit me.

'I needed it to look like –' I swallowed, touched my stomach. 'I cut myself.'

Marc shook his head. 'No, the police said there was a lot, two or three litres. That's too much. Nobody does that to themselves.'

'I was aiming for two,' I said. 'I'd read that would be possible. It was meant to be the final test of my commitment. I was timing myself, but I lost consciousness, came to and I was still bleeding. I thought I'd messed everything up.'

Marc was still.

'I patched myself up,' I said, 'and walked along the bike paths to Selby. It took forever, I was so weak, but the next morning I slipped away on a bus in different clothes. I knew it would hurt, but I thought you and the girls could move on, remember me fondly. I didn't mean for it to become this big thing.'

I stopped myself. I hadn't meant to say that.

'Big thing?' Marc said.

'I knew there would be an investigation,' I said more quietly, 'but I thought you'd trust the evidence. I knew you'd never believe it if I made it look like suicide, so this was the only way. I thought you'd make peace with the fact I was gone.'

Marc looked like he wanted to spit at me.

'I'm sorry,' I whispered.

We sat in silence, our bodies still.

'Can I get you a cup of tea?' I repeated.

I guess those words snaked through his ears and sank their fangs into his brain. Something snapped. 'Tea? You're offering me tea? You ran away from our life, left me for another woman, made me think you were dead, and now you're offering me a cup of tea?'

I froze. 'No! I've never – I would never – there's no one else, there never has been.'

'What about Amelia?' he said, his fists clenched.

'Marc, I'm Amelia. Amelia is me.'

Marc stared at me like he was trying to figure out what on earth he was looking at. I made myself still. I wasn't a person in that moment, but some strange, distasteful object. I watched Marc's jaw move back and forth, his neck thicken with tension. Slowly he began to move his head from side to side. 'No,' he said. 'No.'

'I'm sorry,' I said again.

'No,' he said, a little louder this time, but not exactly to me. 'I've read her letters. I've seen her show.'

'It's kinda complicated,' I said, slipping into my American twang again. The only time I'd had to switch like this was when my mum's phone number rang. My heart had pounded every time the blue and white Skype logo filled my screen and I had to answer as Caitlin. I thought lying to the police would have been the hardest part, but even with my vowels flattened and my fingers muffling the microphone, my biggest fear was that Marc would recognize my voice.

Just like those phone calls, I waited now, terrified and excited, for my husband to piece it all together. I'd never said any of this aloud, but I'd been rehearsing this explanation for years. It sounds strange, but it was almost a relief.

'I made her up before I left Chicago,' I said. 'It was going to be my final project to try to construct an identity, see how easy or hard it would be to get a work permit and a social security number.'

Marc looked at me like I was speaking a foreign language. I turned away, spoke to the wall. I needed to say this. 'We met that summer and I couldn't stop thinking about you when I went back. I still worked on my project, but my heart was no longer in it. Then you turned up at my dad's on Boxing Day and I knew I wasn't going back. I didn't want to. I knew that for certain, but it was still a hard decision. I wanted to keep hold of something. I'd set almost everything up already. I'd even taken a driving test in her name. At each point I kept thinking that this was where I'd get caught, but I wasn't. So by the time I returned there were only a few tweaks left to make, which I managed from England.'

I finally looked at Marc. His face was pale. 'What are you saying?' he said. 'You faked an identity?'

'Borrowed one,' I said. 'I found a girl who died of cot death the year I was born. It was perfect: she hadn't registered for anything, and nobody except her parents had really met her. They'd moved shortly after she was born, so she'd died in a different state and there was no cross-referencing between birth and death offices. So I applied for a certified copy of her birth certificate.'

Marc looked like he was about to throw up. I cleared my throat.

'You're allowed to request that. It's legitimate. Then I used the birth certificate to get a driver's permit and all this other stuff. I even managed to register her for my classes. My plan was to –'

'I don't care,' Marc said, cutting me off.

'I want you to understand.'

He held out his hand, palm flat towards me. 'I don't care any more, Alex. I don't care about your stupid whims and all your fucked up ideas. All I've cared about for more than a year is finding my wife.'

I was silent. I didn't know whether to believe him. I'd wanted to tell him this for years. I knew I couldn't without ruining our marriage, but the stupid thing was I'd always felt he was the one person who'd get it. If he could put aside his pain for a moment, I thought he'd see the magnitude of what I'd achieved. I thought maybe he could be proud of me.

'There was always this big deal made about how good SAIC would look on our resumés,' I said. Marc shook his head in disbelief, but I carried on. 'Everyone in the art world clings so preciously to their work because that's their identity, their justification for being, but I wanted to question how fragile those identities were. If I could make Amelia seem like a real student, I thought I could start this discussion about the irrelevance of the person. I managed to confuse the administrators so much that they merged our student records. Every grade I got was actually being given to someone who didn't exist.'

I couldn't tell if Marc was listening. He sat perfectly still, his gaze focused on the mess of broken glass on the floor. I should clean that up, I thought, but didn't move.

'She was ready,' I said. 'But then I stayed in England and we began our life together. I felt so far away from it all that it didn't

320

seem important to tell you about some silly project I never completed. But I kept thinking about it, and it niggled and niggled until I started wondering if I could still do it. I wanted to see if I could make Amelia graduate. I still had to come up with these pieces she could make for her final year without me being there. It was tricky. Another project I'd been working on was this idea that I could write to my future self. I'd set up this network of mail forwarding addresses so I could post a letter and it would go halfway around the world and boomerang back to me after a month or so. That way, I could be in epistolary contact with my past and future selves. I'd send a letter to England and it'd be sent around Europe and then to New York, where someone would forward it to a box in Chicago, where I'd pick it up. I tweaked my system a little so things ended up in York and it became me writing to myself as Amelia to Alex. It turned into a useful tool for me to work out her projects and imagine the life she was living. It gave her a firmer identity.'

He let me drone on. I could tell he wasn't listening. Something was occurring to him. 'Your mother,' he said.

I snapped my head towards him. My first thought was panic, then pity. 'You found out?'

He nodded.

'I'm sorry,' I said, realizing how pointless my apologies were at this stage. 'I hated lying to you. I really did. But Mum dying, it was convenient. It coincided with my – I mean Amelia's – work really taking off here. She was becoming a big deal and I needed to come out here more often. I told my mum about Amelia that first weekend we spent together. I don't know why, but it was so emotional and she was talking about being married to my dad and it just came out. She was supportive. Right at the end, she was the one who suggested I keep her alive. She said she was the perfect alibi. She also said I could never tell you, you'd never understand.'

'She was right,' he said, folding his arms.

I sucked my teeth, decided to persist. 'It was a little project to begin with. Just something to occupy my mind while you were at work and the only people I had to talk to were the mums at toddler group who just wanted to discuss potty training and their precious darlings' first words or steps or whatever. I needed something creative. It was fun, and harmless. I set up projects over the internet, got people to post the results in chat rooms. I felt like an invisible puppetmaster. I had this virtual life as well as my beautiful real one.'

'Why keep it from me?' His voice was softer now. It undid something in me.

'You were so scared in the beginning,' I said. 'You studied me every second you could, looking for signs I'd changed my mind. Sometimes I felt like you thought I wasn't real, thought I might dissolve in the rain or wash down the plughole. I didn't want to worry you. I didn't want you to think you weren't enough.'

'I obviously wasn't.'

'No, you were. This was just something I did for myself. I never expected Amelia to do well.' I paused. 'But this one piece blew everything up. Suddenly she was being offered grants and gallery spaces, and these journalists were trying to figure out who she was. It was a nightmare in a way. I had to figure it out on a much grander scale. I got myself a second phone, learnt how to cover my tracks online.'

Marc frowned.

'You found me with it once, remember? Not long before – I guess I was getting sloppy.'

'Wait,' Marc said. 'The iPhone at our party? I thought you were acting strange, but you hate iPhones, you refused –'

'I wanted to keep things separate. Amelia had all these skills, all this knowledge about proxies and encryption, because she had to. She needed them to survive. But Alex didn't. I liked switching off from all that, asking you to fix things when the internet cut out, living physically in our world.'

Marc pinched the bridge of his nose, his face screwed up like he was in pain.

'I was terrified of getting caught, of course. Not just by you, by journalists or gallerists, anyone. But it was exciting too. All that attention. It was everything I'd once dreamt of.'

'So you decided you'd kill off Alex and be Amelia?' Marc snapped, looking at me now. 'Her life was more exciting, was it?'

'It wasn't like that,' I said.

He shook his head and stood up again. I held out my hand, panicked he would leave. I wanted him to stay.

'I was doing both. I hated lying to you, but it made me feel alive being able to have it all. We were happier than ever and you didn't have to know that every few months I went to New York, not Dorset. I felt like I'd won the lottery. I hadn't had to sacrifice a thing. If anything, being Amelia some of the time made me a better Alex. Having that creative outlet meant I could be a better wife and mother.'

'Because that wasn't *all* you were?'

'Don't say it like it's a bad thing. Do you know how many times I heard some woman at a PTA meeting or bake sale wish she'd done more with her life? Not wish she hadn't had children or hadn't married, but wish she'd done something that mattered to the outside world.'

'Why couldn't you just tell me?' he said. 'I'd have supported you.'

'Would you?' I searched his face. 'You think you would and you'd probably have tried, but we wouldn't have had what we did if you'd known. We'd have been torn between each of our ambitions. I changed when I met you. I didn't set out to, but I did. I wanted to be what you wanted, what you needed. What you thought I was. And I never stopped wanting that. But the reason I could keep doing it was because I still held on to a little piece of what I was before. I felt secure in my identity. If I hadn't kept Amelia alive, I'd have reverted back eventually. I'd have resented you for the changes I made in myself. I'd have been grouchy and miserable just like everyone else with failed dreams. We wouldn't have been as happy as we were.'

'But you're telling me we weren't,' he said, raising his voice. 'If we were happy and our life was perfect, why the fuck would you leave?'

I was quiet for a moment and faced the window when I finally answered. 'Because of the girls. I realized that when I was younger the future held promise. I believed I was heading for happiness. I knew I might not get there, but I never imagined I'd stop trying. Then I sat in our office one day and realized I'd settled. There I was, writing a proposal for a PhD I didn't want to do, while journalists and curators all over Manhattan were vying for Amelia's attention. I was caring about school fetes and buying the right kind of cereal, when a whole world of war and famine, race and gender, politics and protest was going on beyond the A64.'

I heard Marc inhale as if he was about to speak. I turned to face him, talking quickly in case he interrupted. 'However much I loved you and the girls, I realized it wasn't enough. Because Charlotte and Lizzie were watching me live this half-life. Some of it was magical, of course, but the bits in between: the daft conversations about television programmes, the office politics, the minuscule dramas of my students, the endless committees and meetings, the packed lunches that needed making every day, the house that always had to be cleaned — it all felt so insignificant. What kind of example was I setting?'

I grew conscious of my flailing hands, let them drop to my sides. I expected Marc to laugh or shout, but he just stared at me.

'I felt more like an actor when I was being Alex than Amelia,'

I said. 'And that was so stupid, because not only was Alex a terrible role model for our girls, half the time I didn't even feel like she was a good mother. I tried to turn myself into this smiling, subservient wife, but I just kept getting it wrong, I kept –'

'You're making me sound like some 1950s monster,' Marc said, cutting me off. 'Do you know how hurtful this is? I never wanted you to be a smiling, subservient wife.'

'I don't mean it like that,' I said. 'It wasn't you. *I* wanted to be that wife. I told myself being there for you and the girls made me happy. Then one day Lizzie said she wanted to be like Fran and I felt like I'd just been shaken awake. I realized I'd been telling myself stories about how happy I was in order to make myself so. If I had a bad day, then the next day I'd just rewrite my memory, tell myself yesterday had been great. So each time I did have a wobble, wondering if everything I was doing was wrong, I'd think about my memories and realize how perfect my life was, how momentary and insignificant this feeling must be. I was living in a kind of self-constructed fairy tale.'

'Jesus,' Marc said. 'This is ridiculous. Can you hear yourself?'

'It's what I felt. I wanted us to be happy so much that I devoted myself to making it so. But I also started to have nightmares about breaking down and confessing everything, ruining all that we had. I didn't want to do that, but I worried about the damage I was doing to the girls by erasing so much of myself, by denying what I truly felt. I started thinking about making Amelia full-time. It was a fleeting fantasy at first, and I felt guilty for even entertaining the idea. But I kept wondering about it. I'd daydream during boring seminars where my hung-over second years gabbled about essays they'd only read the introductions to. I didn't know if it'd even be possible. But the more I thought about it, the more miserable I grew as Alex.'

I saw Marc wince.

'Not miserable,' I corrected. 'Certainly not with you and the girls, but restless. I couldn't imagine the future. All I could see was me gradually dissolving into the resentful woman I would have been had I never created Amelia. And Lizzie and Charlotte growing up thinking that was okay. I started working out how I could make it happen with the least amount of pain.'

Marc snorted.

'The hardest thing was to get Amelia a passport,' I said. I had to say this or I never would. 'I'd always used mine when travelling, but that'd be no good if I wanted you to believe I'd died. The paperwork took forever and at one point I was worried it wouldn't be ready in time, but Amelia had been making social security contributions for the past few years and she had an untarnished record, so in the end it was issued. The rest of the plans were pretty simple. I'd given myself a year to organize it. I rented this apartment and began to tie up loose ends. I wasn't sure I'd go through with it, right up to the last minute even.'

My voice fell away. We heard another siren, but it didn't pass as close this time. I listened to the cars on the street below, the occasional horn.

After full minutes of suffocating silence Marc spoke, taking pains to keep his voice measured. 'Do you have an idea of the utter devastation you have wrought upon our family? Upon our children?'

I opened my mouth but shut it again without speaking.

'It's destroyed me,' he continued. '*You've* destroyed me. Look what I've become.' He gestured to his scuffed jeans and four-day stubble. 'I'm running around New York trying to come to terms with having lost the woman I love, while she's wining and dining the city's art critics. While I've been in police stations and making public appeals, comforting our daughters when there's no comfort to be had, you've been scrawling quotations on gallery walls and paying actresses to stick their tongues down people's throats. It's absurd.'

I blinked at the mention of the gallery and Erin. I couldn't speak.

'But, like you said, we're *insignificant*.' He shook his head. 'Everyone changes, Al. It's life. It's being a fucking grown up. Do you think I got everything I wanted? Do you know how tiring it is living with someone who refuses to take anything seriously? How much I wanted an adult conversation some-times? A blazing row even! I'm not a violent man, but sometimes I wanted to slap you. It was like having another child in the house. And all this, you think it's better for our girls? You think you're a good role model now? What sort of role model can you be when they think you're dead?'

'I was going to –' I let out a sob.

'What? What were you going to do?'

I took a breath and wiped my eyes. 'I was going to wait until they were older. Then I'd come back, show them what I'd done.'

'And you think they'd –'

'I know they'll never forgive me,' I said quickly, cutting him off. I didn't need him to spell out how much I'd sacrificed. 'I know I'll never be able to undo the hurt, but as adults I think they might find a way to understand, to be proud of me, and to see how important all of this is.'

Marc was shaking his head.

'I know I will never have a relationship with them again,' I said. 'You have no idea how much that hurts, but I honestly think I can be more to them as Amelia.'

'Jesus Christ, Al,' Marc said. 'Even for you this is ridiculous. You've rationalized it beyond belief. My mum's right about you.'

We held each other's gaze.

'You should have told me,' he said.

I shook my head, scattering tears. 'I couldn't. It would have erased everything that went before.'

'And this hasn't?'

'I saw my parents destroy everything that had ever been lovely about our family,' I said. 'They became these miserable individuals living at opposite ends of the country, unable to mention the other's name. We weren't even left with our memories of the good times.'

'You think memories are what counts?' he shouted. 'You think your daughters are better off with the *memory* of a mother than the real thing? I'll give you a fucking memory. How about Lizzie holding a knife to her skin because she thinks her mum thinks it's cool? How about Charlotte bawling her eyes out because I can't tuck her in like you do? How about Christmas and holidays and birthdays where the only thing any of us wanted was yo—' Marc's voice cracked.

I kept my face still, imagined playing statues with Char.

When he spoke again, it was so controlled and quiet that it made the hairs on the back of my neck stand on end. 'You left us so we could continue our perfect life without you, but did it not occur to you that *everything* in our lives would continue to be about you? That we'd *never* escape you?'

I closed my eyes. I couldn't look at him.

'You weren't sparing us, you know? You were sparing yourself. It would have been much kinder to tell us how crazy and selfish you were, but no, of course poor little Alex couldn't stand the idea of someone being cross with her. Everyone had to like her and get on and remember her as a bloody saint. So what could she do? Make us think she was dead, of course. Ensure we all sobbed and wept so you could feel fully loved as you fucked off to your new life. Does that about cover it?'

I squeezed my eyes tighter as more tears rolled down my cheeks.

'Say something,' he said.

I heard him step towards me.

'You have to say something!'

'I feel awful,' I said, my eyes still closed. 'About you and the girls. About everything.'

'You deserve to feel awful.'

I heard him take another step.

'I've thought about them every day, missed their silly smiles and the tiny ways they grow.' My knees were shaking. 'But I couldn't have stayed. As much as I love them and you, what I'm doing is better for all of us. It's more important.'

'Than being a mother?' he yelled. The volume shocked me into opening my eyes. His face was red. A vein bulged across his forehead, tears streaked his cheeks.

I took a breath and forced myself to make eye contact. 'They have you. I would never have left if I didn't think they'd be okay without me. But I have a chance to do more than wipe their noses and hold them when they're sad. Amelia has a platform, a responsibility to explore ideas, to challenge things. It started out as play, but it's more significant now. It's about far more than my or your or the girls' comfort.'

Marc snorted. 'So you had a *social responsibility* to leave?'

'To do something more than spend my days lecturing uninterested middle-class kids, stopping at the supermarket on the way home and slumping satisfiedly into my own over-privileged life.'

Marc's jaw twitched. I felt like I'd slapped him.

'I wanted to send a note,' I said, 'to tell you all not to worry, to get on with your lives, but that wouldn't have worked. The number one rule in all of the books I read is to cut off completely. I made a donation to my search. It wasn't enough to make me feel better, but I thought it might make up for wasting resources.'

Marc frowned, processing what I'd said. He'd felt grateful for that money. 'Our life was a lie,' he said.

'No.' I stepped forward. We were a foot apart.

'It was a complete fiction,' he croaked.

'Every relationship is part fiction,' I said, kneeling at his feet. 'Nothing between us was untrue. It was just not all that there was for me.'

I looked up, willing him to understand. He wiped his eyes.

'I know it's not enough, but I'm sorry I hurt you.' My tears were falling on to my dress, forming irregular polka dots as they soaked into the fabric.

'I thought you were dead.' His Adam's apple bobbed. 'Or worse.'

'I'm sorry,' I repeated.

'*Sorry?*' I think he wanted his voice to be angry, but it came out more weary than furious. 'How can you sit there and say sorry? You saw us on the news. You must have to make that donation. You saw how it affected us. How could you do it?'

'I had to.'

'Like that? We were friends, we knew each other. I'm not some horrible monster of a husband who made you sacrifice your dreams. You could have talked to me. You *should* have. You should have given me a chance. I deserved that much. Any man deserves to at least know if his wife wants to leave him.'

'But I didn't *want* to leave you, that's the whole point.' I looked him in the eye and his galloping horse of anger missed a step, stumbled and threatened to topple him to the ground.

'Now I'm utterly confused.' He threw his hands to the ceiling in melodramatic exasperation.

'I *needed* to leave because Amelia had to. But Alex never wanted to. So she – I – couldn't have told you, couldn't have made you understand, because it wasn't what I was feeling when I was there with you. I was never a woman who wanted to lose her husband and children. I'm still not. But I was also not a woman who could have stayed. It's more complicated than that. It always was.'

'Thirteen years of marriage and two beautiful children and all you can come up with is "it's complicated"?' Another man would have shouted those words, accompanied them with smashing crockery or a fist hurtling through a piece of plaster. But I knelt at Marc's feet, our pupils glued together like they used to be when we were silly twenty-somethings marvelling at how lucky we were to have found one another. His voice was a whisper, a plea. His horse had sped off without its jockey. Someone had unscrewed the cap and let the air out of his anger. I knew what he wanted was for me to say something that would make him forgive me, something that could make sense of the situation we were in. I wished I could find the words.

'Maybe I'd have sympathized,' he said softly. 'Maybe we could have made it work. Maybe we could have moved to New York.'

'You really think so?' I said. 'You think if I'd told you I'd been leading a secret life since we met, you'd have said, "Oh great, congratulations, let me just quit my job and move across the Atlantic to live in an overcrowded city I'm bound to hate"?'

He glared at me. He wanted to say *yes, I might have*, just to challenge my infuriating certainty.

'You understand,' I said. 'I know you understand. Or you can if you try. I told you it was strange, being a different person with you. I never regretted leaving Chicago, never regretted moving in with you and marrying you, but I still missed the girl I used to be, the woman I might have become. And I don't want our girls to grow up like that. Don't you ever wonder what it would be like if you'd said, "Fuck responsibilities and salaries and mortgages, I'm going to write my novel"?'

I paused. He'd flinched at the mention of his lost ambition and I wondered if I'd gone too far. Of course I had. With everything, obviously, but in particular by bringing up what he hadn't achieved while he was still trying to come to terms with what I had.

'I'm sorry,' I said for the fortieth time. 'I didn't mean that. I was just trying to find a way to have it all: to be your perfect wife and the girls' perfect mother without feeling like I'd lost a part of my core.'

He shook his head slowly from side to side. 'If Lizzie and Charlotte had a perfect mother, she'd be with them right now.'

Before he finished that sentence, my torso crumpled. I buried my face in my hands and my back heaved with sobs as I absorbed, maybe for the first time, what I'd done to our daughters. I knew, of course. I'd thought about them every day, justified it all. I had academic, objective arguments – I still do – but seeing Marc there, hearing him say it, they suddenly meant nothing. Marc watched me sob, his own face running rivers of tears and snot. Maybe a part of him enjoyed watching me cry, wanted me to feel a little of what he'd felt over the past fourteen months. He'd have been justified in that. A line from a song has played over and over in my head since that day: *You can cry me a river, cry me a river, I cried a river over you.*

But my husband is stronger and more compassionate than I am. He felt his insides tear as he watched his wife, the woman he adored, break down before him. Without thinking it through or analysing the complexities of the gesture in this convoluted set of circumstances, he reached down to touch my shoulder. He folded his limbs and sat opposite me on the floorboards.

I looked up at him. His hand rested awkwardly on my shoulder, our first touch in fourteen months. I imagined the heat of his skin unknotting something inside me. I wanted to feel whole again. To feel like Alex: Marc's wife, his love, his flesh.

He removed his hand and reached for the chain around my neck. He lifted the silver pendant from my chest, fingering the tiny paper plane. Then he let it drop and I jerked my body forward. I pressed my lips to his. I kissed my husband when I'd thought I never would again. He tasted of salt and snot. His lips were fleshy and real. I felt him pull away. I held his shoulders, kissed him harder, insistently. I imagined we were regaining ground, remembering ourselves. This was not one of the kisses either of us had missed and imagined while lying in bed alone. It couldn't make up for every hello and goodbye we'd skipped, every spontaneous display of emotion and predictable anniversary romance. I knew this was a kiss that could never be repeated. I felt we were sucking life out of each other, taking what we needed to be able to go on.

Marc turned his head and leant away from me. Without a word, he peeled my fingers from his shoulders and pushed my arms to my sides. I lost my balance on my knees and fell against the floorboards. He lurched to his feet and looked down at me.

I opened my mouth to speak, but nothing came out. He reached for his rucksack and backed towards the door. He didn't break our stare until he stepped into the hall and allowed the triple-bolt door to swing shut between us.

He left me there, littered on the floor with his scent still in my nostrils. I imagine he returned to his hotel. The next morning he may have allowed himself a quick fantasy that I might meet him at JFK, say I was coming home. But I didn't know which flight he was on or even that he was returning that day. And, actually, that's far too romantic a notion, because sometime between exiting my building and passing through passport control, the man I thought loved and cared for me picked up a telephone and dialled the number for Homeland Security. So when the immigration officers banged on my door, when they clipped handcuffs around my wrists and ushered me into the back of a patrol car to speed me through the city I'd thought my home, I was forced to understand that it was Marc who had finally abandoned me.

Mr London Tweets @London321

Is this art? bit.ly/47ukorj #performance #wtf #findalexsouthwood

↩   ⇄   ♥   •••

Angry Fem @sheissomeone

Maybe this is the conversation starter we need. #womensrights
   #timetolisten bit.ly/82gelfh

↩   ⇄   ♥   •••

4 from 40 @workingmum77

Cannot believe a mother could do this! #rotinhell #bitch
   bit.ly/49yirrl

↩   ⇄   ♥   •••

Lucy Loo @Lucyonthenet

Not condoning it, but would we judge a man this harshly?
   #doublestandards #AmeliaHeldt bit.ly/47ukorj

↩   ⇄   ♥   •••

Buzzfeed UK @buzzfeeduk

Ten ways Amelia Heldt broke the law #AmeliaHeldt #isthisart
   bit.ly/57bjhdl

↩   ⇄   ♥   •••

Rosie C Cary @rosiecarywrites

#AlexSouthwood's lawyer painting her a victim = slap in face to real
   victims. Justice for Marc!

↩   ⇄   ♥   •••

Personality Tests Online @knowyourself

Are you an Amelia or an Alex? bit.ly/61yyehd

↩   ⇄   ♥   •••

EVERYDAY ETHICS EXAMINED: AMELIA HELDT'S *EXHIBIT A*

August 2015, *The New York Times*

It's not unprecedented that an artist requires his or her viewer to possess approximately $1,000, a passport and 48 hours of travelling time to fully appreciate a piece of work, but Amelia Heldt's *Exhibit A* does tick a number of other art-world firsts, not all of them comfortable. The line between art and life has been debated for centuries and many artists have deliberately crossed it, hoping to provoke a reaction. Consider Sophie Calle's stalking of an unknown stranger in *Address Book*, Guillermo Gómez-Peña and Coco Fusco's trick on the American public in *Couple in the Cage* and Andy Warhol's living-art *Factory*. But in an act that has sent moralists, critics, lawyers and artists around the globe into a frenzy, Heldt has blown the above out of the water.

Readers in the UK will know Heldt better as Alexandra Southwood, the wife, mother and University of York lecturer who went missing in February 2013. Her face was splashed across newspapers, on the sides of buses and in train stations up and down the UK. Her husband made regular appeals for people to come forward with information and the media had a field day with rumours about her murder, abduction and more.

In contrast, those au fait with the American performance and installation art scenes will be aware of Heldt as a rising star since 2004. A series of glowing reviews, grants and invitations from large galleries secured the name, if not the face, in the art-world psyche. Famously reclusive and thought by some to be the alter ego of another well-known artist (rumours ranged from Miranda July to the resurrected Andy Kaufman), she's racked up awards and acclaim with unprecedented success.

Only a few months behind the authorities, it seems, we discover the two are one and the same. Southwood constructed Heldt's identity while studying as an international student at the School of the Art Institute of Chicago. Upon returning to England, she continued to secure legal documents for her imagined companion. While Southwood dropped out of her MFA course with one semester left to complete, she managed to make Heldt graduate even though she herself was in England for the final showcase and not a single professor could attest to having met the star student. In recent years, other SAIC alumni have spoken publicly of their close friendship with Heldt, creating buzz for a group labelled the Chicago Set. We now know, however, the leading figure and entire backbone of this set never actually existed.

The initial part of Southwood and Heldt's combined story might make amusing reading, but it is the events from February 2013 onwards that leave a sourer taste in one's mouth. Southwood disappeared from York, England, on Thursday, 21 February 2013 after leaving work. Her belongings and her blood were found next to the River Ouse, but no body was ever discovered. The police unearthed few leads and Southwood's husband and two daughters were left to accept she had joined the ranks of the some 250,000 people who go missing every year in the UK. The truth, we now learn, is that Southwood left the country using a passport in Heldt's name and arrived in New York intending to adopt her fabricated identity full-time.

Heldt's latest installation offers the contents of her missing person inquiry as art. She's collected newspaper clippings, video footage, police reports and even recordings of her husband's tearful pleas and signed her name to them as original pieces of creativity. Held simultaneously in York and New York, *Exhibit A* comprises two gallery spaces stuffed with the detritus of both Heldt's lives. In the New York space, we find the remnants of her life in York: minutes from PTA meetings, shopping lists, family snapshots, practical shoes with worn-down soles, TV box sets, academic planners, art history tomes, and other pieces of evidence of a perfectly functioning, middle-class existence. Meanwhile, the gallery in York offers a completely different view of the same woman. The left side of the room is given to documenting Heldt's artwork, dating back to 2002 and including her work with advertising agencies and such celebrated events as *My Terms of Endearment*, *Be My Friend* and *Shot at Love*. Meanwhile, the right side of the gallery is devoted to an explanation of her transition from Southwood to Heldt. With documents beginning in 1999, we learn that Heldt came into existence as a piece of coursework about immigration. As an international student curious about the treatment of 'alien' citizens in the USA, Southwood researched methods of obtaining a Social Security Number, applying through the correct, legal methods as well as purchasing fake documentation on street corners and applying the 'infant death' technique. It was in this way that Southwood created a fictitious room-mate with a Social Security Number and State of Illinois driver's license. The exhibition claims her original plan was to present Heldt along with tax records for illegal immigrants in a piece about the corruption behind the IRS and the Social Security Service.

However, in the winter holidays before her graduation, she dropped out of her course to be with her future husband. Upon returning to England, she began to lead the life we see documented in the New York gallery, but in York we find traces of her gradual deception. Notes to her husband about visiting her elderly mother coincide with airline boarding passes and programmes for gallery openings in Manhattan. Displayed in a glass case are copies of letters from Heldt to Southwood, seemingly the correspondence of old room-mates about their divergent lives, but in fact one woman's jottings about her schizophrenic existence.

The corner of the York gallery where viewers seem most drawn contains Heldt's explanation of the past two years, detailing how she vanished from York and made her way to the US, abandoning her husband and two young daughters. As astonishing as this act is, it is perhaps more astonishing still that throughout the process, with no knowledge of how it would conclude, she had the foresight to imagine this piece and collect the documentation along the way. The brief artist's statement says *Exhibit A* was intended to open in February 2023, a decade after her disappearance, but has been brought forward due to 'unforeseen legal matters'.

The largest unforeseen matter, we learn, is that she was found. Marcus Southwood tracked his wife down in Greenwich Village and turned her in to the immigration authorities. The installation, however, had already been meticulously prepared on both sides of the pond. York gallery owner Don McGee explained that he received a phone call from the institution where Southwood was being held, telling him to access a locked storage facility on the edge of town where he would find all the materials and detailed written instructions to set up the installation.

'I realized right away how controversial this piece would be, and I immediately phoned the New York gallery to see what they were thinking, but we decided together that we should go ahead with it,' said McGee.

Southwood's pleas for extradition were denied and, following a hunger strike and a suicide attempt, she was held in a high security psychiatric facility in upstate New York. Heldt's charges included using false documents to be employed, misusing a Social Security Number and using false documents with intent to defraud the US. Her plea for diminished responsibility due to mental incapacity was denied, and she was found competent to stand trial. She was found guilty on all counts and sentenced to the maximum available penalty of 15 years in federal prison and a $250,000 fine. Her appeal date is yet to be set.

Exhibit A gives a gory tabloid account of a seemingly impossible stunt, but what neither of the exhibition spaces offers is any sense of why. For this, if there is an answer, we must turn to the novel-length document Southwood has produced from incarceration. Displayed in the original in the New York gallery, it has also received a limited print run. Available at both sites, it's an audaciously fictional account of her family's experiences from the day of her disappearance to the moment her husband found her in New York. Though in many ways it is yet another form in which Southwood has managed to deny her family their own voice, their own autonomy, even from the depths of incarceration, the document does add a heavy weight to the question: what is art worth? Attempts have been made to reach out to Marcus Southwood to tell his side of the story, but as of yet he has declined to make a statement to this or any other journalist. Left only with Amelia Heldt's version of events, the viewer at either of the installations is forced to contemplate whether what they are devouring as art is a fair exchange for someone's suffering.

Periodically, across the arts, a story surfaces that sends us into a frenzied discussion of right and wrong. In literature, we've seen Michel Houellebecq and Karl Ove Knausgård justify robbing their families of their privacy; in film, we've had reports of Alfred Hitchcock abusing Tippi Hedren and Bernardo Bertolucci confessing to camera about the lengths he was willing to go to produce a 'real' reaction from Maria Schneider. Some will argue art needs to be controversial to make its point, that exploitation can itself be an aesthetic, or that the end justifies the means. But can art ever be worth inflicting pain? Is it an acceptable reason to break someone's heart, abandon one's children?

I ask these questions without the glib critic's rhetoric readers are used to encountering, but with a truly uneasy feeling in my gut. For it is articles like this and all the individuals who queue to enter *Exhibit A* that will ensure Heldt's place in the art books, thus effectively answering a resounding 'yes' to all of the above.

Reinhardt Lang
Art Features Editor

A Note About the Art

Much of the work in this novel is real and I'd encourage the curious to explore.

With special thanks to Casey Smallwood for allowing Amelia to borrow and adapt her pieces.

Acknowledgements

This book wouldn't have been possible without the love and support of my friends and family. Thank you to my stupendous agent, Marilia, and to my wonderful editors, Jess and Hilary. For being patient enough to read early drafts, thank you to Anna, Bryony, Emma, Fran, Christine, Ban, Kate, Laura, Beth, Amy, Nat, Carole, Angela, and the Bayford Hill Book Club. For supporting me emotionally, morally and at times alcoholically through this whole journey, thank you to my York and Goldsmiths families, some of whom are mentioned above but also: Ollie, Nik, Charlie, Patrick, Neil, Chris, Beckie, Paul, Sam, Ellen, Stef, Martha, Cath, Heather, Nuala and Emily. Thank you to Alicia, Lucy, Francis, Linda, Kimmy and Casey for being excellent human beings. To my sister, my brother and my dad for always being my champions. To my mum for everything, especially her generosity about the dangers of having a writer in the family. And, finally, to Chris, for believing in me when I couldn't.